Term Life

A Novel of Love, Death, and Computer Security

William H. Boyd

BLACK ROSE writing™

First printing

ISBN: 978-1-61296-931-2
PUBLISHED BY BLACK ROSE WRITING
www.blackrosewriting.com

Printed in the United States of America
Suggested Retail Price (SRP) $20.95

Term Life is printed in Palatino Linotype

Thanks to Max Apple and Daniel Keyes for their help and encouragement during my formative years. Thanks to my wife, Laurey, for her patience and support. Walker Percy, pray for me.

Term Life

Contents

I – The Search

It started with a simple Google search. What is the difference between whole life and term life? It was an innocent question. After all, why should I want life in the first place? Well, the responses I received to my simple question were pointed and contrary.

"Whole life protects your future and builds cash value you can access when you need it. You can borrow against it without having to qualify, and if you pay your premiums on time, the price will not increase as long as you live."

It sounded good until I read the response.

"Don't be a chump. (I wasn't sure what a chump was, but I decided to avoid being one at all cost.) Whole life is over priced. You'll never get your money back. Buy term life. Protect your future, and save your cash for more profitable investments."

Immediately, I was in a quandary. Both messages seemed to be saying that my future was threatened, and neither one had much confidence in my present. They differed principally in regards to what I was supposed to do about it. But I didn't know what to do. After all, no one had asked me if I wanted to have a life. So, why should I be compelled to insure it? But just when life becomes untenable, something happens to change things.

My change came outside Central Market on a Friday night after I finished a particularly satisfying vegetarian bisque. I thought the man beside me was going to make a comment about the singer/songwriter who had just finished her set on the patio. Instead, he chilled my soul. That is, he would have if I had had one.

"You know you don't have to die like your father."

"Excuse me?" I said.

He said, "You don't have to die like your father."

"I don't know what you are talking about. I don't even have a father."

"Not now you don't. He's dead. That's the point. Don't you see? He's dead. You're not. But you will be soon enough, and now is the time to do something about it."

"Look here."

"I am looking here."

"I don't think you're very funny."

"I don't either. I am as serious as the grave."

"Some joke."

"No joke. I am talking about life and death, and you're only about fifteen seconds from decking me with a round house kick to the head."

"I am not."

"If you are not, you should be. After all, you beat George Ramirez with that kick in the mixed martial arts tournament in Plano. It took him awhile to get up."

"You were there? You remember me from that?"

"Yeah."

I have to confess. I smiled at this.

"No. I wasn't there. Except in spirit."

"In spirit? Are you trying to tell me you're an angel?"

"Why? Are you a start up?"

"No. And that's not what I meant."

"I know what you meant. Do you believe in angels?"

"No. But I met a girl once who said she was a vampire, and I thought maybe you—"

"Was she a vampire?"

"She thought she was."

"You didn't believe her?"

"Whatever. "

"Vampires! They won't let you die in peace. No, I wasn't there at your kung fu tournament. Look! You're in software. You've been to DEF CON. I looked at your Facebook page."

"Are you my friend?"

"You posted the tournament."

"Ten years ago!"

It was also thirty pounds ago.

"I combed through some of the archives."

"Those aren't supposed to be available."

"Sometimes it's not who you know, it's what you know. Then, I followed you on Twitter."

"Because of my tweets on Open Authority?"

"No! I followed you while you tweeted. I tracked your GPS position here. Honestly, you thought I couldn't find you? Really?"

"Are you a cop?"

"If I'm a cop, you're supposed to ask me for my warrant."

"Where's your warrant?"

"I don't have a warrant. I have a warranty."

"What?"

"I'm not a cop."

"NSA?"

"Would I show up in person?"

"I don't know."

"You did some searches on insurance."

"So? People search on a lot of things. I search on a lot of things."

"People search on the capital of Assyria because they watched an old Monte Python movie. They look up look up the engine size of the BMW that passed them on the freeway. They look up Jill Ferry's cup size because she's in a movie. They don't look up the difference between whole life and term unless they have a reason. Did your father have insurance?"

"I don't have a father. "

"Not now you don't."

"I didn't have a father."

"Were you born by virgin in vitro? Everybody has a father."

"All right then. I never knew who he was."

"But you had your suspicions."

"Maybe I did."

"He shouldn't have had to die like that."

"No he shouldn't. "

"No one should have to die like that."

"No one."

"Least of all you."

"I don't intend to."

"And how are you going to prevent it?"

"What are you getting at?"

"If your father, your suspected father, died like that, there's a chance..."

"Yes, there's a chance I could get hit by a Suburban, but I'm not worried about it."

"You're suspected father was worried. He had insurance."

"Not that much."

"It was something."

"Not really."

"It was 75K."

"Yes. Tax free."

"That's how insurance works. It may not have been much, but you were able to finish college."

"That's when I really wondered."

"Wondered about the connection with him when you got the money?"

"Yeah. Why else would he have done it?"

"Just think if he hadn't had insurance, you would never have known. Or suspected.

"But he did have it. And I don't. Is that your point?"

"Partly."

"Well, you are wasting your time. I don't have a child. Or a wife. Or a sick old mother. No dependents. There's no one to benefit, so there's no reason for me to insure my life."

"Are you sure you don't have any kids? How can you really be sure?"

"I'll worry about that when the time comes."

"It's cheaper to worry about it now. When it comes to life insurance, uncertainty works in your favor. The very thing that keeps you up at night can save you money."

"What keeps me up at night?"

"Uncertainty."

"Oh! But I can save even more money by not buying insurance at all. There is no one I would want to give the money to!"

"You could give the money to me."

"Now why would I want to do that? "

"Not me literally. My company."

"Why? Are you a start-up? And do I look like an angel?"

"No, we'd be selling you insurance."

"To give you money when I die?"

"No, to make sure you don't die like your supposed father. Or like some poor schmuck with cancer or Alzheimer's. Or like any number of people who lack any good reason to keep on suffering when they have no expectation that their lives will ever get any better. To ensure that you live life on your own terms. To make sure your life is truly your own. Now isn't that worth a little insurance?"

I tried to answer, but this stranger I had never met, that I still had not really met, was already receding away into the shadow of the outdoor diners and live music appreciators.

And then I was alone in the crowd.

2 - The Wee Hours

Normally when I am awakened in the wee small hours of the morning, my first thought is not about the joy of life—especially when I am awakened by the Security Information and Event Management system on a Saturday. Batch says when the SIEM wakes him up, he rejoices that he is alive, that he has a job, and that he is privileged to man the watch tower of data security.

Batch's real name is Butch. That is, Butch is his primary nickname, the one he gained in the sixties, and the one the company put on his name plate at the office. His actual real name is Cassidy, Paul Cassidy, but his grade school friends changed Paul Cassidy to Butch Cassidy after the character in a movie they saw once on late night TV. We changed Butch to Batch because his IT career goes all the way back to batch processing on mainframe computers. He is one of the few people I know who has made the transition from the green screen to distributed processing and data security. For awhile, we tried calling him Punch, but the younger guys didn't get the joke. In fact, the name Batch was beginning to require too much explanation, and people misunderstand Butch unless they watch old movies from the sixties.

Lately, I have considered calling him Paul.

I wasn't glad to be on the front lines of computer security that morning, but still for some reason four AM seemed an unaccountably fine time to be awake. After my encounter with the mysterious stranger the night before, I had come home and gone to bed early. As a result, I had had just short of five hours of sleep when my phone rang with a message from the SIEM.

"The SIEM can be very unseemly at two o'clock in the AM," Butch/Paul likes to say. But, as I said, it was four, and two hours makes a lot of difference to someone who is on call one week out of three. I was happy to have made it past the work week. Better a Saturday than a Wednesday. I wouldn't have to drag myself back into the office after dealing with this alert. I could spend the rest of the day in bed recovering. Yet, there was still this one problem regardless of the day of the week. If the world were coming to an end, I was the one who would have to bear the bad news.

My first job, though, was not to awaken the Chief Security Officer to tell him all our employee's social security numbers had been stolen or that all our company trade secrets had been FTP'ed to China. My first job was to determine if this particular incident was a false positive or truly the apocalypse.

Someone in Accounting asked us once what the SIEM was. (We came to ask him why his database server was sending two hundred megabytes of data to an IP address in Las Vega every Thursday night at ten o'clock.) Paul described it as a device that gathered up all the little piles of straw into one big hay stack. Then, it pulled out a few straws and asked you if any of them were needles.

From my iPhone screen with my bleary eyes, I really could not distinguish a needle from a straw, so I opened up my laptop and logged in to our network. It took me some precious minutes before I was able to read the message clearly. Then, I had to struggle to understand what it was telling me.

"Is this a straw or a needle?" I said.

Butch had found a coral snake once in his back yard. He told us how long it took him to work through the color code to determine whether it was "friend of Jack" or the "kill a fella." I stared at this message for nearly as long as he had stared at that red and yellow serpent. Then, I sat back.

It was an attack. It looked like an elevation of privileges attack. Someone came into the web application and tricked the system into giving them access to the very root of the server where you could do any damned thing you pleased.

I started to grab the phone, but I realized I needed more information. So, I combed through the logs, and by five AM I was ready to make the call. I took a long pause, and then I dialed Butch. I hated to do it, but Butch had more mental acuity at odd hours than anyone I knew.

True to form, he didn't miss a beat.

"Hello, Zed," he said before I could say a word. "We have a bug,"

"What? Oh, right. I'm supposed to say that to you."

"So, do we have a bug?"

"We sure do. This looks like the apocalypse."

"Really? How many horses would you say?"

"At least two. Maybe three."

"Well, if it turns out to be four horses, you will have to call George immediately. If it's only three, we can let him sleep a little longer."

"I'm not sure. I can't tell if the hacker's done anything yet."

"Okay. Well, no need to pull out the poison pill just yet. Let me log on, and then I'll call you back, and you can give me the tour."

I sighed as I set down the phone. To the joy of living I could now add the joy of relief. The truth was I hated handling these situations by myself. First, it was good to have another set of eyes looking at a problem. Second, it was good to have another pair of shoulders to bear the blame. It's not that I would have ever tried to shift blame onto Paul or he onto me. It was just that it was easier for George to shoot one messenger than two. The only problem was that the Chief Security Officer insisted on a strict communications plan. If we rated a security incident at level four, then the person on call had to phone him directly. That meant I myself would be disturbing my boss three layers up with something that could prove to be either the end of the company and our jobs or much ado about nothing. Either way the temptation would always exist for him to throw some collateral damage my way and send me back to high tech unemployment.

I had already been through the embarrassment and pain of that situation twice before.

At the lower levels, however, the communications protocol was less severe. Our entire security rating schema consisted of four codes. We called them unofficially the four horsemen of the apocalypse.

1 – Concerning

2 – Alarming

3 – Threatening

4 – Critical

At the Concerning, Alarming, and Threatening levels, I was only required to alert my immediate supervisor Butch. He had the discretion to elevate the threat level to a four which still meant I had to make that call to George. Or, he could leave it in the Concerning to Threatening range. Then, Butch merely reported the issue to his boss Susan the next day. That reduced my risk. It also erased my hopes of becoming a hero. Still, the data security analyst's motto is, "Most heroes are dead."

By six AM Paul had called me back.

"It still looks like two horses to me," he said, "but you know the deal with the horses of the apocalypse don't you?"

"No, I don't."

"You never read the Bible?"

"No."

Why would I?

"Well, the deal is that there are four of them, and they come as a package. If you have seen two, you can be sure that the other two will be coming along."

"Each one worse than the one before?"

"Depends upon your perspective. Keep your eyes peeled. I'll be available on my cell."

By nine AM, I had consumed four cups of coffee, and I was beginning to feel hunger. I decided to risk leaving my condo and running down the street for a breakfast taco. All right. For two breakfast tacos. I could have made oatmeal in my own kitchen, but I gained some reassurance from seeing other people milling about on the street. Also, I could eat a taco with one hand while I hunted and pecked keys with the other.

I had unwrapped the second taco and had peeled back the plastic tab on the grande sized cup of coffee I had purchased at the taco stand, when I saw the third horse. Right after someone had gained the elevated privileges to the application server, he apparently went to a data base server and then sent a large file of data right past the web server sitting in the DMZ and out onto the world wide web. I was not a software developer myself, but I knew this was not the usual way these things were supposed to work. I called Ken, the data base administrator, who had authority to see in his logs what data the guy had taken.

"It looks like he accessed payment information on the data base. It's hard to tell. He used the same account the application would have used, but the application would have sent the data back to the web server wouldn't you think?"

"What would someone want with payment information?"

"Names of customers and how much they were spending?"

"Credit card numbers?"

"That too."

"Are those encrypted?"

"Sure are."

"How do you know that?"

"It's a standard, and we always follow the standards."

"Are you being facetious?"

"No. Not me. But even if I am, I know because I set these tables up. The credit cards are encrypted."

"I see. That's a relief."

"Of course, because they are, you can't verify that's what he took."

"Are the names and addresses encrypted, too?"

"No."

"Why not?"

"It's not a standard."

After that came the conversation with the server guy. Then, it was noon, but at least I had the goods on our guy. I knew that he had broken out of the carefully defined path we of IT had laid out for him and had taken the direct path to the database. He had liked what he had seen so much that he had sent 500 kilobytes of data to an IP that was not of our network. This had to be the fourth horse. I picked up my phone to give Butch the news.

"Good job," he said. "Did anything show up on the DLP?"

"No. Not for this."

"Call the server admin. Have him block any further transfer of data. Tell him to block the FTP ports."

"Right."

"Then call Susan and give her the skinny—"

"Call Susan? What about George? The procedure is we call him first."

"Yes, but Sweet Sue wants to know what is going on before George calls her so she can be that much better prepared. Otherwise, George thinks she's not doing her job."

"He insists we tell him directly, but he expects her to already know when he calls her to make sure she is on the case?"

"I know. That's the difference between procedures and politics. Beware as you climb the ladder, my son."

"Thanks for the advice. The rung I'm on is slippery enough."

"That's what they all say. 512-463— "

"What?"

"Susan's number: 512-463-"

***

By the time I dialed Susan's number, my phone was giving me the battery warning message. I lunged across the bar for the charger cord and plugged it in just before the fifth ring. Fortunately, Susan was not picking up her phone. I prepared to deliver my report to her voice mail.

"Hello, this is Susan Wilson. "

I waited for the tone to leave a message.

"Hello? Hello?"

It was not voice mail. It was the woman herself.

"Oh! Wait! Hello?"

"We've been through this, Gus. I've already said hello."

"How did you know it was me?"

"Let's see...I have your number on my phone, and your name came up when it rang?"

"I didn't know you had my number."

"Of course I have your number. I would have let your call go to voice mail if I hadn't known who you were. You sound out of breath. What have you been doing?"

"Nothing. I just lunged across the breakfast bar because my phone needs charging, and the cord was too short."

"Why didn't you plug it into your computer. You are at your computer, aren't you?"

"Yes, but that would not be a good security practice."

"No, I suppose it wouldn't. I'll bet that's why your calling. Someone is doing some nasty things, someone besides us, and you're on call. That's why you called me. You weren't just interested to see what I was doing, were you?"

"That's right. We have a four horse—I mean—a Level Four Critical Incident."

"I see. Have you called George yet?"

"No."

"Good. I want you to call Butch back and make sure."

"But Butch and I—"

"Yes, I know. Butch and you have already made your assessment. But you don't want to jump the gun and call George without being really sure of your shit."

"He sent data to—"

"Yes, I know. He sent data to China for all we know. Call Butch again. Then, call George. If it is necessary."

My phone rang before I could even hang up.

"Butch, I was just about—"

"Did you call George yet?"

"No. Susan said—"

"Don't. That FTP transfer is a known process. We documented it somewhere. You can double check that on Monday. In the meantime, call Susan."

"Again?"

"Yes. Continuity in the line of communication. If George gets wind that we even thought we had a critical situation, she wants to be able to tell him that she already knew it wasn't even concerning."

So, I called again.

"Well that sucks," Susan said. "I mean I'm relieved nothing bad happened, but still—"

"Yeah."

"You've been up since when? Six?"

"Four."

"That's a hell of a way to spend a Saturday."

"Well, I am on call."

"But if Butch had remembered about that documented process, you wouldn't have had to spend half the day glued to the screen. Sometimes that man remembers too much too late."

I was surprised by her candor about my boss.

"Monday," she said, "I'm calling the application manager. His ass is going to be in a sling. He's not supposed to write applications like that. 'Not enough resources to fix it,' he'll say. And I'll tell him if my guy can spend twelve hours on Saturday tracking down his half-assed program, then his guys can spend a Saturday fixing the damned thing."

"It wasn't really twelve hours," I said.

"Get some rest. Try to get out and have a little fun before the weekend is over."

***

Sure, I thought. There was still some time to take in the advantages of living within walking distance of "The Live Music Capital of the World." Of course, I couldn't go see any live shows because I would not hear the alert on my phone if the SIEM found another needle. I would have to stay out of the loud bars, but there were a few quieter places where I could go. Instead, I fell asleep on the couch, and when I awoke, it was 12 AM. I made a sandwich and went to bed. When I awoke on Sunday I realized I needed to do my laundry. And the dishes. So the remains of Sunday morning and even Sunday afternoon were spent in drudgery. About four PM I finished my clothes only to realize I had run out of groceries. I spent the waning hours of Sunday at Central Market sifting through the organic vegetables and the free range chickens. I didn't actually buy any of that stuff. I just looked. Over by the antibiotic free beef I saw the vampire I had met the other night. She was holding a package of 90 percent lean hamburger and was trying to position it in her hand basket so that the blood from the package did not leak onto her gluten free whole grain muffins. The blood had already leaked on her hand which she wiped off with a paper towel after quarantining her meat with more paper towels in the basket.

I could not tell. Did she have a bit of spinach stuck to the corner of her mouth, or was that a bit of green, decaying flesh drooping from her left lower blood drenched lip?

For some reason I did not stop to say hello.

3 – In Sickness and in Health

On Wednesday I stayed home sick. Monday I spent working up the report from Saturday. Tuesday I spent tweaking the SIEM—looking for a way to tie the clues from incidents across the network a little closer together so that nasty things happening in our systems didn't go unnoticed quite so long. Butch took a look over my shoulder.

"Sir Gawain, does thou look for the Holy Grail?"

"Why do you ask? Is it futile?"

"No, but the road is long and perilous."

"Also, the hours are not billable," said Morgan. "They won't let me go on epic quests. It costs too much."

Morgan was our contractor. He didn't take on-call rotations because he was too expensive, and managing billable hours outside working hours did not sit well with Susan.

"I don't want some strange man waking me up in the middle of the night and then billing me two hundred dollars for the pleasure," she said.

"I'm not sure what you mean by that," Butch responded. "But why do you keep him on then if he costs so much?"

"Because he helps me sleep at night."

"Does she know what she is saying?" I asked.

Butch just put a finger to his lips.

"Some of us," I said to Morgan, "have to be cheap enough to do the thankless jobs," However, pointing this out did no good. Morgan just agreed with me without any sense of shame, and therefore I got no satisfaction. But then on Wednesday I got revenge of a sort. I stayed home flat on my back with no lost pay. I had sick leave, and I was allowed to use it. Morgan, as a contractor, did not, and he would come in with any fever under a hundred and three just to avoid losing those precious billable hours.

Being sick afforded me a certain allowance of comfort but only when I could strike the right balance. If you are going to take sick leave from work, you have to be too sick to work but not so sick that you suffer undo pain or, worse yet, fear for your life. I read once that night sweats were a sign of cancer, so thereafter whenever I sweated at night the thought that I had a fever was the third thing to come to my mind. The first was that I might have cancer. The second was that the air conditioner was broken.

Tuesday night was pretty much sleepless from twelve thirty onwards, so even before I got up to make my assessment—was I sick enough to call in or not—it was pretty much a foregone conclusion. There was no doubt I felt awful, so awful that I had a difficult time getting to the phone to make the call. But, of course, once I was up, being so sick made the call that much easier. When I was sick enough to stay home but not sick enough to feel unequivocally awful, I had to be careful to moderate my phone delivery. I didn't want to sound too well, but I didn't want to sound melodramatic. Both sound fake to your supervisor, and once you begin to hear the doubtfulness in his voice when he says, "Well, okay. Get well, then," you become forever self-conscious about everything that comes from your mouth. You wonder how it sounds and what alternative interpretations it can support. However, when I felt as sick as I did that morning, there was little doubt that I was going to strike the right balance.

I left my message on Butch's cell phone, and then I just stood by the bed with the phone in my hand. A wave of nausea came over me, tightening in my gut then subsiding. It seemed that the slightest movement would bring it back. So, I hovered over the bed half inclined to fall back in and half bent towards the bathroom where I longed to evacuate from whatever direction was necessary the bitterness in my digestive track. Finally, I managed to grab the blanket without bending too far over and pull it back with a shuffle, turn around and fall sort of sideways into the bed. A pang of fear came into my stomach somewhere just below where the nausea had been. This was not going to be pleasant.

It was dark outside, and the street was almost silent. It was still too early for most of the commuter traffic coming into town to work from such awful, distant places as Cedar Park, Buda, and Georgetown. Why did people spend so many precious hours every week in a car so they could live in a house on a postage stamp lot far from all the true amenities of civilization? Of course, then, there was Raj.

Raj lived in my building. Here he was in the heart of downtown within walking distance of all its wonders, but he worked up on the north edge of Round Rock. He had paid for premium real estate like me and still had to commute to work. I wondered if I sent him a text he would bring me over some bland flat bread. Probably not. Everything he ate was most likely spicy. Like me. Then, when the abdominal distress came, neither of us had anything in the house that was soothing. I should keep crackers in the condo for times like this. I decided to try going back to sleep.

My phone buzzed with a message.

"I see your light's on. You okay?"

It was Raj. If I stood up and peered through the blinds, I could probably see him standing outside or peering out his car window.

"Feel like hell. Taking sick day."

"Too much Thai, or too many intrusion detections?"

I always tell Raj he commutes too far, and he tells me my job is too stressful.

"I thrive on the edge."

"Need anything?"

"I'm good. Sleep."

Then the cramps came back. I left the phone on the bed and ran to the bathroom. I hung over the toilet bowl for several minutes, but nothing productive happened. I became aware of how tired I was and of how much my head hurt and my back ached. But the tile floor felt cool and soothing, so I slid off the toilet bowl and embraced the floor: my own private tomb, my own crypt of consolation.

That didn't last long.

On the bathroom floor with no clock ticking, no television keeping time by commercials, and no window to display the movement of the shadows and the sun, time becomes awfully subjective. You try not to move because all motion becomes motion sickness. So, you lie there still like your mother used to tell you to do on that cold tile. The coldness of the floor seeps into your bones and seems to drain away the ache in your muscles. It freezes your gut long enough for the sickness to subside, and then it's like you had entered into a little piece of eternity with off-white squares running off in all directions. But bathroom eternity doesn't last forever. The cramps come back, the comforting chill of the floor gets pushed aside by fever chills, and you find yourself back in time lying at the base of the commode. Eventually the cramps loosen a little, and the chills subside. But nausea still abides, and it seems like the time will never end.

Nothing is worse than nausea. I was reduced to a function of my own evacuations, and when the evacuations wouldn't come, I was reduced to nothing.

Pray!

I never prayed. No one worth praying to.

Pray! Pray to the god of the bowels. Pray for release. Not healing. Not life, but release.

How do you put an end to nausea? I read that people once bought heroin from Sears and Roebuck for that. Hadn't William S. Burroughs given his Christmas Eve fix to a kid with cramps? But then I had also heard that heroin induced nausea. That contradiction must be what people meant by diabolical.

As the chills and the nausea moved through me in alternating waves, my thoughts gained a voice of their own.

"So you don't want to die? We can fix that, but the price of avoiding the fear of death is death."

That couldn't be right.

Cold, cramps, nausea. Cold, cramps, nausea. Lie still.

***

Robert took me once to meet his father. The man was over ninety. He had fought in World War Two.

"My brother was in the infantry. I didn't want anyone shooting at me, so, I joined the navy. But if its not one thing, its another. The first week out of San Diego on the way to Pearl, I liked to have died."

"Why was that? Japanese sub?"

"No! Seasick. For a whole week. Me and the guy in the next bunk shared a bucket. Some just hung over the rail on the deck and 'Bluggh!' I thought seeing the water move made it worse."

"Pretty bad, huh?"

"You wished you could die but you couldn't. Finally, after about a week I started to feel better. I decided to try to eat dinner. So, I went to the mess hall and stood in line. I asked the guy in front of me what we were having. The navy had this dish of dark gravy with chunks of meat on bread. The sailors called it 'shit on a shingle.' The old boy in front of me saw my face, and he said, 'Shit on a shingle!' I almost lost it before I could reach the railing and puke over the side."

Robert hadn't seen his dad in awhile. He had asked if I wanted to come along. He asked me to do things with him from time to time. It was sort of a road trip.

"Who's this young man?" his dad asked when we came in the door.

"This is a friend of mine," Robert said. "He wanted to meet you, Dad."

"Well, he's mighty welcome."

Mighty welcome. I guessed that was how people who lived through World War Two talked. I guessed I had wanted to meet him. Might as well, I had thought. Like meeting history. Nice old man. He had made me feel welcome. He had also made me feel a little ill with his stories of seasickness and the funny way he smelled. I smelled it again there on the bathroom floor. I felt the floor reel, and suddenly I thought I was going to vomit. But when I pulled myself up on the bowl and leaned over the white abyss, it was just the same unproductive nausea. The hole was too small to crawl into, and the rim was too high to crawl over. Disappointed I sank back onto the floor. It was still cold, and I felt welcome.

I wondered how Robert had stood it. His old WWII dad lingered on too long. Robert himself did six months of chemo and spent time beyond measure hovering over just such a bathroom bowl. To make matters worse, his bathroom floor hadn't been tile. He had had carpet. Already I had more comfort in my misery than Robert. Still, I couldn't have stood it. I wouldn't have stood for it. I certainly hadn't stood for carpet in my condo. Of course, the building manager hadn't offered it.

Why had Robert lived so cheap? Surely he didn't have to choose apartments with carpet in the bath. Why would anyone choose cheap?

I decided then and there to stop eating Thai. The internet claimed that hot peppers released endorphins, but the stomach and small intestines cared nothing about endorphins. Digestion trumped brain chemistry.

"My god is my belly."

Could an atheist have a god? Could an atheist have a belly? Is that the best we could evolve?

Either way I would never eat Thai again.

"Either way my god is my belly."

I climbed the bowl again to put an end to all this whichever way the relief needed to come, but still nothing budged. The cramps only intensified. I sank to the floor again seeking death, but death eluded me.

This was not fair. Sickness was just supposed to be a slightly unpleasant vacation from work. It wasn't supposed to be painful. There was supposed to come a turning point, a purging followed by a gentle exhaustion. Then towards evening a little hot soup, some saltines and a little TV or maybe a low key video game. Not this. Not real suffering.

Then, it got worse, worse in waves. Headache. Muscle aches. Cold chills. Withdrawal. Withdrawal without the addiction. Without the rush. Just the pain.

How Robert had endured the pain! Pain even in the cure. In the supposed cure. For there had been no cure, and hardly any respite. I had told him not to worry about addiction. Just let the nurses ease the pain. He said the pain was bearable, but I could see that it wasn't. At least when the doctor gave up on the cure, the nausea had ended. That had been some small consolation.

I would sure have let them ease the pain. I would let them ease it now, but no one was offering. Maybe if I could crawl to my PC, I could get into a game and be distracted. Maybe some actual pain would give me a little edge in the competition. The game should let you submit a medical record to the game master for extra points. How many times had I crossed a barren desert or climbed a sheer mountain face to gain a token or magic talisman. This should be worth twice as much as one of those virtual feats.

"But you would have to endure. You would have to prevail, wouldn't you?"

Screw that. What I needed was a doctor.

Somehow with the goal of seeking medical attention, I managed to stumble, hunched over like Mr. Hyde, out of the bathroom and back into the bedroom. I wanted to fall back into bed and try to sleep, but I kept myself half erect on the edge of the bed and grabbed my phone. I found my primary care physician under the P's in my contact list and punched the number. Butch had once asked me why my doctor wasn't filed under D for doctor. I said that method forced me to search down a whole list of doctors before I found the right one. I preferred to file them by specialty, and once again, I was vindicated—except I would have to get better to tell Butch about it.

By some stroke of good fortune, my PCP had a cancellation for three PM.

At two thirty I took the elevator down to the first floor and went outside. I found a Car2Go a half a block away and drove it to the doctor's office. I figured if I threw up on the way, it wouldn't be in my car. If I had taken a cab and thrown up in the back, I would have had to face the driver. Car2Go provided just the right balance of personal irresponsibility and self-determination.

When I arrived in the office, the waiting room was full. On top of my aching back and stomach cramps, I had a crick in my neck, so I picked up a magazine and began reading about the crowds waiting to climb Everest. In March all the alpine amateurs gathered at base camp waiting their turn for their tour group to ascend.

"Those people are crazy," I muttered. "You wouldn't catch me hanging onto a peg driven into the side of a glacier. This is the closest I want to get to Tibet."

"It's Nepal," said someone in the room. He had heard me talking to myself and answered as if he were allowed in on my personal conversations. Still, I felt the need to answer. He had corrected me. I needed to put him on the spot in return.

"Would you do that?"

I pointed to the mountain on the cover of the magazine.

"Not now. But I've done a little rock climbing. Have you?"

"Indoor rock climbing. That was plenty for me."

I put my eyes back in the magazine. I didn't want make eye contact with the stranger. I didn't mind talking with strangers so much when my stomach wasn't cramping, but I didn't like having conversations with strangers in front of other total strangers. I also didn't want to admit my rock climbing had been done on a plastic wall in the mall.

"What are you here for? Hope it's not the flu."

I could feel all the eyes in the place turn towards me. I had no intention telling this ass hole about my medical condition, but now I was trapped. Everyone was going to think the worst, so I decided to do some damage control.

"No, I said, "I just have some stomach issues."

Then, I looked up. It was the man from Central Market.

"Stomach issues? You mean like diarrhea? Vomiting?"

"No, Look! I don't think—I mean I don't—feel that much like talking."

"Oh, sure. No problem. I was just going to say if that's all you've got, then you just need to get some Emetrol. You can get it over the counter. You didn't need to come in here to see the doctor. Unless you are worried about something else."

"Haven't you ever heard of the HIPA rules?"

"Oh sure. But don't worry about that. Your medical records are safe with me."

He smiled.

"Of course I'm not so sure your doctor can say the same thing."

I wanted to argue with him, but then I remembered that Dark Reading had published an article saying the medical industry was behind the curve in computer security. So, I kept my peace.

"You know," he continued, "it's a dirty little secret that the medical industry has a ways to go in catching up with the financial industry and even the retailers when it comes to computer security. That's saying a lot, isn't it?"

What did this human plague with no sense of personal boundaries know about it? Of course, I had injected a few viruses and cross-site scripted a high profile website or two myself. It was part of my professional chops. To defend against a hack, you had to know how to hack. And it took a little practice. My favorite game at the airport was to hack people's Androids and leave them personal messages.

"Say, Babe, nice tattoo."

"Dude! That chick over at Gate 31 is not going to look at you. Give it up."

Of course, doing things like that at a doctor's office was too risky. The crowd was too small, and the risk of getting caught, too great. Besides, people in a doctor's office had enough to worry about without adding computer insecurity to their maladies. Even I wasn't cold hearted enough to do that.

"I guess the moral of that story is don't pay your doctor with a credit card."

At that moment the nurse opened the door and called my name. I was glad to put an end to the conversation. I wished I had brought enough cash for my co-pay. On the wall next to the patient's entrance there was a wrought-iron version of the medical symbol: a snake coiled around a vertical stick. I had always wondered what that meant. Once I felt better I would go to Wikipedia to find out.

There were no Everest articles in the examination room—only People and Woman's Day. I waited in there sitting on the examination table with my nausea and boredom. When the doctor came in, he peered down my throat, listened to my heart and my gut, thumped my abdomen, and said he couldn't do anything yet.

"It will most likely run its course. Drink fluids. Gatorade. 7-Up. Take some Emetrol. It's over the counter. I think you'll be fine. If you're not better by tomorrow, call me. If you get severe diarrhea for more than twenty-four hours, go to the emergency room."

He keyed some notes into his tablet computer and disappeared.

When I emerged from the office back into the waiting room, the stranger was gone. I left quickly in case he was waiting for me in the hall. He wasn't. Outside the heat of the afternoon felt strangely comfortable. My Car2Go was gone, taken by another subscriber, but before I could call up the phone app to search for another of those little white cars, I saw one just across the street. I crossed in the middle of the block and opened the door. Inside on the passenger seat was a paper sack from a pharmacy. Inside the sack was a bottle of Emetrol.

I had drunk half the bottle before I got home. By evening I was eating steamed rice, and the next day I was back at work resuming my post at the digital watch tower.

By Friday night I was eating Thai.

4 – Here in the Dark

"You know, Butch, I've come to a conclusion."

"What's that?"

"I have a laughably inadequate bucket list."

"That's serious," Morgan said.

"Do we pay you to jump into conversations unasked?" I said.

Butch held up his hand in my direction. "Now! Now! You made a statement out loud. Morgan can ask a question. How's it serious, Morgan?"

Sometimes Butch was just too evenhanded.

"It means Gus here is running out of reasons to stay alive."

"What? I said no such thing."

"Yes, you did. You said your bucket list was 'laughably inadequate.' What is a bucket list but a list of things you hope to do before you die. That implies that your life from day to day is inadequate, and you need a list of special experiences so that your life will seem to have been worthwhile by the time you come to the end. The irony is that once you have done everything on your list, what reason have you got left to stick around? And if you already think your list isn't good enough, that's just pathetic."

"Pathetic? What's pathetic is that people like you—"

"Uh! Uh! Uh! Don't take the bait. You know Morgan is only being provocative."

"His reason for living is to irritate everyone he comes in contact with."

"If that were true, then his work would be done."

On the other hand, I appreciated even handedness. Morgan, to my disappointment, was not fazed.

"That's right. But my work is not irritation or provocation. My work is truth."

"Besides, he's right."

"He's right? You agree with him?"

Morgan turned away from his keyboard and actually smiled at me.

"Only in a sense," Butch said. "I agree with his logic, but I don't accept the initial premise that a bucket list is always a justification for your life. Although...."

"Although what?"

"Although," said Morgan, "if the shoe fits...."

Butch shrugged. "He has a point."

"Why do I even get into these conversations?"

"Because you are searching," said Morgan.

"I'm searching? I'm searching?"

"Again," Butch said, "I don't necessarily disagree."

I decided to let time pass before I said anything else. So, I stayed put in my log files and honed my regular expressions to avoid more false positives in my search for nefarious intruders.

Even though it was tedious, my job was kind of heroic. Of course, Morgan and Butch were doing the same work, so I couldn't expect any special appreciation from them. Still, it ought to count for something, my contribution to society, my addition to the greater good. It should confer some measure of significance to my life. My passing would leave some kind of hole in the fabric of civilization. Surely, I would be missed by someone, and if my life counted for something, surely I was entitled to some small pleasures, some rewards on the road to computer security sainthood.

"What would you do?" Butch asked. "I mean, what would you put on your bucket list?"

I knew he hadn't meant to, but Butch's question put me on the spot, When you've already admitted your bucket list is inadequate, discussing it can only make things worse. I tried desperately to think of something impressive but not embarrassing I could use to supplement it.

What I really wanted to do was something grand, but there were just some things you couldn't say at work.

"I don't know. Maybe...maybe I'd like to climb Everest."

"You mean the mountain?" said Morgan.

"Of course I mean the mountain."

"I thought you were afraid of heights," said Butch.

"What makes you say that?"

"You said you never go out on your balcony, and if one of your guests wants to use it, you just sit in the living room and talk to them through the door."

"I go out on my balcony. It's just not that big, so I let my guest enjoy it without me crowding him. Trying to be a good host."

"Have you ever done any alpine climbing?"

"No."

"Ever climb Enchanted Rock?"

"No."

"Ever climb in the greenbelt?"

"No."

"Ever climb in the mall?" asked Morgan.

"In the mall?"

"Yeah, on one of those temporary indoor rock walls with the harness?"

Exactly where I had climbed.

"Those are for kids."

"How about the stairs? Did you ever climb all the way to the thirtieth floor?"

"No."

"You've got some training to do, I'd say."

"True," I said. "Look! It's a dream. I haven't figured out yet how I to achieve it. It would certainly put a person into an elite class of people."

"Not really," said Morgan.

"And why not?"

"It's too crowded. Every heart surgeon, bored dentist, and trial lawyer is in the base camp waiting to get a crack at the climb. They have fifty people a day going up on the summit. Not so unique."

"Well, what would suggest?"

"How about Airman's Cave?"

"What is Airman's Cave?"

"Two miles of limestone passageway starting at the Barton Creek Greenbelt. You're securely on the ground the whole time. No digging your fingers and toes into cracks and hanging onto sheer vertical rock three hundred feet up."

"I haven't heard of this before, " said Butch. "You said it's in the greenbelt? Where does it go?"

"Ever been to Barton Creek? The cave used to be the underground stream course that fed it. Ever been to Barton Creek Mall? You were standing over part of the cave."

"Really?" said Butch. "Did you know there's a cave over by Lakeline Mall? But that one is locked up."

"Oh, Airman's Cave is locked up, too."

"It's locked up? So, my new bucket list item is to break into a locked cave?"

"The city opens it once a month."

"So, why would I want to go into this cave?"

"For the same basic reasons you would climb Everest: self mastery, overcoming fear, seeing things that only a few have seen, doing something that just a few have done. Far fewer people have explored Airman's Cave than have climbed Everest."

"But a cave?"

"It's a whole lot cheaper than a trek to Tibet. It's still a feat of physical endurance, but a lot less training is required. And there's nowhere to fall."

"Actually, the usual access to Everest is in Nepal," I said. "What's so hard about going in a cave?"

"There's quite a bit of crawling. Your knees and elbows might get sore."

"Why would I want to crawl over rock till my elbows were sore just to say I did it?"

"Why would you want to risk your life in freezing cold just to say you did it?"

"There's a spectacular view. What does the cave have? You've seen one crawl space, you've seen them all."

"This is not a shimmy under your 1940's house in East Austin to fix leaky plumbing. This is a crawl through the Cretaceous. Oh, there is the Aggie Art Gallery and the cavern with walls covered in geodes. If you can reach it."

Then, he whispered, albeit quite audibly, "You have to read a map. There's no GPS. Of course, it you are afraid of the dark..."

At that the conversation died. Butch went off to a meeting, and I burrowed back into my network logs. Morgan returned to whatever we paid him exorbitant amounts to do. At five o'clock, they left. As usual, I stayed on.

Around seven o'clock Susan came by to ask if I were on the trail of a stuxnet infestation. I told her no, and then she suggested that I go home.

"Are you on call?" she asked.

"No. Not this week."

"Then, go home. But the next time you are on-call, call me. It makes me feel secure to know there is a strong man standing over me."

As I walked out the door, I wondered what she meant by that.

Sometimes I wished I didn't live downtown. Other people stopped by the store on their way home. Every store I wanted to visit was out of my way. I had to walk home and get my car to go anywhere except to a restaurant or a club. There were moments when I wished I cooked, that I kept wine in a wine fridge or even beer in the refrigerator. But I didn't. Nearly everything I consumed was handed to me over a counter or delivered to my door in a box or a bag. I did go to Central Market on occasion, but I usually just ate in the cafe. Sometimes, I bought fresh roasted coffee beans. Once I purchased five pounds of organic apples. About four pounds rotted in the bag.

That night I went to Chipotle to eat on the way home. I stopped at my the condo just long enough to get my car keys. It was a badge of honor for me not to take my car to work. To prove the point, I seldom carried my keys. I kept my cubicle unlocked, and I opened my condo with a password on my iPhone. This evening, however, I needed my own transportation. I went to the garage and found the Abarth.

Of course, the Abarth was in the same spot it always was, but it wasn't in the right spot. By all rights my parking spot should have been on the down ramp just beyond the stairs. Then, I could have backed out and driven straight down one level and out the exit. Instead, the building authorities took advantage of my car's truly compact construction to stick me in the most awkward spot in the garage. I had to open my door just half way to avoid hitting the wall while ducking the pipe that ran level with my head. When I pulled out I had to honk my horn lest someone hit me coming up, and I had to drive up a level before I could head back down. For all that they gave me a twenty dollar per month break on my maintenance fees. They also gave me no choice. If I hadn't loved the Fiat so much, I would have considered buying a full-sized truck to force them to give me a better place.

I squeezed in the car, honked the horn, and backed out downhill. Then, I yanked up the handbrake, let out the clutch, punched the accelerator, and released the brake. When I first got the car, the engine stalled at this point three out of five times. I kept the engine alive only by means of burned rubber. Finally, I learned the Zen of leaving my parking spot and could do so in a state of peace. That is, I could accelerate up the ramp without spinning my wheels, but I made the two turns to get back to the down ramp under at least 0.65 G's, and the sound of my tires gripping the concrete echoed up and down the garage. My custom, aftermarket exhaust reverberated past the firewall and into the condo living space.

My neighbors were glad that I didn't drive much. They all approached the parking garage slopes differently, but they all had automatics.

I headed south from the garage and took a right on Sixth Street. I didn't stop at any of the bars or restaurants but continued on to Lamar and headed north. I arrived at Whole Earth Provisions by eight-twenty. I knew I didn't have a lot of time, but I could not go in unprepared. Even if the sales staff tolerated ignorance, the other customers would not. I spent fifteen minutes with Google and Wikipedia learning what the well dressed cave explorer should wear. I was disappointed to learn that Whole Earth did not carry the knee pads or suits I saw on the internet.

"Go to Academy for soccer pads," the sales clerk said with a certain disdain in his voice, and I left there with only a rock climber's helmet and a headlamp. When I got out the door, it was after nine.

Academy would have to wait for another night.

By the time I got home, I was beginning to feel buyer's remorse, but I put on the helmet and lamp and crawled under the bed. Thanks to my maid service, the floor underneath was pretty clean. I didn't sneeze or get short of breath.

It was a tight squeeze, but I made it all the way and came out of the other side. When I got out from under the bed, I jumped up and turned out all the lights. Then, I resumed my place on the floor. I crawled across the bedroom to the closet and went inside, all by the light of my headlamp. I pushed aside shoes, old gaming consoles and fallen clothes and worked my way around the edge of the closet floor. My clothes and shelves hung above me like stalactites. I emerged from the closet and headed for the living room crawling like a GI in Call of Duty. When I got to the coffee table, I couldn't get under it because of cross piece bracing the legs, so I gave up. I switched on the real lights and pulled off the helmet. I probably would need to go back to get the fit adjusted, but I was pretty pleased with the headlamp. My knees were sore, and I had a rug burn from the Persian rug by the sofa. Still, I hadn't done badly. I spent the rest of the evening looking for an application from The City of Austin Parks Department to enter Airman's Cave. I couldn't find one. That seemed a little strange, but I remained undaunted. I went out on Sixth Street and tried a few watering holes. The bars were no help, but, finally, I found what I was looking for at Starbucks. The girl who brewed my decaf espresso (a man's got to sleep) gave me a URL for The South Austin Caveman. I checked out his web site and sent him an email while I sipped my espresso. Then, I went home to bed. It was twelve thirty AM. At one thirty I woke up dreaming about bats. I went back to sleep with the light on. Thus, when I woke up, the room was not entirely dark.

5 – The Birth Canal

The Cave Man's name was Richard Magdon. He was very cordial in his emails except he wouldn't give me any real information. We corresponded back and forth for awhile, but he made no disclosures about the cave. Then, one Thursday evening he sent me a message asking me to meet him at Kerbey Lane Cafe.

"Richard Magdon? Do they call you Dick?"

"I'm not sure who 'they' are, so I can't really tell you what 'they' call me. But my friends and my clients call me Cro."

"Oh. 'Crow' with a W?"

"No."

"Oh. Well, okay. I'm interested in—"

"Here's the deal, Gus. I do take people into Airman's Cave. I'm one of the few tour guides the city will let in, so if you don't go in with me, you're probably not going in at all. I'd be glad to take you into the cave. In fact, I'm taking in a group this weekend. That group is already full, and after that I'm going to Peru to take a party into La Gruta de Guagapo. I won't be back for a month. When I do get back, it will take me at least a few months to gather another group and get reservations with the city to go back into Airman's. But that's all right, because, unless I am mistaken, you don't have much experience in caving."

"I've been to Inner Space Cavern."

"Did you take the wild tour?"

"Yes."

"How much did you pay?"

"Uh, fifteen dollars."

"No you didn't. That tour costs a hundred dollars."

"Well, maybe it was a different tour. No, I think I had a coupon."

"Doesn't matter. You aren't ready. But, if you will follow my advice and try some of the caves I suggest, then by the time I have organized another excursion into Airman's, well, you'll be first on the list."

"Really? You're that strict about it?"

"I'm afraid so. You see, I take cave exploration very seriously, and it is against my professional code of ethics to take anyone into a cave who is not mentally and physically prepared."

"I am very disappointed," I said. I felt compelled to make an issue of this cave. "But I understand. I would not for a single minute want to see you violate your professional code of ethics as a cave man. But, you see, Airman's Cave was the last item on my bucket list, and with the delay you mention, well, I seriously doubt if I will be here in six months to complete my list. I think—".

I stopped and swallowed hard.

"I fear I will have to go unfulfilled."

"No," said Cro. "No! If you need to enter Airman's Cave to fulfill your personal goals, I am there for you," and the cave man grabbed my right hand in a hearty shake. "I am all about helping people reach their personal best and achieve their dreams. Say no more. I will find a way to squeeze you into this tour."

"Thank you," I said, somewhat touched and genuinely surprised. I hadn't expected him to buy it, but then, I noticed he was not letting go of my hand. In fact, he was squeezing it harder.

"But if you hold up our progress or make me have to drag you out, I'll make sure you never leave the light of day to go underground in this state again. You'll have to go to Arkansas to find a burial plot."

"I understand."

"In that case," he said, "welcome to another quality Cro Magdon Tour! Let me get you to sign the release forms."

I signed the form, three separate forms in fact, with my finger on his iPad, and he sent me PDF copies. I released Richard Magdon Enterprises of all liability in the event of my injury or death. I agreed to hold the City of Austin free from indemnity. I agreed not to enter into any other underground tour contracts with any other entities to go into Airman's Cave for a period of six months. I swiped my American Express across the card reader. I paid his two hundred dollar fee and a fifty dollar surcharge for joining the tour late. I put up a refundable $5,000 bond in case the city had to rescue me, and I paid a non-refundable thirty-five dollar insurance premium to cover any additional rescue and medical expenses on top of the bond. When everything was duly signed and filed, Cro shook my hand for the last time.

"I will email you the map and the instructions. We'll see you at the mouth of the cave at five AM Saturday morning."

"Really? Five?"

"Absolutely! We've got a lot of crawling to do on Saturday."

Evening and morning and it was Friday. I walked to work and stopped a Distributed Denial of Service Attack with only a network firewall and a little JavaScript. It did it nearly single-handedly. Butch was out of the office, and Morgan offered just minor advice. Susan was so pleased she gave me a gift card to an Argentine steak house as a reward. I thought about using it that night, but it was not on Cro's recommended pre-caving diet.

"What the hell," I thought, but then, I remembered the bond. Besides, the certificate was a dinner for two, and I had no one to invite. So, I drove home and went to bed early.

Evening and morning, and it was Saturday.

The weather was surprisingly cool and damp when I arrived at the mouth of the cave at 5:18 AM. I was expecting a lecture from my guide, but Cro was already in the cave. The members of the caving party were entering one at a time after him. There were still three people waiting their turn. There was also a City of Austin park ranger. He looked at me with a certain measure of suspicion and disgust.

"Is your name on the list?" he asked.

I showed him my ID. He didn't seem satisfied, but he did look mollified.

"Have you been in the cave before?" he asked.

"No, but I've already put up my deposit."

"Doesn't matter to me. I'm not going in there after you. I just don't want you getting stuck and holding up the tour."

"Getting stuck?"

One of the three waiting cavers turned around and looked at me.

"Are you Gus?"

"Yeah. I had a little trouble parking—"

"Cro said you'd be late. He said I should make sure you got in okay—if you made it in time. Which you have. You can go next after Maize. I'll follow after and give you instructions from behind. For now, watch Maize."

"Maize?"

"Yeah. That's Maize."

I turned around and looked to see a woman heading into the cave. She was wearing a climbing helmet, headlamp, and pads on her knees and elbows. She had a small pack dangling by a cord from her left hand.

Maize looked vaguely familiar, but I couldn't see her face.

"Hey! You got extra batteries for that lamp?"

"Yeah."

"No you don't. Cro said you wouldn't. Here."

He handed me a pair of triple A's."

"Not in your shirt pocket. You haven't got a button. Pants pocket. And take off that pack. You'll never get through the Birth Canal with that thing on. Didn't you read the instructions?"

"The Birth Canal?"

But he was already pulling my pack off my shoulders.

"Push it ahead of you," he said, "till you get through the canal."

"But..."

"Go! Follow Maize. Go!"

I turned around hoping to see a friendly, encouraging face, but all I could see was a pair of legs scrambling to push a torso into an impossibly narrow hole in the rock. I dropped to my knees in amazement to peer in after her. I could see her light reflecting off rock somewhere ahead, but beyond that was darkness. I watched as that pair of legs wriggled into the hole. When the neon soles of her shoes had receded into the depths, the caver behind me gave me a push.

"Lie on your belly hands above your head and wriggle."

For reasons beyond my comprehension I obeyed. I scooted like a soldier under barbed wire, and so I maneuvered my body into the canal just past my hips. That was the point when my knees hit the mouth of the cave.

"Now what?" I said. I didn't know who could hear me even though I could hear voices and laughter up ahead.

"Straighten your legs," said my coach, his voice coming from where the ambient light of the city still reached. I obeyed and felt myself being pushed from behind. "Now wriggle and pull with your hands. Push with your toes."

My fingers and toes followed instructions even though my brain became as impassive as the rock, but progress was slow. Then, the caver behind pushed me. He pushed on my feet far enough to get me out of his own way. Once he was in the canal himself he couldn't push anymore, but he wielded a force that impelled me forward nonetheless. I made another twelve inches in response to his beratement. Then, I came to a realization I had been avoiding for the past several years.

I had become fat. My waist had expanded into a tummy like the Buddha in the Thai restaurant where I ate more meals than I cared to count. My chin drooped. My arms had begun to expand for reasons that had nothing to do with the gym, and my cholesterol was high. Within my arteries plaque had undoubtedly formed so that my red blood cells were even now struggling to pass through the vascular walls even as I was struggling to pass through this cave. Only I was not passing through the cave. I was stuck. Cold damp fear came upon me. I was going to die where I lay. My arms were above my head. If my headlamp had gone out, I could not have lowered my arm to reach into my pants pocket to retrieve Cro's extra batteries. I could not raise my knee or position my foot to push me any further. In my own foolish attempt to pad my bucket list, I had already kicked my bucket over. My heart pounded against the rock pressing upon my chest. I remembered a film I had seen on the IFC channel in which a man awakened in a coffin to discover he had been buried alive. I, however, had crawled into this hole myself. On top of this, I still had no life insurance and no reason for it. I had nothing of me to leave behind, and no one to leave it to.

Just then, at the point when all reason and hope had left me, I heard a voice, a female voice. I couldn't see her because my pack was in the way, but I could hear her in front of me in the tunnel.

"I'm stuck," I said in response. "I can't move. I'm going to die. I want to die."

"You stupid son of a bitch!" I heard from the caver behind.

"John, be quiet. You're not going to die, not here anyway. Take a deep breath. Deep. Hold it. Hold it. Now exhale. All of it. Don't inhale yet. Now, squirm your way forward."

"I can't do it."

"You can do it. Don't talk. Breathe in. Deep. Deep. Hold it. Hold it. Exhale. Shimmy."

"I'm too fat."

"No, you're not. Cro wouldn't have let you in the tour if you were. Have you ever crawled under your bed?"

"Yes."

"Then, you can do this. Think like a worm. Inhale. Fill the space with your body. Feel yourself expand right up to the wall of the cave. Push against it with your ribs. Now release the pressure. Shrink back away from the cave walls. You've created a space to move. Now, think like a worm. Move your hips. Inch forward.

My shoulders moved an inch.

"That's it. I can hear you do it. Little more. Now breathe. In and out. In and out. Deep. Hold it. Puff out. Release and squirm. Squirm. Inhale deep. Exhale. Squirm."

She talked me in, one breath at a time. I exhaled. I squirmed, only inches at first, always only inches, but more of them each time. When I inhaled, I shoved my bag as hard as I could forward and let go. When I exhaled I made for that bag and didn't inhale again until I reached it. Over and over. Shoulders and hips, fingers and toes. And then my bag slid away out of reach. I thought I had lost my lifeline, my little attainable goal. But then the birth canal filled with light. I closed my eyes and became blind like the worm. But I had fingers, and now someone was grasping them. It was Maize. She had come back in head first and was inching backwards to my forwards. The pull she created drew me. I no longer had to think about breathing. My hips and shoulders moved in coordination, and the squirm became a scramble.

Then, her light left my face. She fell away. My fingers found an edge. My elbows found the same edge. I pushed back against it with my hands. My torso fell forwards. I reached down with my one hand to the floor of the cave and pushed back with the other. Then, my hips were out of the tunnel. I put both hands down and walked on them till my knees emerged. I was out of the birth canal and into Airman's Cave.

6 – The Underground Horizon

Only when I was in the cave and out of the way of John, the caver behind, did I get a good look at Maize. I realized she was my vampire I had met on Sixth Street and seen at Central Market with the organic beef.

"I think we've met before," I said.

She didn't answer, but grabbed my arm and pulled me forward. I heard the sound of either palms or orcs' feet slapping against rock. The caver behind me who had tried to impel me forward by the sheer force of insult was emerging from the canal like my second born twin. I noticed he was no more adept at squeezing out of an impossibly tight stone orifice than I had been.

"Please move along. We have two more cavers trying to get into the cave."

I turned to see the voice that was speaking to me and saw it was Cro's. I had forgotten he was even on this tour. Then, I remembered what the caver behind had said. Cro thought I would not be prepared. He probably had not expected me to make it even this far. The fact that I really had not been prepared made no further difference.

"Come on," I said to Maize, "let's continue on with this quality Cro Magdon tour."

After everyone had come through the birth canal, Cro Magdon took his place at the head of the group and led us on into the cave. I kept up behind Maize trying to stay well ahead of John who remained the caver behind me throughout most of the excursion. I never learned his precise relationship to Cro, whether he was paid to bring up the rear and drive on the stragglers or whether he was in fact a zealous amateur frustrated by those with less enthusiasm than he had for crawling into utter darkness. Whatever his motivation, I took great pains to stay out of his way for the rest of the tour.

Once when I was eight or nine, I found a stretch of long sewer pipes lying on top of the ground along the major street at the other end of my block. Normally I stayed away from that road and its traffic, but that night those pipes offered enough apparent protection from fast moving cars for me to ignore my mother's warning to stay off that busy street. My friends and I crawled for several blocks through those pipes on our hands and knees. We got back on our feet to dart from one pipe to another and to cross the side streets between blocks. Then, we ran quickly in a crouch like soldiers advancing from one hedge to another. We took joy in running without standing up.

That sewer line had presented us a more spacious thoroughfare and more wholesome atmosphere than did Airman's Cave. For hours we could not stand up. Sometimes the floor beneath our hands and knees was hard rock. Sometimes it was slimey clay. Sometimes it consisted of broken and jagged chunks of rock that had fallen from the ceiling. I soon came to believe that we had crawled not into the womb of the earth but into her small intestine. After coming through the birth canal, I had been glad to have space to crawl on all fours and sit upright. After a quarter mile on my knees, squirming on my belly again was a relief. But then, my knees and palms still had to push, pull and scrape to propel my body along. My belly left a slime trail of my own epidermis even through my shirt. I felt like a western movie cowboy being dragged across the desert from a horse except I was having to drag myself where no horse could ever have fit. When we were finally able to stand on our feet, waves of relief moved down my arms, my chest, stomach and legs, but most of the time, what passed for standing in Airman's Cave would have been called crouching anywhere else under the sun.

I took whatever pleasure there was to be had in the cave from keeping as close to Maize as I could. I made a game of reaching for her heels every time I lifted my palm from rock though I never touched them. I kept my headlamp focused on her blue jeaned butt, and whenever it faded from sight, I pulled whatever strength I had left out of my panic and pushed on till I could see her again. This became my sole motivation for going deeper into the cave. By the end of the expedition, it had become my sole motivation for getting out.

Did I say I spent all my cave time scooting, crawling, creeping and stooping on rock? That was not so. Much of Airman's Cave was actually wet clay. In fact, when we reached the first chamber where we all could gather together in a circle and see each other somewhat clearly for the first time, the floor, walls and ceiling were plastered in the stuff. And it was all red.

"This is how you know you are in a different geological stratum," said Cro. "Where in Austin can you find clay east of I35?"

Because of the color of the clay and because we were in Austin, previous cavers had called the chamber The Aggie Art Gallery, and they had filled the chamber with misshapen clay sculptures. It looked like a kindergarten open house. At least, the skill level was like kindergarten if not the subject matter. We turned off our headlamps and looked at the gallery by the light of a single lamp placed in the center of us all. Every one of us was already filthy, the mud and fossilized muck of another geological era ground into our clothes and skin. I wondered if I would even be able to recognize any of my fellow cavers on the street after this. I was glad I had had cornea laser surgery and no longer had glasses to keep clean in a place like this. I felt more evolved. Perhaps we would know one another again above ground, tattooed as we all now were with Cretaceous limestone. As I looked about our party, I felt Cretaceous myself. I was older than most of the group. Except for Cro himself, everyone else was in his or her twenties. I tried to project a sage and augustly image, but Maize did not seem to notice. We sat next to each other but did not speak. We looked around a little at our fellow cavers and at those pitiful sculptures, but mostly we looked straight ahead to the light in the center of the circle. Even though I did take quick and frequent glances at the side of her pretty face, nothing in that hole under the mall was quite as lovely as the light itself. It seemed that we had brought it with us not to illuminate the cave but so that we could see the light itself for the first time.

After the Aggie Art Gallery we plunged on into the darkness. The cave seemed to mock me. I could hear the team voices ahead expressing delight at every change of strata; I found every change to be a disappointment. Whenever the cave opened up and presented us with a clear path in which we could stand up and walk, it closed up again in short order. I was glad to get out of the clay, but the rock was abrasive. Then, the rock became smooth, but that made it harder to get traction. Every change of condition became first a relief and then a different kind of obstacle. If this was a better choice for my bucket list than climbing the ice of Everest, it was not apparent to me.

At the end of one tunnel the cave opened up into a wide vista. It was as if one western desert mesa had been inverted and suspended above another with no visible supports between them as far as the eye and lantern light could see. It was a vast panoramic horizon under the earth no more than fourteen inches high. I wondered that the ceiling did not come crushing down upon me, and yet the upper mesa seemed to float firmly above the lower one. Every time I rose off my belly to push on I feared I would dislodge it. It never moved, but I did. My hands began to slide. I slipped sideways into the horizontal void to my left, or was it to my right? I rose up on palms and knees to lodge myself between the upper and lower firmament, and then the two reversed positions, and the upper became the lower. Apparently, the two were interchangeable. I became a spider crawling on the ceiling, my back occasionally scraping the floor. How did the upper and lower switch positions so readily? It must have been the rotation of the globe. The entire earth moved around me as if I were on the central axis. Then, I was falling again. Then, I was upright. Sideways and falling. Inverted. Falling. Upright. Then, the spin stopped.

I scanned the length and breadth of that subterranean horizon to find its boundary, but my headlamp could not find one. Then, I saw another tunnel. It looked like a black portal in the darkness, a hole in the wall where there was no wall. I could just see the soles of Maize's shoes disappearing into that hole. I followed her like Alice following the white rabbit. Inside, jagged rocks lay on the path, rocks that had fallen from the ceiling, rocks we had to crawl over. Above us were more rocks waiting their turn to fall. I was alarmed at the prospect and amazed at the irony. The vast expanse of the twin mesas had held, one suspended just above the other in subterranean space, but the rocks in this narrow tunnel were falling. Perhaps the stones here knew which way was down.

The way was filled with obstruction, but Maize was airy and thin. With her I became most thin and somehow slid across the broken floor and under the overhead compression. But my lightness of being did not last long.

An hour past the panorama, my muscles hardened like the rock and fused with the stratum. I could no longer move. I was becoming petrified, immobile in stone itself. Sweat flowed out like water I had seen seeping out of the sides of hills along the highway after a sustained rain. It flowed from me into the rock. In a year or so, it would join in the Edwards Aquifer. From there it would stream out of the kitchen tap of some homeowner in San Antonio. In ten millennia would the earth thrust up this stratum and then someone find my mineralized body beside the newly laid South Lamar rail line? Not in a million years!

As the sweat poured out fear seeped in from the darkness to displace it. I felt it in my gut. I could taste it. It was a metallic taste just on the tip of my tongue that turned to numbness in my lips. I wanted to run, but I couldn't even stand. I tried to crawl, but I was frozen. I remembered a pistol I had seen in a Cabelas ad, one made to fit in your pocket. I wished I had bought it and that it was in my pocket now. I wished that I could reach it if it were.

Then, I saw a woman's face lit up in the cave. It must have been Maize, but I couldn't quite recognize her. I couldn't see through my sweat. No, my eyes weren't burning. It must have been tears that blurred whatever was left to see.

"Don't be afraid," she said. We two alone were in that tiny space. "Come on, Gus. I'll lead you through this."

I felt my crystallizing body break free from the rock. There was just enough gap between me and the stone for me to slide through. I kept sliding. My knees hurt. My hips hurt. My shoulders and neck hurt from holding my head on the horizontal. Even my toes and fingers hurt, but I followed that light till I could see Maize's green soles again. Then, I followed those soles. When those disappeared I followed the trail from my headlamp till I found her soles again.

And so I made it to the part of the cave called the One-Legged Man. There I could stand up for the first time in hours.

The One-Legged Man section had a high ceiling for this cave but the passage was narrow, barely wide enough for one. That would have been fine. I could have walked through it with only an occasional scraping of my shoulder against the wall if it had not been for the big rocks blocking most of the lower half. That meant I had to raise my one leg and lay it across the top of each rock while my other leg squeezed down into a small crevice to the floor. So, I pushed against my cocked, raised leg to drag my extended leg through the crevice. Then, the next step I pushed my other leg against the cave floor so I could drag my knee and shin over the rock. My greatest fear was that my hip would go out of place. My second was that I would lose a shoe and be unable to reach it.

At the end of the One-Legged Man, Cro had called a stop to wait for everyone to catch up. I envied the ones who had already made it and were already enjoying their rest. As it was a couple of my fellow cavers pulled me off the last rock and dragged me to what I was sure would be a very short-lived respite. Cro squeezed past the others and greeted me personally as I struggled to refill my lungs and straighten my legs. I was sure by now this was an orc passage under Austin, not a grand dwarven mine under the mountain.

"Great job, Gus. You made it. You are nearly halfway."

Somehow, I was able to croak out a question between deep gasps.

"Halfway? We're only halfway to the end of the cave?"

"More than half. You're practically there."

I smiled. I think I smiled. My facial muscles hurt doing it, so I must have. That made the pain in my body unanimous.

"Eat something. Drink. There's a tunnel off to the left where you can pee and take a dump. Rest. We make our final push in ten minutes."

I looked down at my shoes. My laces needed retying, but I couldn't bend over or work my fingers to do it.

I looked around for Maize, but my lamp began to flicker. I couldn't pick her out.

"Where are those batteries I gave you? You better change them now, and switch off your lamp whenever you can see by someone else's light."

It was the caver from behind.

"Why?" I said. "Cro said we were close to the end. This other set of batteries should get me out with juice to spare."

"He meant halfway to the end of the cave, not to the exit. We still have to turn around and go back."

"Go back? Doesn't the cave come out somewhere else?"

"No. Didn't you look at the map Cro sent you? You go out the way you came in. Adjust your knee pads, and conserve your batteries."

I had looked at the map, but the fact that the end of the cave on the map was not another exit to the surface of Austin had escaped my notice. With that realization, I felt all hope drain into the rock. I spent the last of my energy getting into the tunnel to the left. There the last dribble of my bodily fluids slipped through a fissure and begun a descent towards the Edwards Aquifer. If any moisture had remained in my body, I would have cried.

Then, I saw Maize's face again. It was right next to mine. She did look rather vampirish in the last of my LED light.

"Here. Eat this."

It was an energy bar.

"Drink your water."

She pulled an energy drink out of my pack and held it before my face.

"Can you see this? Don't drink it. Not till we get closer to the entrance. Your energy will crash."

So, I ate and drank, and on that oatmeal raisin bar, twenty ounces of Aquafina, and the hope from the green glow of the soles of Maize's shoes, I somehow made it to the very end of Airman's Cave. We all huddled there like doomed men each of whom had completed the last item on his bucket list and was now waiting his turn to die. In turn, Cro was taking each of us separately into one last hole. No doubt he was offering every person a final resting place there at Cave's End. I decided if he made the offer to me, no matter what it cost I would accept.

I was the last one to enter that hole. Cro went in first. As I followed he reached his hand to my helmet and shut off my lamp. I was engulfed in utter darkness. His hand grabbed mine and pulled me forward a few more steps. The taste of fear returned to my tongue, but now I knew there was only one escape from the fear. I was about to tell him he could put my burial expenses on the same credit card that I had used to pay for the tour when he struck a match and lit a candle in a small lantern. I thought I had been transported back a hundred and fifty years to a time when miners crept without electric lights into such dark places looking for gold. I saw Cro's face. He was looking at me as if he were wondering what was wrong with me. What was wrong with me? Did he not recognize death when he saw it? I was about to ask him that question when he jerked his head over his left shoulder. I followed the tilt of his head, and then I saw the walls of the cave.

Every thing around us glittered. The entire subterranean room sparkled in the light of a thousand candles all kindled from that one candle. The ceiling was set with stars, stars close enough to reach. I reached up and touched one. It was moist.

"Isn't it beautiful?"

"What is it?" I said. "Is it gold?"

"No. We are inside a geode. To be perfectly honest, most of this cave tour is about endurance. Can you overcome your claustrophobia? How far can you crawl? There isn't much to see. Until now. Most people never make it this far, but here you are."

He said nothing about his doubts about me, the ones revealed to me by the caver behind.

"But I got you here, and now I will get out. Once you exit the cave, my liability ends. Avoid bright lights and alcohol for the first few hours."

And he did get me out, he and Maize. Back through the One-Legged-Man, back through the horizontal panorama with the severe vertical pinch, back through the clay, back through three rest stops and another battery change, all the way to the birth canal. Cro went out first and set the lantern where we could see it. That is when I first realized it was dark outside. I was the second to the last out. Someone else took my bag, my helmet and my headlamp. I stripped down to basics. I waited till I could see the light, unblocked by the caver before me, and then entered the canal. Maize entered behind me. Whenever I stopped, she tapped my foot and told me to exhale and wriggle, but the canal was not as tight as it had been going in. Five miles of crawling on my hands and knees and my belly had taken several pounds off my weight and a couple of inches off my waist. When I emerged my pants were off my hips. I managed to pull them up as Maize wriggled out of the cave.

"And that is it," said Cro. "Thanks everyone for good caving, and a good morning to you all."

With that Cro Magdon was gone, and so was everyone else except me and Maize, the vampire girl. For her sake, I was glad it was not daylight. As for me, by this time the city darkness seemed bright.

"What time is it?" I asked.

"I don't know. I left my phone in my car. You have a watch."

"I do? I can't move my wrist to see it."

She gently grabbed my wrist and twisted it around so she could see.

"Twelve thirty. We've been in the cave almost twenty hours."

I nodded without real comprehension.

"Come on," she said. "Where's your car?"

I couldn't really remember, but she found it. She opened the door and looked inside.

"This won't do. It's a standard, and you can barely walk. Besides, you'll get clay all over your nice seats. You're covered in it. Here's what we'll do. We'll lock your car back up, and we'll leave it here. We'll take my car."

I liked the idea of we, but I protested about leaving my Abarth behind.

"But someone will break in or steal it."

"I don't think so. Besides, you're insured."

I marveled that she knew that. It was true.

7 – The Bathroom Window

Maize's car was an old Suburban. She practically pushed me into the passenger seat and then climbed into the driver's seat beside me. Even the front of the vehicle seemed large, much bigger inside than the cave. I thought of the compactness of my own car, like a cave in itself. The Suburban was spacious but not in good repair. Maize had seat covers stretched over the front seats, and the headliner drooped. That, I supposed, was why she wasn't so concerned about the clay.

"I could have put you in the back, but you would probably fall asleep, and I need you to navigate."

"I live downtown. You can take Fifth Street."

"Got it."

I turned around slowly to look at the back seat to see just how wide it was in case I did want to lie down. There was no back seat. The remainder of this vast vehicle was empty.

"Oh, that," she said, as if she knew what I was thinking. "My friends and I took the seats out. I used to be into vampirism, and we would put a coffin in the back and take turns lying down in it and riding around town. It was pretty cool arriving at Sixth Street, opening the back and having the dead man sit up and climb out."

"That could be cool." I said, trying deliberately to be ingratiating.

"But I hated it. When it was my turn, I made them remove the lid. I couldn't stand being shut up in there. Even with the lid off I couldn't take it. So, when the old Caravan that we used to haul the coffin around in died, I bought this old Suburban and offered it up instead. I told them I only had liability, so I had to drive. That way I got out of riding in the back. They didn't mind because no one else could park the thing, especially at night. So, I avoided the coffin. I also avoided getting my bicuspids fanged. I told everyone I couldn't afford it. If I had worked for the city or had been on disability, I could have had my fanging paid for, but I didn't see any future in it. Also, I don't like the taste of blood."

"Turn left on Brazos."

"I thought I could do it. I died my hair black. My skin is fair. I put more red blush in my cheeks. I tried to be gaunt, and I wanted to be dead, but I wasn't. And vampires are supposed to live forever, right? Well, Mike died. Mike, my friend."

She said "friend" with a little deliberate hesitation.

"He laid in that coffin right back there. He drank blood. He never went out in the daytime, and he still died. After that, I gave up on the undead thing.

"Right here. You can park on the street till seven."

"You mean till Monday?"

"Yeah, I guess so."

I had forgotten what day it was.

"Today is Sunday."

I nodded. She climbed out of the car, came around, and opened my door. I could barely turn my hips to get my foot on the step. My right knee almost buckled before my left foot reached the curb. Maize held me up and got me into the building. As the elevator rose I felt like a coal miner being rescued from a cave-in. Maize turned to me as we ascended. By the elevator light I began to see she shared my own condition. Her hair was plastered down from sweat. Her clothes were caked in dried mud. Her face was smudged. Her fingers left clay on the elevator buttons. Only the soles of our shoes left no muddy tracks because in the cave we had spent so little time on our feet.

"You know how you are supposed to be able to be anything you want to be? What you are intrinsically doesn't matter? What you decide yourself to be—that's what they say matters?"

"Yeah," I said being agreeable again.

"Don't you believe it. When we get inside, can I use your

shower?"

I thought of a line from a country song I used to hear on Robert's car radio: 'She doesn't know she's beautiful.'"

She guided me past the sofa and the recliner all the way to the bathroom. I sat down on the toilet seat, and she stripped off my shoes and socks from my feet and the shirt from over my head. My neck and shoulders were as stiff as stone, and the cold dampness of the cave clung to me still. I shivered there on the toilet seat, but Maize did not relent.

"Stand."

She pulled my pants and boxers down to my ankles.

"Step!" she said and pushed me out of my clothes and into the tub. She drew the water up to the overflow.

"Soak!"

So I soaked. I soaked until the water became opaque with ancient sediment. While I soaked, I heard the shower running. I wanted to get up and join Maize in the shower, but wrapped in warmth, my tightened muscles began to relax. My clay covered body became like putty. The warmth of the water flowed in replacing the cold, and I began dissolving in contentment.

I awoke to the sound of water draining. I was cold again.

"I found this brush. I don't know what you used it for, but it has to be cleaner than you are right now. Man, you have a lot of hot water in this apartment."

"It's a condo. The hot water's tank-less."

She drew more water and began to scrub. I think she was wearing my T-shirt, but it no longer mattered. I was six again sitting in the tub while my mother hovered over me. I was in the hospital, and the nurse was lifting the bandage to see if the hernia incision in my groin was healing. Sex did not hold first place in this relationship. Sex would come later, after I got better, after I had recovered. After I had grown up.

I awoke in bed. The sheets were clean. I was wearing clean underwear. No one else was in the room. It was three o'clock in the afternoon, and the room was filled with light. I got up quickly, but stiffness fell on me again like a panther. I straightened up anyway and stumbled about the condo. Maize was gone. By the front door lay a gray garbage bag, cinched and tied. I stooped and opened it up. There were my clothes from the cave. There also were a woman's clothes including a bra, just as stained as the jeans. We had entered the depths of Earth, and the Cretaceous had embedded itself in our clothes and in our flesh. I shuffled back to the couch. The leather was cold. Normally in Austin that was a good thing but not now. I put my hands on the coffee table and lowered myself to the rug on the floor. It reminded me of the cave.

Maize had been here. She had scrubbed me clean, put me to bed, used my shower, and either put on some of my clothes or run down the street naked. Maybe she had just run down for Thai and would be right back.

I sat on the rug a long time. After I tired of sitting, I laid down on it without sleeping. I lay there alone staring at the leather couch where I often went to fall asleep. Butch said he usually fell asleep on the couch until his wife told him to get up and go to bed for the sake of his back. I started in bed and got up to lie on the couch where loneliness was not so stark. The couch was much more cozy for one than the king sized bed was. Robert had always slept in a twin bed like a child. Maybe he had understood the advantage of a narrow bed for a single man.

I would have let Maize have the bed all to herself if she had asked. I would have gladly taken the couch and the cold to gain even the residual warmth of her in my bed. My bed was much larger than a coffin. It would have been the perfect place for her to sleep. Why did I think she needed anywhere to sleep? She probably had an apartment with a roommate. Maybe she had a bed mate. I lay on the floor and waited.

Today was Sunday. That led my mind to Monday. I had to work on Monday. Then, I remembered the Abarth was still parked off South Lamar. I jumped up off the floor, but I could only reach about two thirds of full standing stature. My back, my legs, my hips—they all arrested me in mid stretch. I walked like Igor to the bedroom where I crawled into clean clothes. Then, I reached for my keys. The condo key was there, the one I kept in case the power went out and the keypad didn't work, but the fob to the Abarth was gone. My Car2Go card was missing.

I grabbed the condo key and headed out the door. I would have run down the stairs, but hours of crawling had taken all the run out of me. Instead, I waited for the elevator. I rode down to street level in what seemed like geological time. It was cold in the elevator. I must have crawled through the remnants of an Ice Age in the cave and brought it with me to the surface of Austin. How come only past geological eras had names? What -cene was this? The Austi-cene? I felt the heat of late afternoon on my skin, but the cold was still in my bones, unreachable by the sun.

In the lobby of my building I began to wonder just how was I going to get to my car and how was I going to get it home? The fob that I was now missing was actually the spare. I had lost the original months ago. Someone was walking the streets with my first fob in his pocket sweeping beside parked Fiat 500's hoping the locks on one of them would pop so he could drive it away. Maybe he had finally found the one that matched.

Yet, when I reached the sidewalk of Brazos, there was my Abarth. At least, it looked like mine. It was white with red highlights. It had the moon roof, the spoiler, and the black wheels. It said "Turbo" on the side. It was parked at the curb precisely where Maize's Suburban had been. That is, it was parked where the front half of the Suburban had been. The second half of that Suburban spot was occupied by a Car2Go. Both of my usual vehicles were sitting right there in front of me, but there was no benefit to either. Without my fob and without my card, both were lost to me. I looked at the plates of the Abarth; I realized I did not know my own license plate number. I had it on my phone in a picture of the plate. I also had the image of my registration. My phone—it was not on my hip in its swivel case. It was not in my pocket, and it was not back up the elevator in the condo. It was in the hands of the man from the City of Austin. I had given it to him before I entered the cave, he the keeper of valuables, the public servant whom you could trust to hold the stuff of your life while you engaged in adventures. I hadn't thought much about giving him my phone at the time. He wouldn't have been able to get in and use it. I had a great password, and everything in it was backed up to the cloud if he tried to sell it. But now I needed my data. I needed my phone to call the locksmith to come and open my car. I needed my data to prove to him that the car was mine and that I was not simply impersonating the owner. I needed Maize.

But I had a backup procedure. My phone data was as close as iTunes on my computer up the elevator and in the condo. In a pinch, I could Skype to the locksmith from my computer. Problem solved, but the question remained. Why did Maize return my car but keep the key? No, that wasn't the question. The question was, when was she coming back?

I started for the door to my building, but somehow my feet went in another direction. I followed my own unconscious inclinations down the block and around the corner. On my right I passed the Catholic Church just across the street. Whenever Raj walked past the Church, he made this rapid sweeping motion across his face and shoulders. Whenever I passed the place, I made a more singular motion with one hand, but tonight my shoulder refused my arm that much mobility. Instead I made an imperceptible nod to my right as I rounded the corner and went into the source of all comfort: Joe's MyThai Kitchen.

"Good evening, Gus. How are you, Joe? You want the regular?"

The owner of Joe's MyThai Kitchen was named Joe, and he called me Joe as well as Gus. Each name he used for me served a different purpose. "Gus" showed that he knew who I was. "Joe" brought us on intimate terms. It made me one of them. Joe was Chinese. He spoke Mandarin with his staff, but with me he spoke with the flavor of pigeon English that Chinese laundry owners used in old movies. The Austin Chronicle said his little hole-in-the-wall was renowned for its eclectic Asian fare mixed in with a surprisingly authentic Thai cuisine.

There was not a single Thai in the place.

"Let me see the menu, Joe."

I never asked for the menu whenever I walked in. I nearly always ordered the Vietnamese vermicelli noodle bowl with shrimp, lobster sauce, and egg rolls. I never said I wanted that. They just knew. This time, I wasn't so sure, so I let my eyes go up and down the column for what seemed ages.

"Give me the Vietnamese vermicelli noodle bowl with shrimp, lobster sauce, and egg rolls."

"What a surprise, Joe. Glad to see you being adventurous. Say, what happened to you? You look like someone dragged you through the mud."

"No, I dragged myself."

"You sit down. You eat here. After dinner, I walk you back home. You don't look too steady."

"No, I need to call someone to open my car. Can I use your phone?"

"Sure. Sure. You use my cell. I keep the land line open for customer orders. But why do you need to call someone to open your car?"

"I've got to get it off the street before the city tows it. They've already got my phone. I can't let them get my car."

"City tow phone? Never heard of that. But why you call someone else to open own car?"

"It's a long story. I—"

"Joe likes long stories. Why don't you use the car key?"

I started to explain, but my words halted somewhere over the back of my tongue. There on the table was my Fiat fob, my key, and next to it was my Car2Go card.

"Where did you get—"

"Not from little bird. From pretty girl. She had white skin and dark hair like an Asian, but her face and arms looked like you. All smudged. She was wearing a man's T-shirt. Was it yours? She asked if I know you. I described you good. She believed me and trusted the key to Joe. I wonder why she have Gus's key. I wonder why she don't just knock on his door? Maybe you don't wake up."

I ate my noodles, shrimp and egg rolls there at the small table by the inner wall just a few feet from the take-out counter. After my meal, Joe walked me, Gus, to my car. I made an illegal U-turn on Brazos and pulled the car back into the garage. After I parked, Joe helped me out of the car and back to my condo.

"You use Joe's phone until you get your phone out of hock. If the city give you trouble, you tell Joe. He's got friends."

I nodded. I had no doubts of it. I managed to send a quick email to Butch telling him I was going to be late to work on Monday. Then, I lay down on the couch. It felt cool, like the cave, and close. Unlike the cave, there was no need to crawl, and in the closeness of the couch, I could forget that there was no one to crawl after.

Nevertheless, I followed those green soled running shoes in my dreams until morning.

8 - The Evolution

The exhaustion of the cave pressed down on me like the strata of geological ages. I crawled and crawled with the rock pressing me down. I swam through seas of solid mineral, always chasing that little green light. I reached for it, but it always slipped out of sight. It was driving my car. I was peddling a rental bike. The rocks caved in, and I was trapped. Yet, in the tunnel, there was a gleam in the wall. It looked like gold, but it was as soft and wet as clay. I tried to make a ring from it and wrap it round my finger, but it would not adhere, and once removed from the wall, it lost its luster.

There was a bumper sticker on my Abarth left there by someone putting stickers on all the cars in the parking lot. It depicted a fish with legs. I had seen that fish with legs in the cave. It was a fossil in the wall illumined by the gold.

"Evolve!" said the message on the Abarth. Trailing the fish with legs on my tailgate were four or five little fishes, little fishes with Karate gis and names on them: Amber, Cole, Silver, Rocky. Honor students. Athletes. After school ninjas.

"But I can't catch the green light! I am trapped underground."

"You are extinct," said the man with the bumper stickers, and I was.

My bones came to the surface in a drill bit. I was just the faint outline of fish bones. They rinsed me out of the rock and flushed me into a pipeline. I poured out of a nozzle into the tank of a car. I could not tell what kind of car. The inside of the tank smelled of rotted fish and dinosaur dung. The man with the stickers pulled the nozzle of the pump out of the tank.

"Burn!" he said.

The car pulled out of the gas station and was driving away. I was disappearing. The car was fading away. Only darkness remained. It was crushing me.

Then, a door opened. A hand reached out. I was in a coffin in a big SUV. The lid slid away. Gentle gray light opened my eyes. The hand tugged on my hand, folded on my breast, and I sat up. I was on Brazos Street. I walked past the parked Abarth and went up the elevator to bed, but the bed was empty.

And endless geological ages stretched before me, but I had much to do now.

So I got up.

The light was dimmer than the light I was used to when I normally got up. The sun still looked orange peeking between buildings across the street. St. Mary's almost glittered. It was all new to me, this early morning light—something you could almost look at instead of shielding your eyes from. Still, I had miles to go, so I opened my Mac, and I got to work.

First, I sent an email to Butch telling him I would not be in till noon. He answered back immediately.

"That is what you call being late? I would hardly have noticed."

"Very funny," I typed. He knew very well I always made it in by ten thirty. "Eight-thirty Pacific Time" Morgan called it. Then, I started looking for my phone. The GPS showed it was at the Austin City Hall. I sighed in relief. My phone was only a mile away and being held in official custody, not in the hands of some miscreant. But I remembered seeing homeless people sleeping on the steps of the building—not that I had seen this often. The homeless of the city were usually up and about their business before I got up and went about mine, but once I had seen them after I had pulled an all night-er at work. Surely the park ranger had not given my phone to a homeless person. I decided to get there as soon as the doors opened.

I was too stiff and sore to walk or bike that distance, not that I avoided walking. I always walked to Sixth Street. Even a Car2Go was hard to park down there of an evening, and not even the Car2Go with all the ecological enlightenment it conveyed could save you from a

DWI. So, I always walked to Sixth Street. It was only seven blocks to City Hall. Seven blocks—I had crawled further than that. If Maize were still here, I could manage it. Now it was beyond my limit.

Instead of walking, I took a Car2Go. I arrived to find a one half parking spot right in front of the front steps, more convenient than even a handicapped spot. I stepped out of the car practically onto the sidewalk. There amidst the homeless who were shuffling off with their sleeping bags to get breakfast at the Methodist Church and the City of Austin employees who were shuffling in to work stood my would-be insurance agent, my Central Market stalker. Before I could collect my wits to avoid him, he had already handed me my phone.

"I charged it for you. You don't need the pass key to do that. Don't worry. I didn't break in."

"How did—?"

"I can see you've got questions. I bet you're hungry. Why don't we grab some breakfast and talk?"

I should have turned right around, got back in the Car2Go, and left. But I didn't. Instead, I checked my phone. It opened with my biometrics. No calls had been made since I handed it over to the city. No data had been uploaded since then either except for what the locator service would have used. And the battery was full.

"I put a quick charge on it. It was getting low."

"All right," I said. "We'll talk."

Last year I had gone to Blackhat. There I met the hacker who broke into our network. That had been the incident which had kept me up all night—me, Butch and Morgan. We had stopped the attack script before it managed to use the password stolen from the Linux administrator. The hacker had sent our Linux admin an email about discount tickets for driving Lamborghini's around The Circuit of the Americas, an email which, against all training and better judgment, our guy had opened. Now, there we sat at Blackhat, the hacker himself and I myself, across from one other on the adjacent sides of the corner of the bar. He explained quite openly how he had made it so far into our systems, and I described how we had stopped him. All the while we talked so nonchalantly, I was sweating in my boxers at the bar thinking how very little we had known about the attack at the time and how narrowly we had escaped.

We took turns buying rounds of drinks. I was drinking Silver Patron, and he, Makers Mark. By the end I had switched to Makers and he was sipping Patron Reposada. I never asked his name. His name tag said "Mr Root." I was going by the name "Mr. Underhill." We shook hands and parted like two chess players who had reached stalemate or two comic book antagonists who had fought to a draw but knew they would meet again. I thought I saw him at Comic-Con later that year, but if it was he, we didn't speak.

If I could sit and drink with that hacker who almost stole our corporate crown jewels, I could eat breakfast tacos with this cyber-insurance stalker, so the two of us got into my Car2Go, and we drove.

We went to Starbucks. I was drawn to the comfort of large, nutty sweetbreads and pastries, not savory egg tacos with salsa. Also, I thought the place offered a good balance. On one hand it was a public place where I did not have to be alone with the stalker. On the other hand, it offered a kind of public privacy where you could talk safely about anything.

"Who are you?"

I decided not to make the same mistake I made at Blackhat. Somehow I intuited that if you knew a person's name, even if was a false name, you had made him vulnerable. Besides, if he used the same false name in other contexts, I could trace him on the internet. Butch had space rented on a Cray three dimensional processor to look for such correlations in the malware we had found on our boxes.

"My name is Mr. Smith. John Smith. No, not really. My name is Lloyd London. Here's my card. Funny how we still use these paper things in the digital age."

"How did you get my phone?"

"I retrieved it from the city. I know you would have found it eventually, but, frankly, time was of the essence."

"It was?" I framed my response as a question even though I completely agreed.

"Yes."

He leaned a little closer across the table. "The man who had your phone was just a bit too vulnerable to temptation to be left with your phone for very long."

"He was?"

"Yes. You see, he's been looking into getting a rather expensive operation, and even though the City of Austin insurance will pay eighty percent, that co-pay and deductible are pretty steep. So, he's been searching for alternative sources of income—on the TOR, if you know what I mean."

"How do you know that?"

"Insurance—it's my business, but you already knew that."

"You've been stalking me. You've tracked my computer use and my social media. You've traced my position from my phone. I can't do anything without you knowing it."

He doesn't know about Maize, I thought, and he couldn't track me in the cave.

"What do you want from me?"

"I don't want anything from you. I want you to have what you need for the future. Can we be frank?"

"I don't know. Can we?"

"I'm going to ignore that. I am going to be frank with you, and it's up to you if you want to be frank with me."

"Oh, what the hell. You know everything anyway."

"Not everything. I'm being frank. Not everything, but enough."

"Enough to know what?"

"Enough to know that you are unprepared for the future. You are unprepared for tomorrow, much less what is coming in forty years."

"I wouldn't say that," I said. After all, I had my bucket list, and I had just accomplished the first item on it. I could not think of a second item, but I would.

"You sound like a life insurance salesman."

"I told you. That is what I am."

"Life insurance? You want to sell me life insurance? I told you already I don't have anyone who is depending on me. I don't need it."

"Why did you search for it?"

"We've been through that. I was just curious."

"About something you don't need?"

"No. I wondered if there might not be something more to it than I knew about."

"Ah! Now we're getting somewhere. Gus, I am here to tell you that there is. What do you know about life insurance?"

I felt relieved. Now he was beginning to sound like an ordinary salesman. I had almost decided that he was either Russian Mafia or NSA.

"It's like an old joke," I said. "Life insurance is about you betting you are going to die while the company bets that you won't, but you are hoping the company wins."

"That's pretty good," said Mr. London. "I hadn't heard that before."

That's because you don't know anyone old, I thought. My mind went back to Robert and his father, the World War II vet. I was well connected to the past.

"That is the way it used to be. You bought a policy in case you died."

"In case you died? Was there any doubt?"

Lloyd London smiled.

"You bought a policy in case you died before your dependents were taken care of. But you raise a good point: 'in case you die.' We'll get to that. The trouble with that kind of policy, the trouble with term life, is that the only benefit you, the policy holder, gets from the policy is peace of mind. The insurance industry eventually realized that that was not enough. So, it invented whole life which builds a cash value that you could use in this life. You collect it. You could borrow against it. You could use the death benefit to shield your loved ones from destitution when they were younger and more vulnerable, and you could save the cash value for them long after you had stopped paying the premium on the death benefit as a nice little inheritance."

"Very nice. But the financial advisers all say you can do better in the stock market than buying life insurance."

"You can build a larger cash value in stocks than you can with whole life."

"So, you admit it."

"Sure."

"But the death benefit—"

"The death benefit you still need for your dependents. Still need. But it is true, you can make more from mutual funds than you can build in cash value in a whole life policy. Rather, you can now."

"Now because the market is rising?"

"Now because the ordinary man has access to the market. When whole life was invented, the common man could not invest in the market. There were no mutual funds like there are today. No discount brokerages. A man had to buy and sell in significantly sized lots and pay a hefty commission. You could have done it, perhaps, but not most people."

Not Robert, I thought. Nor his father, an ordinary man if ever there was one.

"This is all very interesting, but I am in funds. I have no kids and no wife. If I had a wife, she would be working so I could keep my money in the funds. So—"

"So the policy has changed. That is, the policies have changed."

I looked at him dumbly and not with as much cynical indifference as I would have liked.

"Pardon my little professional pun. The products have changed. Whole life, as your grandfather knew it, is not dead. It has been transformed."

"Ah!"

Now I knew why I was not indifferent. I was enjoying this. I was waiting till this salesman tipped his hand, That's all he was—an ordinary salesman equipped with sophisticated data mining and analysis technologies. But, in the end, he didn't want to steal my identity or disrupt my cyber presence. He just wanted to sell me something. It struck me as just a little pathetic that he should expend so much sophisticated technological and personal effort to convince me to spend money when he could with the same technology more easily steal my money.

"So, Mr. London, what has whole life become? I am just dying to know."

"That, Gus, is exactly the point. You are dying: slowly, imperceptibly, but surely."

"Surely," I said. "Sooner or later."

"Surely but maybe not soon enough."

"Not soon enough? What are you talking about?"

"I asked you before, and I have to ask you again. How did your father die?"

"And I told you—"

"—you told me you had no father. But I say you did because I have collected the data and done the analysis. But I don't have to tell you because you already know. You didn't need Big Data to know. You figured it out by more intuitive means."

"I don't have a father."

"Not now you don't, but only because he's dead."

"My father was just a sperm donor. I never knew him. He never came to me and said, "Gus! I am your father."

I stood up to leave.

"No? Then why did he put "son" in the relationship field when he made you the beneficiary of his life insurance policy?"

I sat down.

"He put that?"

"Yes, he did."

For the next few minutes it seemed to me that Mr. London could read my mind, not just my database. He answered every question that I was unable to express.

"You didn't know that. You never saw the policy. The company called you and told you that you were the beneficiary. They were just an insurance company. They never thought to tell you that you were also a son. If only they had. Right?"

I nodded.

"Robert Stauer never signed your birth certificate. Your mother never named him as your father. She went to apply for AFDC. She never went to the Attorney General to apply for child support. If she had, they would have compelled her to name your father. There is no record of him or her in the child support system. But Robert was there with you. He supported you without compulsion. He picked you up from school when your mother worked. She had to give approval for that, you know. It's in the school records. He bought your clothes for years. I can tell you the number of his credit card, if you like. You always suspected, but you always resented because nothing was ever said. But that was due to your mother. She insisted it be that way."

"You don't know that."

"True. I only infer. It is possible that your mother wasn't sure Stauer was your father. But it would have been so easy to find out. She didn't have to find out. She already knew."

"You attribute all these motives to her, but it is all speculation."

"No, that's where you're wrong. I'll admit I am speculating about your mother. There are no medical records of her discussing your father's identity under privilege with any psychologist or legal adviser. But I do know about Stauer and you because I have seen both of your DNA records."

"You've seen what?"

"Hey, calm down. They will throw us out of here. This isn't a bar. They don't allow for emotional revelations in here. We have to remain under the social radar."

I sat down again meekly. I believed him. He had proven his hacker credentials to me already. Besides, he was right. I did know. That is, I never had any real doubt that Robert was my father. That is why I had always resented him, resented the fact that he never told me and resented the fact that he was not richer, or smarter, or more heroic.

"So, you see, Gus, when we talk about how Robert Stauer died, we could also be talking about you. You have his DNA."

"He was such an idiot. He could have ended it so much sooner, but he wouldn't."

"And you would."

"Damn right! I wouldn't suffer like that."

"Texas doesn't allow it. Doesn't allow assisted suicide."

"There are ways. There are other states. Texas allows guns, doesn't it?"

"And you would do it?"

"I told you I would."

"You would leave chemotherapy and travel to another state where they allowed assisted suicide? With all that pain, you would get in a car, or a plane, or a bus and travel that far?"

"In those circumstances, I would just use a gun."

"You would?"

"I would!"

"You will?"

"What do you mean?"

"I should think it was obvious."

"I don't have cancer."

"Not yet. But there is a better than average probability."

"Why? What else do you know?"

"I'm just saying."

"There's no guarantee I'm going to get cancer."

"How did Robert's father, old man Stauer, die?"

"I don't know. I only met him once."

"It was congestive heart failure."

"How long did that take?"

"A couple of weeks. Only it really took a year or so. Things just intensified in the final two weeks. It's a long time to suffer."

"You're telling me I should worry about congestive heart failure just because..."

But I didn't finish the sentence.

"Because why?"

Because I had not really thought about it before. That old man had been my grandfather. Robert introduced me to him before he died.

"He'd be mighty welcome."

"My point is—"

"Your point is that if it's not one thing, it's another."

"My point is much more pointed than that."

"Well, medicine keeps improving."

"That used to be true, but even so, medical improvements have tended to take something that had been relatively quick and stretch it out over a long, painful time."

"Like I said, I'll relocate. The law will change, or I will get a gun."

"Will you?"

"Why do you keep asking that question?"

"Have you ever fired a gun?"

"No."

"Ever hold one in your hand?"

"No."

"Then you've never put the muzzle of a gun in your mouth and pulled the trigger?"

"Of course not."

"Unloaded, of course. Just dry firing as they call it."

"No!"

"Never played Russian roulette?"

"No!"

"But you will. When the time comes, you will buy a gun, load it, put the muzzle in your mouth, and pull the trigger."

I didn't answer for a moment. I felt the cave pressing in.

"If I am in enough pain, then—"

"Does it have to come to that? Must you be caught between severe pain and fear waiting to see which outweighs the other? Is that how you must end your life?"

"Look," I said. "I know I need an advanced directive. Maybe I need a will. Maybe I need life insurance, but I'm still trying to learn how to live my life."

"I understand. Believe me. But you have already begun to think about the end. You are ahead of many people. You have begun to realize that part of the key to living the good life now is making sure you don't lose it all in the end."

"Excuse me, but isn't that what happens when you die? The end comes, and you lose it all?"

"Not if you plan well. Not if you build up a legacy that you can pass on to someone who is left to receive it, and not if you make sure that you go on your own terms when it makes the most sense for you. You will not believe how much freedom that allows you when you know that you will live a life well ended. That is why I am here. That is what I offer you: a life well ended which frees you up to enjoy a life well lived!"

"I don't understand. What are you saying?"

"Death comes for us all. You can't avoid it. You can't bargain with it. You can't reason with it. You can't play chess with it. You can't cheat it. But you can plan for it. You see, the trouble with death has always been that it comes at the wrong time. For some it comes too soon, and for some, it comes too late. We, my company, that is, mitigate that risk. We can't prevent death from coming too soon, but we can ensure that it doesn't come too late."

"Well, I suppose that's better than nothing. You do what?"

"We can't prevent an untimely death, but we can make sure you have something to leave behind. It used to be that people just provided for their families. Now you can endow a scholarship or fund a charity. You can make a name for yourself with your death."

"No. No. That's all very interesting, but what was that other part?"

"Look at the time. Don't you have to get to work? Listen, we'll talk soon. You write down your questions, and I will answer them. Okay?"

"No, wait! What do you mean—"

"We'll talk. All will become clear."

With that Mr. London was out the door.

9 – The Drink

"What happened to you?" Butch said. It was Monday morning.

Morgan eyed me carefully.

"You've been in the cave," he said.

I nodded. I thought that would be easier than speaking. It wasn't. After my meeting with Lloyd London and after retrieving my phone, all my stiffness had returned with a vengeance. I could barely move.

"Cave?" said Butch. "What cave?"

"Airman's Cave. The one we were talking about before. The one I told him to put on his bucket list. How far did you get?"

"All the way."

"Well, I have to hand it to you," said Morgan. "I didn't think you would even attempt it, and I wouldn't have thought you would make it to the end."

"Was it worth it?" asked Butch.

I thought of Maize putting me to bed.

"Yes," I said.

"So what's next on the bucket list, or are you ready to die now?" said Morgan.

I thought of Lloyd London. Was I?

"Not yet."

"I'm glad to hear it," said Butch. "But maybe the next item on the list shouldn't almost be the last item on the list. You look like Lazarus come from the tomb."

I nodded in agreement, but I didn't know what I was agreeing with. Who was Lazarus?

"Maybe I'll catch the guy who put the malware on our system last year," I said. It didn't sound like the normal bucket list item, but it seemed worth doing.

"You'll never catch him," said Butch. "You did the best you could just to stop him."

I had never told Butch or Morgan that I had met the guy at Blackhat and had drinks with him. I could have reached out and grabbed him by the wrist, but I would not have been able to hold him. Without proof I would have had to let him go, and we both knew it.

I devoted the day to crawling through the network logs, looking for clues left by someone who had been there before, looking for that imprint left embedded in the wall or that malicious script hanging from the ceiling of a server waiting for the night to open its shadowy wings and fly ominously towards some open window. Towards late afternoon Butch asked me to scan a new application for vulnerabilities. At six I left the office with my computer to grab some dinner.

I say I left the office. There was a restaurant on the first floor of the building only thirty-six steps from the elevator. I know because I counted every one of them. I moved across the floor in a semi-hunched posture as if I were still moving through tunnels with low ceilings. The waiter took one look at me and seated me in a dark corner. He seemed to realize that I had recently emerged from a cave and still wasn't ready for light. I opened my computer and was about to connect to the restaurant's public Wi-Fi with a Virtual Private Network, but our company's secure network was available even in my dark corner. Apparently the network guys liked this restaurant. I had never eaten there before. It wasn't Thai. The menu was downtown Tex Mex. So, I ordered a Negra Modelo and a plate of enchiladas de mole and focused on my scan.

I heard one of the chairs disturbed on the floor.

"Hey, Geek! Buy me a drink?"

I looked up, and there was Susan, my manager, standing at my table. I had never seen her outside of the office. I started to rise. In the office we were casual, but outside I somehow thought I needed to be more formal. Maybe it was the extension of our on-call protocol that we had followed on Saturday.

"Whoa!" she said as I tried to scoot my chair back to stand. "At ease."

She sat down across from me. I had thought she was kidding about the drink till she intercepted my beer bottle bottle just as the waiter placed it on the table.

"Is this the best you can do?" she asked. "Bring me a Mexican martini."

The waiter looked at me for acknowledgment. I nodded.

"House tequila or premium?" he asked.

"Premium!" she said. "He can afford it. I pay him enough." Then she looked across the table at me.

"Do you want one? This beer won't get you very far."

"I'm not going very far. I'm going back upstairs to work. This is just my dinner break."

"Too bad," she shrugged.

The waiter looked at me again and left.

"I forget," she said, "that you work such late hours. I was going to say it was a pity on such a pleasant evening, but I do feel a lot more secure knowing you are still on the job."

She looked at my computer. She looked at me looking at my computer. "What are you doing? Looking for porn?"

Fortunately, I didn't have a mouthful of beer.

"No. I'm scanning a new app."

"Oh! Well, tell me. Is it vulnerable? I won't breathe a word."

"They all are, one way or another."

"Sons of bitches," she said. I wondered if she meant the hackers who exploited the vulnerabilities or the coders who inadvertently created them.

"They don't do it on purpose," I said choosing to answer for the coders. Secretly, I had always wanted to be a coder, but I was terrified of deadlines, and I never had confidence that I could ever sit down and make things work.

"Don't you live around here?" she said.

"Yes."

"That makes it easy."

I acted like I knew what she meant, but I didn't.

"If we get around to asking, 'Your place or mine,' the answer will be obvious."

This time I spat beer on the table. Fortunately, my mouth wasn't too full, and I missed the computer keyboard. Still, drops of Mexican brown ale ran down the screen.

Susan handed me her napkin.

"By the way," she said, "the answer is 'D.'"

"'D?' Is that the answer to a test question?"

"No. It's Jill Ferry's cup size. That is the most common search on the internet. Don't ever let anyone in the office say that I don't understand technology."

I dabbed the screen with her napkin and tried not to look directly at her.

"Of course, I don't believe it," she said.

"You think the search engine companies manipulated the search counts to please her publicist?"

"Do what? No, I don't think she is a 'D'. I think she's a 'C'."

"Oh."

"Maybe a 'C+' at most."

I started to ask her if there was such a thing as a 'C+', but I decided I had better not.

The waiter came with her martini and handed me a screen wipe. Such a technology friendly place. I would come more often if I could always get a secluded table.

Once Susan got her martini, she stopped talking. My enchiladas arrived, so I closed my computer and pushed it to one side. I did not want to risk mole sauce on the keyboard.

"Careful, Senor, the plate is hot."

I nodded. I was glad for the heat, not only because I liked hot food but more so because, with the computer pushed aside, it was my only protection, that hot plate of enchiladas.

"Would the Senora like to order something to eat?"

I looked up past my plate at her. I realized that I should have asked her that question out of courtesy even if she had invited herself to my table. She shook her head and smiled.

"Are you sure?" I said. I had never noticed before that Susan was a Senora. I had figured she was older than me by ten or twelve years, but I had never wondered if she were married. Yet, there on her left hand, the hand that held the Mexican martini glass, was a rather discreet gold band, discreet because there was no diamond with it.

"I'm sure." She smiled right at me over the rim of the glass. Her eyes sparkled over the salt.

"Do you need to get home to your husband?"

I held the fork of Spanish rice still over the plate, not fully raising it to my mouth until I heard the answer.

"No. He's out of town."

I lowered the fork.

"Out? Out of town?"

"You got it, Geek! I am free and available."

For a moment I wondered if he were involved in some long distance wife swapping arrangement, and Susan's side of the arrangement had not yet arrived at the airport. I had no doubt that, if it were true, she would tell me.

"Is he away on business?"

My food was cooling. I steeled myself against any surprise and took a bite.

"No."

I tried the re-fried beans. Unlike the rice, the beans held their heat. Steam trailed from the fork all the way to my mouth.

"Vacation?" I said.

"Not hardly."

I scooped up more beans. I was beginning to feel the heat.

"Oh," I said as I put the fork in my mouth. With any luck my allergies would flare up so that I had to breathe through my mouth, and then I would end up chewing with my mouth open. That was something I had trained myself not to do in the hopes of getting second dates. Now, I hoped for a relapse. I followed the beans with more rice, but the rice had little flecks of jalapeño in it. In its own way it was hotter than the beans. I felt my sinuses clearing. I could breathe through my nose. A bead of sweat rolled down my temple.

I took a gulp of beer and tried to relax.

"Then why, if you don't mind my asking, is your husband out of town?"

"His mother is dying."

"His mother is dying?"

She sipped more martini.

"'fraid so."

My hand and my head hovered over my plate.

"You didn't go with him to be with her?"

"No."

"You don't like your mother-in-law?"

"I like her fine. She's a peach."

"You couldn't get off to go?"

"I could. There's nothing going on here that Butch can't handle."

"Then, you could still go."

She nodded. I now felt vulnerable for being so bold. I took a bite of rice to regain my detachment.

"True."

I knew I was entering dangerous waters, but I had to keep going. I took another sip of Negra Modelo and then cut into my enchiladas. This last question would best be served with chicken.

"Then, why don't you?"

"Because I don't do death."

"You don't do death?" I said with my mouth full.

"Sure don't. My husband is much better at that. I may send him to be with my own mother when her time comes."

I sat there frozen amidst the steam and my own sweat.

"Don't mind me. Go ahead and eat. Go on."

I took a second bite of enchilada. She downed the rest of the martini. The waiter came and stood beside her. She handed him the glass.

"I don't suppose you can wrap up another one of these up so I can take it with me?"

"No, Senora."

"Pity," she said. "Damn city council. Well, Gus, it's been grand. My husband will be calling soon with the news, and when he does, I want to be home sitting down with another couple of drinks in me. He needs me to be strong, and I've got to be ready. You married?"

"No."

"Of course not," she said.

I wondered what she meant by that. She stood up and smiled down at me.

"Work hard. That's what I pay you for. And thanks for the drink."

She smiled again. Without the salt on her glass lifted to her face, her eyes did not sparkle so much.

As she walked out, I felt a huge sense of relief and disappointment. I dove back into my plate for consolation, and, unlike Susan, I ordered a second beer before I returned to the office to finish my scan and take another crawl through the SIEM.

I left the office at 10 PM. There were no Cars2Go handy, so I tried walking. It felt good to be standing erect in the open air, and it gave me a chance to search the streets. I saw no black Suburbans parked anywhere along the way. When I got to my building there was no Suburban parked in front of it either. I took the elevator up and went straight to bed.

I saw Maize standing beside me with a basket of laundry. She asked me if I had any blood to drink or, at least, some red wine. I said no, absolutely not, and sent her down the street for tequila and lime instead. After she left, Susan sat down on the bed, stretched out next to me with her head supported by her hand and leaning on one elbow.

"Well, the mother-in-law is dead," she said. "My husband called to give me the news, and all I could say to him was, 'Well, Baby, you're next.' Have you got anything to drink in this place?" But Maize had not yet come back with the tequila, and I couldn't help but think that, under the circumstances, that was a good thing.

10 – Dark Identity

The sun reached between St. Mary's and the Rusk Building and yanked me out of darkness. I sat up in bed. Butch always marveled that I got up every morning without an alarm clock. I told him I lived in tune with nature. When you live with your window facing east but shielded from the dawn for a couple of hours till the sun has gained some strength, it isn't very hard to wake up naturally. But it isn't very pleasant. I lay back down and put my head under the pillow.

Perhaps Robert had had the right idea. He always had insisted on getting up early, and, whenever I had stayed with him, he had insisted on me getting up early too. He said that when we got up in the dark, we could ease into the day. We could accustom ourselves to the light.

"After you've spent the first hour or so of the morning moving about in the dark, you welcome the light when it comes instead of trying to hide from it."

"If you would turn on the lights, you wouldn't be in the dark," I said, but I was only being difficult. I didn't want the lights on. Not only did they hurt my eyes, I felt exposed. I felt ashamed for reasons I never tried to discover. So, I shunned the light, but once I was awake, I no longer wanted the dark either. The real trouble was that I was afraid of the dark, and that fear awoke with me in the predawn. This put me in a dilemma. Either I drew back into the dark where the fear was, or I moved into the light where shame awaited. I could never decide which I would really choose. So, Robert turned on a dim lamp, and after I had lain under the covers wide awake for a few moments, I could get up. He gave me the compromise of having just enough darkness to hide from shame and just enough light to drive away fear. Sure enough, after a few minutes of that, I was ready for the daylight.

Only now, with Robert gone, I followed the opposite philosophy. I stayed up under bright lights until I could remain awake no longer then dove under the covers of unconsciousness until the darkness was gone and the light was simply undeniable. Then, I would go to work.

Except I didn't want to go to work. My shoulders were even stiffer than they had been on Monday. I needed another sick day. I thought of Robert still going to work while he was taking chemotherapy.

Damn his example!

Maybe I could work from home.

Damn again. I had left my computer at the office. Now I would have to drag myself in after it.

Once I had dragged in, how could I face Susan now knowing what I knew? What would I say to the bereaved daughter-in-law who didn't do death? What did her husband think of her staying away at such a time? What would I have thought if I had had even a girlfriend when Robert died who had refused to go with me to that final bedside, or to the funeral, or to the grave? I had done death, but I didn't want ever to do it again. If someone had loved me, she would have at least gone with me to the edge and looked down.

I thought of Maize rising out of the coffin in the back of a Suburban without seats. She was so slender she had slipped through the Birth Canal easily. I had followed her almost willingly into darkness.

I decided if I had the right kind of breakfast, I could make it to work. I slouched to the bathroom as I had done in the portions of the cave with the higher ceilings and stood in the shower under the pulsing jets until I could stand up straight. More bits of clay and dried blood washed off my belly, knees and elbows; ran down to the tub at my feet and down the drain. Did the drain water run into Waller Creek and then into Lady Bird Lake, or did the sewer pipes, running underground, somehow return the water to drip down the crystalline walls of Airman's Cave again?

How would I know? I didn't understand plumbing.

Getting the right breakfast was going to be a problem. Eating at the Mexican restaurant the night before had broken up my rhythm. I usually ate Thai in the evening and Mexican in the morning. Now, I was thrown into a great reversal. Joe didn't open his Thai place till lunch time, and that was too late for breakfast even by my standards. The obvious solution was to break with protocol and go to Starbucks, but that reminded me of the mysterious Mr. London. I cleared my head completely with Honduran food from a food truck by a construction site.

I got to work early for me. Butch and Morgan pointed that out in tandem. Butch put his hands on my shoulders and scanned me head to foot for abrasions, smudges, and misaligned skeletal components.

"You look better than yesterday. You are standing straighter."

"Oh, to be young!" said Morgan. Morgan was all of forty.

"The trouble with being young," Butch said, still looking me over, "is not having enough sense to stay out of dark, tight places and off sharp rocks. But, if you survive, you recover quickly."

I did not feel like I was recovering quickly. I sat at my desk hunched over and shifting every few minutes to stretch and reposition my tight muscles. As I stared at my screen, I kept my ears open for Susan. I was used to not seeing her at work, but her presence hovered over us nonetheless. Butch received phone calls from her, and Morgan and I both could tell when she was on the phone just from hearing Butch's side of the conversation.

"Yes, we are investigating a possible probing of our domain...No, I wouldn't say that. We see no evidence yet of any actual breach....No, I didn't hear what the other managers are saying....No, I don't....No, I....No, I wouldn't say that....No, I don't think that is a fair assessment....No, I wouldn't say that at all. I think you can tell your boss that we have are investigating....No, don't say that.... We can't give him a guarantee....You could remind him of your budget request that got denied....You don't have to say he denied it. Just say it was denied....Well, was it him? If it was....No, I wouldn't go that far. Yes....Cover....Yes....Cover but verify....That's clever....No, I wouldn't say it was hanging out...He's just trying to get you nervous....You don't put forth your best image when you are nervous...."

Butch's phone was quiet all morning. I put Susan's name into the address line of an email. There next to it was that green dot that said she was on-line. I thought about sending her an email asking if her mother-in-law had indeed kicked the bucket, but that would have been too personal, I judged. I didn't send the email, but I kept the draft open and checked the light. Towards one o'clock it went gray, but I did not know what that meant. It could be that she had left the office and gone home. It could be that she went to a meeting and turned off her computer. According to Butch, she was the only person in the company who turned off her computer during the day. I shook my head in amazement when I heard that. Morgan suggested maybe she was smarter about computer security than the rest of us.

I expected Morgan would say something about her today since he made it a point to know everything going on in the office, but he, like the phone, was quiet into the afternoon.

The computer systems were quiet, too. It bothered me that, although I spent my days and nights watching over them, I did not know what that meant—the systems being quiet. I had no idea if they were performing well, if we were processing our business transactions efficiently or meeting the service levels expected by our customers. I did not know if the information on our websites was true and accurate or if our Big Data were truly big enough. I only knew there were no alarms going off, no unexplained system anomalies, no signs of intrusions. It was a rare day. The sun was high and illuminating every crevice and corner. It made me nervous.

I decided to take a spin through the dark side to see what was lurking below the horizon.

We subscribed to reports, produced via Big Data analysis, to show us what was appearing in the hacker networks. I could read every morning what was on the hit parade of malware: what were the top selling exploits, what was the going rate for credit card numbers and personal information on the black market. I could see how much it cost to buy a zero day exploit, and I could even see ratings of them from customers. Ratings came in stages. First, there was an initial projection of how damaging an exploit was expected to be. These were only based upon word of mouth or subtle black market advertising. Some of it was based upon the reputation of the exploit producer, but this was always suspect since no one was supposed to know who the producer was. Then came the first reports from the early adopters telling how well the exploits had performed. Much later came the white hat analysis of the exploits from the labs who found them in the wild and who let them attack their test environments so they could assess their potency. Much, much later you would see the news reports of companies who had been attacked. Last came the post-mortem reports from the security people who had determined how an attack had been conducted and what exploit had been used. Sometimes the security community could tie an actual attack back to a zero day exploit, and then we could all evaluate how well the exploit had worked and how well the expectations for it had been met. This in turn helped feed the reputations of the entities who wrote the malware so they could charge more.

And therein lay the virtual rub.

"Every producer of malware needs a reputation," Butch once said, "but in order to get a reputation, you have to have an identity."

"Why does he need a reputation? Isn't it better that he not have an identity?"

"You've just conceded his point," said Morgan. "You've agreed that reputation requires an identity."

"I have?"

Butch nodded that I had.

"Whatever," I said, "but why does he need a reputation?"

"Without a reputation his malware will never command a good price. Even if someone buys his exploit kit for $9.99 and uses it to bust open the NSA or shut down the Iranian nuclear program, his next exploit will still only sell for $9.99 unless he can build a reputation. That requires an identity. Then, he can build a brand."

"But doesn't he want to remain secret?"

"If he wanted to remain secret," said Morgan, "he wouldn't write malware. He would only buy it. Slam the bitcoin on the bar, buy the tool to crack the safe, break open the bank, take the money and run."

Morgan thought that it was in keeping with Paul's Butch Cassidy nickname to use western movie metaphors as much as possible.

"But don't malware writers put their wares on the market to avoid being connected to the robbery? Otherwise, they would write it and use it themselves. In fact, wasn't that how it used to work?"

"Yes," said Butch, "back in the day. But even so, back to your point, the malware writer is not selling exploit kits on the Dark Web to avoid having an identity. He is just putting distance between his identity and the crime."

I knew what they meant. The crime was breaking and entering and stealing data. Writing the malware itself was not a crime until the courts could connect the malware to actual data thefts. Even then the authorities needed one more thing—the identity of the malware writer. Therein lay his difficulty.

The malware writer needed an identity to make more money, but he didn't need his real identity. A false identity would do, one made initially out of whole electronic cloth but carefully woven until it became a full blown digital reputation. It seemed to me even preferable. First, if your reputation became sullied—if every hacker who bought and used your wares got caught—then you could ditch your identity and assume a new one. Second, if the police did catch up with your online identify, they still had to find you, the holder of that identity. They usually made it a point to charge you under your real name.

"You, know," I said, "why can't one identity on the web be just as vulnerable as another? Your bitcoins can be stolen on the web just as well as your money in the bank. Why couldn't your pseudo-identity be stolen and used to steal your on-line connections and reputation? What would a person do who had lost his virtual reputation?"

"If I were a successful malware writer and someone had stolen my identity," said Morgan, "I would demand justice."

"You would have to appear in court to do it and prove that you were you," said Butch.

"Who is really you?" said Morgan.

"I don't know, Morgan," said Butch. "You've got me there." The room became quiet. I turned my attention to reading the latest security analysis.

Security analysis was like anything else. Some analysts very conservative and disciplined in their approach. Others would incorporate more speculative indicators in their reporting. Either way you could judge the analysts in the same way you could the exploits—by their track records. The whole endeavor was not unlike the weather forecasting. One meteorologist predicted a freeze, and another kept the temperatures in the higher thirties. It all depended upon which projection model the meteorologist used. Neither used the same model because they were in competition, and each had his professional opinion regarding which one was better, but neither one really knew. Neither did the security analysts, not until after the fact. That, Morgan claimed, was why there was Big Data about Big Data. Someone figured out he could do analysis to see how well other people's analysis worked.

To my mind all this analysis was useful, but I found there was no substitute for diving into the exploit marketplace myself and poking around. I formed my own sense of things from checking several key indicators. One of my favorites was the price of bank account numbers for accounts that contained more than $100,000 and which came complete with passwords less than thirty days old. I also kept tabs on smart thermostats that still used their factory default passwords or that had no authentication mechanism to them at all. You could buy the IP addresses to those in lots of a hundred to use to stage attacks on the banks.

Basically, malware and stolen digital property were like drugs. The more there were on the marketplace, the lower the price. Low prices were a gauge of how ineffective the interdiction efforts against them really were. Of course, Big Data could tell you that, but I liked to see it for myself. Besides, I kept accounts in various places myself, and I checked regularly to see if any of them had appeared in the markets yet. Some of these accounts were my own real accounts, and some I created simply to see if they would be stolen. Some were more than just accounts. Some were the keys to the honeypot. We had created, Butch and I, several honeypots for the company, several traps within our network and our cloud accounts designed to be appealing to hackers. Here we looked for signs of intrusion, but out there on the Black Web, we looked to see if our stuff had been stolen without us knowing. Data was not like physical items. No one could steal your car without physically removing it from the place you left it, but data could look undisturbed and yet have been hauled out of the server on a virtual truck in the dead of night and scattered across the four winds of the web. And then there were your precious secrets, or even your precious identity, up for sale. To add insult to more injury, you could be sold multiple times, not just once. The more your secrets and self were sold, the more you were diminished and the less value you had in yourself. Out on the black internet the market sold copies of your company secrets, the identities of your customers and of your employees. Woe to the one who was put up for sale. In prior days robbers might kidnap you and sell you as a slave, but at least then you had value to the one who bought you. You knew you had been bought for some price, and as your new master refused offers from others to buy you, you could see your value increase. In the identity markets of the internet, anonymous buyers bought you in replications at $100, $50, or even $25 an instance.

When I looked at a report prepared from massive scans on the web, all this seemed removed and merely technical. When I walked through the identity markets myself and saw the names and numbers of real human beings, some of whom I knew, it gave me fresh resolve to resist the cyber-barbarians who were out to rob us of the last vestiges of our civilization.

Once I had seem the name of someone I knew for sale on the Black Web. It was a woman I had pursued vainly through the clubs and down the alleys of Austin. In person you could not buy her for love or money, but in the cyber-market, her bank account number, her name, and her bank credentials were available for $125. That was because her credentials were virgin, and her account held over $100,000. I wanted somehow to warn her, but I decided there was nothing I could do. She would never listen to me, and if I had shown her the website, she would have accused me of stealing her data myself. As for me, I've changed my password a dozen times to ward off a threat, and I have closed four or five financial accounts. I managed to stay one step ahead. Of course, one time it was Morgan who tipped me off when he found my identity for sale. I thanked him in suspicion and disbelief.

I think I would have done the same for him.

All through the afternoon I checked the markets. I looked for my company's data, but I also looked for Susan's name and for Maize's. What would Susan do if I saved her from certain on-line disaster?

"Thanks, Geek," she would say leaning across my plate of enchiladas and lifting a glass of top shelf margarita to my lips. I would take the sip, but she would keep pouring until either the glass was drained or I had choked and spewed half the glass all over the both of us. Either way, she would only laugh, and I might rise from my embarrassment and rise to the occasion.

Or, I might not.

I stayed in the office until ten again. I ate at the same Mexican restaurant downstairs, but I drank my house margarita all by myself. Back at my desk, I reflected on what a failure I was as the Geek Protector of Fair Damsels in Distress. Perhaps it wasn't my fault. You cannot protect a damsel who is not in distress. You can protect one who is in distress but does not know it, but you will not get a reward.

As I walked home the issue seemed abundantly clear. I was no good as a rescuer, and the only one in distress was me.

11 - Grave Tuesday

My favorite online gaming avatar was a monk—not that I played much anymore. In my maturity I preferred the search for real villains in the cyber world to fighting against other avatars with mere virtual weapons. Of course, some of the people you meet in games are the same ones you meet at security conferences like Blackhat sitting on the other side of the table.

In fact, it had been a game that had led me to a career in IT Security. Back in my youth my favorite role playing game was hacked. The hackers didn't steal any credit card numbers or take source code so they could develop and sell cheats to the game. No! They added more money to the game's virtual treasury. They made more game gold so that gamers could buy more avatar powers and skills within the game and rise faster to the higher levels. It didn't work. Instead, the game suffered inflation. The value of gold in the game fell ten percent over night, and I was stuck on Level Four for a month. I couldn't afford to buy the key to the gate that opened onto Level Five, and I never managed to acquire all the skills needed to find the key on my own. I finally gave up on the game entirely. It was my first glimpse into the destructive and disruptive potential of computer hackers. I began to consider how to make the online experience more secure. I talked several of my friends into putting better passwords on their online accounts, and I wrote a script to search through the system logs of a PC to look for changes that could indicate tampering with the system. Word got around about my defensive efforts, and I became a target. Hackers from my school began trying to penetrate my defenses just to see if I could call them out. One managed to freeze Windows on my machine. It took me a week of crawling around in the poor resolution of Safe Mode until I found the virus. I removed it from the system folder and put it on the Apache server I had built in my new cloud account. Then, I crafted an email about skate boarding, a sport all my hacker friends pursued. I put a link in the email to a site for our local skateboarding shop. Rather, that is where the link appeared to go. It actually went to my server where I had put the virus I had removed from my own computer. Then, I sent the email to the same guys I suspected had sent the virus to me. No one admitted to the attack, but no one ever bothered me again, no one from school anyway. I hear one of them say that he had received a C in English because his computer froze the day before the term paper was due, and he couldn't open his paper to finish it. He had had to stay up all night and rewrite the paper from scratch. The second version was not as good as the original.

How did I get the virus? I opened an email attachment that was supposed to contain nude pictures of the best looking girls in the school. I knew immediately that there was something wrong when an HTML page slowly came up with a poor resolution picture of someone I had never seen before. The file I had opened had been much larger than it had needed to be for such a low definition picture. I knew then that I had been had. But I learned another valuable lesson. I learned to avoid online pornography, even the soft core variety. As a result I suffered a lot fewer serious computer viruses, and I think my attraction to real women actually increased.

However, in my current situation I was stalemated. One woman seemed almost available yet still unattainable. Another had been right there within my grasp but then had disappeared. So, I took a cue from my old avatar, the monk, and went on a brief, secular retreat. I didn't go back to playing games. I did more research into the dark side of the web. I stayed out of restaurants with margaritas and enchiladas. I went back to eating at Joe's MyThai for dinner. Since Joe had no alcoholic beverage permit, I took to buying beer one bottle at a time at the convenience store down the block and drinking it at home instead of in the approximate company of women sitting at a bar. And so I began to lose hope. Loss of hope begat loneliness, and loneliness sent me back out onto the streets. Still, I fluttered about like a night bird or a bat, never alighting anywhere, never nesting. In the evenings I saw all the women going to the bars, going in and coming out. In the late afternoons when I took a break from the SIEM to walk around the block, I could see the women from the condos walking their dogs on the sidewalks like New Yorkers, retractable leash in one hand, plastic bag in the other. I wondered if I needed a dog to walk so I could meet them. Most of the dog walkers were married though. They had joined their incomes to their husband's incomes to live the high rise city high life, and the dogs were their children. No hope there. So, loneliness became longing, and longing burned down to smoldering despair. And despair? It didn't cool. It kept burning under a layer of ash, sending up an occasional wisp of smoke or a brief moment of small flame. Otherwise, you would hardly know that the fire of despair was even still there.

Somehow, all this made me think of Mr. Lloyd London. I wondered where he had gone. Just when I thought he was going to reveal to me what he was about, he had disappeared. What he would say about my situation?

"And just what is your situation?" I could hear Maize saying in my head.

That was just the trouble. I felt certain I was in a situation, but I couldn't really describe what it was.

Would Maize truly say that, and say it to me? She hadn't. Like Mr. London, she had disappeared and had not come back to ask me anything. I had no idea how to find her again. Even if I were to go into another cave, I didn't think she would appear. Lloyd London was another matter. I had conjured him once unawares. Surely, I could conjure him again with the right search in Google.

So, I made a few searches asking about term life insurance. I went to some sites that compared the ratings of several insurance companies. I waited a few days. Nothing appeared but insurance pop-up ads on all the other sites I visited. I went to a site that gave price quotes on term life. I got an email from an agent, but no Mr. London. Lloyd was not on Facebook or Linkedin or Twitter. No one was selling his stolen credit card number on the Dark Web.

I drank coffee at Starbucks, ate twice a week at Central Market, and used Car2Go everywhere I went. He did not appear. Now, I really felt alone. Butch and Morgan were my only company, but they went home in the afternoon. I stayed in the office until eight or nine. If some alert came up, I interacted with Butch by phone or instant messaging. The only people I saw after six were the cleaning people, and none of them spoke English.

During this time I began to develop a strange sensibility. Around eight forty-five when the lights in the windows of the other buildings were becoming visible and the distant wail of the vacuum cleaners had faded, I had the strange sense that I was not alone. One night I dimmed my monitor and looked for reflections. No one was behind me. I got up and strolled around the floor. I checked the offices. No one was in them. I looked out the window. There were people on the street. I wished them well from afar, but they were not keeping me company. Something or someone else was. It followed me about the floor. It stood beside me in the marketplace of the Dark Web. It was not robotic. It was not Google. It waited in the evening until the last employee on the floor was gone and the cleaning crew had left. I began to expect it to come. I would not leave the office until I sensed it even though I sometimes had to remain until ten. Then, I would walk home seeing the people I passed with new appreciation. Sometimes I smiled at them. I even smiled at the homeless. Somehow we were all in this together. What it was exactly that we were in, I didn't know. I wondered if they knew, the homeless, but how could they? What resources could they possess to discern anything? What search engine could they use?

Sometimes I gave them a little money, and I began to realize I was seeing some of the same ones every night in the same places. I also found that they recognized me. That alarmed me, so I changed my route. Then, I met new homeless, and those became familiar. I varied my route constantly. I tried to change it randomly, but apparently I fell into a pattern because one of the homeless men began to address me as I came down Brazos. He didn't just ask for money. He spoke to me as a person.

"Hey," he said, "it's Captain Tuesday. How you doin' there, Captain?"

"Captain Tuesday? Why do you call me that?"

"Because you look important, and you always come by here on Tuesday. Say. You ain't been drinkin', have you? You're walkin' pretty steady for a drinkin' man. Don't tell me you been workin'. Man! You been workin' and this late at night."

I think I shrugged without moving my shoulders.

"You been workin' and makin' that high tech Austin money. Say, you got a little of that high tech Austin money to spare?"

I was taken aback. For all practical purposes this anonymous man knew me. He knew my habits. He knew I walked this way on Tuesdays. He guessed pretty close to my profession. I stood there as he spoke, and I listened in amazement. Then, I reached into my pocket and pulled out my money clip. I saw his eyes light up. I felt vulnerable holding this clump of bills in front of this desperate man, but he knew me. There was no point pretending. The smallest bill I had was a twenty. I peeled off that high tech Austin Andrew Jackson and handed it to him. I knew I was setting a bad precedent, but what else could I do?

"There it is," he said. "There's a man who knows who he is. Thank you, Captain."

I may have smiled. I'm not sure. I may have nodded, but I definitely moved on down the block. Did I know who I was? I was Captain Tuesday. Why Captain? Flattery, I supposed. Still, it was an identity. I liked it better in some ways than Gus. It was more secure. He didn't steal it from me. Rather, he gave it to me. No, I paid him for it. I gave him almost as much money for that name as my credit card number was worth on the black market. As I sat down at Joe's MyThai to eat my late night dinner, it seemed to me that I had come out ahead. But I changed my route home the next night, and I didn't use that stretch of Brazos again for another week, not until Tuesday. When I came back to Brazos, there he was again.

"Captain Tuesday," he said.

I smiled this time and handed him another twenty. I had it loose from the money clip and ready in my right side pocket.

"Why you so good to me, Captain?"

"It's a long time till Tuesday," I said.

He observed the bag in my hand.

"You're comin' from work! I thought maybe you was comin' from chasin' the women on Sixth, but you're comin' from work!"

I just shrugged.

"But you out there the rest of the week, right Captain?"

He looked me over again. He looked me in the eye in the dim light, and I looked away, but not immediately.

"No. No you're not. You're just workin'."

From then on I took the same route home every evening. I decided to give the man four dollars every night. At five days a week that would still be twenty dollars, but I discovered he was not there every night. I didn't see him again until the following Tuesday. When we met, I pressed twenty one dollar bills into his hand, the accumulation of the past week.

"I'm walking this way every night now," I said. "I thought you'd be here, and so I thought I would spread out the donation. But I guess not."

"Oh, I couldn't stand bein' here every night."

"You couldn't? Why not?"

I began to be afraid. Was there some danger on this section of Brazos that I couldn't see?

"Because I was afraid of seein' you every night, and I couldn't take that."

"You couldn't take seeing me?"

"No, Man. You too sad."

He looked down at the street as if embarrassed. Then, he looked me briefly in the eye.

"No offense. I'm just sayin'."

"No," I said. "No offense."

"Well, thank you, Captain. See you next Tuesday."

And he hurried down the street to the convenience store or the food truck or to the homeless shelter to spend his twenty dollars. I stood there watching him go. I kept on standing there in the same spot facing in the same direction after he had gone. I waited for awhile to see if anyone would come by that I would recognize, but there was no one. So I went home.

In the wee hours of the morning I reached out across the bed, but there was no one there either. I was alone after all.

The next morning I awoke up at seven o'clock. I got up, showered, dressed, and ate cold cereal on my balcony. My routine was disrupted, and I had no sense of time. I arrived at work at eight o'clock.

"What are you doing doing here so early?" said Butch.

"Is it early?" I said.

No wonder the sun was lower in the sky.

Later in the day Morgan broke the silence, but he did not turn around in his chair to face me.

"How is your bucket list coming along?"

"Not so good."

"Not so well."

Morgan wasn't being excessively condescending. He just couldn't help himself.

"That too."

"Your last list item didn't work out," said Butch. "Did it?"

"I wouldn't say that. It was definitely a challenging experience. I'm glad I did it. I never want to do it again."

"So, in that sense, it was satisfying."

"I suppose."

"Well, I suppose you can't expect more than that from a bucket list. Have you come up with another item? Have you thought of something to top the cave?"

"No."

"Oh. Well, in that case I guess you are ready to go anytime."

"Yes," I said. "Any time."

12 - Entire Life

Then, that evening there he was at Joe's MyThai, sitting at my table next to the carry-out counter.

"Well," I said, "if it isn't Lloyd London. You know, you better get yourself better data analytics. I did all kinds of searches on insurance days ago, but you didn't show up. Now the iron is no longer hot."

"I tried to come sooner, but the Prince of Persia withstood me."

"What are you talking about?"

"Look, can we go somewhere and talk?"

"Isn't this somewhere?"

"I mean somewhere that's more nowhere."

Somehow I knew what he meant.

We found a Car2Go and drove to Central Market. Lloyd ordered us each a large Greek yogurt smoothie, and we sat at a table outside. There was a live band and a large crowd for a week night. Yet, we were able to speak with low voices and still hear one another—not that I kept my voice particularly low. I was ready for Mr. London to make a full disclosure, and if he did not, I was going to make as much disclosure as I could.

"So," he said, "what is it you wanted to talk to me about?"

"Isn't it obvious? I need some insurance."

"Did you find someone to be your beneficiary?"

"Not exactly."

The one prospect I couldn't find, and the other, I couldn't reach. No one needed me or my benefit.

"You want to benefit yourself?"

"Yes. I want—what is it called?"

"The one consumer advocates tell you not to get? Whole life?"

"That's it. I want whole life. I want something that builds cash value for the future while providing me protection for today."

"You've been reading the literature. Who's going to get the benefit if you die before the cash payout matures? You see? You still have the same problem."

"I'll give it to you. You can be my beneficiary."

"I'm touched, but no. That would be a conflict of interest."

"I'll give it to my boss or my co-worker. I'll split it between them."

"No doubt your boss would consider it wise to give you raises to make sure you could afford to keep paying the premium."

"That's true. He would consider that a conflict of interest. All right. You've got me. I still don't need insurance, not life insurance anyway."

"No, you had it right the first time. You do need life insurance, but not the kind you think."

"What kind do I need then?"

"You need entire life."

"Entire life? I don't think I read about that one on the internet."

"That's because you can't buy it on the internet. It is only available through personal agents like myself. And I'll tell you right now: there aren't very many of us. If you think you want to shop around, you're going to have a hard time doing it."

Robert's father had sold life insurance door to door.

"You knocked on the door of total strangers to sell them insurance?" I asked him the day we visited.

"I collected door to door, too."

"People were home, and they actually came to the door?"

"You don't sell door to door," I said to London, "do you?"

Lloyd was sipping on his smoothie. He shook his head, and then he swallowed.

"Not unless I'm invited first. I'm like a vampire that way. People think their homes are sacred. I think that's why they are almost never there."

"So, what is entire life?"

"Your entire life is not complete until...?"

Now I was the one sipping the straw. With my lips still pursed and my mouth still full of Greek yogurt, I answered him like Scooby-do.

"Ri ron't row."

I swallowed and pulled my mouth away from the cup.

"It's a mystery," I said.

"I see," he said. "So life is not complete until you solve the mystery?"

"I never really thought of it that way," I said. "But I suppose that is true."

"I like that, Augustus. I will remember it."

I felt cheated. I had not meant to say something profound.

"Well," I said, "at the risk of sounding cynical, life is not complete until you die."

"Actually," said London, "that is more in line with what I would have said."

He took another draw from his straw. We seemed to be trading sips. I held off so I would be ready to respond when my turn to speak came again.

"Is there life after death?" he asked.

"No."

"Is there a reward or a punishment after death?"

"Of course not."

"Can we live forever?"

I thought of Robert lying on the bed, moving his lips slowly, dryly, trying to speak, trying to tell me one last thing.

"Who would want to?"

"Ray Kurzweil?"

"That's true," I said. "But he probably only wants to outlive Bill Gates."

"He's already outlived Steve Jobs."

"That's also true," I said.

Lloyd raised his cup.

"Here's to life," he said.

"To life," I said. We knocked our cups together and then sipped Greek yogurt smoothies in unison. The yogurt was cold like ice cream only with a twang.

"I wonder if this stuff goes back to Alexander or only to Anthony Quinn?" I said holding my cup aloft. "I saw him on TCM the other night in Zorba the Greek."

"I think it goes back further than that. When I drink Greek yogurt smoothie from a straw, I like to think am kissing the living lips of Helen of Troy."

"How is that?"

"The bacterial culture that was on her lips survives in the living cultures of this yogurt."

"Really. Well, I don't suppose the rest of her made the transition."

"No. I don't suppose it did."

We each took another sip.

"I'll tell you who did become immortal though," he said.

"Who's that?"

"Marilyn Monroe!"

"You mean because she's on film?"

"There's more to it than that," Lloyd said. "Lot's of women have been on film."

"It's because her films are on TCM," I said. "Turner bought the rights. You see them in your home. Robert Osborne sees to their restoration personally. Ben Mankiewicz tells you all the back story from his family history in Hollywood."

"Not exactly. The woman still sells calendars. She became a sex goddess before porn on the internet. How did she do that?"

"She slept with the President?" I said.

"No. I'll tell you how she did it. She died young. She died before she could go down hill, while she was still gorgeous. So, we never saw pictures of her getting old. She stayed eternally young in our eyes."

"She still died."

"Yes, but she died before she could decay."

"So, she died at the right time?"

Lloyd smiled.

"That, my friend, is entire life."

"What?"

"That is entire life. You just said it."

"Entire life is dying? We all die."

"Exactly!"

"That's it? That's the big secret? That's what you have been stalking me for weeks to tell me?"

"Not exactly."

"No, not exactly? Then, how about this question? 'That is what you have been stalking me for weeks to sell me?'"

"Not completely."

"Because if it is, I'm not buying."

"No, you're not buying that."

"I'm not buying."

Lloyd took another kiss from Helen.

"I'm not buying," I said, "because I've already accepted it."

"You've already accepted the belief that you are going to die? Believe me. In this world today, that is a gift."

Thank you, Robert.

"No," I said, " it is not a gift. It is costing me plenty. And, it is not a belief. It is a fact."

"That is interesting. Have you ever done a comparison of the birth records and the death records?"

"No."

"Have you ever seen the actuarial tables, the ones we use to determine insurance rates?"

"No."

"Have you ever read a scientific study which followed a thousand people from birth until they all died?"

"No. Who would even do that?"

"Then, how do you really know?"

"The Social Security Administration should have some records. If everyone didn't die, they would be bankrupt already."

"But you haven't submitted an open records request to find out."

"Of course not."

"Then, how do you know everyone dies?"

I took another long draw on the straw before I attempted to answer that one. I heard the slurp. I had hit dry bottom.

"It's just common knowledge."

"Everyone you know has died?"

"No, but I have known people who died. I met a man who had

outlived his contemporaries. Most of them. And he died, too. I think he died. I wasn't actually there."

Robert's father—I had gone to see him once after Robert died. Old Dad was still alive. I had not gone back again. Now it was undoubtedly too late.

Lloyd kissed Helen again. His cup seemed to hold more than mine, or, maybe, half his slurps had been bogus while every one of mine had been genuine.

"Look, London! What are you trying to say? You just said it was a gift to know you are going to die. Now you are trying to cast doubt on the idea."

"No, not casting doubt, and I'm not denying anything. I'm merely asking you how you know you are going to die when you don't know of a scientific study that verifies it. You doubt such a study exists, and I think you are right. After all, why would anyone do a study to prove something they already knew, even if they didn't know why they knew it"

He held up his cup and toggled it back and forth in the air above the table.

"Did you run out? Do you need another?"

"I'm good."

"I don't see how. You haven't had any dinner."

"How do you know that?"

"I intercepted you before you could order, didn't I? MyThai? Do you want something to eat?"

"I don't think so."

"Do you want another one of these?"

"I like this table. I don't want to get up."

"I'll get it. You sit."

"I don't know if I want you buying me anything."

"Afraid of the obligation? I can use your credit card."

"I'm not going to give you my credit card."

"No, not the -7791 Discover you're not. Not the one with the $50,000 credit limit. But the -0621 Visa is only a $2,490 limit. You could risk that. Do you want to know the security number on the back?"

"You've stalked me. You've gathered information about me and followed me. You've —"

"I haven't done anything that Google hasn't done. Not much anyway. The difference is that I appear before you in person and lay my cards down on the table. Or, in this case, I lay your cards on the table. Don't worry. They are not for sale."

"Why? What is this all about?"

"All for a good cause."

"You collected personal information about me for a good cause?"

"I had to find out if you were a good risk. I believe you are. Look, I was kidding about the credit card—not about your numbers but about using it. I'll get the next round. You just sit here and decompress."

"How do you know I will still be here when you get back."

"You'll be here. You want to know the secret, and you know that if you leave, I will find you. Besides, we've become friends."

"Friends?"

"Sure. Who else talks with you like we've been talking here tonight?"

I reflected upon the evening's conversation and about my normal conversations with Butch, Morgan, and even Susan. And Maize? She talked to me, and I loved it, but what had I said to her? 'Turn left here.' Lloyd London was right, and when he came back with another pair of smoothies, I was still there waiting.

13 – The Terms

As Lloyd London weaved his way down the terrace steps of Central Market back to the cafe counter, I sat numbly at our table reviewing what it was that I had come to know. The list was short and tenuous. I was going to die, but I could cite no science to make that claim. Knowing my eventual fate, that I was indeed going to die eventually, was a great blessing, but my stomach was in a knot at the very thought of it. Every Google search I made brought Ray Kurzweil closer to his goal of eternal life, but what would a Google search for eternal life yield but a catalog of all the same old, tired religious myths? Why couldn't people just accept the inevitable? Why did the inevitable have to arrive so slowly and with such pain? Why did I have such fear of it whether it was slow, sudden, deliberate or indifferent?

Where was Helen now, and why did Marilyn still look so good?

Why did Maize dive into caves but eschew coffins? Why did Susan avoid her mother-in-law's funeral? Why was my list of questions longer the list of what I knew? Why was my bucket list so short? Was I ready to die, or was life simply not worth of prolonging? Did Kurzweil know something I didn't, or was I the one who had pulled back the thin protective, outer layer of life to expose the raw aching secret of our tenuous existence?

"Got it all figured out, Gus?"

Lloyd London was back with two full refills of the smooth and the Greek, and I had forgotten the most imminent question.

"No, but I think you have something to tell me."

"I don't have all the answers."

"Still..."

"All right. Do you remember the question I asked the first time we met?"

"No."

"You don't? It was quite a difficult question, one designed to give you a great deal of consternation."

"I don't remember."

"I didn't enjoy asking such a question even though I spent a great deal of time and effort finding just the right one to ask and just the right time to ask it."

"No."

"Okay. Well, let me ask it again."

"No."

"I'm afraid I must, you see. It is essential."

"No."

"If I can't ask it again, and I can't get your answer, then our time together really is at an end."

"No."

Lloyd London rose from the seat he had only retaken moments before.

"Augustus Bishop, I bid you a good life."

"No."

"No? You don't want a good life?"

"No, I don't want to die like my father."

"Ah!" he said, and he sat down.

"I want to live a good life, but I'm not sure I know how. I know I'm going to die, but I don't know how I know it. I don't want to die like my father. I don't want to live like my father."

I paused, waiting to hear what I was going to say next.

"But I wouldn't be here where I am today if he hadn't lived like he had. So, I owe him, but I can't repay him, and I can never be free of the debt."

Lloyd nodded. My hand was shaking, I put down the cup of Greek before I dropped it.

"He took care of me my whole life. He didn't have to, but he felt obligated. I hated him. I hated who he was. I hated his own lack of success. I hated his dependability, but I depended on him. I hated the fact that I depended on him. I hated myself for depending on him. For years I thought I had no father. I just had this fool who kept buying me clothes and picking me up after school and keeping me on weekends but was never there on holidays, never eating birthday cake with me, and never seeing me compete in my karate tournaments. But I knew who he was. I never admitted to myself who he was, but I knew. I knew."

"Sounds better than a lot of fathers. Why did you hate him?"

"Because he was just such a fool, and such a nobody. And he never told me. He never told me. Then, at the end he died this slow, agonizing death. And I had to be there for him. I didn't want to be, but I did it. When he finally died, it was a relief. I saw it in his face. I saw it before he was gone. I was still wrung out, but he was relieved, and then he was gone. He was gone, and he was relieved. I wanted that relief, but I never want to go through what he went through to get it."

"I see."

"And I never told him. I never told him."

"Told him what?" he asked.

I didn't answer.

"I understand," he said, "and I can help you with that. It is precisely for that purpose that I have been pursuing you these several months."

Months? I would have said weeks, long weeks, but still only weeks. For the first time I realized what should have been obvious: that Lloyd London had been collecting data on me, watching me, long before he first approached me at Central Market. None of that mattered now.

"Help? How?"

"I can ensure that you never have to die like your father."

"How can you do that? The man was my father. We are talking heredity."

"I know. That is the point. How can I do it? By ensuring your life."

Lloyd spoke like a New England-er. His -ens and -ins were clearly distinguished from one another unlike a Texan.

"Don't you mean insure?"

"No. I mean ensure."

"You want to insure my life?"

"No, I want to ensure your life."

"But you were talking before about insuring my life."

"Well, yes, but that is an ancillary aspect to the process. You said yourself you have no dependents. My purpose was not to convince you that you did. In fact, you actually don't although that is subject to change. You may not think so, but it is."

"I don't understand."

"It is very simple. Why should a good life come to a bad end? A good life requires a good end. A bad life should not continue unnecessarily. Why should you have to suffer, and why should others suffer because of you?"

"You shouldn't. They shouldn't. I shouldn't."

"No," said Lloyd. "No indeed."

"So it seems," I said, "that we are in agreement, but I still don't know what we are talking about."

"How?" asked Lloyd.

"How what?"

"How are you going to ensure that your life comes to a good end and not a bad one?"

"I don't know. I guess you try to live the best you can and don't screw up in the end."

"No," said Lloyd. "You ensure your life comes to a good end the same way you ensure that you don't have to suffer. How are you going to make sure you don't have to suffer? How are you going to ensure that you don't have to die like your father?"

"That's easy," I said. "I told you before. Either I move to Oregon, or I buy a gun. Here in Texas I buy the gun."

"You know how to use a gun?"

"What's to know? I'll watch YouTube."

"So you will end your own life when the time comes?"

"Better than pain. Better than suffering. Better than humiliation."

"What if you can't do it? What if you fail the screening at the gun store because you are under psychiatric care for depression? What if you cannot hold the gun because you have arthritis from a lifetime of typing?"

"Texas will change. We will get assisted suicide rights here like they have in Oregon. The Austin City Council will make this town an assisted suicide sanctuary."

"I would say two things about that. One, don't underestimate the power of the right wing to overturn the laws. And with that don't underestimate the fickleness of the public. Two, never forget that when the government gives you the right to end your life, it also assumes the right to make the decision for you. It is very likely that you will die not at a time of your own choosing. Rather, you will die at a time determined by someone else for the sake of his convenience, not yours, and to ensure the fiscal soundness of the government agency dispensing your care."

"That is a depressing thought," I said. It drove me back to the lips of Helen of Troy.

"You may or may not get the right to die. You may or may not be able to keep it. But either way, you will not be guaranteed the right to die at the right time."

"The right time?"

"Rutger Hauer said it in Blade Runner: 'Time to die.' It says it in Ecclesiastes: 'A time to be born, and a time to die.' It's all a matter of timing."

"So I should rush down to Academy now before I am diagnosed with depression and buy a gun while I still can?"

"If you do, make it a revolver, a thirty-eight. Hunter S. Thompson used a forty-five, but I don't recommend it. A revolver can lie in a drawer for thirty years and still fire. Really, though, I don't recommend a gun at all."

I was going to respond with something to the effect of, "Oh, you don't, do you?" or "You don't say?" but I couldn't muster the sarcasm. A sense of dread was settling over me. Lloyd London was serious.

"What do you recommend?"

"Timing really is everything. Did you ever notice that Father Time carries a scythe just like the Grim Reaper? The only difference is that Father Time doesn't dress in black."

It was true. I hadn't noticed. In fact, I couldn't tell the two apart.

"What do you mean by timing?"

"Did you ever see a pro ball player who stayed too long in the game?"

"You mean the guy who tries to play one more season, but he finds out he doesn't have it anymore and should have quit while he was ahead?"

"He ends up humiliating himself and damaging the team."

"But the thing is you never know," I said. "Some athletes get put out to pasture by their team, but they go somewhere else and do great things. You just never know."

"Not necessarily. There are indicators."

"Are you telling me that you can tell when an athlete should retire and when he should keep playing?"

"No. That is not our market. We leave that to others."

"So what are you saying you can do?"

"I'm saying we can tell when the time is right for you."

"To retire?"

"No."

Lloyd returned to his cup of yogurt. He raised his eyebrows and looked at me as he bent down to drink.

"You mean to die?"

Lloyd took another long sip and raised his head. I asked him again.

"Are you saying you can tell me when to die?"

"Not tell you. Ensure you."

"Ensure me?" This time I was careful to enunciate the "e" rather than slipping into the short "i" vowel sound.

"You have already said that you would rather die than suffer, but I would bet that you would be willing to suffer if you could recover and improve your quality of life. You did get lasik eye surgery, did you not?"

"Yes, but not even I would call that suffering."

"But if you had an ailment that could be cured by medical treatment, by painful medical treatment, you would do it."

"I suppose so."

"You would. The fear of death would drive you to undergo even a painful cure. But prolonged suffering with no resolution in sight? That's another matter. In that circumstance, a man would welcome relief. You would welcome it. But you have to be able to discern which is which. You have to be able to tell the difference."

"And you can do that?"

"Yes, we can."

"So, if I were facing cancer, you could tell me whether I should undergo chemotherapy or move to Oregon. Or get the gun out of the drawer." I said it cavalierly, but I shuddered at the thought.

"There's more to it than that. You see, you need to decide yourself when to die, but you need to do it while you are still able to think clearly. You could do it by the calendar, but that doesn't protect you in case of early decline, and it doesn't maximize your potential."

"Maximize my potential?"

"Yes, the time to go is when the sufferings of life exceed the current satisfaction level and the potential future rewards. That is the time to go. In fact, the best time is before the suffering comes, when the satisfaction level is high, but the potential for suffering exceeds the potential for future satisfaction and well-being. You cannot determine when that time has arrived, but we can. We have the data. We have the analysis. You decide you want to live to your full potential and satisfaction, and we determine when those parameters have been met."

"And then what? Do you send me a text? 'Gus, it's time.'"

"No. Once you've made the decision to accept our services, we relieve you of the burden of having to determine when precisely to act."

He took another sip. I hovered over my straw.

"What do you mean by not having to decide when to act?"

"You don't have to decide when it is time. You don't have to evaluate from a state of emotional distress whether or not your life is still worthwhile much less try to decide if it is likely to improve. You don't have to move to a different state. You don't have to find a helpful doctor. You don't have to pull the gun out of the drawer, stare at the barrel for an hour, and finally put it in your mouth. In effect, you don't have to worry about the end of your life. You are free to live, to enjoy, to prosper, and to exit peacefully and gracefully."

"That's the part I don't get. How am I free to exit gracefully?"

"It's very simple. We take care of it."

"You take care of what?"

"We take care of your exit."

"My exit?"

"We take care of your departure."

I gave him a very confused look.

"We take care of your death."

"And how do you do that?"

"In a variety of ways. We are very sensitive to the context. We strive to avoid the pain, but that is not always feasible and not even always appropriate."

He took another sip. I sensed something was coming, so I quickly followed suit. I hid behind my cup and straw lest some coming revelation arrive and find me unprotected.

Lloyd disengaged from his straw and raised his head.

"Let's face it," he said. "Death is just as personal as it is universal. The size that fits one man needs significant alteration for another. It's not something you should just buy off the rack and wear, so to speak."

There ensued the longest period of silence between us since we had met. The Central Market open air cafe was still bustling with activity, but I felt like Tom Hanks on the bridge in Saving Private Ryan. Silence blanketed the scene until I broke it. Something in me, almost everything in me wanted to remain in that silence, but I broke it nonetheless.

"Are you telling me that you are selling death?"

"No. I told you. I sell entire life."

"But life is not entirely complete without death," I said.

"That is right."

"And since we have to die anyway, why not do it when it is most convenient?"

"I won't promise you that it will necessarily be convenient."

"But you will do it when—"

Lloyd London returned to his straw and waited for me to finish my statement. I was waiting to hear what I was about to say, too.

"You ensure that the person dies when he has nothing more to gain, and everything to lose."

"Well put. I could not have said it better myself."

"Thank you," I said. "I don't think I understood what you were talking about until I said it myself."

What was I saying?

"You know," Lloyd said, "this is what I love about this job. The policy sells itself."

"The policy?"

"Yes, the policy. Well, technically it consists of three policies, but we market it as one because we sell the three as a bundle."

By this time I was no longer incredulous. My own words had caught me. For at long last I had figured out the mystery of Mr. Lloyd London, and the fact that I had done so myself made me willing to hear him out. My lips returned to my straw, and I drank deeply as I listened.

"First, we offer life insurance which gives you protection. Only this is whole life, not term. What's the difference? Term life only pays a death benefit. Whole life builds a cash value, and that cash value persists even after you are no longer paying the premium. Term life you have to keep paying till you die, or it won't pay. It's almost like a ransom. And you remember the old joke."

"Joke?"

"You told it to me."

"Oh, yeah. Right."

"With whole life, once you have paid in full, you stop paying. The cash value remains—it even draws interest—until you die and pass the cash to your benefactor or until you draw out the cash value yourself. Along with that you get Accidental Death and Dismemberment. This insures you against sudden, premature death or loss of quality of life due to loss of limb. Standard stuff. Finally, comes *le piece de resistance,* the entire life benefit, the first of its kind: life ensurance. Quite simply we ensure you against a life of pain, futility, and undesirable elongation. We promise you not immortality, which not even Google can deliver, but mortality, mortality refined, mortality with the bitterness removed so that in life you need taste only the sweetness. Now, I ask you, is there any other way to live?"

"Not that I can think of. But, just how do you remove the bitterness and leave only the sweet?"

"We offer you entire life ensurance."

"And life ensurance removes the bitterness? How?"

"By means of the death benefit."

"And the death benefit does what?"

"It's very simple, Gus. The death benefit ensures the benefit of death. Make no mistake. Death is a benefit when it comes at the proper time. Our company, for the benefit of our policy holders, ensures that it does."

"Wait a minute. I could get hit by a bus when I walk out of here. You're going to prevent that?"

"No! No! No! That is not an untimely death. It is quick. It may not be painless, but the pain is over soon. Moreover, it is a pain that precludes a worse eventual pain. As for it coming too soon, well, that is in the very nature of death. That is what you have life insurance for: it enables you to leave a legacy if, unfortunately, death comes too soon. If it comes too soon, accidental death and dismemberment enables you to leave a much larger legacy."

"And life ensurance?"

"Think of it this way. Life insurance is for the time when death comes too soon. Life ensurance is for the time when death can't come soon enough. And, let's face facts. In this postmodern age, death comes too late more than it comes too early. How many people go through life fearing death, dreading that sudden knock on the door during the day and longing through the night for the knock that never seems to come? How many people are sitting in assisted living homes alone, unable to sleep, unable to rest, full of regrets, and wishing they could have gone sooner like some of their friends? Those are the people, I have to say, who could have used life ensurance."

There began to arise in me a flood of questions. I didn't so much need the answers so much as I just needed to ask the questions, even if I was covering the same ground again.

"But government sanctioned assisted suicide—"

"—is unreliable and untrustworthy. Its very availability depends upon the opinions of the majority or on the cant of the most fanatical. Where it is in place, the authority to decide when to apply it lies more with the state than with you, and the decision to pull the trigger, if I may be so crass, rests more upon the considerations of the government's convenience than with your need to draw your own life to a peaceful and timely close. To put it bluntly, the motivating factor will be economic, but you and I both know there is more to life than money."

I weighed his words silently, waiting for my next objection to bubble up, but Lloyd London was faster.

"And, by the way, the same holds true for the hospitals, government or private. The hospitals want treatable conditions with no chronic repeat customers. They will decide when to treat you and when—"

He paused for emphasis.

"—and when to give you your, shall we say, final discharge. It will no more be a medical decision with them than it will be with the government. And they won't weigh the value of your life. But we will. Now, it is true that sometimes we make use of the hospital and the government. Both of them act under our guidance at times. That is, we may use official government or medical means to deliver your benefit, but we are not limited to those. The fact that government sanctioned assisted suicide is available or that the hospitals in your area are culling patients who do not meet their care model does not prevent us from ensuring your complete life. And that mission means our company will do whatever we can to protect you from untimely death so that we can deliver you a timely life completion. Not too soon, and not too late. Just right."

"But how are you going to prevent the hospital from culling me, as you put it?"

"We have access to medical and financial data across the world."

"So you can predict the decision the hospital is going to make and head it off."

"More or less."

"And what about the opposite? How do you get the hospital to act 'under your guidance' when their data would say that I should be treated but your data says it is time for me to go?"

"We have access to medical and financial data across the world."

A literal chill went down my spine. I pushed my yogurt smoothie aside. It was too cold to drink. That cool beauty Helen was stone cold to me now.

I knew it well enough. There were two kinds of access to data in a database. There was read access, and there was write access. Those with read access could see how things were. Those with write access could determine how things were going to be. Now, it became clear. There would be no diagnosis that did not fit with the data in the hospital database, and there would be no course of treatment that was not prescribed by doctors' orders in the database because Lloyd London and his company had write access to the data.

"What if—" I couldn't speak. I tried to swallow, but my throat was dry. I pulled the smoothie straw back to my mouth. The cold went all the way down to my stomach and stayed there. The sweat which I had not noticed breaking out on my neck dried. I found it strangely comforting.

"What if I am not in a hospital? What if I am not sick? What if—"

"What if you merely are sick at heart? That is where we start to get creative."

"Creative?"

"Yes. Our methods are varied and unpredictable but always appropriate."

"But not always painless?"

"Not always. Sometimes a measure of pain is appropriate. Some clients require pain to know they are alive. Some need pain to assuage their guilt. Sometimes pain is simply unavoidable, but we don't use it lightly or maliciously. We don't inflict pain for our own enjoyment nor do we use it for the enjoyment of our clients. In any event we do not inflict or allow prolonged suffering."

"Do I call you when I feel the time has come?"

"No. We relieve you of the burden. You see, the client is not the best judge of when the time has arrived. He can be fooled by circumstances which are only temporary. He can't see what is coming, good or ill. We have the best data analytics in the industry. I believe you would agree with that from what you've seen already. We will keep watch over your life, and when the time comes to bring it to a happy close, we will be there. You don't have to figure out when that time is. You just live your life. You don't have to wrestle with your conscience or your fears. You don't have to search the web looking for someone who can help. When everything is ready, we will be there. If we seem to be delaying during a difficult time, rest assured you've probably got more quality life to come. Just be patient. Once life truly is as good as it gets, or rather, once life has been as good as it could be for as long as probable, then we will be there. We will not abandon you to endure the long, slow decline."

I thought of Lloyd London sitting in my doctor's office intercepting me just before I went in to be examined. I remembered the Emetrol and my phone retrieved from rogue forces in the city. I felt as if I had reentered the cave, passing through that impassable birth canal into darkness with no glimmer of green shoe to lead me on or to bring me out. Without Maize I had only Helen seducing me into the ruins of her shattered city. Night was descending upon Central Market. I asked the only question that remained.

"What does it cost?"

Lloyd London smiled. Even through the darkness, he smiled. I smiled, too. I know that I did because I felt that unfamiliar muscle contraction in my cheeks. I returned to the yogurt, to Helen and her once more comforting chill.

"Well, since you ask, I have to warn you. It isn't cheap."

Somehow I knew that.

14 - The Bargain

The Central Market closed at ten. We followed the remaining patrons into the parking lot. I followed London. Our Car2Go was gone, and I wished for once I had taken my Abarth. I considered checking my apps for other Car2Go's or even cabs, but Lloyd kept walking. I figured he had found another Car2Go using his own, superior data analytics, but we did not stop. We crossed Lamar at the light which turned green for us as we approached. It seemed like a fairy tale or Star Trek. London kept a steady pace, I a step behind, until we found ourselves at Kerbey Lane Cafe. It seemed like the city on the edge of forever. Strangely I was scarcely winded when we arrived, but I was voraciously hungry.

It was ten thirty. We ordered the pancakes and coffee. It was still hours from my bedtime, but I felt like a kid staying up late and not doing my homework, gleeful in a way I had seldom felt during my life. Neither of us spoke until the food arrived.

"How expensive?" I said.

Lloyd reached for the syrup.

"At your age you could easily get term life for thirty-five to fifty dollars a month."

I started to speak, but he cut me off with a wave of the syrup pitcher.

"But you don't want term. Whole life—well, to tell you the truth no one buys whole life anymore. Too many radio and TV consumer advocates telling them to buy term and invest the rest in mutual funds. But they are right. Whole life is too expensive, and too incomplete. Entire life is expensive, but it's affordable.

I nodded in agreement as if I knew what he was talking about, as if we had just left a session of the insurance agents' convention and were now digesting what we had learned.

"Here's how it works," he said. "You pay a level premium for twenty years."

"A level premium? That means it never goes up or down."

"That's right. The policy has three components. First, it contains a term life component. Very cheap. Second, the policy contains a whole life component which builds cash value. Third, there is the entire life piece itself. You can pay the policy ahead, if you like. Once you have reached your cash value, you're done. The cash draws interest, the policy remains in force, and you are done with your entire life. You continue on with the term at the premium level that matched your age and health at the time you began the policy."

"Done?"

"That's right. Done. You can borrow from the cash, but you have to pay it back with interest."

"Oh. Interest.

"Four percent. Ten years. Like a car loan. But, if you don't borrow, you don't pay another dime."

"Really?"

"Really."

"And then?"

"And then you're covered. When you go, your dependents are provided for. That way, you aren't stuck thinking you need to stay around to take care of them. It is quite liberating."

I stuck a fork full of whole wheat pancake in my mouth and chewed on what Lloyd had said.

"Liberating how?"

"From burden and concern. From responsibility. You know that people live longer who don't worry, and loving someone, especially someone you can take care of, can give purpose to life."

"It makes sense," I said slicing off another section of pancake although I had never thought of it before.

"But sometimes the two work at cross purposes. The source of your purpose can become the cause of your anxiety, and then you do need an escape hatch. That's where the entire life and the term life work together. Term gives you the freedom to depart when you need to by alleviating any concern you may have for the ones you are leaving behind. Entire life gives you the freedom to love without having to sacrifice your own life to do it. See how it works?"

I nodded with my mouth full until I could swallow.

"And I don't call you to say it's time?"

"You don't have to keep your finger on your pulse and constantly be taking the temperature of your life. You are free to live your life to its fullest. We make use of the most advanced data collection and analytics to discern when your life has indeed reached its entirety. Again, you are free from having to do all that yourself.

"Now, I will admit that the data collection disturbs some people. I think it is a selling point. That is why I have demonstrated it to you, because I knew you would appreciate it."

"Well," I said, "it would help if you had a website I could read—"

"No website."

"No website," I repeated. "How do I know—?"

"You will have two contacts. One will collect your premiums, and one will visit you from time to time to see how you are doing. That second person will be me. I will be your personal agent. I will watch over you, offer you guidance, and I will participate in your ongoing assessments and reviews. The company will make no final determination without my participation. So, you see? We will continue to be friends."

"Do you have an email?"

"No."

"Do you have an office?"

"Wherever you and I meet and sit down together, that is my office."

"But how do I reach you? I don't suppose you have a phone number."

Lloyd London shook his head.

"You already know how to reach me. You've already done it. When you need me, I will know it. Usually I will know it before you do."

"What about the premium?"

"The premium—we will get to that."

He stuffed his mouth with pancake. I knew the answer to my question was going be delayed, so I did the same. I felt the whole wheat warmth descending as it were on an elevator down into my belly. It radiated out from there. Coffee carried the warmth even further to my extremities. I was suffused in a sense of well being. We ate on in silence save for an occasional grunt of appreciation for the pancakes and the warmth. Even after the waiter took our plates, we sat back in the booth in quiet satisfaction sipping coffee as if we had the whole night before us, as if the night were the day and the day were filled with the promise of the darkness and all that incubated within it. When the check came, Lloyd picked it up and held it between two fingers over the middle of the table.

"There is no contract to sign. Tuesday next week you will meet a man on the street. He will say to you, 'So, have you found what you have been looking for your entire life?' You answer, 'I believe that I have, and what I have, I want to share.' You look perplexed. I'll write it out for you. Then, you will give that man one-hundred-sixty-seven dollars in cash. As you hand it to him, you will say, "Thank you for letting me share,' and he will answer, 'You are entirely welcome.' That will be your weekly premium. At the end of twenty years, you will be paid in full on the whole and entire life components. You can prepay like I said. If you do, there will be a ten percent discount. To do that you will have to go through me. We can discuss it at one of our meetings. Once you've paid the full amount, what we call the whole life face value of the policy, you are done."

"Done?"

"Done."

"What does that mean?"

"Done as in done paying premiums. Paid in full."

"Oh," I said, "but what happens then?"

"You live your life. You live your life in the confidence of knowing you are fully protected."

"But what about the term? I thought you paid that until you died. And I thought we both agreed, I didn't need term life because I have no dependents."

"You have been paying attention. You are free to buy your own term life policy with any insurance company you like to protect your dependents whenever you acquire any worth protecting. This is different. This is a little insurance pool we provide as an added benefit for our customers."

"You provide an added benefit? A term life policy on the side as an added benefit?"

"Yes. You see, many of our clients are in the same situation as you are. They have no family. They have no dependents. So, we like to pair them off so they can cover one another."

"Cover one another? I don't know anyone else with this policy. Why would I want to cover a stranger?"

"Insurance is a way of sharing the risk so you can cover the loss. You cover another person so that, in the event of your death, his or her entire life policy can be paid in full for him. Someone else does the same for you."

"And that's part of the package?"

"Yes, it is."

"It's like you are telling me who to love."

Lloyd London shrugged his shoulders.

"These days sometimes somebody has to," he said.

Then, he paid the bill. It felt good to have someone pay for my dinner, but I knew not to let myself get carried away. This was just a loan.

Outside we walked the half block of Kerbey Lane to 38th Street. There we found a Car2Go. Lloyd put me in the driver's seat and stood by the car.

"Big decision, I know. Life insurance traditionally took care of someone else. What the policy holder got out of it was the peace of mind that those people who depended on him would have money to continue their lives. Entire life is the first life insurance that takes care of you."

He shook my hand. There was money in his palm.

"You don't have to pass the premium like this if it feels awkward to you, but notice that the two one dollar bills are on the front and back of the stack? You sandwich the one-hundred-and-sixty-five between the ones."

I peeled back the first bill—a one. Behind it were three twenties, two fifties, a five, and another one.

"Why this arrangement?"

"Security cameras. This way they can't pick up the amount you are passing."

"The police will think I am buying drugs."

"No they won't. Nothing will be passed back to you."

I handed Lloyd back his money. That is, I tried to hand it back. He held up his palm and shook his head.

"First month's premium on me. If you decide not to buy the policy, keep the money. I know I caused you a lot of grief the past few weeks."

Then, he closed the door of the Car2Go and disappeared at the corner of 38th and Kerbey Lane. I knew better than to try to follow him. I started the car and headed up to 35th to Jefferson. I turned left and drove south to 29th. From there I took Guadalupe to 5th. On the way I thought of the cave, its mouth just a few miles away, running under some of these streets. I thought of Maize's green shoes, always just out of reach, and now, completely gone. I remembered Susan downing tequila with me at my table because she could not face her mother-in-law's death. I thought of Robert and, even more, of his father in that nursing home waiting for another visit. Which of these griefs could I blame on him?

On Monday, I took the Abarth to work. I wanted the freedom and the insulation from the street—that is, from the people on the street. But on Tuesday I found myself walking down the ramp and out of my parking garage without the Fiat. When I turned the first corner, a homeless man was sitting on the sidewalk leaning against the building.

"How are you, Sir?"

I was taken aback by being called sir.

"All right, I guess."

"So, have you found what you have been looking for your entire life?'

I stopped.

"What did you say?"

"I said, 'So, have you found what you have been looking for your entire life?'"

I paused. I felt naked on the street. People were passing by, but I felt certain that they were watching to see what I would do.

"You heard me the first time. I'm not askin' you again."

"I believe that I have, and what I have, I want to share."

I handed him the same bundle of bills Lloyd London had given me.

"Thank you for letting me share."

"You are entirely welcome."

"Well, I guess we did that right."

"Yes, Sir. Thank you. You won't regret it, not for your entire life."

The next Tuesday I saw the same homeless man at a different corner. He saw me first, and asked me the question.

This time I answered him immediately and put the money in his hand. As I walked away to my office, I had to admit to myself that I did feel fully protected.

15 – Blackhat

Butch came by my desk and tapped on my shoulder. I was wearing my noise canceling ear phones, so, of course, I jumped.

"Sorry," he said. "I sent you an instant message, but you didn't respond."

"I couldn't hear the ding with these on," I said.

"You didn't see the blinking icon?"

I looked down at the lower right corner of the system tray.

"Oh! There it is. Sorry. What's the problem?"

"Susan wants to see you in her office."

"Really? When?"

"Now."

"What's going on?"

"You'll find out."

For just a moment I had a tinge of panic. In my mind I went from promising career to unemployment to property foreclosure to begging on the street in milliseconds. But then I remembered my new ensurance policy. It had only been in effect a few months, and all the implications of the coverage had not fully percolated into my consciousness. Or was it my unconsciousness? Either way, my life had not yet become fully informed to the benefits of being entirely ensured.

"So now what?" I had asked Lloyd on our second meeting after the policy had gone in force. I had made nine premium payments by then. I had kept count. Lloyd had given me an old fashioned calendar like Robert once had with pictures of beaches and light houses at the top of each page and squares for the days of the week. Each month was on its own separate page, but since it was on paper, you couldn't change the pictures. Twelve pages made up the year. He had showed me how to mark a little X on every Tuesday: Premium Day.

"What now? You just live."

"I don't feel any different," I had said. I thought I was being facetious, but Lloyd answered with a reassuring straightforwardness.

"It takes time. You'll get there."

Maybe he was right. As I got up from my desk and rounded the corner of our cubicle suite, it occurred to me that even if I got fired and lost my condo, with the policy in force, things could only get so bad.

Susan had an open door policy, but her door was practically always closed except when she was managing by walking around. She seldom walked around. So, I had to knock.

"Come in, Gus."

"How did you know it was me?" I said.

"When I beckon, you come. I have the power."

She waved her fingers in front of her face as if casting a spell.

"How would you like a special new geek treat?"

"Geek treat?"

"How would you like to go to that Blackhat Conference?"

I didn't know what to say. I didn't know what surprised me more: the fact that Susan even had the vaguest idea what Blackhat was or the fact that she didn't seem to realize that this treat was not new. I had attended last year.

"I'd love to. That would be great."

"I asked Morgan in the hall when he was on his way to the can if there was a good security convention I could send you to. The contractors always know these things. He told me to send you to DEF CON, but I looked it up. That has something to do with national defense, and your job is not to protect the country. Your job is to protect this company. I don't know if he doesn't know what he is talking about, or if he had to pee so bad he just said the first thing out of his mouth. Besides, wouldn't you rather go to something called Blackhat than something called DEF CON?"

"Absolutely!" I said.

I was happy to go anywhere that didn't involve getting fired.

"I knew it. Get yourself a black cowboy hat—not one of those wimpy red hats the Linux guys talk about—some boots, maybe a whip."

"I don't think you can carry one of those around."

"It's Vegas. You can do anything. Remember though this is a business trip. Don't be ringing up any call girls, not on my expense account."

"No, Ma'am!"

"Does sound like fun, maybe even the geeky parts. My husband would be so worried about me. Anyway, go make your reservations and learn how to protect us."

"I will."

"One question. Is this a conference for people who protect computers, or is this a conference for people who want to break in?"

"It's for protectors, but the hackers attend, too."

"Sounds even more exciting. But be careful. I don't want you going over to the dark side."

"Maybe you should give me a raise to make it less tempting."

I was feeling unusually bold.

"Maybe if you caught a few rats, I could talk my boss into a better grade of cat food. He keeps telling me you guys aren't worth what I pay you now. He has a compliance mindset, but I think you guys can do us some good. So, put on your black hat and go learn how to think like a rat so you can catch one and not become one."

"We have to learn to act like rats to demonstrate how attacks could be made."

"Why would you want to demonstrate an attack? So you can convince the execs to keep paying you to build walls?"

"No," I said, but I was not so sure I was being honest. "You have to think like an attacker so you can be a good defender. Sometimes you have to convince management to pay for a new wall. Sometimes you need to understand how to reinforce the one you've got."

"Sounds good. Sounds hypothetical."

"Well, yes, but wouldn't you rather deal with a hypothetical threat than a real one?"

"I don't buy mouse traps to catch hypothetical mice. And I don't send my cat to a convention about rats so that he can become one. Watch out for the rats. Catch me a big one and drop it at my door."

When I got back to the cubicle, I approached Butch at his desk.

"Did you put her up to this?"

"To what? To sending you to Blackhat? No. It was all her idea."

"Are you going?"

"No, I'll be here holding down the fort."

"Really? She's sending me and not you?"

"That's right."

"What about him?"

I jerked my thumb in Morgan's direction.

"Why don't you ask him?" Butch said.

"I'm going, but I am using my own nickel," Morgan said.

I turned to Butch. "Our man here tried to send me to DEF CON instead. Blackhat was not big enough for the two of us."

"Not so," said Morgan. "I figured we could use the coverage: I go to one conference, you go to the other, we share our gleanings, and our group benefits."

I felt a tinge of shame. He made sense, but I wasn't willing to admit it.

"I think it is good that you two go together," said Butch. "I am going to schedule a meeting and go over the conference schedule so we can plan what you boys attend. I may not be going with you in the flesh, but I will be going in spirit, if it is possible to have a spirit in Las Vegas, and I am sure that there are some sessions I will want to attend with you spiritually. In the meantime, you two need to get with Susan's secretary and book your flights. I know we are not paying for you, Morgan, but I thought you boys might want to sit together."

Dread crawled up my spine.

"Sorry, boss," said Morgan, "but I plan to drive."

"Drive?" I said. "Through the desert?"

"I like the desert. Think of it as doing penance on the way to Las Vegas."

"What is penance?"

"Being sorry for my faults and my sins. Of course, you might not want to call driving a Mustang Cobra penance unless you ordinarily drive a Ferrari."

"No, I should say not," said Butch. "On the other hand, there is still some degree of mortification just in being in the desert, especially if you drive with the top down."

"True. But I am only driving from Albuquerque. Driving all the way through Texas in August is too much penance for me."

"Oh! You're flying to Albuquerque and renting a car to drive the rest of the way? Sounds wonderful. Makes my staying behind to work seem penitential."

"You are welcome," said Morgan as if he were doing Butch a favor. Butch nodded as if he agreed.

I still didn't know what penance meant, but I suspected that flying in a plane next to Morgan would qualify. I would have thanked God that Morgan had made other plans if I had believed in him, in God that is. Morgan was in the flesh. I had to believe in him. Then, for a moment I considered driving to Las Vegas in my Abarth. I fancied myself passing Morgan's rented Cobra at one-hundred-and-forty miles an hour. I thought the Abarth could do one-hundred-forty, but I never had pushed it. A drive through west Texas would be the perfect time to find out. But what if the Cobra swallowed the Abarth and I had to endure Morgan's stare as he passed? Better to take the plane. Maybe Susan would spring for business class.

"If you are going," said Gus, "you better register today."

"That's right," said Morgan. "some of the sessions are already sold out. I got the last seat in 'Advanced Web Attacks and Exploitation'. You had better hurry."

"Are you springing for the courses, Boss?"

"You'll have to clear that with Susan."

Immediately, my phone rang. It was Susan herself.

"Hey, I need a justification from you to go to this conference, just a page I can give to my boss so I can clear the budget for this. Explain what you plan to study and how it will help you do your job better."

"You don't have the money yet?"

"Don't worry. We've got the money. I just have to get his signature. I've got him sixty percent convinced, but he wants to hear it from you. I'm meeting with him tomorrow afternoon, so get it to me in the morning in case I have to de-geek it a little. You need some geek in it or he won't believe it, but not too much or his eyes will glaze over."

At first I tried downloading and sending her the letter that letter that Blackhat provided on their website. It was designed for you to give your management to convince them to send you to the conference. Susan shot it right back.

"What is this?" she responded. "It reads like a sales brochure." So I wrote up my own version. I explained how sometimes you had to learn how to think like a hacker to catch a hacker. I talked about the data analysis we did and how I wanted to enroll in 'Crash Course in Data Science for Hackers'. It was five the next day before I got a response from Susan. She had secured the money for me to go to the conference and take the course.

"George didn't quite understand," she wrote. "I told him it was like Jodie Foster going to see Hannibal Lector to catch the serial killer. I told him data science was like Harrison Ford matching the assassin's voice from the cell phone to the drug cartel's intelligence officer. You have to make it simple for these guys. Put the conference and hotel on our company credit card, but I would put the flight on my own card and request the company reimbursement, if I were you. That way you get the frequent flier miles."

By the time I had card in hand and could get to the website, my course was sold out. So was the course in Software Defined Radio. That course might have given me a chance actually to do the Harrison Ford trick of intercepting a cell phone call. Instead, I got the final spot in 'Cyber Intelligence Gathering Using Maltego' and the last seat on the last plane that would get me to Vegas in time to attend.

So, naturally I arrived late for my flight. I wished I could blame it on an urgent alert from the SIEM, but it just took me a long time to pack. I had to do my laundry. I had to pick my desert wardrobe, and I had to harden my laptop computer against intrusion. You couldn't just walk into Blackhat and not expect trouble. But then everyone knows that the best defense is a good offense. Maybe I should set up a honeypot on my machine. There could be a prize at Blackhat for catching the most flies. If I installed Cold Fusion on my Mac and set up a virtual instance of Windows, that would be irresistible. But that would be too easy. I could install Android in a virtual environment. That would be tempting. I should offer a real challenge and put Z/OS on my machine, but that was getting ridiculous. Then, I realized I was out of time.

I considered driving the Abarth to the airport and charging covered parking to the company, but I couldn't bring myself to do it. There was no telling who would swing open the door of his or her FU-250 pickup and scrape off the paint right below my window. So, I left the Fiat safe in the garage and took a Car2Go to the Omni Hotel. From there I took a cab. My luggage fit much better in the trunk of the cab than it had in the Car2Go Smart Car, even though the cab was a Prius. I marveled at my carbon credits all the way to Austin Bergstrom.

The airport was so jammed that the TSA didn't make me remove my shoes. When I got to my gate, Southwest had already boarded the all the C boarding passes. I was the last one aboard. They closed the gate as I walked onto the jet bridge. The steward smiled as I entered.

"Last seat in the back," he said. "Good thing you don't need the overhead." He was holding the detached seat belt he used for his safety demonstration. I walked all the way to the last row. The seat in the middle of the right side was the only one available. I stuffed my computer bag under the seat in front of me, placed my tray table in the locked position, and fastened my seat belt. But I didn't study the card in the seat pouch before me or look for the exits over the wings. If we went down, I was ducking out the back. Instead, I looked at the drink menu.

"I'm with you," said a female voice on my right, the holder of the window seat in the last row. "I consider the cocktail bar to be the most important safety feature on the plane. You would think, though, this being Austin, that they would put some tequila on the menu, but I suppose there is more profit margin in gin."

I turned in surprise. It was Susan.

“I hope you have a ten dollar bill on you. I forgot that Southwest only takes cash for their booze, and they don’t give change.”

I dug into my back pocket and pulled out my wallet. The engines revved, and the plane lurched forward.

“I have a ten.”

“Good. In that case you can buy me another drink, Geek.”

16 – The Flight

"So," said Susan, "we start from 541 feet at Austin Bergstrom and end at 2001 feet at Las Vegas. That's 1,460 feet. I could do that on foot. But before we get there, we climb to 35,000 feet to cruise. That's twenty-four times higher than our destination."

"You did that math in your head?"

"What's that all about? All that rising and falling?"

"Avoidance. Avoiding the birds. Avoiding the buildings. Avoiding the smaller planes. Avoiding the drones. Avoiding making a bunch of noise near the ground. Besides, I'm not sure but there may be some mountains between here and there to clear."

"There's no mountains between here and Dallas, and you still make the grand climb on that flight. I think it is partly showing off. 'Look how high I climb.'"

Susan raised her hand above the level of the seat before her.

"Here I go up. Now here I come down to you. I am descending to your level, Las Vegas."

Her hand landed gracefully upon my non-upright seat back tray like a plane landing upon a desert butte, but we were still over Leander and rising.

"Surprised to see me?" she said.

"Yes," I said.

"I could only talk Butch into letting you go if I went along to make sure you stayed out of trouble. No, I'm kidding. That's not why I'm going."

"I would have guessed you were going for the gambling."

"The gambling? No, I do enough of that at work. I'm going to Blackhat."

My facial expression betrayed me.

"No, that's not right. Really—"

She put her hand on mine.

"We are going to Blackhat."

"Why are *we* going to Blackhat?"

"We are going because of you."

"We are going because of me?"

"That's right. Because of the wonderful sales job you did to justify going yourself. George bought it."

"And George told you to go too?"

"No, I told me to go too. I decided."

"You decided to go learn something about data security?"

"Damn straight."

"What about Paul?"

"Butch volunteered to stay behind and man the fort. He said you should go. That's the kind of boss Butch is."

I realized afresh that Susan knew Paul's nickname and used it. I also wondered if he hadn't jumped at the chance to be in the office without his boss. If only he hadn't thrown her together with me.

"So you're going to Blackhat?"

"You needn't sound so shocked."

"But you know the main session doesn't start yet. The first few days are courses. Computer security courses."

"I know that. I signed up for one."

"But those are technical courses."

"Yeah, Baby."

"What did you sign up for?"

"Oh, I picked one of those three letter acronyms. I chose one that had the word 'hack' in it. Hack something."

The conference course list was still in my browser cache. I scrolled through the offerings.

"'Hack'.... 'Hack'.... 'HackWave'?"

"Maybe."

"SDR?"

"That's it. SDR. I told you it was a three letter acronym. But where does the 'hack' come in?"

"SDR—that's Software Defined Radio."

"Yes. I remember now. I looked it up."

"Do you know about that, about SDR?"

"No, but that's why I signed up for the course."

"Yes, but I'm sure there is some technical background that you need going into the course, and without that, you are going be pretty lost."

"I know. That's why you're taking the course, too."

"Me? I'm taking the course?"

"Yes."

"But I didn't sign up."

"That's good because if you had, you'd be taking the same course twice."

"How is that?"

"Because I signed you up."

"You signed me up?"

"Of course. How else was I going to understand all that geek-ery? Gus, you look worried. Don't worry. You'll do fine."

No wonder the course had been full when I had looked at it. I had helped fill it. A feeling of dread began to come over me. I was not my own master after all.

"Wouldn't you rather just lose at Blackjack?"

"Why would I want to do that?"

I started to say something about it being better to lose at a game you thought you could win than to begin to understand how thoroughly the game was stacked against you, but I didn't know how to get into it. Besides, I wasn't really so sure I believed it myself. Instead, I fell back on another question to which I wasn't sure I wanted to know the answer.

"What about your husband?"

"He's not coming on this trip."

"I figured. I just wondered—"

What did I just wonder?

"You wondered why he would let me go to Las Vegas by myself? I told him I wasn't going by myself. I told him I was going with you."

I didn't know if Susan's husband had played high school football or chess, but I could picture him going to Academy and buying a Glock. He would get a matching locking case that could be checked in with his baggage at the Southwest ticket counter. There I was uncertain. Would he fly to Las Vegas to kill me or just lie in wait until I came back?

"He knows about me?"

"Not yet, Darling, but I will tell him."

"Where is he now?"

"He's gone this week to his mother's."

"I thought she died."

"Oh, she did. He's gone to deal with the estate. Get the house ready to sell. I just hope he doesn't come back with a U-Haul full of crap. That woman had awful taste in furniture, and she had a whole collection of these horrid little figurines."

Susan held one palm above the other to indicate the height of the average figurine and shuddered in her seat belt.

"Who's gonna buy all that stuff? That's what I'm afraid of."

"I don't know," I said.

"But I don't want you to get the wrong idea. I'm not on this trip to escape my husband and his dead mother. I'm going to learn more about computer security. I figure I'll either learn enough to get more confident about this stuff so that I can sleep better at night, or I'll develop a full blown case of paranoia. If that happens I'll tell my husband to just pile up all that Precious Moments shit around the bedroom, and I'll go into full blown denial."

"It can be overwhelming," I said.

"But you're up to it, and with you helping me with my homework, I will be up for it, too."

"Up for what? For SDR class?"

"For that, but mostly up for the threat. For the attack. It's coming. I know. I read Dark Reading."

"You do?"

"Hell yes! Why do you think I have trouble sleeping? You don't think it's my husband who keeps me awake at night!"

"I never really thought about it—"

"Maybe when this estate shit is over he'll get his wood back and I'll lose sleep over something better than penetration tests. For now you will be my Obi Wan."

She smiled, a big, outright, unaffected, almost shy and self-revealing smile.

"Teach me the ways of the force."

"I'll try."

"Good. Keep your light saber on your pocket for now. We're still on the plane."

About that time the stewardess arrived to order our drinks. I gave her my ten dollar bill.

"I'm sorry, Sir. I can't make change."

"This is for her"—I pointed to Susan—"and me. Gin and tonic and —"

"Scotch on the rocks," said Susan.

Scotch on the rocks! It figured, and it was apparent to me in the midst of atmospheric turbulence that my choice of drink, rather than showing my sophistication, had instead unmanned me, and while Susan threw down her scotch, I sipped my gin shaken with shame and tonic.

Somewhere past the peanuts and over the Rockies, she turned away from the window and the snow capped peaks and looked me squarely in the face.

"Okay, 'splain it to me, Lucy."

"Explain what?"

"S—D—R!"

"Software Defined Radio. It turns your computer into a radio."

"You mean like Pandora or KLBJ online?"

"No. Those are internet streaming services—radio over the internet. SDR uses your computer as a radio. It uses the computer to decode the radio signals. The computer does the work of a bunch of radio electronic circuitry."

"What's so exciting about that? Am I just replacing a dial with a mouse? What does that have to do with security?"

"Let me see your phone."

I signed her up for the Southwest Airlines WiFi and put the charge on my own credit card. Then, I found an SDR application in the on-line store and downloaded it to her phone. A colored graph of peaks and valleys ranged across the screen like the Rocky Mountains.

"You see? This is a whole range of radio frequencies on the screen. Think of it as the dial on an old fashioned radio where you could see all the frequencies you could hear and you turned the dial to move the needle to the one you wanted. Only with that system you didn't necessarily know if a station was there until you turned the dial to that spot and listened."

"My dad had a car with an old fashioned radio, and when we were on long trips, he would turn the dial back and forth until he found a station."

"Right," I said. "Well, here you can see everywhere there is a signal. The SDR draws a graph across the screen."

"It looks like the graph on a heart monitor."

"Sort of does. Only here each peak in the graph represents a different radio signal. You touch the screen in the peak, and you are tuning in that signal."

Susan picked a peak on the graph, and the sound of Morse code came out.

"Who would use Morse code in this day and age?"

"I don't know. These are not real signals. This is just a recording. You would need to plug in a radio receiver and an antenna to get actual radio signals."

"I'm still not seeing where the hack is. I suppose there is something to be said for making a computer into a radio, but it's still just a radio."

I found myself in an awkward position defending Susan's own choice of Blackhat classes to her. It hadn't been my choice after all.

"Well, think about what else is just a radio: satellite signals, for instance."

I was searching for the topic as I said it. The airline WiFi was not too bad, but not so fast that you could pull up things as quickly as you could think of the questions. So, while Google rifled through its big data, I had to use my imagination. Susan bored easily.

"The WiFi component of this computer is a radio. The wireless router in your house is a radio. A wireless mouse or keyboard, the Bluetooth earphone with your phone, your cell phone itself, your garage door opener, all your wearable devices, OnStar in your car—they are all two way radios. Look! Here's an on-line video of someone picking up the weather satellite images with his SDR."

"Hmm. That's pretty cool. Lots of information there. Everything your weatherman isn't telling you. But it isn't hacking, is it? I mean, the information was always there in the air."

"Well, in a manner of speaking. It's hacking in the sense that no one ever expected you to be able to get the information for yourself because you had no affordable way to get it. But now you do."

I pointed to the image on the screen.

"That little thing that looks like a thumb drive in the USB port is the radio receiver. It only costs twenty-nine dollars. And it's a hack in itself. It was made to be a TV receiver you would plug in your USB port to turn your computer into a TV, but someone figured out a program to use it to receive all sorts of other signals as well."

"So hacking is turning something computer-ee into something no one expected it to be turned into."

"That's right."

"But I still don't see how picking up free open radio signals is hacking."

"Well, what if it was something the provider really expected to sell, something he never expected you would be able to access without buying the device or the software he provided to receive it? Only now, you come up with another way to get it without buying his access device. Now, he has to figure out how to keep you out until you pay for the access to it. He never had to spend the money to protect it before because he never expected so many people to be able to get it before."

"I can see that."

"Now, let's extend that. What if it wasn't weather images from a taxpayer funded satellite you were seeing on your SDR? What if it was the signal from someone's wireless keyboard to his computer?"

"You could see what they were typing?"

"Well, it's more complicated than that. We would have to crack his encryption."

I could see the disappointment rising in her face, and I hated to disappoint a woman.

"But it can be done. Not terribly hard."

She brightened.

"Then we could tell the guy in the next seat is going to Porn-R-Us instead of the in flight movie."

"Oh, we could do more than that. We could capture his password."

"To the porn site?"

"Or to the bank."

"Or to his office HR account?"

"That's right."

Susan looked around.

"Do you think there are wireless keyboards on the plane?"

"No, but the WiFi signal itself is a radio signal."

"We could intercept that."

"That's right"

"I've heard of that, but I've never heard of the wireless keyboard interception."

"It is supposed to be such short range that no one worried about it being intercepted."

"So they didn't protect it."

"Not at first. And not always well enough."

She smiled. I nodded. I even smiled, an open, non-ambiguous smile. Susan was actually catching on. This was a thrilling prospect. I might come back from Las Vegas with a boss who understood our business. Did Butch foresee this and throw us together for that purpose? My smile half fell back into ambiguity. Did I want management to understand what I did? Part of me did. I valued the appreciation and support that came with that understanding, but I also feared the transparency. I didn't have anything to hide necessarily, but I enjoyed the independence of working in the dark. When I was alone in the office late at night I liked to turn off the lights and just work by the light of the computer monitors. It gave me the sensation that I was on the shadowy trail of secret, hidden knowledge. But that sense only lasted until the cleaning crew came on the floor and turned on the lights to vacuum. If I were a late night janitor, I would leave most of the lights off, but maybe that was not technically feasible in their line of work. Perhaps, they couldn't fully trust the technology of vacuum pumps, hoses and filters and needed to see the dirt.

Susan smiled again and got a far off look in her eye. Her smile and that look thrilled and concerned me. I began to wonder if I had created a monster.

"So, for twenty-nine dollars, which ought to get us free shipping, we could plug something into our computer that could read other people's keystrokes if they have half-assed security."

"You got it."

"But what's good security today may be half-assed tomorrow."

"That's right. That's how the security game works."

"So we're going to this conference to get the lowdown on what's half-assed today and what may be half-assed tomorrow."

"Right."

"So we can be whole-assed."

"I don't know how to answer that question."

"This stuff strikes me as being pretty hard, but you make it sound almost easy. I find that reassuring and frightening. Have you ever done any of this yourself?"

I thought of the woman I sent messages to at the airport once—not emails or instant messages but right across her browser.

"Only for the purposes of research."

"I see."

She grabbed the neckline of her blouse and tugged it up. I felt suddenly ashamed, and we didn't speak until the captain announced our approach into Las Vegas.

"You know I thought we were going to a conference on security."

"We are."

"We are going to learn how to be the good guys, how to defend our company from the bad guys."

I answered with a nod. She was partly right.

"But they call this conference 'Blackhat,' and it is in Las Vegas of all places. I think we better bring our virtue with us."

"Our virtue?"

She nodded. I noticed her neckline had slipped again. As the plane descended shuddering in the cloudless sky, I saw that it was entirely up to me whether my eyes descended into that cleft of flesh or whether I raised them up to accept the challenge Susan presented to me in her face.

I turned my eyes away from her towards my seat back tray.

"When we get to the hotel," I said, "I had better harden your computer."

"Harden my computer. Sounds interesting. For research purposes?"

I felt ashamed again.

"No," I said, "for real protection."

"Okay, Geek. I'm counting on you."

"As soon as we have landed, call your husband to tell him you're here."

"Good idea. Can't let the old man worry."

"And as soon as you hang up, turn off your phone."

"Why?"

"Your phone is a computer and a radio, and there will be lots of guys at the conference who are—"

"Doing research?"

"Yes."

"I see. Do I need to remove the battery too?"

"You can't. It's an iPhone."

And so we descended into Las Vegas in fear and loathing.

17 – The Dark Onion

The first thing we did after settling in at the hotel was buy a pair of walkie talkies and a couple of hats, not tin foil hats but white cotton and straw. The Nevada sun was intense, but in Las Vegas we found we needed to get out-of-doors frequently to recover a sense of reality. So, we needed protection from the sun. Austin heat was bad, but I never thought it was apt to kill me. Going out in the Vegas sun seemed like eating Japanese blow fish: a little taste gave you a controlled and enjoyable exposure to imminent death. In Austin I had never been able to bring myself to wear either a cowboy hat or one of those wide brimmed gardening hats, but just getting in and out of the taxi convinced us we would need protection here. A few minutes in a casino convinced us we would need to seek regular shelter outside. In such a paradox, hats were our only hope.

Susan had brought a Round Rock Express cap with her, but she immediately realized it would not be enough. She chose something akin to what Audrey Hepburn would have worn had she ever gone to the desert. I picked out what I could only describe as a Mississippi river boat gambler's hat in cotton. It had a blue ribbon that encircled the base of the crown.

"That's a nice splash of color," I said.

"You watch too much remodeling TV," said Susan. "Splash of color! That band is there to hide the sweat marks."

I thought she was wrong though. The Vegas sun sucked the sweat right out of your pores before it ever had a chance to bead up on your skin or dampen your hair.

We both already had sun glasses. So, wearing our shades and our off-white hats we strode into Blackhat like western movie actors who had forgotten to remove their shades when they stepped onto the set.

Our rooms were in the same hotel but on different floors. I was both relieved and disappointed by that fact. However, I had not even finished hanging up my clothes when Susan was knocking on my door.

"Okay. Geek, what is with the walkie talkies and what good are they if you won't turn yours on?"

"No good, I suppose. I just hadn't had time—"

"I've been trying to call you on every damn channel, but you don't answer."

"I got these for us to keep in contact when our phones are turned off."

"But they don't work when you don't turn them on."

"No." I said. I had envisioned being the one to call Susan. I hadn't anticipated that she would be calling me.

"You know at home when you're on call, you call me when there is an issue. Here I get to call you. If someone is trying to break into my damn computer, I need you there ASAP. Right?"

I nodded. More and more I was finding my half-baked boss possessed unassailable logic.

"And another thing: a walkie talkie is a radio, right?"

"Yes."

"So, with these HackWave SDR's we are getting, we should be able to do the same thing. Talk to each other. Turn them into walkie talkies."

"Yeah, I suppose so. I don't know how much power the HackWave puts out, but we might be able to do it."

"But we would not be the only ones able to do it. What about all our HackWave buddies in the SDR class?"

"Yes, one of our classmates could listen in on our conversations, if that's what you are getting at."

"That's what I'm asking."

"But listening in is not what I'm worried about. If he can listen in to our SDR conversations, he may be able to launch some sort of attack in our computers, but if he tries to hack our walkie talkies, what can he get?"

"Not much."

"Right."

"Believe it or not, I was just trying to save the company money. If our SDR's are radios, we could have used them as walkie talkies, and then I wouldn't have had to explain that expenditure to accounting."

I hadn't thought of that.

"I suppose we could, but we would have to carry our computers with us all the time."

"Well, I plan to do that here anyway except in the pool. In this heat I doubt I'll be caring about the hot tub. But if we are worried about our phones, why aren't we worried about our computers, whether we use them as walkie talkies or not?"

It was a good question. I talked about the hardening I was able to do. I told her we could turn off Bluetooth and wireless except when we needed them.

"But we need our computers to participate in the conference. Software defined radio can't define the radio if there is no computer to run the software. Right? So we have to use our computers. We have to make ourselves vulnerable."

"We do."

"So you could say this whole conference is an enticement to draw us here so that we can be hacked. 'Come and learn about computer security!' Only you may just have to learn the hard way. This was my idea for us to come to Blackhat, and boy did I fall for it."

"I never thought of it that way," I said. I had always looked at it as an occupational hazard. "But, see, if we know there is danger, we can turn it around. We can catch the hackers."

"How? By acting like victims? By becoming bait?"

"There is a term for setting up a place on your computer just to entice hackers."

"And why would I do that?"

"So you could study their methods and better protect your real assets. The term is honeypot."

"Ooh. I want a honeypot. Can you set me up a honeypot?"

I had to admit, but only to myself, that the idea had appeal. There were surely geeks at Blackhat who, in seeing Susan, would want to hack into her box. I figured you could tell by looking at her, never mind by talking to her, that she was management, not technical. That alone made her an appealing target. Besides the other reason.

"You have too much access at work to sensitive data," I said. "I don't think it would be a good idea to turn you into a honeypot."

"No?"

She looked disappointed.

"Too much access? Like what?"

"Like financials. Like personnel. Like my social security number."

"But you have access to all the servers."

"Just to the logs."

"Okay. I'm too valuable. You be the honeypot."

"Okay, I will. But first I need to harden your box."

"Excuse me?"

"Your box. Your computer. Make it harder to break into."

"Oh. My computer. Harder but not impossible."

"That's right."

"So, in a way just by being here I'm a honeypot."

"I suppose so."

"Me and my box."

"Mostly your box. Although there is social engineering."

"And what is that?"

"That is a technique to trick you into revealing something that allows someone to get into your machine or into one of your online accounts. Like finding out your dog's name or your date of birth and then trying those things as passwords."

"What good would that do? Excuse me. What bad would that do?"

"Well, if you used your dog's name to log into the company system, someone could find that name on Facebook. Your login ID is not secret, so they could try the dog's name with your ID, and they would be in our system. Or, if you used your date of birth to log into your bank—"

"The bank won't let me do that. I have to type my password out in letters and numbers and capitals and symbols. Then, I can't remember it. I lock myself out out and have to reset to more letters and numbers and capitals and symbols. I hate passwords. They're no fun anymore."

"Security's a bitch," I said. "Present company excluded. No! Wait! I didn't mean that like it sounds."

My entire career flashed before my eyes, but Susan looked more beleaguered than offended.

"I hear that," she said.

"You do?"

"You bet. I'm the head of security, aren't I? Every time you guys find a problem, every time I make somebody fix something in their application, every time I tell Bob he can't do something he wants to do or his ass will be in a sling, I become the bitch. They wouldn't say that about a man, would they?"

"No. I'm sorry. I didn't mean—"

"It's okay. I would rather be a bitch than an asshole. It's much more feminine and becoming don't you think?"

Susan's laptop was in better shape than I expected. I closed some firewall ports, changed some defaults, turned off straight FTP, eliminated file sharing, and tightened up her browser settings. Then, I found the conference WiFi network.

"When you want to use the internet, don't use the hotel public WiFi. Use the one set up for Blackhat. Only conference participants can use it. Then, log onto our company VPN: Virtual Private Network."

"Oh that's what it stands for."

I think she was being facetious.

"You will be browsing then through our protected network."

"You want me to use the Blackhat network because only the hackers and security experts can get in it?"

Once again I didn't have a good answer.

"Only long enough to get from their network over to our network. Except when you do any security type exercises for the conference. Then, you should just stay on the Blackhat network, and we'll do nightly virus scans on your box."

"My box? What about your box?"

"I'll scan mine, too," I said. "But I am more used to getting on the Dark Web."

"The Dark Web? What is the Dark Web?"

"It is like an alternative universe of the World Wide Web.

Remember that dark alley in Harry Potter where all the evil spells are for sale? It is the place where all the really bad internet stuff is."

"Bad stuff? Like what?"

"Well, if you want to buy an exploit kit, that is where you would go."

"An exploit kit? Like if I wanted a computer virus to infect Bob?"

"More or less. An exploit kit would include all the components you need to break into a computer system. You pay the money and follow the directions. And, once you have successfully broken into a system and downloaded data, you go to the Dark Web to sell it."

"Sell data?"

"Like credit card numbers, social security numbers, bank accounts, trade secrets."

"How do you get into the Dark Web?"

"You have to use something called 'The Onion Router.' It allows you to enter an alternative network and to navigate anonymously."

"How much does that cost to set up?"

"It's free. It's open source."

"Free?"

Susan reached over and patted my cheek.

"We're screwed, aren't we?"

"Well, I hope not. We are taking every precaution."

"It's okay. I'm a big girl. It's kind of like sex, isn't it. Everyone talks about safe sex, but sex is never truly safe. Neither is this. You done here now?" she said pointing to the computer.

"Yeah."

"I'm going swimming. You want to come?"

I wondered if my face betrayed my sudden flush of excitement and embarrassment.

"I don't have any swim trunks."

"Well, you can't do without those, not even in Las Vegas. I'm sure you could buy some around here somewhere. Just don't get a Speedo."

I surely blushed at that suggestion, me with my abundant Thai food diet.

"I guess I don't have the figure for that."

She picked up her computer and smiled.

"Only the few do."

As she opened the door, she pointed to the walkie-talkie.

"Channel eleven. After midnight we switch to channel six. Got that?"

I nodded.

"See you before the sun goes down," she said and closed the door.

After Susan left I put on my gambler's hat, my dark shades, and my computer shoulder bag, and I went down to the lobby. Blackhat was actually being staged at a hotel down the street. Our hotel had a shuttle to take us there, but I looked down at my belly. I thought of the pool, and I decided to walk. I never went swimming in Austin except once at Barton Springs. The water had been so cold I couldn't stand to enter past my calves. I spent the rest of the time hanging out under the shade trees trying to hide my physique from all the people with better bodies.

Elements of Blackhat spilled over into our hotel. I could see people I had met from years past down at the front desk checking in. Whether they recognized me in my hat was another story. For the moment at least I took refuge in anonymity. I wanted to get the lay of the land: who was here, who looked to be at the top of his game and would be most worth seeing, who should be avoided because he was on the professional decline, and who was simply too dangerous to approach. In years past I hadn't cared about that. I had figured danger was my business. This year I felt protective like a father taking his little daughter swimming in a lake—steering her past conversations she should not hear and making sure she knew where the holes were so she did not sink in over her head. Once Robert had taken me swimming in a place in Oklahoma named after some water fall. I had stepped in a hole and disappeared under the water. Before I even had a chance to inhale, Robert grabbed me and pulled me back into neck high water. I had not been slim even in those days, and Robert had always been slight, but he pulled me out of danger as if it were an everyday event.

I had been out in the heat for about a block when I heard rumbling. It was not thunder in the desert. I knew that sound from my own parking garage. It was another Abarth with custom pipes like mine. It could have been my own car if mine had not been back in

Austin in its cramped little designated parking space. I turned to look. This one was black. My car was white. Who would buy a black car in Las Vegas? The window rolled down.

"Want a lift?"

I pulled off my sunglasses to see into the interior of the car. The upholstery was red leather. The voice inside rumbled in tune with the exhaust. It was Morgan. In all my surprise over Susan coming to Blackhat and in all my efforts to equip her for the experience, I had forgotten that he was coming to the conference.

"I thought you were renting—" I began.

"Get in before the traffic piles up."

I knocked off my hat as I ducked in the door, and the wind blew it down the sidewalk. Morgan rumbled along beside me until I chased it down. I reentered the car and sat down hat in hand.

He pulled away from the curb and roared into the traffic.

"Buckle up," he said.

I had never been the passenger in an Abarth, only a driver. I found myself less satisfied but more anxious when I was not the one behind the wheel.

"I thought you were renting a Cobra."

"It wasn't available when I got to Albuquerque. They gave me this instead. Besides, this has paddle shifters. The Cobra was a standard."

"You can't drive a standard?"

Morgan paused.

"No."

"Maybe you should put that on your bucket list. My Abarth is a standard. It is white, though. The Abarth name is in red."

"Sweet. Where are you going?" he said.

"The Mandalay Bay Hotel."

Morgan tapped the down paddle and turned right into the entrance drive of a hotel. The Black Abarth roared like an F1 car coming in for a pit stop.

"Here we are," he said.

So we were.

"I have to put the car in the garage. I'll see you around during the reception."

"Are you staying at this hotel?"

"Of course."

As he roared away, I stood at the curb and watched. I felt as if I had lost a testicle.

People were already walking around inside with name tags. I wondered how secure the registration data base could be.

"In for a penny, in for a pound," I muttered. That was an old Robert-ism. It had to be a saying with English origins. I wondered why no one had ever converted the currency to American money. It must have been because the pound carried more weight in the collective linguistic memory. Too bad I couldn't register for Susan and bring her her badge *a fait accompli,* but she would have to provide her own credentials.

After I checked in, I stuffed my badge in my pocket and began mulling around the floor. I realized I was still wearing my hat and sunglasses. It gave me a sense of superiority to be able to see who people were without disclosing who I was. The trouble was I couldn't read anyone's name indoors through my dark lenses, so in essence, they were just as anonymous as I.

I took off the glasses and the hat and walked around the ballroom. I could see some of the major players in the industry already setting up booths. You could tell who was hungry by who was already here. I noted that our SIEM vendor was setting up. I decided to avoid them later in the evening after I had had too many opportunities to drink. I really didn't want to come up to them full of false ethanol bravado and tell them how their product kept me up at night chasing rabbits. Susan would tell them she slept better because of the SIEM and all its alerts, and they knew who really controlled the budget in our company.

I looked for the booth from HackWave, but no one was there. I started to go when I heard a voice behind me just discernible above the din rising gently in the room. I recognized it immediately.

"Hello, Mr. Underhill. Opened any interesting emails lately?"

"Mr. Root," I said. "How's the phishing? Have you caught any financial companies lately?"

"A small one here and there. They're still biting. They are always biting."

"I was thinking you might pay us another visit. I watched for you, but you never showed up."

"Oh, but I did. I knocked, but you apparently didn't hear me. Maybe you were asleep. Too much of that loud, live music you Austin guys are so famous for."

Mr. Root might have been bluffing. I certainly was. I had kept watch for him ever since he first showed up inside our firewall. When he disclosed himself so brazenly at Blackhat, I doubled my efforts. He might have stayed clear of us in the past year, but he might have placed exploits on any number of our servers that I just hadn't recognized.

"I don't sleep much. Funny. You are not wearing your name tag."

"Neither are you, but then again, I'd know you anywhere. Isn't this is the nice part of Blackhat? Meeting old friends?"

"Is that what we are?" I pulled my badge out of my pocket and slipped the lanyard over my neck.

"Very clever. The name is turned away where it isn't visible. Did you practice that, or is it really blank on both sides? No, don't turn it around. I like it that way. Besides, Gus, I'd know you anywhere. Have a good Blackhat. See you around. We'll have another drink together. Exchange tricks."

With that, Mr. Root turned and walked out. I tried to follow him but lost him in the lobby. I put on my hat and glasses and stood out in the declining Las Vegas sun.

18 – Waterfall in the Desert

I found Susan by the pool with her computer open on her lap. She was wearing an orange bikini that showed distinctly through a white T-shirt. She was still wearing her Audrey Hepburn hat. As I approached she reached past a tall glass on the table next to her lounge chair, picked up her walkie-talkie, and waved the antenna in my direction.

"Who's idea was this, and yet who keeps forgetting to carry his radio?"

"I'm sorry. I had something to do. What is that black device plugged into your USB port?"

"That, my missing-in-action little geek, is a HackWave transceiver."

"Where did you get that?"

"From the Hack Man. He came by the pool and asked me if I was here for Blackhat. I told him I was not only here for Blackhat but I was taking the SDR class. Funny, he said, he was teaching the SDR class. I showed him my registration, and he showed me how to insert this little thing in my jack and boot it all up. Went all the way back to his hotel room to get it while I laid here and baked in the sun. So now I've got a jump on the class. I tried to call you to come and share the experience, but no walkie, no talkie."

I could feel my face turning red with disappointment as much as shame, but Susan had already shifted.

"I should make you go upstairs and get your own radio, but take mine and say something."

I usually did not mind being the geek. In Austin, geek-hood was a badge of honor, but in Las Vegas standing in my blue trunks holding a walkie-talkie next to a mature woman in a bikini, I felt like I was twelve.

"Say something."

"What do you want me to say?"

"No, into the radio."

"Testing. One, two, three."

"Come over here. Look at this."

I had to squat down enough to get my head past the brim of her hat and put my chin practically on her shoulder to see the computer screen.

"No, keep talking."

"I never know what to say in a microphone."

"Hold down the button."

"So, the class instructor gave you your HackWave in advance?"

"You bet."

"And he helped you set it up right here by the pool?"

No wonder he wasn't in his booth.

"That was awfully nice of him."

"I thought so. Of course, I wasn't wearing this T-shirt at the time. Speak again. There! See? No, keep talking. Right there. That tall squiggly line—that's you."

"So, we're at 467.6375 MHz."

"You mean I am. Your radio is not even turned on—"

"Click on me. My signal. Right there. Click on the line and pull up my signal. See if you can hear me. I'm talking. Talking. Talking. Hello. What happens in Las Vegas stays in Las Vegas."

No discernible voice could be heard.

"Oh, you know what it is? You don't have the program object to decode FM."

"I know that. The guy got the waterfall display working, but he ran out of time to set up the decoding parts. It's already in the software download. It's called New Radio. You just have to set it up. Do you suppose we could do that after dinner?"

So at seven o'clock Pacific Time I was in Susan's hotel room sitting at the mini-bar learning how to set up her SDR.

My first hurdle was figuring out that New Radio was spelled GNU Radio.

"I could have told you that," Susan said. "It says so when you boot it up."

Once I figured out how to search on 'GNU', I easily found the code that turned her SDR into an FM radio, but it took half an hour before we could hear the walkie-talkie over it. I stood out on her little balcony and described the lights of the Las Vegas Strip to Susan in frequency modulation.

"Can you hear me?"

This time I was using my own walkie-talkie. She answered from hers.

"Just like you were on the balcony outside."

I came back in the room.

"I meant on the computer."

"Yes. You came through on the SDR, but I had to answer you on the talkie. Why can't I answer over the SDR? Is that more code?"

"Yes."

"Let's try that."

This time we set Susan's walkie-talkie in the far corner of the room. I still sat at the little bar and Susan hovered over me. I could feel her hair at times on my left ear. Her hand occasionally touched my arm. Somehow I kept on working.

"OK, go over there and try speaking into the radio."

Her voice sprang from the laptop speaker. She carried the little radio in her hand and laid across the bed.

"You did it Gus. I'll have to give you a bonus." She stretched her arms upward and arched her back above the king sized mattress. "But not yet. Here," she said holding out the radio. "Take this and go forth into the casino and tell me what you see."

She was sprawled obliquely across the bed, her head near the right foot. She held the walkie-talkie aloft. I had to lean over the bed to take it from her hand.

"Other duties as assigned," she said smiling. I smiled, too. I tried to control it, to keep the corners of my mouth reigned in, but they spread to the breadth of her arms as she stretched them out in both directions.

"Well, go on."

I left like Lancelot on a quest.

"Okay! Ground floor. Can you hear me?" I said.

"Yes."

"I'm now entering the casino area. Lots of people. Making my way through the slot machines."

"Are you catching the vibe?"

"No. Well, maybe. It's exciting. Actually, it's kind of depressing. The slots are full of older people. They shove in a quarter. They pull the lever. Their eyes light up as long as the wheels spin. When the wheels stop, their eyes go dark. Shove in another quarter. Maybe this time. Nope! Another quarter. Still hoping."

"I don't think they are hoping," Susan said. "I think they are waiting to die."

The suggestion surprised me, but I could see what she meant. Then, I had an inspiration.

"It's too bad they have to wait," I said.

"Well that's a morbid thought. I'm sure the casino doesn't like that line of reasoning."

"Why not?"

"They're making money, Honey."

"What if Vegas sold one way trips? People come here. They spend some money. They don't come back."

"Where do they go?"

"They just check out."

"What do you mean," she said, "by 'check out?'"

"Just walk out into the desert into the sunset and fade away."

"It's a bit of a walk from the Strip to the desert."

"The hotels could offer a bus ride out to the end of civilization. The bus would let you out, and a little sign would tell you which way to go. If you wanted it to be like a movie, a crop duster could chase you. Or, they could hand you a canteen, and when it was empty, you would throw it away and stumble on till you dropped. The billboards could read, 'Come to Vegas. Why wait?'"

"Geek! Step away from the slots."

I moved on.

"I see the poker tables. If I can make my way over there—"

"Good idea."

"I think I may be making people nervous. They see the walkie-talkie, and they think I'm the hotel security."

"Hotel security? I don't see them on the waterfall."

"Well, you won't. They use a different set of frequencies. You'd have to move the SDR to another part of the spectrum. Okay, I've made it to the tables. I'd read you someone's hand, but I bet I'd get thrown out."

"How are the people dressed? The women, I mean."

"Oh, I don't know. Varies. Some look like they come from Dallas. Some look like Austin."

"Do you see much decolletage?"

"Much what?"

"Low cut dresses. Do you see many of those?"

"Yeah. Some. Why?"

"I want to know how to dress. Especially at the poker table."

"I see. I mean—"

"What do you mean?"

I was afraid to say what I meant.

"Wait. Uh-oh. I think the security folks have spotted me. They are talking into their own two way radios and watching me. I don't think they like the fact that I am talking to you."

"Why should they care?"

"They think I'm looking at someone's poker hand and relaying the information."

"What good would that do me? I'm not there playing, and you're not telling me how to play."

"They don't know that."

"You better get out of there."

"I am. Heading back to the slots. Uh oh….No, sir….No, I was just watching the game….No, I couldn't see any cards. Just what was on the table….I was describing everything to my boss….Still up in her room….No she hasn't come down….Not the game so much….She wanted to know what the other women were wearing….No, I won't….I'm leaving…..Wait! That's mine! You can't have that. No. Wait. Give that back!"

I climbed the stairs to get back to Susan's room. I never used stairs under normal circumstances, but this time I saw the stairs sign and went in on impulse. No one else was in the stairway, and it felt good to be alone in an enclosed space. I also needed to inflict a certain amount of pain upon myself after losing Susan's walkie-talkie and nearly being expelled from the casino. What did Morgan call it when you tried to pay for your failures? Penance?

I knocked on her door sheepishly.

"Come in."

The door was unlocked.

"I asked you a question. You didn't answer. I kept saying, 'Roger,' and 'Over,' but all I heard was nothing."

"They confiscated my walkie-talkie."

"You mean, they confiscated my walkie-talkie. Figures."

"Oh, yeah. That's right. You can keep mine."

"Oh, thanks. That will do me a lot of good. Never mind that. Over here, Geek. Look at this. I have a question."

Susan was sitting on the bed with the computer like a high school girl doing her homework. I was to be her tutor. I looked around and noticed there wasn't a chair, not one that would let me see that screen. I climbed hesitantly and hopefully onto the bed and sat down beside her, next to her, shoulder to shoulder, hip to hip, leaning back on the pillows against the wall she had already placed there. I started to look down at the screen, but she turned and looked straight into my face, straight into my eyes. I dared not look away.

"Do hotel security people use radios?"

"Um, I think so. Sure."

"Then, why can't we hear them?"

"I don't know. I imagine they're on a different frequency."

She slid the computer onto my lap.

"Here! You drive."

She stayed right next to me looking down on the screen. Beads of sweat rolled down my neck and brow from my hair. My hands trembled. She seemed not to notice.

For the first few seconds the computer screen was blank to me, opaque and expressionless. Then Susan began managing.

"Look up hotel security radio...No, not alarm clocks. Stupid search thingy."

"Engine," I said. "Search engine."

"Oh, look. There's a radio. Two way radio. Not walkie-talkie. Look up two way radio."

"Okay," I said.

"Where's the frequency? Scroll down. Down. I don't care about that. These things are all made in China. Probably all have back doors to the Chinese spy agency. How could we tell?"

"The radio itself could not reach China, not even the nearest Chinese embassy. It could send out a Wi-Fi signal though to the nearest router. But what....Oh! They're digital."

"What's digital?"

"The radio transmissions. These two way radios are digital."

"What does that mean?"

"It means even if we tune into the right frequencies we won't be able to hear what the security guys are saying."

"We can't?"

"Not without more software."

"Well, check the frequency first and see if we can see any signals there. Then, we can look for more GNU software."

The phone rang.

"I'll get that," she said. "It's my room."

The hotel phone was on the night stand, but it was on my side of the bed. She leaned away from the headboard, spun around past my lap, and picked up the phone on the fourth ring.

"Hey, Wood. How's it...Doing homework....No, the class starts tomorrow...We're getting an early start....No, no gambling....Maybe later, but I don't know. There's a lot to learn. Got to get my money's worth....Well, it's my budget....Am I getting my money's worth out of Gus? You better believe it."

My head turned round from the screen at the sound of my name. I had been exposed without my knowledge or consent, and to Susan's husband at that. Fear knotted my stomach and filled my loins.

"He's helping me with my homework....He's right here on the bed with my computer looking up something. He's been teaching me about the Dark Web....Yeah....Sure. Hold it a moment."

She held out the phone in my direction. I stared at the receiver in panic.

"He wants to talk with you."

My palm was sweating as I held the phone in my hand. I waited a moment so he wouldn't realize how close I was, as if Susan were in the next room and not on the same mattress. I looked at her pleadingly. Susan urged me on with a nod of her head.

"Hello?"

"So, how are you and Susan getting along? She's not asking too much of you, is she?"

I knew Susan couldn't hear the question, but I answered diplomatically.

"No, not too much."

"You've got to watch her. She'll wear you out and ask for more, if you let her."

"I'll be careful."

"Say, I just wanted you to know that I am glad you are on this trip with Susie. I was worried about her until she told me you were coming. I know, she volunteered you, but that doesn't matter. You stepped up, and I really appreciate you taking care of her."

"Oh, well, uh—"

"So, don't let her keep you up too late. Tell her you've got to get to bed. Got to get some sleep. Many's the night let me tell you."

Tell me?

"Well, that's all I wanted to say, Gus."

"Really?"

"Again, thanks for helping Susie."

"You're welcome. Woody. Goodbye."

I handed her back the phone.

"Bye, dear," she said, but she was looking at me even as she cradled the phone, and she was smiling.

"What is it?" I said. I couldn't help but smile, too. After all, I had escaped.

"You called him Woody."

"Yes. That's his name, right?"

"No. He didn't tell you? His name is Glen."

"Glen? But why—?"

"I'm the only one who calls him Woody. Used to embarrass him in front of his mother. Used to be a term of endearment earlier in our marriage. Then, it became ironic."

She sighed deeply then moved back to the pillow next to me. She pointed to the computer. So, what have you got?

I was glad to change the subject.

"I found some activity."

I pointed to a sharp rise on the screen.

"Looks like you've got something there. Do you know what it is?"

"Not for sure."

She reached down and touched the rise on the screen. I shifted the computer uncomfortably on my lap. Rushing, harmonic sounds burst forth.

"Sounds like my dad's old modem."

"I think it's digital."

"What does that mean?"

"It's like your cell phone. Instead of laying the sound waves from your voice over a radio wave, it sends a digital representation of your voice, like the graphic coordinates of all the peaks and valleys of what you say."

"So you have to get the GNU program for the SDR to reproduce the graph and turn it into a voice?"

"Yes, as soon as I figure out which digital protocol they use. Apparently, there's more than one."

"That's good."

Then Susan took a deep breath and paused.

"You can do that tomorrow. Tonight I'm throwing you out."

"Really? It's only...eleven o'clock...Pacific Daylight Time."

"I know. I know. 'The night is still young,' but I'm not, not as much as I used to be."

"I wouldn't say that."

"Oh, you wouldn't? Why wouldn't you?"

I didn't dare to answer that question. I remembered how good she looked in the bikini. I put her computer down and crawled off the mattress.

"Wait!" I said. "I shouldn't have left that on the bed. It might overheat."

"Don't worry. I'll get it. You go on home to your room. What's the matter, Gus? You look disappointed. Well, if someone asks why you left my room so early tonight, you tell them it was for eating crackers in bed, not for looking up digital radio protocols. I'll see you at breakfast."

I walked out of her room, down the stairs and out the door of the hotel onto the sidewalk. The heat of the evening hung over my head like a reproach. I wondered if I should turn around and go back. Knock on her door. Go back and put an end to my disappointment. But I didn't dare. I just kept walking. The neon signs flashed angrily on my face, indignant at their inability to lure me in to casino or bar or even distract me for a moment from my regret.

I paused by a fountain and stared at the brightly illumined water until my shirt was damp from the spray. When I returned to my room, my cheeks were still moist.

19 – What Stays in Vegas

Susan's poolside rapport with the SDR instructor was evident when we arrived in his class. She quickly became the teacher's pet, and even though I sat next to her in class, the teacher hovered over her whenever she asked him a question and ignored me completely. Whenever I asked a question, he answered very perfunctorily. Then, he turned to Susan, a rotation of a mere twenty degrees, and gushed forth with enthusiastic elaboration. It seemed very much like high school. I began to funnel all my questions through her. The instructor was completely oblivious. I could ask him about adding the codec for a digital signal to my FM demodulator, and he would deflect me towards the GNU libraries to find it myself. I could then turn to Susan and feed the same question to her. She would ask, and the correct module would be practically installed on her machine before the next break. The major topics of the class became the questions that we asked. I became the application server, and she, the proxy. All the geeks surrounded us during the breaks. They asked her questions which she would defer to me to answer. Yet, however how many questions I answered, they kept feeding the follow-ups to her. At first, I was happy to be seen in her company.

"So," she said as I talked her through another SDR configuration, "have you changed your mind?"

"About what?"

"About me, your know nothing boss, coming with you on this trip. You've become Doctor Who, and I am your just-another-pretty-girl-you-picked-up-on-earth companion. I ask all the dumb questions. You give all the smart answers. Yet behind the scenes, I set the Doctor up for success. And I pull in the ratings."

"On the contrary," I said, "you've become my trophy boss."

She smiled at that answer. I basked in her reflected glory, and she knew it.

Then, I began to get jealous. I was afraid to go to the bathroom during the breaks, afraid that Susan would be surrounded by such a dense crowd that I would never make it past them to get beside her again. I was like a moon in close orbit, a moon that feared becoming a comet slipping from a daily orbit to a distant revolution, out of sight for decades and only coming close every seventy years. A dry and sterile moon with a full bladder and a stuffed colon.

Finally, I had to give in. I spent twenty minutes in the men's room, fully ten minutes past the end of our last break of the afternoon. When I returned from washing my face, I fully expected someone to have taken my place in the seat next to hers. For reasons I did not comprehend, no one had.

"Everything come out all right?" she asked.

If Morgan had asked that question, I would have come up with an appropriate answer. With Susan all I could do was try to deflect.

"What is that?" I said pointing at a full color picture of the earth displayed on her screen.

"My NOAA weather satellite feed. The friggin' weathermen on TV can't seem to get it right. This way I get my own view of the weather."

I smiled but swallowed hard. Someone had taken my place as Susan's geek while I was away. I began to see just how untenable my position was. I simply could not hope to hold on. This one installed her SDR. That one gave her satellite weather. All I had given her was FM two way radio. Then, I thought of Woody—Glen—on the phone. Did he feel the same insecurity? Is that why he called and asked to talk to me, to give one man's subtle warning to another? Could any man hold onto Susie?

Did Glen have a gun?

We spent the afternoon learning how to hack into WiFi. My explanation on the plane seemed paltry by comparison. The instructor was setting up a hot spot for us to attack when Susan suggested we look at the hotel network.

"We'll just use the network I'm setting up," said the instructor. "I'm sure you'll find plenty of interesting things on it to check out."

"Not unless someone logs onto their bank during class."

The instructor laughed.

"I'm sure no one here is going to do that. As for the hotel, we want to be polite guests while we are here. No hacking the hotel."

Susan cupped her hand over her mouth and whispered to me.

"I thought we were supposed to be finding real vulnerabilities in real systems so they could be fixed before the bad guys found them."

"We are," I whispered, "but people don't want to know the truth."

She nodded as if she agreed. Management though she was, she seemed to understand. It thrilled me to be in her confidence again.

"Tune your radios to the 2.4 gigahertz range. Raise your hand when you see the signal."

We spent the afternoon hacking the hot spot. We spent the evening in Susan's room surfing through the signals that appeared in the hotel. We found the hotel security were using a digital protocol called P25, and when I loaded the GNU methods to decode it, we were suddenly privy to all the inner workings of the hotel. We learned that slot machine forty-seven had paid off. We found that a guest from Idaho was winning at black jack at table six. Hotel security were dispatched to both locations to ensure the safety of the one and to verify the honesty of the other. We discovered there was a tipping point in a casino. Guests needed to be winning enough to keep up the level of excitement and expectation in the room, but too much winning made the house nervous. I thought of my own encounter with security the night before. We learned that there was a call girl working in the room down the hall from us, and I learned that the hotel took note of the fact that I was in Susan's room for the second night in a row. I was embarrassed by the disclosure, but Susan was unfazed.

"Perhaps we should do some loud moaning so that the security staff don't get the wrong idea," she said.

"The wrong idea?"

"Yeah. We don't want them to know we are in here hacking their wireless."

"Oh!"

"That was good, but make it a little louder. You know, more like 'Ohhh!' I don't know about you, but once upon a time at our house—"

The phone rang again.

"Speaking of Woody," she said and picked up the phone.

"Oh, no," I said.

She covered the mouthpiece and whispered fiercely but half-laughing as she did.

"Not now."

She uncovered the phone.

"Hi, Wood...Oh, we're just lying around doing some penetration testing. That's what you do at a computer security conference. A hotel in Vegas is a great place for it, let me tell you, but don't you ever think you are keeping a secret here, because you're not...No, not long. Soon....Yes, he is. You want to talk to him again?"

I shook my head vigorously.

"No, he's shy. Woody says 'Hi.'"

I nodded up and down. I waved. I buried my head in the waveform on the screen.

"No, me too....Really. Okay. Don't start without me. Bye, Wood."

She hung up the phone. She looked at me with a knowing smile. She laughed and shook her head.

"That was a short conversation," I said.

She nodded.

"You got any good ideas for what to do with the rest of the evening?"

I sensed a turning point in our relationship.

"Maybe," I said. "Do you?"

"I sure do."

She leaned towards me. I could feel the desert heat pulling the sweat from my brow even through the air conditioning of her room. This was it. If I were ever going to make my move, now was the time.

"Gus, have you ever been involved with the things of the internet?"

"The things of the internet? What are the things—oh! You mean the Internet of Things. IoT. No, but I've always wanted to."

"So have I," she said.

So let's do it, I thought.

"Ever since this afternoon, but I've got things I need to do tonight. What I need you to do right now is go back to your room and research it. From a security standpoint, that is. Use your computer. I'll just bet the casino is full of things of the internet. Maybe you can find some."

She pushed me towards the door.

"Wait!" I said. "What if you need me?"

"I need you to do research. Don't call me. I'll be off-line. Research!" she said and closed the door.

I stood in the hall stunned despite the fact that she could see me through the peephole, despite the hotel cameras recording my expulsion and dejection. Without the benefit of SDR to eavesdrop on all the hidden conversations, the hotel was silent. I turned and went to my room.

For the record I did try to research the Internet of Things, for I surely expected to see Susan in the morning, and she would ask. She would want a progress report just like at work, but I didn't get very far. I couldn't get past the first paragraph of anything I opened to read. I lay in bed worrying like a kid who has not prepared for a test. What was I going to tell her when I saw her at breakfast? It wasn't going to suffice to say that I could spell "IoT" but nothing else. Worse than that, if I asked the burning question I wanted to put to her, what would her answer be?

"What did you do last night after I left? Did you find another man? Did you call another geek?"

I needn't have worried. She did not appear at breakfast. She did not come to SDR class. I sat next to her empty seat, and everyone in the class was dismayed. The look on the instructor's face said the same thing as what was written on the face of every student.

Where is she? Where did she go? What did you do wrong, you who had more opportunity to do something than any of us? Were you not man enough?

But after the initial shock, those interrogative and accusatory looks subsided into sidelong glances. Everyone knew that I had failed, but no one dared ask me anymore questions.

At lunch I broke away from class and wandered aimlessly around the casino. I saw the winners at the poker tables throwing their hands in the air in triumph and opening their arms to sweep in their winnings, and I saw the losers threw down their cards in disgust and shake their heads. Then winner or loser reached for another chip and tossed it on the table to play another hand. I had no other chips. I felt certain I had played my last hand.

I was on the way back to class when there she stood in the lobby dressed in T-shirt and jeans with her luggage on either side. I wanted to say, what happened? Where are you going? I thought we were good together. Why are you leaving? But you don't say such things to your boss. So, I just stood there and said nothing, and that was even worse.

"I'm leaving, Gus. I'm going back to Austin."

She shrugged her shoulders and looked at the bags on either side of her.

"I guess that's obvious."

I nodded.

"I'm glad I ran into you. I was afraid the airport shuttle would arrive before I had a chance to explain what was going on. I would have called you on the walkie-talkie, but we only had the one."

"Giving up on the Internet of Things?"

"No. I just had to make sure that what happened in Vegas stayed in Vegas."

"I see. What happened in Vegas?

"Well, not so much what happened as what almost happened. Actually, it did happen. Depends on how you look at it."

Now I felt like the one asking technical questions without the technical vocabulary.

"I don't understand," I said. "What almost happened? You mean when we hacked the hotel?"

"Oh, that. No, I was thinking more of where we were when we did it."

"Your room?"

"My room. My bed. Don't tell me you didn't notice. It would hurt my pride."

"Oh. Well, yeah. I noticed."

"You noticed. You could barely keep your mind on the screen."

I sighed deeply, a long, shuddering sort of sigh.

"I thought you—I thought we—I guess I misread your intentions.

I think I'm bad about that. I—"

"No, you didn't, and that's the trouble. You read me right—mostly."

"I did?"

"It was SDR, Gus. I put out the signal, and you picked it up. You thought I was wide open. You were just making up your mind when to come in. The truth is—"

Now she was the one catching her breath.

"The truth is you were not getting in. It was all a honeypot. I wanted you to think you were getting in, but I had no real intention of letting you past the firewall."

"You were just playing with me?"

"Yes and no. I was serious about the hacking, about the whole security thing. But the whole lets-do-this-on-the-bed approach, that was to keep you interested in being my teacher. And to feed my ego. Mostly my ego."

"But you were not interested in—"

"In you? But I was. Not in that SDR instructor. I never even got his name straight. That was all purely mercenary. You are different. In fact, well you don't know how close I came to...."

She smiled, and I saw tears welling up like an unexpected oasis in the desert.

"I telling you this to say how sorry I am for leading you on for my own amusement. There was no way this was going to end well whether we did anything or not. And, you may not believe this, but I violated the sacred trust between a boss and her employee."

"Sacred trust?"

"That's right. That's another reason I'm going back to Austin—to preserve what's left of that trust. You see, I still want you waking me in the middle of the night on the phone with security issues—over the phone. I don't want to have to sever that relationship."

"You mean you would fire me?"

"No. It's not your fault. I'm the one who would have to go."

"George would fire you?"

"No! I'd resign."

"You would resign?"

She nodded.

"So, you're leaving? You'll miss the rest of the conference, the keynote speaker, the hotel hacking."

"I wouldn't say that aloud in the lobby," she said. "I only wanted to come for the class anyway. You can fill me in on all the speakers and the networking once you get back."

I looked past her and saw the airport shuttle bus had arrived. She turned and looked over her shoulder. I stood there and watched her pick up her bags.

"Shuttle's here. I've got to get back to Glen and confess all this to him."

"Glen?"

"My husband."

"Sorry. I'm still used to you calling him Woody."

"Yeah, I told you 'Woody' started as a term of endearment; then, it turned into an irony. Now it's become a lost hope. Almost a prayer. The priest said that maybe if I went back to calling him Glen, it would give him the freedom to become Woody again."

She picked up her bags and turned towards the door.

"Priest?"

"Yeah. That's where I've been all morning: Guardian Angels Cathedral. Confessing."

"You went to confession? In Las Vegas?"

"Yes. I told the priest how badly I've been treating you. And Glen. And even that SDR instructor. You ever go?"

"Me? To confession? No!"

"Neither had I. Not until I converted."

"What? This morning?"

"No. A few years ago."

I followed her through the double doors and out into the heat. The cool air from the lobby followed us outside for a couple of feet then retreated back inside.

"Why? Why did you—convert?"

She dropped her bags next to the luggage bay of the bus and turned towards me. We were close again, not shoulder to shoulder and hip to hip like we had been on the bed, but face-to-face, maybe even soul to soul if there were such a thing.

"Why? It's a long story."

She turned and stepped onto the first step of the bus, but then she looked back over her shoulder.

"Basically, I realized that if the whole God thing weren't true, there wasn't any reason for me to keep on living. See you back in Austin."

Then, the bus pulled away.

Immediately, the geeks in class began asking me where Susan was. I told them she had been called back to work for an emergency. Everyone seemed disappointed, our instructor most of all.

Later in the afternoon a few people began to ask me direct technical questions, but I couldn't answer them. I realized that all the work I had done for the class, every bit of it, had been done on Susan's machine. I had never even installed the SDR software on my own. In effect, I went from being the smart kid who did the cheerleader's homework to being the ne'er do well who had not done his own. Everyone stopped asking me for any help.

That night Blackhat held a meet and great. I did not attend. Instead, I went into the casino and wandered aimlessly about. This was not my first Blackhat in Las Vegas, but I had never so much as put a coin in a slot before. I had always held the gamblers in secret contempt. I was there to pursue cyber-security. This time I envied them. People enjoyed putting themselves on the edge of disaster. I watched a basketball player for awhile at a high stakes poker table. He kept tossing more and more chips into the center of the table. Everyone thought it was the winning that kept him there. The crowd that had gathered around trilled in excitement every time he won another hand. It seemed to me that what he relished was not actually the winning but the sheer fact that he was not losing. Every hand he played he looked a little deeper into the abyss, and with every win, he pulled back from the brink with a renewed sense of relief. He rejoiced every time he raked in a pile of chips, but he wasn't glad to have won more money to keep. He was glad to have won more money he could potentially lose.

I left the table before he lost it.

I had forty dollars in my pocket. It was left over from the sixty I had when I stepped on the plane and that I used to buy Susan and myself two drinks each. I bought forty dollars worth of chips with it and went in search of a game. The basketball player was already gone, and the stakes at his table were too high anyway. I saw a table for Texas Hold 'em and sat down in a vacant seat. I tossed in my five dollar ante, and the dealer gave me two cards face down. He laid five cards down face up. That was when I realized I did not know how to play the game. I faked my way through the first hand and tried a second, but the dealer caught on and threw me out. I had thirty dollars left. All the other poker tables were full, and I couldn't bring myself to try blackjack. That single card coming off the deck like a swooping desert vulture unnerved me. By the time I found myself at the roulette table, I was beginning to shake. I decided to end it all on number nine black. The wheel spun round, the ball hopped and stopped on the very black nine. I had won one hundred and seventy-five dollars. I took the money and went out into the street.

Las Vegas bustled as much outside as inside the hotels and casinos. Flashing lights beckoned me to innumerable pleasures, and doorways invited me on uncountable anonymous adventures, but there was only one place I could think to go. I returned to the fountain where I had stood the night before hoping to stand in the very spot where I had been letting the spray blow over me and dry in the desert air.

Unfortunately, there was a man standing in my spot. I hesitated for a moment, but I had nowhere else I wanted to go, so I took the place to his right. He didn't turn to look at me. He stared straight ahead. We both stared straight ahead like two men at a urinal.

"Nice hat."

I reached up. I had forgotten I was wearing it. No wonder the water was not hitting my face.

"Thanks."

"Keeps the spray off, but I bet you bought it for the sun."

"That's right."

"So, have you found what you have been looking for your entire life?"

I turned and looked at him in amazement. He still looked straight ahead and smiled at the fountain. There was nothing left for me to do.

"I believe that I have," I said, "and what I have, I want to share."

I reached into my pocket and gave him the entire one hundred seventy-five dollars.

He took the money and turned his back from the fountain for a moment. Then, he gave me back eight dollars in change.

"You look perplexed" he said. "I'll spell it out for you. It's Wednesday. You are a day late, but Mr. London is a forgiving man. He doesn't charge a late fee. We knew we would get our money. Now, don't you have something to say?"

I stared at him dumbly.

"You will give that man one-hundred-sixty-seven dollars in cash. As you hand it to him, you will say—"

"Thank you for letting me share?"

"That's right, and he will answer, 'You are entirely welcome.' Good night."

I stood there for a long while just holding the eight dollars in my hand. When I finally put it back in my pocket and turned back to my hotel, the money was wet.

20 – A Beautiful Friendship

The morning that the Blackhat Conference proper began, I ran into Morgan again. He appeared in the lobby of the auditorium before the keynote speech. Apparently he had been there at the conference all along even though I had not seen him since he gave me a lift in his rental car. Those two evenings alone with Susan had kept me out of the regular off-hours conference circuit. Otherwise, we would most certainly have met and would most likely have sparred over some issue or the other. Then again, maybe not. I began to notice that the rules of our relationship had changed. We seemed to have reached an uneasy armistice. At Blackhat the enemy of my enemy had become my friend.

Morgan had indeed taken "Advanced Web Attacks and Exploitation" just as he had told me in Austin that he would, and he was only too happy to tell me about it. Over the course of the morning, I began to feel as if I had taken two courses at the conference, mine as well as his. I, on the other hand, said practically nothing about SDR. Morgan did not seem to care. He said nothing about Susan. I wondered if he even knew she had been here. If he didn't, then there was no way he could know how much we had been together. At the office Morgan knew everything. In Vegas he was out of his network.

"So," he said, "did you see the Chinese group?"

"No."

"They claim to be from the Apple factory in Shanghai, but I met an Apple guy from Austin who said he was unaware of any manufacturing delegation from Apple coming here."

"Maybe they just didn't tell him."

"He was in a conference with Shanghai just a week before this."

"Maybe they had to meet their production quota before they could come and didn't have time for small talk."

"You know, for a computer security professional you are awfully trusting."

"So you don't think they're Apple. Who do you think they are? Microsoft?"

"No. I think they're PLA Unit 61398."

"You think they're with the People's Liberation Army? The hacking unit?"

"Why not? How better to probe our defenses?"

"Oh. Well, if they are, they're not fooling anyone."

"They fooled you."

I actually smiled, At home arguing with Morgan just made me angry. Here I found it a welcome diversion.

"I only just now heard from you that they were even here. That hardly counts as being fooled. Being fooled takes time."

"Okay. Fair enough. But you've got to be on your toes around here."

"Don't I know it. I did hear that there was someone eavesdropping on the hotel's two-way digital radio communications and that this person or persons heard chatter about suspicious behavior around the game tables."

I should not have said "or persons".

"Was it you?"

"Was it me where? At the tables acting suspicious or listening to security?"

"Either."

"Both."

Morgan smiled.

"I'm proud of you. Was that SDR?"

I nodded.

"That was Susan's idea for you to take SDR, wasn't it?"

I nodded again, but as I did, I felt a disturbance in my countenance. My smile turned bittersweet. I felt myself sliding into sorrow. I steeled my face to hold back any revelation of my emotional state.

"You know," Morgan said, "that woman is smarter than we give her credit for."

I nodded again.

"Better looking, too," he said.

This time my mouth began to quiver like Mel Gibson's mouth in Signs when the veterinarian apologized for running over his wife. I turned my head and feigned a cough. Maybe Morgan had lost some of his customary sensitivity, but I was sure he had seen the movie, so I hid my face till the quivering stopped.

A pure, burning pain ignited right there in the hotel within my heart—my metaphorical heart I supposed, since the physical heart was only a blood pump. Overnight it had merely smoldered, but now, just before the welcome address to Blackhat, the ember had erupted into flame. Disappointment by women was a constant paradigm in my life. In a room full of geeks I was not going to be unique in that. This time, however, was different. Not only was the pain of loss was more acute, but now there was something else besides. It was insane, but along with the pain, I felt a growing sense of joy. First, I thought it was the relief that comes with resignation. "Oh, well," I would say to myself, "par for the course" even though I never played golf. But that kind of relief dulled the pain. This joy existed with the pain as if the two were conjoined. I had never experienced anything like it before. Was this what Robert meant when he talked about consolation? But what reason did I have to be consoled?

We were well into the keynote address, deep into the dread of the latest threats to cyber-civilization, when I realized what it was. I had lost Susan as a love interest, as a sex interest, but in losing her I had somehow come closer to her, maybe closer than I had ever been to any woman before. Standing in the lobby three feet apart, we had connected. We had loved one another, loved one another by letting go of one another. I felt like Humphrey Bogart putting Ingrid Bergman on the plane with her husband at the Casablanca airport only this time it was a bus, and this time it was her idea.

But Bogart had Claude Rains walking with him in the mist. Who did I have? I had Morgan walking with me into the desert. Was this the beginning of a beautiful friendship?

Morgan leaned over and whispered.

"Apparently, our speaker doesn't know the Chinese are here in the room."

The keynote speech had highlighted the hacking efforts of the Chinese government and spared no criticism.

"I can't see their faces," I said. "I don't know if they are angry or pleased."

"You can tell that guy is in software, not hardware," said Morgan.

"Why?"

"He's not worried about his manufacturing costs going up. When the Chinese hear all this, it will cost him twice as much to build a computer chip as it had last week."

"Maybe," I said, "the next time he goes to the Apple Store to upgrade his phone, the price will ring up higher for him."

"Just for him? How would they do that? Oh, I know."

We both said the words simultaneously.

"Big Data!"

"That would be hard," Morgan said, "because the prices are printed on displays."

"They could add in hidden fees and taxes that no one else was charged. You don't compare prices with the other guys in the store, and they don't buy the exact same things you do."

"He might check comparative costs on-line and come back to the store to complain they had charged him too much. But then they could lure him into buying a bunch of add-ons he couldn't resist."

"Apple would do that anyway," I said. "But what if the Chinese did just the opposite. "What if, instead of making the prices ring up higher for him at Apple, what if they made the prices for the add-ons ring up lower for him."

"So he would end up buying more?"

"Yeah," I said. "No matter where he goes, they always offer him something extra that is so targeted to his interests and so sweetly priced that he can never get out without buying it."

"He never buys another TV or SSD without getting the three year warranty because—"

"—because it is too cheap to pass up!"

"This is getting scary. Sounds too much like real life. Real life on Big Data. Nah. They won't do all that. They'll just hack his company servers and put malware on all his software products."

"Then," I said, "they will plant stories in the media exposing the malware, and he'll go bankrupt."

We paused for a moment.

"That's pretty scary," I said.

"I know," said Morgan. "I think I liked the Chinese better when they were communists."

Throughout the introductory remarks and during the keynote address we wondered. We always knew—had I not even told Susan on the plane—that Blackhat was a mixture of hackers and defenders, but having such a large group of foreign nationals of questionable intent in the premier security conference put a different spin on the question. I found myself wondering what Susan would do if she were still here. I imagined she would walk up to them during the lunch break and say, "I wonder if you guys could settle a little bet. My geeks say that you are members of PLA Unit 61398. I say you're just software pirates from Taiwan. So, which are you?"

But Morgan and I would never have had the nerve to take such a direct approach.

"Our boss would just walk up and ask them," I said.

"Our boss could get away with that."

"They might even tell her the truth straight out."

"That's what happens when you take men from a country where there are one hundred eighteen males to one hundred females and expose them to western women."

"Our women are our greatest asset, maybe our most powerful weapon."

"No argument from me, boy."

"Morgan, what would you say the ratio of men to women is in this room?"

"Just looking around, I'd say three to one."

He paused for a moment.

"Come to think of it," he said, "maybe the Chinese should have sent us some of their women."

That evening we went to the casino. For me it was a matter of pure distraction.

Morgan asked me, "Why do you want to go to the tables when you could be interfacing with your fellow professionals?"

"A man can stand only so much joy in Las Vegas."

He accepted that statement at face value. He even followed me, but once we got in, neither one of us was all that interested in the games. No one anywhere seemed to be winning. No crowd had gathered around any particular table to celebrate anyone's streak of good luck. I decided I would rather go cruise the Dark Web to look for zero day exploits than to watch people voluntarily hemorrhaging money, but Morgan grabbed my arm.

"Look over there at the poker table. It's the Chinese!"

"You mean there are Asians at the blackjack table?"

"No, I mean the guys from Blackhat are playing Texas Hold 'em. There are three of them at the table. See? That one on the right looks like Chairman Mao. There's two more just watching. Go buy some chips and get in the game."

"Why me?"

"You've already scoped things out. Go on. You can add this game to your bucket list. You can say that you engaged in an epic struggle at the Texas Hold 'em Table with agents of the PLA. You'll be like James Bond in Casino Royale."

"It's not the same group of Chinese."

"I tell you it is."

"Texas Hold 'em? I don't know how to play it."

"So what? Neither do they. I'll Google it while you get the chips."

"I'm taking all the risk and you—"

"Only the first three hundred. If you need more, I'll kick in the next three hundred. Now go!"

He pushed me towards the cashier and headed for the table. I saw him taking hold of an empty seat and pointing back at me. Then he put his hand on his head like he was putting on a hat and pointed at his shoe. I supposed his shoe was black, because the entire group nodded all around. I went to the cashier and laid down my credit card. I imagined Susan beside me. She was asking me why I was so cheap. Epic battles required epic budgets. I found myself asking for three-fifty. I wondered if Morgan would match me dollar for dollar. It didn't matter now. I was committed. Morgan had turned on his phone at Blackhat to consult with Google, something I had refused to do. The Chinese were counting on me. They had no interest in playing among themselves. They needed a true Texan to pit their skills against. The sovereign State of Texas, if not the entire free world, depended on me.

"Okay," I said to Morgan back at the table, "how do you play this game?"

The first three hands I lost sixty-five dollars. I didn't have a chance. Successful poker playing depended either upon counting the cards and calculating the odds or in reading your opponents' faces. I had no clue what cards anyone had, and I could not read the faces of those inscrutable Asians. On the fourth hand, however, I got lucky. For the next hour, I managed to stay alive. By the second hour of play I had begun to think I knew what was going on, but I needed to put that knowledge to the test. Chairman Mao kept raising the bet. Everyone else thought that the honorable chairman was bluffing. I was pretty sure he wasn't, but if everyone else folded, I would never know without losing myself. Therefore, my plan was to stay in long enough to convince one other member of the Gang of Three to make the entire Long March. I would get out just before we reached the river and the point of no return. That way, I could reserve a little cash. The other member of PLA would ford the river and force Mao to reveal his hand. Then, I would confirm what I suspected about the chairman. From then on I would know how to play him.

Unfortunately, the entire PLA folded at the river except for Mao. If I were going to test my theory, I had no choice but to match his bet. When the dealer called in our bets, I was proved right. Chairman Mao had not been bluffing. I half smiled as my two thousand dollars fell into the hands of the Chinese. At that point, the dealer declared a break, and Morgan pulled me aside.

"You just lost two thousand dollars."

"I know. Not bad for someone who started with three-fifty."

"How much have you got left?"

"Three-fifty."

"Three-fifty?"

"Not bad for a beginner, don't you think?"

"I do not think. You are no better off than when you started."

"That doesn't worry me. I think I can win it back. I have my opponents figured out."

"Figured out? You think you have them figured out?"

"Yes."

"You just lost two thousand dollars in a single pot. You didn't have a very good hand, You should have gotten out before the betting doubled at the end. Did you think that guy was bluffing?"

"No, I was pretty sure he wasn't. "

"You were pretty sure he wasn't? Then, why did you stay in?"

"I stayed in to confirm my theory."

"Let me get this straight. You lost two thousand dollars on purpose so you could prove a theory?"

"Think of it as an investment. Now that I have confirmed it, I know how to play these guys. I can win the money back. I invested two thousand now for a bigger payback later. I know when Mao is bluffing, and he thinks I'm a patsy."

"Let's suppose you have figured all this out. Have you noticed that the stakes are getting higher? On the next hand you won't have the money to make it past the turn and cross the river! You just sank yourself!"

"I don't think so. But if you think I'm under funded, why don't you kick in the three hundred you promised? None of this so far was your money, so why should you be upset? You didn't lose anything, and you still don't have any investment in it."

Morgan looked stunned. I don't think anything I had ever said to him before had had such a silencing effect. Now I wanted to go in for the kill, but the moment I opened my mouth, something made me soften the blow. In fact, I turned the sword on myself.

"How about this? If you like, you can buy your own chips, and I will give you mine. You can continue the game."

Morgan shook his head.

"No, you've got the experience. It's different when you are sitting in the chair than it is just looking over someone's shoulder. I'll give you the three hundred."

So he did, and I stayed in the game. After another hour I was up about six thousand dollars. I was beginning to think it was time to quit, but Morgan disagreed. He didn't have to tell me what he wanted me to do. With my new found skill in reading faces and judging intents, I could just tell. As far as Morgan was concerned, this was a fight to the death. We stayed in till Mao had lost all his money and had walked out of the game.

At one AM. Mao stood up and asked for a break. He had about seventy-five dollars in chips. Morgan was smiling. Mao came back to the table with one thousand more. In the next hand, I had two queens face down on the table. At the turn, the dealer laid down three kings. I went in for the kill and made the chairman lay down every dollar he had. At the river, he turned over two aces, and things went south from there. At four Morgan put his hand firmly on my shoulder. I stood, and we moved a couple of steps from the table. We were like a couple of foreigners resorting to our native language for a private conversation in the middle of the crowd.

"We're done here."

So much for the fight to the death.

"But I've still got three hundred and change."

"You've got change. The three hundred is mine."

"Wait a minute. Poker funds are fungible."

"Last in, first out. I'm out. If you want to go back to the bank, you are on your own."

I turned and hovered over the table for a moment. I picked up the chips and put them in Morgan's hands. I gave Mao my poker face one last time. It was mostly straight except for a fold around my eyes and a bend at my lower lip. For the first time all evening Mao was smiling. He could read me like a book. Then, I turned to the dealer.

"I'm out," I said.

I left the casino and western civilization in the hands of the Chinese and went out into the desert.

Even with all the lights and asphalt of the city, you could still tell you were in the desert, and the desert seemed to be the right place to be for someone who had lost everything. I wandered the streets until I came back to the same place as before, to the fountain. I did not do it intentionally. I wasn't looking to meet anyone or for anything to happen. It just seemed, once I was there, that there was nowhere else better to be standing at night in Las Vegas.

A fountain in the desert! I supposed that the builders of the city had intended that to be a symbol of hope, of the triumph of man over nature. All that water pent up by the Hoover Dam powered the lights installed under the pool of the fountain. The electricity generated at the dam drove the pumps that impelled the water through pipes underground until it spouted up and spilled over those lights. Once again I stood close enough to feel the water on my face and see the lights play upon my hands, but it did not make me forget the desert. Standing by the water, standing on the edge of darkness, I felt the desert's drying presence even more keenly. The water wetted my face and the light illumined my skin, but the desert penetrated, as it were, into my soul.

Once again there was another man at the fountain off to my right. We could see each other without turning. It was not the same guy who had collected my premium. We stood side by side staring straight ahead like two guys at a urinal until he spoke.

"This is a good place to come at four in the morning when you're losing, isn't it?" he said.

"I think it's closer to five."

"Five?" he said. "Goes to show its later than you think."

We stood and let the falling water speak for us awhile.

"You know," he said, "when you're winning, when I'm winning, I want to spend money. I want excitement. I want to keep on winning. When I lose, I want to walk out of the hotel into the desert and just keep on walking. You feel like that?"

"I don't know. Maybe."

"But instead, I come here. It's like an oasis. But it's still the desert, and I can still take that walk if I want."

I just nodded.

"I was up ten thousand dollars at blackjack, but then...."

The water washed our faces as the desert dried our bones.

"It happens," I said.

He snapped his fingers.

"Like that."

"Yeah."

"Say, you don't have any money, do you?"

I didn't answer.

"Don't tell me you lost, too?"

This time I looked down.

"I'm sorry. Damn! That's tough."

Then he looked closer without shifting an inch, closer into my drying soul.

"Wait! There was a woman. You lost her, too. You don't have to say nothin'. I can see it in your eyes. I'm sorry! If I had realized, I wouldn't have asked you for any money. But you see, it's like this. If I had just a little cash, I could get into another game, and..."

We stood looking at one another a moment. I reached in my pocket. I still had twenty-five dollars left over from my roulette winnings. I gave him the money.

"Thanks, man. You don't know what this means to me."

I didn't watch him go. I just stood watching the fountain. I could scarcely imagine his desperation or the futility in his life: always placing another bet, always playing another game. One thing I did know. I was never so glad that I was so well insured.

21 – The Sacred Trust

Austin was a hundred degrees when I returned, not as high as the temperature of Las Vegas when I left there, but this was not a dry heat. I took my hat on the plane and wore it into Austin Bergstrom Airport. I saw myself in the men's room mirror. I looked like a sadder, wiser, and fatter Stevie Ray Vaughn. However, that was only an illusion. I felt myself no wiser. Oh, sure, I had thought myself wiser in the desert, but I lost it in the time shift from Pacific to Central Time. Instead of gaining back two hours of my life, the insights I had earned vanished like desert mirages. Besides all that, Stevie's hat had been black.

Before I stepped out into the heat from the terminal I had never realized how dry Austin was. To be sure, there was humidity, and it hit you immediately when you left the air conditioning, but all that moisture in the air did you no good. Lake Travis was still twenty feet low, and unless you could drink your own sweat, the heat was still going to drain you like a vampire bat. All the moisture there was was in your sweat. It clung to your skin, and it never reentered the water table. It was a good thing it didn't. All that salt would have contaminated the springs. The startup company that could figure how to desalinate perspiration could make a fortune.

As I peered around for a bus or even a taxi, I saw a Car2Go pull up in front of me. I went up to the car to tell the driver I would take the car back to town if he were here to catch a plane, but he told me to stow my luggage and get in. I recognized the voice. It was Lloyd London.

"I know this looks like stalking, but honestly, I was in the neighborhood and thought I'd offer you a ride."

"You just saw me standing here and decided to pick me up?"

"Yes, and no. I knew you were here, but I wasn't tracking your location. It was partial serendipity. Honest."

I got in the car. I had to put one of my bags in my lap.

"So where you been all week?"

"Las Vegas."

"Blackhat?"

"You know about Blackhat?"

"Sure."

"Of course you do. That's why you don't offer payment on-line."

"Partly."

"Partly. But you knew I was in Vegas. You knew I went to Blackhat. All that was in the partly."

"Yes, but we didn't know precisely where you were. We got a little concerned."

"Concerned? Why?"

"Because you, my friend, were off-line. You turned off your phone. Although..."

"Although with the iPhone and the hardwired battery, you cannot completely power down."

"Yes. Apple! You gotta' love it. But you weren't on the computer that much, either. Pretty strange to go to a computer conference and not get on a computer."

"Oh, I got on, but I used someone else's machine."

"You didn't log onto anything with any of your known identities."

"No, I didn't."

"That was wise, no doubt, with all those hackers milling about. Still, I've got to tell you...."

"Tell me what?"

"I would not advise you do that much in the future. People in our business begin to get nervous when clients disappear."

"I didn't disappear. You found me. You collected your premium. That was you, wasn't it? Your man?"

"If it hadn't been our man there, it would have been another of our men here waiting at the airport terminal door. You would have been in arrears. People in our business also get nervous when clients don't pay their premiums on time—not me so much, but other people."

"I forgot. I was out of town and preoccupied. That's the honest truth."

"I believe you."

We both were silent for a moment while London merged into traffic. In a Smart Car that was not easy to do.

"What do you mean by nervous?" I asked.

"Well, not really nervous. It is more a figure of speech. What I meant was that when a client stops doing the things he normally does, our analysts pay attention. In this case, you were off the grid."

"We had power at the hotel. You mean I was off the network, off the web."

"That's right, but it's more than that. You were off the data stream. When a client changes habits, it flags his account for an analysis. When a client leaves the grid, it triggers an evaluation. We knew you were at a conference, so your account only received a review concerning probable cause."

"Probable cause?"

"Yes. An analysis to determine the probable cause for your change in habits. But after three days off the grid, you were on the countdown for an evaluation. Good thing you used your credit card and bought those chips. That put you back in the good graces of the Big Data. You were doing something we would expect in Las Vegas. All was well."

"Look, I paid my premium as soon as you asked. And you did ask. You knew where I was. You knew exactly—"

"Yes. When you won at roulette, you showed up on Casino Cam as big as life."

"You were looking for me on the casino security cameras?"

"It's more a case of found you on the casino camera. We found you, and then we could relax, because we had reestablished the data stream. Of course, we still didn't know what your state of mind was—whether you were happy or depressed. But then you won, and that is always an encouragement."

"I won," I said, and then I thought more about what I had said.

"I won. How did that happen?"

"Don't you just love roulette?" said Lloyd. "I mean, what are the odds you could ever win? But roulette always has a kind of romance about it. I think of Casablanca and of the young girl in the movie who goes to Bogart for help. She desperately wants to start a new life with the young man she loves. He's sitting there at the roulette wheel digging them both deeper into hopelessness. She's so innocent, but she's willing to give innocence away for his sake. He's so naive that he thinks he can beat the odds and the house. And there's old Bogey who sees this and tells him to put all his money on number...Well, the point is we found you, and we collected our premium. But it was never about the money. We can get the money. I mean, who needs automatic bank drafts? We can always collect our money. The point is you. The point is that we as a company must always be vigilant to fulfill our commitment to you."

"Your commitment? Oh, you mean the policy."

"Yes, your benefit. Your death benefit. We always have to be measuring, and discerning and deciding when the time is right to pay the benefit. That's what you pay us for. That's why you signed up. It's a sacred trust, and there aren't many of those left in the world."

"Why does it matter if I am out of the data stream for a couple of days?"

"I don't tell everyone this stuff, but since you are an IT person, I can talk a little shop. You know how Big Data works. You scan gigabytes, terabytes of data. Then, you look for correlations and for trends. Insurance has always been about data analysis, but modern technology has become a game changer. Anyway, we watch your trends, and when you make an unexpected change, we zero in. Well, when you go off the grid, that becomes more difficult. In fact, going off-grid is a sign in itself that something may be developing. So, we get concerned, but we have less data for our analysis. That's when we have to bring human judgment to bear. And, when humans get involved, then someone has to make a determination. I mean, someone in the company has to make a formal determination."

"I thought it was an evaluation."

"The evaluation precedes the determination. Analysis begets evaluation begets determination."

"I see."

"You see? I'm not sure you do. There are two schools of thought in my business because there is always an element of doubt. Because there is doubt, there has to be a benefit of that doubt."

"Oh, that makes sense," I said, "in a vague, abstract sort of way."

"The two schools divide over the question of which side of the doubt gets the benefit. My thinking is to give the client a little time. Unless the trend has been declining for some time, these sudden aberrations don't amount to much. My grandmother always said, 'Cheer up. Things will get better.' It was that Great Depression mentality. But, she was right. Things often did get better, and I think they sometimes still will. The other school, however, their philosophy is, 'Invoke the policy, and pay the benefit.' That school—it tends to be comprised of the younger generation. I'm a little old school—I think that suffering can be short-lived and can even be somewhat beneficial. The newer school—they are more immediate, less tolerant of what I think are just momentary sorrows. They are less patient."

He drove on in silence for a couple of miles as if he wanted all this information to soak in.

"Well, I just wanted you to know that, as your agent, I will always protect your interests as I see fit. So, to put it bluntly, I thought there was still hope, and I was right. However, when the time comes, if the Big Data is temporarily blind or not all that clear....But don't worry. I won't let you down. I think I am a pretty good judge of the times."

I don't know how many miles or long a silence ensued after that. Then, Lloyd spoke again.

"Oh, look. You're home."

Indeed, we were on Brazos in front of my building. Lloyd swung the Car2Go nose first to the curb.

"I hope you can get your own luggage."

I nodded and got out. There was traffic coming, but the rear end of the Smart Car hardly stuck out any further than the door of a typical parallel parked car. The traffic easily went around me without even having to swerve.

"Thanks," I said to Lloyd.

"Keep smiling," he said. He backed the car out into a break in the traffic flow and entered the stream. I followed his tail lights past St.

Mary's Cathedral as far as Eleventh Street where he turned left. I wondered if I could break into Car2Go's database and see who he really was. Probably not. There was no telling how many identities Lloyd London had. Even so, I trusted him, and I wondered if there was anyone I could recommend him to. Susan was my first thought, but after my last conversation with her, I doubted she would be interested. Butch would not understand. Morgan might be interested, but I was not so sure I wanted to share with him. The next time I saw London, I would have to ask him if he were interested in referrals. I remembered I was not supposed to talk about entire life with other people, but that did not mean I couldn't recommend my friends and co-workers to London. As I rode the elevator up, I counted my list of friends. I was only on the fourth floor. By the time I reached my condo door, I had reached the end of my list and had reviewed it twice for omissions.

The condo was cold and empty. I had forgotten to change the thermostat before I left. Maybe Joe could use a policy. What if his Thai restaurant were to fail? Surely a person could use insurance to deal with a situation like that.

I dropped my bags and went back downstairs and around the corner to Joe's to help reduce the risk of any business failure before he could get insured. Other than Joe who was manning the takeout window himself, there was no one else in the place that I knew.

22 - The Sands

When I arrived back at work, Butch practically met me at the door.

"Where have you been?"

"At Blackhat?"

"I mean since then. I mean all weekend."

"I've been at home, resting from Blackhat."

"I tried to call you, but I kept getting your voice mail."

"Oh! I turned off my cell phone while I was there to keep from getting hacked, and I guess I forgot to turn it back on."

"You turned off your cell phone because you were afraid of hackers?"

"I wouldn't normally do that, but I figured if I was going to tell Susan to do it, I should set a good example."

"You were with Susan at Blackhat?"

"Yes. You knew that. I didn't know she was coming until I got on the plane."

"That's another thing I want you to tell me about, but first things first."

"What? What's going on?"

"Have you checked your email?"

"No. I've been off the grid."

"You didn't have any power?"

"No, I mean I've been offline."

"I'll say. Check your email."

He stood there waiting. He didn't even move to let me get to my cubicle. Being offline seemed to have even larger repercussions than just making my insurance agent nervous. I opened my laptop on the nearest piece of furniture and powered it up. Once I opened email, I began scrolling down.

"Yeah," I said, "that's a lot of email."

"How many?"

"How many?"

"How many unopened in your in-box?"

I looked at the count in the in-box folder.

"Ten thousand-three-hundred-and-forty—damn! That is a lot of emails."

"It is. You should see how many were on the server."

"Were on the server?"

"Yes, before we took it down. As of Friday evening, however, there were ten-million-three-hundred-eighty-five thousand give or take."

"Are you serious?"

"We took down the server, we blocked your incoming email, and then we brought the server back up. We scrubbed most of the emails, but we left you the first ten thousand to research."

"You left me ten thousand? Wait! Who were the rest addressed to?"

"You guessed it. All those ten million give or take emails were addressed to you, copied to Susan, and copied to me."

I looked around for a chair, but there wasn't one near enough. So, I just stood there in the lobby absolutely still.

Butch stood before me nodding, affirming his own statement, but I sensed there was more.

"Would you like to know who were they from?"

My legs became unsteady. Butch did not wait for my answer.

"They were from all sorts of people. From all sorts of companies: IBM, Microsoft, Apple, Oracle, Adobe, Sailpoint, Amazon—"

"Technology companies?"

"—Discover, American Express, Frost Bank, MasterCard, Chase Bank—"

"Financials?"

"—The World Health Organization, The Knights of Malta—"

"There's such a thing as the Knights of Malta?"

"—The Trilateral Commission—"

"That's got to be bogus."

"—The Central Intelligence Agency, Stratfor.com, Gartner, Whitehouse.gov! The list is endless."

"It can't be endless. You said there were only ten-million-three-hundred—and change."

"There were so many we could not come up with a list to block them all, so we blocked everything coming to you. Once we got the server back up, it stopped accepting your email. You will be getting no more email. I hope that isn't inconvenient."

I shook my head.

"It is going to take you awhile to read the ones you've got."

"I can't read all—"

"Oh, you need to read them. You need to read them so you can figure out why all these people decided to send you email. I've read several hundred of them myself. I hope you don't mind."

He waited till I gave him an answer.

"No," I said, "under the circumstances...."

"I haven't read them all, but all the ones I have read say pretty much the same thing. Maybe as you work your way through them, you will find a different message than I found. Maybe the nine-thousandth email switched subjects."

"I need to sit down."

"Oh, yes. By all means. Go sit down. Get yourself some coffee. When you're ready to start work, then maybe the rest of us can take a little break."

I had never seen Butch so sarcastic before. It was not just insulting. It was disturbing.

Morgan was there at his desk when I got to mine. The little matters of our loss to the Chinese and of the three hundred dollars that had come up between us in Las Vegas seemed almost comforting by contrast.

"You'll have to overlook Butch if he seems a little out of sorts," he said. "He's been up forty-eight hours. It really upset him that he couldn't find you. Now that you are here, I think he will go home and crash."

"What happened?"

"Read your email. Man, you really stepped in it."

Standing in the lobby I had only seen the number of emails. Now I began to examine them. They came from a vast variety of sources. I scrolled down through a hundred or more and did not see a single source repeated. Then, I noticed the subject line. It was not literally the same from email to email, but they all followed a common theme.

"To: Augustus.Bishop@FairWare.com

cc: Susan.Wilson@FairWare.com

Paul.Cassidy@FairWare.com

From: Steve.Jobs@apple.com

Subject: What Happens in Vegas Does Not Stay in Vegas

In my day no one really got ahead sleeping with the boss. But then again, who was sleeping?"

"To: Augustus.Bishop@FairWare.com

From: Albert.Einstein@princeton.edu

cc: Susan.Wilson@FairWare.com

Paul.Cassidy@FairWare.com

Subject: What Happens in Vegas at a Constant Velocity Does Not Stay at Constant Velocity

From my point of reference you spent a relatively long time in Susan's room. However, I did observe that you were not at constant velocity. It is as I said. There are no simultaneous events in the universe, are there?"

"To: Augustus.Bishop@FairWare.com

From: J.Edgar.Hoover@fbi.gov

cc: Susan.Wilson@FairWare.com

Paul.Cassidy@FairWare.com

Subject: What Happens in Vegas is Under Constant Surveillance in Vegas

At 7:30 PM the male subject was observed entering into the hotel room of female subject Susan Wilson. Male subject was not observed entering the female subject. The computer camera was pointed the wrong way."

"To: Augustus.Bishop@FairWare.com—"

"There are two questions," Morgan said, "Butch will be asking when he wakes up. Who sent those emails? Why did he send them? What really happened in Vegas? Okay, that's three questions. I've been up awhile myself. They are actually letting me bill overtime for this. Butch has already asked what the hell you were doing in Vegas. I told him that you were studying SDR and losing at cards to the Chinese. I also told him that if you were screwing Susan, I was unaware of it."

"I appreciate your directness," I said.

I was glad he had not been any more direct than that.

"To: Augustus.Bishop@FairWare.com

From:Frank.Sinatra@TheSands.com

cc: Susan.Wilson@FairWare.com

Paul.Cassidy@FairWare.com

Subject: What Happens in Vegas is not Nearly as Important as Doing it 'My Way'

Sorry you couldn't meet me while you were in Vegas, but I guess it was kind of hard since I am dead.

Maybe when you're dead, too, we can stay at the same hotel."

I laughed nervously in spite of myself. Morgan smiled.

"Was that the Sinatra one? I liked that one the best although I am partial to Einstein."

"You read these, too?"

"A few."

"And Susan?"

"Oh, yes. We had to stop her email, too. And Butch's. I think we may try turning hers back on. What do you think?"

"I—I don't know. What did she say?"

"I think her exact words were, 'Son of a bitch!' She spent a lot of time in George's office."

"George knows about this?"

Of course. The escalation policy.

"Sure. He was here Sunday talking to Susan. They are both here today."

"Already?"

"Most people get here before ten, you know."

"To: Augustus.Bishop@FairWare.com
From: Jack.Nicholson@TheShining.com
cc: Susan.Wilson@FairWare.com
Paul.Cassidy@FairWare.com
Subject: All work and no play makes Jack a dull boy, even in Vegas

You probably want me to give your company executives a good explanation for what you were doing so long in your boss's hotel room. Frankly, I'd rather have needles in my eyes. You were just inches from a clean getaway."

"I didn't do it," I said. "I mean, I didn't do 'it' with Susan."

"Oh, I believe you, Man. You were just helping the boss with her homework. She was a babe in the technical woods, and someone had to protect her."

"Exactly."

After all, that was true enough. Then, I noticed something which somehow managed to slip past my agitation and fear.

"You know," I said, "I've never seen this before. I've seen email addresses get spoofed, but they at least looked like probable email addresses. Some of these are like parodies. They're anachronisms."

"Yeah," said Morgan. "Some of these people are dead. They were dead before email existed."

"Some of these domains look like they would belong to places that obviously don't exist. Not anymore. 'TheSands.com'. I think The Sands Hotel was a popular Las Vegas Hotel back in the day, but it is long gone now."

"What I find fascinating is that the subject matter of these is all the same, but the subject line and the text for each email are unique. Surely someone did not write these all by hand. Did someone write a program to produce these? Are the robots that good? What would Frank Sinatra say about sex in Las Vegas? What would Einstein say? You're lucky you didn't get one from Jesus."

"Did you check to see?"

"No, but put that in the search and… What do you know? You did. You got an email from Jesus, from Jesus Martinez."

"Not the same."

"Maybe your spoof-er didn't write a program. Maybe he hired a bunch of people in the Philippines to write these."

"They would have to be culturally savvy to do this. It seems like a lot of trouble. Not the way I would go about attacking a company."

"You see this as an attack on a company?"

"Obviously! Don't you?"

"Partially, sure, but mainly I see this as an attack on you."

"On me? I suppose so."

"You suppose so? You know so. I mean, basically, the attack is over. We lost email for a weekend, but it's back up. The damage to FairWare Software is contained, but to you? The attack on you persists. On you and Susan."

I winced at that. I winced because Susan had been implicated, too, and her reputation had been damaged. I winced because the accusation had almost been true.

"You know," said Morgan, "I am pinging these emails, and as we expected, there is no Albert.Einstein@princeton.edu. Princeton University may remember full well that old Al won the Noble Prize, but the princeton.edu email server has never heard of him. And the same is true of J.Edgar.Hoover@fbi.gov. But, Frank.Sinatra@TheSands.com comes back with a response. That is a real email address. I doubt if Old Blue Eyes is reading it, but the address does exist. So, is that just a coincidence?"

"No," I said, "it is not. Princeton.edu and fbi.gov are real domains."

"Yes, you said that."

Morgan was being more like his old self, but I ignored it and answered him as if he were not being a butt.

"Princeton and the FBI are real institutions," I explained with patience, "and they own those domains. This e-mailer could not create a real email address on someone else's domain. The Sands, however—"

"The Sands blew away before the Internet was invented. That's obvious. So what?" Morgan said.

"But don't you see? That means the domain was available. Our guy could register for that domain and set up a real email called Frank.Sinatra@TheSands.com."

"That's cute," said Morgan, "but why would he bother?"

"Well, it makes the connection to Las Vegas," I said. "It makes it appear Frank Sinatra saw me in Las Vegas because he spent so much time there."

"Except Sinatra would have paid no attention to you in Vegas no matter who you slept with."

"I suppose not."

"And he's dead."

"Well, he said that in the email."

Morgan shook his head.

"It's a lot of trouble," he said, "just to bring down a server. You know, until now I was ready to blame the Chinese for this. I was ready to say that the PLA was pissed off with you for almost beating them in poker. See? I just granted your claim that you could have won if I had given you more money—although you could have kicked more into the pot yourself if you were so sure. And the Chinese recognized it so they wanted to complete your humiliation with this attack."

"That's ridiculous."

"Well, of course it is. The PLA could not have done this. They could have brought down our email server but not with such, such poignant cultural irony. That is the clever part of all this. It is the also the real, destructive element of the entire thing. It is not just the window dressing on a denial of service attack. The guy who did this did not use you to bring down our email. He brought down our email to get to you. The question is, 'Why?'"

I said nothing, but my nothing was revealing.

"You know something, don't you? I knew you had to have some idea. Let me guess. Some other Blackhat geek was hitting on Susan, and he got jealous because you got her attentions and he didn't."

I thought of the SDR instructor, but I knew this was not his work. No one else in the class had done it either.

"You do know something, but you're not telling. We will see. Maybe Butch can drag it out of you once he's had some sleep, but

George may beat him to it. I imagine you'll be in his office within the hour."

I sat up in my chair at that, but I still didn't answer.

"You could tell me. I know, I'm just a scumbag contractor, a hired mercenary. But in this situation when your job is on the line, the scummy, lowlife contractor may be the last friend you've got."

"How's that?" I said. I said it with a thick layer of dubiousness spread out on the top of my voice, but inside I felt a rising panic. Until that moment, I had not grasped the obvious fact that my job was in jeopardy. The Abarth was paid for, but the condo required a high, steady income to keep the downtown wolf from my door. If I couldn't make the payments, I could sell and pay off my mortgage, but then I would have to move out of the central city. I might even have to go live in Roundrock or Cedar Park. Then, there was the matter of my insurance premiums.

"I have no ax to grind," Morgan said. "I gain nothing by seeing you go down. I am not interested in getting Butch's job and in stepping on you to get it. I'm only here for the money, but I would also like to see a little justice done on the side. I'd like to take this guy down, and you may have some idea on how to do that. You are a pretty good security analyst when you are not pinned to the wall like this."

"When there's an incident, we are always up against the wall."

"True. Whenever there is a breach, someone loses his job. I know. Why do you think I became a contractor?"

"I have no idea who did this," I said. "If you want to help me find out, well, I suppose that would be a good thing. Although, whoever did this was at Blackhat observing my movements. You were at Blackhat. You could have been watching us."

"This is true. And I'll give you another reason to suspect me. This guy must know you well enough to single you out for a rather personal attack. I could be that guy."

"You could."

"Motive and opportunity."

"Motive and opportunity," I agreed. "You were there and you have the technical know how to pull this off. And as for motive, you did sent me to a dark, wet, narrow cave supposedly to help me fulfill my life before I died."

"But it could just as well have been an attempt on your life, or at least on your sanity."

"That's exactly right."

"It may not be an explanation of motive, but it is evidence of motive. After all, no one tries to kill someone for no reason."

"But I survived."

"You did. You did indeed."

"You're damn right. I crawled all the way to the end of that hole."

"You crawled all the way to Death's front porch."

"To the waiting room of Hell," I said. And then I paused. "I do have to admit: it was still pretty cool in there."

"And you crawled back out!"

"I saw the light at the end of that tunnel, and I crawled back."

We both smiled. I realized Morgan and I had come to an agreement. I didn't like it. I added another accusation.

"But you sent me there to get lost in the darkness. When your plan didn't work, you came up with one to drive me into a hole of personal and professional despair. Motive!"

"But you must have found some hope when you got to the end of cave, or you would not have turned around and crawled back out to Austin."

"Maybe I did, but who would believe you sent me there to find hope."

"Probably no one."

"You're right. No one. But that was an ordeal, let me tell you. It may not have been a trial by fire, but it was a trial by tight spaces, dark, rocks and mud. And you knew it would be."

"I had an idea. But the real question is why did you go? Did you go there to find life or to find death? Did I send you there to find life or death?"

"I feel like I'm Clint Eastwood hanging on to a cliff on the Eiger," I said, "and you are George Kennedy offering me a rope."

"But you suddenly realize I walk with a limp like the man you were sent to kill, so you have to wonder if you can trust me."

"That's about it."

"But the tables are turned, aren't they. You think I was trying to kill you, but if you are Clint, you are the one coming after me because I'm George Kennedy."

"That's right," I said.

"But George threw Clint a life rope. He knew Clint was there to kill him, but he offered him a life line."

"And, after that, Clint let George go," I said.

"He did indeed."

He did indeed.

23 - The Email Address

I had only been in George's office once. It was the time of the previous hacking. That time I had had my counsel, Paul, with me. On that occasion George never showed up. We had waited till his assistant told us he was detained and that we should go back to our desks. He never called us back in, so the whole issue died. Butch pronounced it dead when he handed me my bonus two months later. It was two percent lighter than was customary. A slap on the wrist, Butch had said. I hadn't known whether to be mad or relieved. However, since the money had already been deposited in my bank, I had taken the rest of the afternoon off and had gone to the Fiat dealership to put a down payment on the Abarth. Turbo-therapy Butch had called it.

This time George was sitting there waiting, and I was without benefit of counsel. This George was not George Kennedy, either. At least he was not the George Kennedy of <u>The Eiger Sanction</u>. Maybe the George Kennedy of <u>Charade</u>, all filled with rage and ready to push me off the roof because I had cost him money. Susan was not there either. Normally, having her in the meeting would have been a bad sign, an indicator of trial by management, the kind of trial in which the verdict is foregone and the only outstanding issue is the severity of the sentence. This time, and under the circumstances, her absence was a blessing.

A blessing? There was no such thing, was there?

"Close the door."

I obeyed meekly. I knew there was no escape. Yet, my mind was furiously reviewing various strategies for defense. These strategies came from every movie I had ever seen covering such a situation, and they ranged from devising a plausible explanation to telling the truth. George closed the door on both extremes.

"Paul has gone home to get some sleep. This meeting is just between you and me. I don't care what happened between you and Susan. It is none of my business. All I need to know are these few things."

"Number one: 'Were you at any time feeling coerced or manipulated into performing any act which made you feel uncomfortable?'"

"Well, lying on the bed is not the most comfortable position—"

I was going to say, "to be typing out configuration settings for an SDR digital voice decoder," but George cut me off.

"Just 'yes' or 'no'!"

"No."

"Number two: 'Did Susan at any time offer you any kind of managerial rewards such as raises, bonuses, promotions, time off, or job reassignment in exchange for sexual favors?'"

"There were no sexual—"

"Ah-ah-ah! Just answer the question."

"No."

"Number three: 'Were you at any time threatened with loss of future raises, bonuses, promotions, time off, or job reassignment; or with loss of current pay or employment unless you kept silent about sexual activities which occurred between you and Susan Wilson whether voluntarily or involuntarily; or were you threatened with any such losses in exchange for your silence concerning activities, sexual or non-sexual in nature, which occurred between Susan Wilson and other persons?'"

"No."

I was glad Susan had never used the words 'between you and me,' or 'You didn't hear this from me, but...' On the other hand, I was no longer sure I was so glad nothing had occurred between us. If I was going to suffer, at least I should have something to suffer about.

"I am relieved to hear your answers. HR informs me that there are serious potential violations of federal sexual harassment law in a situation such as this. Swift and decisive action is required to mitigate severe legal liabilities. I am glad to hear that such actions are not required in this case."

George paused at that point and began to type on his iPad. I realized that he had been referring to a document on the screen and was now entering my responses. I considered asking for a copy but thought better of it under the circumstances.

"This concludes the HR portion of our interview," George said.

Then, he stood up.

"What the hell is going on here? What did you do at that conference to bring all this on my head?"

Fortunately, he did not give me time to answer that question.

"I don't need this! I'm trying to put together an IPO here. I stand to make a lot of money. You stand to make a lot of money. You don't need to be...screwing it up."

I nodded. He was right as far as it went. I must have smiled faintly.

"Do you think this is funny? Is this your idea of a joke?"

"No."

"Then, why did you do this?"

"Do what?"

"Do what? Send all these damn emails?"

I couldn't believe what I was hearing.

"Send them? I didn't send them. Why would I do that? Why would I put myself in a bad light? Someone sent them to me."

"I know that. But you did something to bring this about. You opened some email somewhere that brought all this on. You pissed someone off. You screwed your f-ing boss."

"Is that what Susan said happened?"

"I'm not the one answering questions. You tell me."

"All right. I will. That is not what Susan said happened. Susan has integrity. I learned that about her in Las Vegas. Second—"

I couldn't come up with a second point. I wanted to tell George that he had a serious security problem, but I could not think on my feet. I could not come up with a way to shift his focus onto the email denial of service attack without further implication of myself. After all, the emails were all addressed to me.

"Your job is not to lecture me on security. Your job is to keep this enterprise secure. Not only have you failed to do that, you have become the very cause of our insecurity. I can't have that. I won't have it. Do you hear me?"

Once Robert told me that a soft answer turned away wrath.

"What's wrath?"

"That's when someone is so mad they could kill you."

"That makes no sense. If someone wants to kill me, I'll just kill them instead."I realized that I had not done much killing in my life. Perhaps, I had believed Robert in spite of myself.

"Yes, sir."

"I suppose you are going to tell me it won't happen again."

"No, sir."

I realized it was an answer that could mean either, 'No, I'm not going to tell you that,' or, 'No, it is not ever going to happen again.' George picked up the meaning without me clarifying.

"You're damn right you're not going to tell me it will never happen again because you can't guarantee that it won't happen again. Can you?"

"No, I can't."

"You're damn right you can't," he said.

Later, as I left George's office, I realized that was the probably the answer that saved my job.

George paced to the right and back again to the left behind his desk. He looked down at his iPad, and then he sat down.

"These things are not that easy to deal with. Are they?"

"No, Sir, they are not."

"Email is working again. That's a good thing. You're cleaning off the server. Right?"

"Right. Once we've gotten any forensic data there is to be had."

"Just clean it off. I don't want to see any of that shit left on it. And then, I want you to find out where those emails came from and fix it so whoever did this can't come back and do it again. As for you, you're on notice. I'm holding you responsible. I can't help but think that you know more about this than you're saying."

When had I had the opportunity to say anything about it?

"However, these things can be difficult to prove. It takes effort to find evidence and build a good case before you can terminate an employee for cause. It's not impossible, just difficult."

He leaned over his desk and looked at the space between me and the desk's far edge.

"What is not difficult is for an organization to take stock of its changing circumstances and decide that the services of one or more individuals no longer fit into the company's strategic vision."

He looked up from no man's space to stare straight into my face.

"That happens all the time."

"Well," Morgan said when I returned to my desk, "I see you are still employed."

"How do you know?"

"You still have access to the network."

"Oh. I do?"

"But I also see that you are standing up. That either means you can't sit down yet after the ass chewing you received, or you're still not so sure you are going to stay employed from one minute to the next."

I was going to say no, but instead I merely nodded. Morgan was not looking at me, but I know he still saw me nod my head in his mind's eye. He heard my unspoken words.

"If I were you, I would lay off the coffee until my nerves settled, and then I would go ahead and sit down before I got carpal tunnel typing on a low desk from a standing position. I'd say there's a seventy percent chance that you will survive the day and a sixty percent chance you will last the week."

"What makes you so sure?"

"I flunked quantum mechanics at MIT and went into economics instead. I also talked to George before you got here, one scumbag contractor to one scumbag executive. I told him the fact you were so targeted by these emails suggested you held a key defensive position for this company and that someone thought you were an obstacle that needed to be removed."

I didn't say it, but I had the sudden impression that Morgan had saved my bacon. Not only had he saved me from George, but he had saved me from my own self-recriminations. There was a word for getting something good that you didn't deserve when you should have received the very opposite, for someone giving you merits you could not have earned yourself but desperately needed. Robert used to talk about it. I couldn't remember the word.

"By the way, while you were getting read the riot act, I looked up the domain of that Frank.Sinatra@TheSands.com email address. Can guess where it is hosted?"

"Rackspace?"

"No. Amazon!"

"Could you see who the name was registered to?"

"No."

"Man, this guy is pretty fast. He saw me go into Susan's hotel room on Sunday night, and by Friday or Saturday he had registered this domain, written all these emails, spoofed all the addresses, and launched this attack. If I had done all that in such a short amount of time, I would have forgotten something."

"You mean like forgetting to make your DNS registration private?"

"Yeah, something like that."

"I don't agree. I think you were targeted ahead of time. You've been to Blackhat before. There was a strong chance you would be going back. It is no secret that you work for FairWare, and it is also no secret that Susan is head of Data Security for that company. If you go to Susan's Facebook page, you can get some interesting information about her."

"I've never been to her Facebook page."

"Well, why go to her page when you can go to her room? Just saying. But if you were to go to her page, you might be able to pick up a few useful things. One, Susan is quite a fox, and she knows it. Two, she may be a bit of a wild child."

Having sat next to her at the pool and having lain next to her on the bed, I was in no position to argue either point.

"So?"

"So maybe someone doesn't have to put spy cameras in Susan's room or gain control of the camera on her laptop to see you in her room. Maybe you don't have to go to her room or even be seen with her at all. The very fact that you two are both in Vegas, that you are a young, unattached heterosexual male, and that she is fairly hot and knows it are enough for someone to make some plausible and rather intriguing insinuations about you two."

"So I should have argued this with George?"

"I think not. You already admitted to Butch that you helped her with her SDR homework, and the company purchasing records will show that you were on the same plane, maybe even on the same aisle. I wouldn't strain credibility if I were you."

"Then, what's the point?"

"The point is that this attack could have been set up well in advance. The potential for a compromising situation was already there."

"You could guess that I was going to be at Blackhat, but Susan had never been. Who would ever expect her to go this time?"

"No one. The guy had a hand. He was hoping the house would deal him the Susan card. If it hadn't been that card, then he would have played a different hand, maybe one involving a call girl. That would have been embarrassing, but not as effective as this."

"On the other hand," I said, "what if someone were to have sent Susan an email, one tailored to appeal to her and aimed at enticing her to go to the conference herself?"

"Now you're thinking!" said Morgan. "I was wondering when you were going to start helping me out here. Like a phishing email without the payload."

"A phishing email without a payload is less suspicious. Nothing to open. No reason to be suspicious of it."

"So we have an idea how this might have been set up," Morgan said. "Now what?"

"Do you happen to have a cloud server on your own account? I would like to launch a few inquiries of our own aimed at TheSands, but I don't want to do it from the company domain."

"Not really."

"Well, I do. I was hoping to use one not connected to me either, but maybe it is better this way."

"Are you going to hit him back?"

"I don't know. First, we had better secure the fort. What if I see to the perimeter and you start looking for any packages that may have been delivered recently?"

"Delivered since when?"

"I suppose in the last year."

"Too many. Take too long."

"How about you look for anything delivered since we went to Blackhat?"

"That should be doable."

"In between scans, I'll do a few probes at TheSands.com."

"Hey, I may get bored. Just because I am contract scum, why shouldn't I have any fun?"

"Okay. Fine. If you want to build some not-so-fair-ware of your own, send it to me, and I will upload it to my server. From there we can send the goods to Mr. Sinatra."

"Maybe we can get him singing 'The worst is yet to come' before this is over."

"Maybe we can at that."

24 - The Wrong Box

We went to work. Morgan checked the firewall logs. I went to the SIEM. Neither of us could find anything suspicious that had come into the company network except the thousands of emails, and none of those contained any hidden scripts or links. None of the email addresses appeared to come from the addresses they said they came from except Sinatra's. His email, indeed, came from TheSands even if he himself had not sent it. Morgan had tried sending emails to Albert.Einstein@princeton.edu, J.Edgar.Hoover@FBI.gov and the rest. Every one of them bounced back as undeliverable except the one to Frank, and Frank did not reply. The network guys blocked incoming traffic from TheSands.com, and we left in the wee hours of Tuesday to get some rest. When we returned at eight AM, a painfully early hour for me, Butch had come back to the office. He stayed in the office with us till eight that night double checking all the usual vulnerabilities, testing all the known defenses, and rounding up all the usual suspects. Everything appeared to be intact. Then, Butch got on the phone. I think he called Susan, but I could not tell from the conversation. If it was she, he spoke in more guarded tones than normal. After he hung up the phone, he sent us home. Morgan and I were happy to have the pressure lifted, but we knew the situation was not yet well in hand. We obliged Butch and went home, but our work continued. I configured a number of cloud servers, ready to spin up on demand. Morgan collected an arsenal of malwares. He even bought a couple of zero day exploits, just in case. I registered a number of internet domains, all privately, all under assumed identities. We had to be sure that nothing we did could be linked back to us or to FairWare, but we still had no intention of doing any harm, only in performing some rather insistent probes. Then, on Friday evening, the SIEM issued an alert.

Butch had already gone home. Morgan was packing up to leave. The cleaning crew was running the vacuum on the other side of the floor. It took us an hour to determine that it was a false positive, but it gave us the excuse we needed. I called Butch to tell him all was fine but that we wanted to monitor things for awhile. That gave us cover to stay in the building without suspicion from management. Of course, what we were about to do, we could have done from a bar on Sixth Street or from Waco. The office, however, was more convenient. As the vacuums' whine faded into the far reaches of the floor, Morgan and I began our counter-offensive.

"I've decided to give you access to my cloud servers," I said. "There's no point in you having to ferry anything you want to run on them through me."

"So you trust me?"

I was going to say, "The enemy of my enemy is my friend," but I didn't. I merely said, "Yes."

"Tell me this, then. How did you ever get the name 'Augustus'?"

"My mother read Lonesome Dove while she was pregnant."

"Your name is more 'western' than Butch's. In that case, we better saddle up. We've got a long drive ahead of us."

We tried various ways to enter the TheSands.com to see who and what dwelt in that mysterious domain. I sent an email to Frank.Sinatra@TheSands.com from a G-mail account so that Frank could not trace it back to me or to FairWare, not easily anyway. Morgan provided a malicious payload to include in the email. It was really a piece of spy-ware designed to report back to us what was on the server and who was accessing it. He had bought it on the Dark Web with a gift card he had been saving for just such a rainy day. I wrote the email as if The Sands were not a Las Vegas hotel but just another web domain in need of security software. Sinatra was just another server administrator, not a deceased singer. That was the first volley.

We prepared other emails from other accounts to go out at

different times. It was rather a pitiful attack in comparison to the one we had suffered. That attack had been well targeted. The attacker had known me by name. He knew whom I worked for, what room in the hotel I had spent my evenings in and with whom. He seemed to have read my mind. As Morgan had said, he was attacking me. We, on the other hand, were striking back at a pseudonymous email address. We were punching at the cloud. We knew nothing about the person behind the email—except I did know who was responsible. I had met him twice. I recognized him by sight. I did not know his name. I wanted to send him pointed emails that said, "I know who you are Frank. I remember seeing you at Blackhat on lo those two occasions." But telling my nemesis what I knew would have revealed to him how much I did not know. I would only have exposed my ignorance and desperation. There was no point to that.

We set up our emails to go out in delayed succession over the course of several weeks so they would not appear to be a coordinated effort. We decided not to spoof any addresses, but used the ones we had set up for the purpose.

"We don't want to imitate his attack," Morgan said. "What is the old saying?"

"Imitation is the sincerest form of flattery," I said.

"Right! How is it you always know all the old sayings?"

"My—uh—my father taught me. I learned in spite of my best efforts to ignore him."

"Your father? Hmm. My father just knew enough to get away from my mother."

"Too bad," I said.

Why did I think it was too bad? What could have been so great about Morgan's father? He had fathered Morgan. What kind of recommendation was that? Maybe there was more in that recommendation than I had thought.

"My mother was the one who split," I said, "as far as I can figure. Neither one of them came out well, but I think maybe she brought the worst on herself."

"Do you visit your father?"

"He's dead."

"Really? My father lives in Vegas. Anyway, we've got the emails set to go out. Do you want to try a direct assault on TheSands.com?"

"Might as well. Although if we get in, I'm going to be suspicious. Even if it is hard to get in, I'm going to be suspicious. I can't help but think this server is a honeypot, just waiting for us."

"Might be, but what else do we have to go on? We may get caught in the trap, but eventually the trapper is going to come to collect our pelts, and that is when we turn the tables."

"When we're dead?"

"When we're mostly dead."

"I suppose," I said, "there is a degree of protection in being almost dead. The worst is over."

"That's the spirit."

But TheSands.com was well protected. First, it was a domain without a website. That was like a house without a door. When you entered the web address in your browser, nothing came back. Yet, when you pinged it, you could see that it did exist, but what could you do about it?

We tried FTP to see if we could land on a server and then explore the folder structure, but FTP was not activated on the server. Butch had his script on the ready to attempt to crack the FTP password, but there was no password to crack. We probed every port we could think of. TheSands.com was dumb except when Sinatra spoke, and then the conversation went only one way.

Shortly after midnight we gave up and left the building. We wanted to show FairWare that we were zealous for the company's security, but if we stayed too late on a Friday night without any evident reason, our superiors might get suspicious. We could not let Paul or George know what we were doing. It was one thing to defend the company against intrusion, another, to make a counter-strike against the intruder.

Outside we walked together to the parking garage, even though I wasn't parked. We walked up the ramp in the garage avoiding the stairs. No one was there to come careening around a corner and run over us. If there had been, we would have heard him first. I suddenly wished I had driven the Abarth instead of walking.

"There's my car," said Morgan. It was a dirty white Camry. I half expected to see a car seat in the back, but there were only a couple of cardboard printer paper boxes full of various things. "Where's your car?" he said. "Wait! You didn't Car2Go, did you? Because I didn't see one parked out front."

"I didn't either."

"Get in. Use the app, and I'll give you a ride to the nearest one."

As we turned the corner to move down the ramp, I saw a red Ferrari parked by the wall.

"Who's car is that?"

"That's George's 308. He bought it in hopes for a brighter tomorrow and drove it to work one day. That evening he couldn't get it started. Rumor has it he can't afford to get it fixed, so he leaves it here until he raises the money. It's probably safer here than in his own condo garage. Anyway, we all figure that when the company has its IPO, George will sell enough stock to fix his car. When you see the car is no longer here, it means that George has got his stock."

The nearest Car2Go was halfway to my condo. When Morgan heard that, he took me all the way to my front entrance. There was that natural pause as he put the transmission in park.

"Look'" he said. "There's something to be said for doing this kind of work under cover of darkness. I'd rather do it while our target is asleep."

He turned to me in that spacious car, spacious in comparison to a Fiat. His blue eyes burned even in the dim light. In that moment he was more like Butch Cassidy than Butch-our-boss Cassidy himself. From that time on, to the both of us, Butch became merely Paul.

"The attack on you was personal."

"You said that already."

"I think you know who did it. At least, I think you have an idea. That's why you are going the extra mile to strike back beyond our perimeter. I'm not going to ask you who it is, if you even know a name. I'm just going to ask for a time zone. Your best guess, if that's all you have."

I steeled myself in the passenger seat of that Toyota to make no admission of guilt, no confession. I started to say, "I don't know," but instead I said, "Pacific."

"Are you sure?"

"No. Gut feeling."

And, in fact, it was my best guess. From the moment we shared tequila shots at Blackhat, I had thought the man who claimed, with all credibility, to have broken into our system was from California. Maybe he had come from Redmond, but he had not struck me as a Windows man.

"Then we need to shift our tactics," Morgan said.

"How so?"

"When we are staying up to hit him unawares, he is still awake. It's only eleven o'clock in San Jose. If we want to get him while he is asleep, we need to change our timing."

"Oh, no. Not the morning. I can't do morning. I won't do morning."

"We could do it from here."

"Here? From my place?"

"Exactly. We do our counter measures for a couple of hours. We have breakfast. Then, we go into the office about nine—"

"Oh no!"

"Or even eight-thirty. You need to get off this ten o'clock crap. You throw your whole day off."

***

Morgan threw my whole day off. He had me getting up at five AM. I couldn't face going out in the dark to find breakfast. I felt like a vampire trying to get one final feeding in before dawn. To avoid roaming the dark streets in search of a Taco truck, I was forced to cook. I found, however, that I liked my own breakfast tacos as much as the ones out on the street, and when Morgan arrived at a quarter to six, the eggs were just coming out of the skillet. I had to admit, to myself at least, that getting up gave me a big psychological advantage. If I, as vampire, was hurrying in Austin to avoid the central daylight dawn, the Pacific time zone gave me an extra two hours to open any window in California and flutter into that house. It was still four AM there, and, as I had learned from many a conference call, Californians arose late.

But this Californian had his garlic out, and all his doors and windows remained closed to us.

At the office the suspicion and dread hung suspended in the air like a fog. Paul was less forthcoming, more perfunctory. Often, he gave instructions to me through Morgan as if Morgan were the employee and I were the contractor. Susan became totally invisible. Occasionally I put her name in the cc line of an email to see if the green light appeared by her name to show she was on-line. Her light would come and go; it almost seemed to flicker and dim. We thought Paul was in touch with her although Morgan and I could not be sure. Paul did not mention her. When he spoke of management, he only spoke of George.

So, morning by morning I dragged myself out of bed in the dark, hosted Morgan at my table, and sought the one window to TheSands that would let us in. Day by day we searched the company logs and the server files for evidence that we had been compromised ourselves.

And all this time I continued to encounter the man on the street once a week and to pay him the premium on my insurance.

Then one afternoon Morgan insisted that we go for a walk. It was one of those rare Austin days when there was a threat of rain. We were on the far side of the block when he broke the news.

"I think I've got something."

"Really? Did one of our phishing emails get through?"

"Not yet. But I think I found something on one of our boxes."

He turned and faced me directly.

"It looks like a security patch from Red Hat."

"That's it?" I said. "That's nothing. We get those patches every month. I don't know if you have noticed, but Red Hat is our vendor for Linux servers. You expect to see a Red Hat security patch on one of our Linux boxes."

"Not when the box isn't a Red Hat box you don't."

Then, I remembered. We had one server that was not a Red Hat server. It was some other flavor of Linux.

"We have that one box. It's got some kind of weird dependency."

"That's right," Morgan said. "There's some old software running on it that won't run on a Red Hat server."

"And that server has it's own set of patches. The server team hates it."

"So?" he said.

Why did Morgan always have to ask leading questions? This time, though, coming up with an answer to his question was not just a relief. It was an enlightenment.

"So," I said, "someone put the wrong patch on the wrong box."

"That's right. Now, did our guys do that?'"

"Could be," I said. "Someone goofed up and put that server on the deployment script with all the rest."

"But you just said our guys hate that server. Doesn't seem likely they would forget and put the one odd box on the deployment script with all the rest."

"No," I said, "no it doesn't. You think it's suspicious?"

"I think it warrants looking into."

"Well, if one of our guys put in on there by mistake, it needs to come off, but beyond that, I don't know."

"That's true," Morgan said. "But what if someone else put it on there by mistake? Not because he wasn't paying attention but because he didn't know any better."

"Because he's new?"

"Because he doesn't work here."

"If he doesn't work here," I said, "he shouldn't be putting security patches on our box."

"And that suggests…?"

"Mistletoe."

"Mistletoe? Excuse me?"

"When I was growing up, there was a tree outside my father's apartment. It looked just fine all summer, but then in November the leaves fell off, and there was one patch of green that remained. It was mistletoe. You couldn't see it because it blended in with the other leaves, but when those fell, it stood out plain as day."

"Stood out," said Morgan, "as the parasite it was."

"It's odd," I said, "the very thing that enabled it to hide on the tree eventually gave it away."

"Now, who says there is no God?"

I was going to say that I said so. I was about to say that a loving God wouldn't allow malware to be put on servers in the first place and that he wouldn't allow thousands of emails to flood a company to accuse an innocent man of screwing his boss. But I didn't say any of that because for a moment I thought he had said something else. I thought I heard him say, "Who says there is no father."

But I must have been mistaken.

***

When we got back to the office, Paul was waiting.

"Where have you guys been? You've got a company to protect."

"What?" I said. "Has something happened?"

Had Paul discovered the Red Hat package?

"George has something to announce. We were all supposed to have been in his office ten minutes ago. Don't you guys read your text messages?"

Paul shook his head. As he led us past the cubicle farm to George's office, he looked less like Paul Newman as Butch Cassidy and more like Strother Martin on the payroll mule train.

"Morons!" Morgan whispered. "I've got morons on my team."

"He can't be firing us," I said. "We'd be going in one at a time."

"And he can't be giving us raises. He would call you in alone, and I'd be notified by my vendor. Most likely he'll be telling us, in a round about way—"

"That we're morons—"

"—but indispensable all the same. Temporarily."

I smiled at that even though my stomach was beginning to burn. We entered George's empty office and stood in a loose semi-circle around his desk. George entered right behind us. He did not seem to be aware that we were late. I moved aside to let him pass, but he stood just inside the door.

"Gentlemen, I'll make this brief. As of this morning Susan Wilson is no longer in the employment of FairWare.com. Effective immediately Paul Cassidy is acting manager of Security. I know you all will give him the same kind of support that you gave Susan in the past. Paul will also be acting Executive Director of IT in my absence."

Paul looked at George as if he were Jesus on the mountain top. His feet almost came off the floor.

"Well, that's it. Everyone back to work."

I stepped aside again expecting George to be getting back to work himself at his desk, but he disappeared out the door. We turned to Paul for further information.

"All the protocols will remain the same for incident reporting and response," he said. "You both will report directly to me, and I will inform George of anything requiring his attention."

"Where is George going to be?"

"Palo Alto."

He did not follow us back to our desks. In fact, he did not return to his desk for the rest of the afternoon.

"'No longer in the employment of FairWare.com,'" Morgan said as we made our way back.

"Does that mean she was fired?"

"She didn't 'leave to pursue other opportunities.' That statement would have meant she had resigned after being given the invitation."

"Resign or be fired."

"Exactly."

"There is one other possibility," Morgan said. "She resigned, under pressure, but not because she was forced to. She did it out of protest. She did it preemptively, and so they didn't even give her the courtesy of saying she had left to pursue a brighter future. They didn't want to admit that she did it under her own volition because that implies they had no control. So, they just said she's gone."

Sometimes I thought Morgan, the contractor, was amazing. For someone not part of the company, he read remarkably well between the company lines.

I didn't respond though. I was fighting back a crushing sense of guilt. Resignation, termination, termination disguised as resignation —whichever one of these possibilities was the case, Susan's exit was my fault. Regardless of the fact that nothing had happened in Vegas, Susan had taken the fall for me. What was I going to do for her?

When we arrived at our desks, Morgan turned and looked me in the eye. I don't know if he saw the turmoil I was trying desperately to hide behind my poker face, but if he did, he wasn't going to stop there. He seemed intent on penetrating past the turmoil to my essential self. I, on the other hand, had never really thought I had an essential self. Even so, I tried to hide it.

"Do you know what this all means?"

"No." I said.

"The IPO. George is going to work on the IPO. That means Paul is going to have his hands full being George. He won't even have time to be Susan. And do you know what that means?"

"We have complete responsibility for security now? I'm on call twenty-four by seven for the next several months?"

"It means we have free reign. What is the most important priority regarding security when a company is aiming to go public?"

"No bad publicity!"

"Exactly! So what is our job?"

"To keep us out of Dark Reading and out of The Wall Street Journal?"

"Yes."

"I don't know. Now that Paul is manager, he's going to want to manage."

"Paul is going to be busy with other stuff, and the main thing he wants, the only thing he wants, is for us not to give him any bad news. If he reports anything bad to George, he will be busted back to security team lead again. He may talk about the protocol, but he doesn't even want to hear anything bad. That means that we have to handle this all by ourselves."

"That's what I was saying," I said. "We are on our own."

"But it also means we can handle it the way we want."

"As long as we stay out of the news?"

"Right."

"Paul won't be looking over our shoulder?"

"Only perfunctorily. And if he does decide to get involved, we drop the hint that we are on the brink of a security incident, and he will back off immediately. He will throw up his hands and tell us to do whatever we have to do."

And that is exactly what Paul did. We didn't have to say a word. He somehow knew that the moment he asked us any questions or gave us any directions, a giant sink hole would open at his political feet. So, Paul went about doing what an acting manager/acting director does on the verge of an IPO, and we began our investigation into the Red Hat update that landed on the wrong Linux box.

25 – The Patch

The company IPO gave us the perfect cover. We started our work early and remained late into the evening, but so did everyone else. To Paul's mind we were only being diligent and adding value to the company. He didn't suspect us of doing anything nefarious or desperate. We moved about the office with a sense of urgency but not panic, and the office seemed to take its cue from us. We set the tone. This was how you were supposed to behave to prepare for becoming rich.

"Keep up the good work," said Paul.

"Yes, Sir."

If it had been Christmas, visions of sugar plums would have danced in his head.

Morgan sent me to see the server admins to ask them about the suspicious Red Hat update. I knew I would have to approach them delicately.

I chose Aston as my informant. Aston wore a silver pony tail even though he was under forty. We called him Server Dude. I asked him about the patch.

"Why would anyone think we would put Red Hat patches on that box?" he asked. "Do they think we don't know our business?"

"No! Nothing like that. I just want you to take a look."

I convinced him to log onto the server.

"Why is there a Red Hat patch on this box? This is not a Red Hat box.

"I don't know why. I was hoping you could help me understand."

"We don't put Red Hat patches on non-Red Hat boxes. Period."

"Is that a policy?"

"No! Why would we have a policy to tell us not to do something stupid?"

"I guess you wouldn't."

"Why would we write a policy that says we are not going to put patches on the wrong servers? You might as well have a policy that says, 'Don't make any mistakes.'"

"That would be ridiculous," I said. I didn't tell him that Paul, in his former incarnation as Butch, had once suggested that we adopt a very similar policy ourselves.

"This is not just a bug fix."

"It's not?"

"No. It's a security patch. I remember. It was a very significant one."

I didn't tell him that I didn't remember it myself even though it was my job to know such things.

"But it won't do any good on this box."

"How do you think this patch got here? Did someone put this server in the wrong list?"

"Well, if someone did, it's not in the wrong list now. This is not the latest patch. We've installed another one since, and this server does not have it. Let me see who put it there."

I watched him stare into that black screen with the white text that Linux guys favored. It seemed to match the dark world they inhabited, dark, at least, to anyone watching over their shoulders.

"Well, whoever put that patch on this server used the same administrator's security account the patch script uses. It's not the same account we human beings use when we install things on servers. If we did include this box in with all the others by mistake, we didn't make the same mistake twice. That's all I can tell you."

"Okay, well thanks anyway."

"Sorry, but this brings up bad memories. I remember applying this patch."

"You do? I thought you didn't."

"No, I remember applying both of them to all the Red Hat boxes."

"Both of them?"

"Yeah, the one you found, and the one we put on after it. I remember because we applied them three days apart."

"Isn't that unusual? Did Red Hat find a bug in the first patch and have to provide a fix pronto immediate?"

"No, they were both just regular monthly patches."

"Then, why did you apply them one after the other?"

Server Dude leaned in close to my face. I almost backed away to preserve my personal space, but I didn't dare miss what he had to say.

"Don't breathe a word of this. We forgot to apply the first patch. There was so much other crap going on that our schedule slipped. Then, we got the notification from Red Hat about the next patch, and we thought, 'What the fudge?' We thought about just skipping the first patch, but that would have violated policy. Plus, if anyone came around to audit us—you know, in preparation for the IPO—it wouldn't look good. So, we applied the first patch, and three days later, we put on the second. Now we are caught up."

I told Morgan.

"Someone put the wrong box in the list of servers that they were going to get the patch," he said. "Then, he realized his mistake and took it out of the list in time for the next patch. That's all. I thought we had found something."

But then I had an idea.

"Suppose that file never was in the patching script," I said. "What if a hacker gets into our network and sees we are running Red Hat Linux on our servers? He realizes, then, that if he wants to put a malicious payload on our boxes, he can disguise it as a Red Hat security patch. No one will notice. Only he doesn't notice that we have this one odd box that isn't Red Hat, and he puts this file disguised as a security patch on it anyway."

"But that means," said Morgan, "that he put the file on all our boxes. We only noticed it on this box because it was the odd one out, but the malware, if it is malware, is on every box. Now, we do have a problem. How are we going to get the bad file off all our boxes without management knowing about it and freaking out?"

"No," I said. "We don't have to worry about that because our guys have already taken care of it. There was one other thing our hacker didn't know. We were nearly a month late applying that Red Hat patch. He thought he was writing over a patch we already had done with his own infected version. Instead, our guys wrote over his file with the correct patch."

"So, you are saying that our Red Hat boxes are all likely okay."

"Yes. The only box we have to worry about is the one you found had the file on it."

"What do we do then? Do we remove it?"

I didn't answer. I took a deep breath. It is surprising sometimes how difficult it can be to breathe.

Morgan asked again.

"Is that what you want to do, Gus?"

"No," I said. "I want to do what Susan said I should have done during another security incident months ago. I want to watch the box. I want to listen to every port the box has open, and I want to examines every packet it sends or receives. I think it will give our hacker away."

"Are you sure that is a good idea? Are you sure you just don't want to wipe the file off the box and be done with it?"

"Yes. If we do that, our guy will only come back, and then we will have even less of an idea where he is or what he is up to."

"But maybe by that time, George and Paul will not be so likely to connect the attack to you. If they find out now about this file on the wrong box, they will tie it together with the emails and blame you immediately."

"That is a chance I will have to take."

"We are playing poker again, aren't we?"

"Maybe so."

"You're the employee. That makes you the boss. I don't have a bet in this hand."

And so we laid low and watched the box.

The box only had four ports open: one for a database, one for regular internet traffic, one for file transfers that were not secured, and one for secured, encrypted file transfers. The box talked a lot to the database. That was normal, but it also made a number of encrypted file transfers: SFTP's. The trouble was, we had no idea what our box was sending, and did not know where the files were going. The destinations for these encrypted transfers were just nameless IP addresses somewhere out in the cloud. There was no way for us to tell who owned them.

"If only the box would send a regular FTP," Morgan said. "Then, we could at least see what it was sending. We'd know if we were being robbed blind, and maybe we would get an idea who was robbing us."

I thought of Chairman Mao at the Texas Hold 'em table, and I had another idea.

"I'm going to call Server Dude," I said, "and tell him to close the secure port."

"Port 22? Once again, I have to ask. Are you sure you want to do that? Won't it just tip off the hacker?"

"It might. It might also induce him to tip his hand."

"Like I said," said Morgan, "in the absence of Paul (who is busy plugging his ears), you are the boss. I'm just the contractor. My role is to advise and do the heavy lifting. But in this case, you are going to have to talk Server Dude into this yourself."

He crossed himself again. "Go with God, my son," he said.

"There you go with God again," I said. "Are you trying to hedge your bet?"

As soon as I had said that, I regretted it. I was not hedging my bet. I was all in.

It was just three nights later that Morgan awakened me up from a fitful sleep. I had been crawling through Airman's Cave. Ahead of me were the glowing soles of a pair of green running shoes. Try as I might I could not catch up with them, and I was stuck in the Birth Canal, trying to get in or trying to get out. Aston the Server Dude was behind me telling me I was trying to crawl out the wrong port, but how could that have been the case when he was following me and complaining because I was slow? Then the phone rang. I tried to be as responsive as Susan had been when I had called her with news. This was news all right. The call was from Morgan.

"What is it?" I said.

"ET phoned home."

"What? He did?"

"Yes. I put an alert on the box. He sent a plain FTP file transfer. I am able to read it like a book. How did you know he would do that if you closed the secure port?"

"I'll tell you later when I get into the office."

"All right. If you want to be cagey. It's just as well, because that is not the best part. Guess where he sent the file?"

"I don't know," I said, but I realized that was wrong as soon as I said it. I did know.

"TheSands.com!"

"No," said Morgan. "Well, okay, he did send something to TheSands, but that is not the only place he sent it. I think the other place is more significant."

"Where was the other place?"

"I'll tell you when you get into the office," he said.

Turnabout is fair play. That was another Robert-ism, but it sounded even older than he. I bet it came from the other side of World War II, from his own father.

"I'm coming in," I said, "but not yet. I want to get a little more sleep."

And I did. I slept more during the next few hours than I had all night.

I arrived in the office at my usual time, not my be-ever-vigilant-on-the-brink-of-the-IPO time, but my normal ten o'clock Austin/eight o'clock California standard time. I was rested. Morgan looked a little peeved.

"Okay, mastermind. Why did you close port 22?"

"I have to go first?"

"Yes. You give me your explanation, and I give you the news."

I was glad that Morgan and I had reached a greater level of understanding and cooperation, but it was good in a way to be back on the same old footing.

"Okay. I closed port 22 because the box was using it to send encrypted files that we couldn't read anyway."

"That's obvious. That's not the reason you did it."

"You're right. I closed the encrypted traffic port because I hoped that the hacker would then turn around and send something over the unencrypted port."

"But why would you think the hacker would do that? Why would he build a piece of malware that resorted to the wide open port when he could use secure port? That would be stupid."

"That's right. That would be stupid. No competent hacker would do that, but a developer would."

"What does that mean?"

"If I am writing a piece of malware, I'm writing a piece of software just like any other piece of software. It presents me with problems. It doesn't do what I want it to do at first. I have to set it up to send files that my target—you in this case—can't read. I can't let you read them off the wire because I don't want you to know what I am up to. So, I'm going to send those over the secure port. But first I want to see if I am sending anything at all. After that I will worry about the security. So, I just set up a simple test to send the data to my browser. Once I see I am getting what I want, I put in the code to use port 22 to do a secure file transfer. That's ironic, isn't it? I have send the data I stole from you securely so you can't see that I am stealing it. Only I have a little more trouble getting that to work, so I put in a switch. When port 22 is open, I use the secure file transfer. When it is closed, I default to the old code that sends the data without any security to me so I can work out my bugs. All I have to do is turn the port on to use the secure path, or turn it off to use the open path. Once I have all the issues worked out, I leave port 22 open, and the program uses the secure path every time."

"You sound like you've done this before."

"Only, I forget to take out the old code. After all, it's not like I have someone reviewing my work."

"Oh!" said Morgan. "I think I see. When we turned off the secure port, the program reverted to the old code which used the non-secure port, and so we got to see what it was doing."

"Yes. That was the idea."

Morgan gave me his most suspicious look.

"Amazing deduction, Sherlock. Actually, it was more like Edgar Allan Poe than Conan Doyle. Poe wrote the first detective story, you know, and he called his detective's approach to solving problems ratiocination. It involved reason and imagination. Well done. I would never have thought of that, and even if I had, I would never have thought it was worth trying. Now, would you like me to tell you what Old Blue Eyes is up to? I assume only Frank Sinatra would be sending data to TheSands.com. You see, he did send the data to TheSands, but it was still encrypted. He encrypted it before he sent it, so even though it went over the open port, I still couldn't read it."

"Oh," I said. "So, I was wrong."

"But," Morgan added, "he also sent information about what he sent and where he sent it to another site in plain text, and that I could read. Do you know where he sent it?"

"No."

I was beginning to get tired again.

"Golden Gate Software: GGS."

"Who is that?".

"They're a lot like us," said Morgan. "A lot like you, anyway, since I am not an actual employee here. Same size as this company. Same kind of products. A competitor, I would say."

He showed me their website.

"I should have known," I said.

"Why should you have known that? I didn't. I still half expected the Chinese."

He looked at me quizzically. I changed the subject.

"Look!" I said. "They're hiring."

"Let's meet the staff," Morgan said.

We opened a web page of pictures and biographies looking for someone we knew. Halfway down the list I caught my breath.

"What is it?" he asked.

"Nothing. I thought I recognized someone."

"Who? Which one?"

I pointed to the screen.

"Who is it?"

"It says right here."

"I can read. But who is it? Who is the man behind the name?"

"I don't know. He just looks like someone I may have seen at Blackhat."

"So? I've seen lots of people at Blackhat. None of them took my breath away. None of the men anyway. Did you talk to this guy?"

"Maybe."

"Maybe? Let's go for a walk."

"Why? It's getting hot out there."

"Come on. Lock your screen. It's not that hot yet."

We were on the other side of the block before Morgan spoke again.

"All right. Spill it. Who is that guy."

"I don't know his name. At least, I didn't know it before we saw his bio on the web site. We met once at Blackhat. Actually, we met twice. The first time we had drinks together. He wore a false name tag. It was obvious."

"What did you talk about? The Dark Web? The show girls? The odds at the blackjack table?"

"No. We talked about computer security."

"Whose security?

"Our security. FairWare's security."

"Were you asking him for advice?"

"Not exactly."

We waited for a car to pull out of the parking garage. We walked in silence past a homeless man on a bench. He was not the one that I knew. It was the wrong corner.

"FairWare had a breach a couple of years ago. This guy approached me at Blackhat that same year and in so many words claimed responsibility for the attack. We had a long conversation about it all, professional to professional over bourbon and tequila. Like I said, he wore a false name tag. I did, too."

"Only he figured out your name."

"Yes. Seeing that we were in Vegas, I'd wager he knew my name before he ever came up to me. It was part of the game. I've been watching out for him ever since, waiting for him to show himself in our system again. I saw him just briefly at this year's Blackhat, but he didn't say much."

"But then the emails came, and you suspected him because of the Blackhat association and your past history. But you didn't know he was the one who did it until now. Not until we traced him back to his company website and saw his picture."

"Right. Until then I just guessed. I hoped it was him."

"You hoped?"

"Well, yes. How many secret enemies can a guy afford to support? One is enough. I gotta' tell you, Morgan, it was a shock to see his face on the website, but it was also a relief."

"Of course it was. I understand completely. You still don't know, do you, why he picked you?"

"No. I still don't know that."

"I would like to think," said Morgan, "that his actual target was this company, but you stood in the way. His primary motivation, at first anyway, was to steal something from the company. But then, he began to see you as someone he wanted to attack in particular. He saw in you something he hated."

"Something he hated? Why? Because I stood in his way?"

"Partly. But part of it just seems personal."

"Yeah. I think I sensed that. I don't know why."

"Don't take this the wrong way. Sometimes someone sees a weakness in someone else, and he hates that person because he has the same weakness in himself. He hates himself because of his own weakness, but he never admits it. Instead, he hates the other person. Kind of a displaced hatred."

"That's just lovely."

"But I think he saw something else in you, something that he hated because he feared it."

"Oh, this is beginning to get crazy."

"Hey, keep Austin weird!"

"This guy's from San Francisco. He has plenty of weirdness of his own."

"So you were right about him being from California."

"I suppose so."

We walked on. We had already circled the block, but as we approached the street with our building, we turned north and walked away. Neither of us was ready to go back. Neither wanted to be within camera distance of the front door.

"So, what do we do now? We can block the IP for TheSands and for GGS.com. We can clean off the script from server. The trouble is-"

"He'll be back," I said.

"Yeah. He'll be back. So, I ask the question again. What do we do?"

"I don't know about 'we'," I said. "I think I need to look for a job."

"Look," Morgan said. "I understand you are under stress here, but I don't know if getting another job right now is the best thing. I don't think it is necessarily the best thing for the company, believe it or not, and I don't know if it is the best thing for you either."

"Oh, I don't want to get another job. I just want to look for one."

"Just look for one? Why? Where?"

"San Francisco, of course."

"San Francisco? Of course!"

26 - Cold California

It took me two weeks to get the interview. I used the Pacific/Central time zone difference to my advantage. I booked a flight for an early Thursday morning leaving Austin before I would think about arriving at work. The flight arrived in San Francisco in time for an eleven o'clock interview with those late rising Californians. I would be able to fly out and still put in a half day of work during the latter half of my usual hours. Paul let me have the time off without question. He was anxious to believe that the security crisis had passed, and maybe he was hopeful that I was interviewing and might leave for employment elsewhere. It all worked to the benefit of my plan.

During the flight I installed HackWave and GNU Radio on my laptop. I sat in almost the same row of the plane where I had been with Susan going to Las Vegas. This time I was by the window. Her memory was nearly as distracting as her physical presence. I wished that things could have been different, but I was glad that they had turned out the way they had. I had gained something when Susan had left Las Vegas, but I could not figure out what it was.

I arrived at the airport with only my carry on bag. I hired a taxi to take me into town and arrived at the offices of Golden Gate Software with just five minutes to spare. As the receptionist took me to the conference room for my interview, it occurred to me that my plan had a flaw. My man might not show. Someone else could be there instead. He could be out of the office or called away on an intrusion incident of his own. Maybe he didn't start work until noon.

When the conference room door swung open, however, there

were three men waiting there for me. My target was number three. As I walked in the door, I began to fear that he somehow knew in advance I was the one who had applied for the job even though I had used an assumed name. I had to tell myself that was not likely. Morgan had created a plausible Facebook page for the job candidate I was becoming, and I had crafted a Linked-in account for him as well. It all looked good from the surface, but if my mark had dug a little deeper, he would have seen that my online trail was rather short and my online identity was rather thin.

Apparently he had done no such digging. I think the company had placed the resume before him only moments before I walked in. The shock on his face as he looked up from the resume to see me walking in the door told me that my stratagem had worked. My entrance was perfect.

The first of the three men rose from the table.

"Welcome, Mr. Schultz. Welcome to Golden Gate Software. My name is Dhan Hoc, but people around here call me Number One. Star Trek, you know. Part of our office culture. I wanted to tell you so that it would not throw you if you heard it from one of my co-workers."

"Sounds like fun."

"Would you like some espresso?"

"Please."

We shook hands all around. I made it a point to look my man Number Three in the eye.

"And you," I said, "I think I know you. I think I've seen you at Blackhat. Did we meet?"

"I don't think so."

"Your name is—?"

"Boris Burns."

"Yes," I said. "That's right. I'm Harry Schultz. I know your reputation. I have followed your work closely."

"Mr. Schultz," he nodded. "You have?"

He ended in an uneasy smile. His voice had lost every trace of that James Bond villain tone that he had assumed during our prior two conversations.

"Let's get started," said Number One. "We don't like to ask questions in our interviews like 'What kind of tree would you be?' or

'What key piece of current technology do you think will be obsolete in five years and what will replace it?' We prefer to ask direct relevant questions that get right to the point but allow our candidates to show us who they are. Okay so far?"

"Fine."

"How you think you could enhance the security preparedness of Golden Gate Software and where do you think our greatest vulnerability lies?"

"Thank you for not asking those other questions," I said, "although I admit I tried to prepare in case you did. I would have said redwood for my tree because this is northern California, but actually the only redwood I have ever seen is the kind they make decks out of. I have no idea what will be obsolete in five years except I hope it's performance reviews because they never seem to have any bearing on your salary anyway."

"We couldn't agree more. We got rid of reviews last year. I suppose that makes us ahead of the times."

"California is always ahead," I said, "despite being two hours behind."

This was going better than I had expected. I almost wished I could maintain the fiction and see if I could get the job as Harry Schultz.

"But now tell us where our greatest vulnerability lies and what you would do to enhance our preparedness."

"On my way here this morning, I was thinking about this. I mean, what else is a security professional going to be asked about in an interview? I suppose the truism is that our greatest threat comes from what we don't know. In my present job I spend considerable time on the Dark Web familiarizing myself with what there is to be afraid of. I do that so I will know what to expect from an attack when it comes. And my company has been attacked. Quite recently, in fact. Yet, I was just as surprised as if I had never looked up the price of a zero day exploit on my TOR browser. I was taken aback even though I had tried to prepare. By the way, in case you guys ever go looking for other jobs, you shouldn't do what I just did. You should not admit to a prospective employer that your current company got hacked on your watch."

No one said a word. Boris still looked uncomfortable but no more so than Number One.

"It makes me wonder, however, how you would react if you had a breech. So, for the purposes of this interview, I have devised a little demonstration. The idea is, of course, that if I can show you a weakness, I can show you how to protect yourselves from an attack on that weakness. By my own admission, however, I have to say that conclusion doesn't necessarily follow. Just because I can find one chink in your armor doesn't mean I can find the critical flaw, the one that can be used to bring you down. It certainly doesn't mean I can protect you from either the chink or the flaw. Besides, I have begun to change my mind."

"Change your mind?" said Number One. "About what?"

"I'm not so sure anymore that the greatest threat lies with what we don't know. I think the biggest danger may be in the things that we do know, that we know very well, but that we are powerless to change because they paralyze us with fear."

I couldn't tell if they were embarrassed by my blatantly philosophical statement or if they were uneasy with what I said. I was afraid I had overplayed my hand and that the interview would be cut short.

"What was the demonstration?" said Number One. "We'd like to see it. We have no fear here at Golden Gate."

"Really? I have fear. Lots of it. That is why I have insurance. But my demonstration is twofold. First, my name is not Harry Schultz. My Facebook account is false. My Linked-in information is fabricated. I have never worked at any of the places listed there although they do reflect my actual experience. Here is my real resume."

I opened my bag, pulled out three copies, and handed them around. Boris raised an eyebrow of recognition, but the look of uneasiness still clung to his face.

"Augustine Bishop," said Number One. "But how do we know this is your real name?"

"I think Boris can confirm that. You see, we have met before. In fact, Boris, I think I may have received some email from you recently. Something related to Redhat."

I saw Boris's Adam's apple move downward.

"Yes. I think you have."

"My point is, gentlemen, that even with social media and big data, we can still be deceived. Now this deception would not have stood very long. I would not have passed your reference checks even if I had survived this interview. Boris would have spoken up. He was only biding his time, and we both knew it. But I did get in the door. In the parlance of network security, I got past the DMZ, and I am now behind the firewall."

This time Number Two spoke. Boris was still tense, but Number Two looked positively indignant at my mention of the firewall. He must have been in charge of the network.

"You are not behind our firewall. You are in our conference room, and you have access to our guest network, but you are not in our internal network."

"But I am," I said, "or I could be soon."

I now pulled my laptop out of my bag with the HackWave connected to the USB port. I opened the book and showed them the waterfall of radio transmissions.

"I'm sorry I did not get here earlier to be more prepared. I just had to make some guesses about your network, but here are all the wireless transmissions to your routers. It looks like nearly everyone here is working wirelessly. Let's just click on one. Look! ASCI. Plain text. Harmless enough, but if we wait long enough, someone will enter a password, and then—".

I snipped the imaginary password out of thin air with my two fingers like scissors.

"—and then I'm in."

"I think we have seen quite enough," said Number Two. He stood up from his chair. Number One waved him back down.

"Sit, Jim. If he had meant us any harm, he wouldn't have shown all this to us. And, Mr. Bishop is quite right. Quite right. He could grab your password or mine out of the air."

"That's right," said Boris. "We access all our internal websites without using secure connections."

"That is correct, Chekhov," said Number One. "I hate to admit it, but Mr. Bishop here has us at his mercy. By the way, Boris's Star Trek name is Chekhov. It goes with Boris."

"Of course," I said. "If you had called him Frank, I would really have been surprised. You know, Frank as in Sinatra. That would have made no sense, would it?"

"No. None."

"After all," I said, "Frank comes, I think, from Francis, and Francis was a saint."

"We don't allow saints here," said Number One. "I mean not in San Francisco. Not that type of saint."

He leaned a little towards me as if he were examining me very carefully.

"You might pass muster though," he said.

I winced a little at that, but I couldn't very well argue the point.

"Tell me, Mr. Bishop. What did you do when you were recently hacked?"

"First we were hit with an email attack, but that was just a diversion. You know how email attacks are. They are directed at people. These were meant to discredit and demoralize, and they did, but we knew we needed to keep our eyes open, and eventually, we found where we had been penetrated."

"Was it through the emails?" asked Number One.

"I don't think so, although I can't really say how it got there, this script that we found. But we started watching to see what it would do, and eventually, we were able to trace it back."

"Back to the site where it came from?" said Number One.

"Back to the person who instigated the attack."

"Really?"

No one spoke for several moments while the officers of the Enterprise took all this in.

"Now that you have found the perpetrator," said Chekhov/Boris, "what are you going to do?"

"Nothing. Yet."

Number One and Jim seemed almost relieved as it they were the perpetrators and were happy to learn that they were not going to be prosecuted.

"That word 'yet'," said Boris, "it sounds like a threat."

"It would be if I were speaking to the person who hacked our system. For him it would be a threat. But I wouldn't call it that. I would call it a warning."

"What is the warning?" Number One asked. "What are you going to do ultimately?"

"We are going to do nothing, not unless our perpetrator attempts any further intrusions into our systems. Then, we will act."

"But what will you do? Besides quarantine the script and stop the attack?"

"We will expose him. Like I said, we know who he is. First, I will let him know that we have identified him. Then, I will make it clear that if he does anything else, I will reveal his identity to other people as well, people to whom he would not want it revealed that he was a hacker. People like his employer. Or his family."

Everyone seemed to know what I was saying, but since I was being interviewed for a job, I thought I needed to be very clear.

"It is a funny thing in our internet society. There is nothing more valuable than an identity. Everyone wants a genuine identity, but they also want a second identity as well, one they can hide behind. Everyone wants to keep his own identity whole and intact, but everyone also wants to be someone else. It is safer. No one wants his true self to be known, not someone involved in nefarious or shameful activities, and there are a lot of those on the web."

"I assume you have the technical wherewithal to do this," said Number One.

"I do."

"You also seem to favor more of an offensive response to computer security rather than a purely defensive posture."

"No, I favor an offensive response to computer insecurity."

That was something Morgan would have said.

"I mean, it depends upon the circumstances. If I am able to make my network fortress secure, then I can afford to remain purely defensive. If I cannot do that, then I must move beyond my boundaries to eliminate the threat."

"So, going on the offensive is an admission of weakness," said Boris.

"I suppose that is true, but it is a truth that everyone recognizes. It's not like I am admitting something that my opponent doesn't already know, and it doesn't do me any good to pretend."

"No, it doesn't. But, when it comes to computer security, we are all weak, are we not? We could all justify going on the offensive."

"Only when someone is there to take persistent advantage of us. Otherwise, a little weakness is not such a bad thing. One can be too strong and too secure."

I did not know what I meant by that.

"But what is weakness if it is not being vulnerable? And, how can there be such a thing as vulnerability or weakness, if no one takes advantage of it?"

"All I can say to that is try being strong all the time and see where it gets you."

Boris smiled as if to say, "I intend to," but his smile trailed off at the end as if he himself were not completely convinced.

"Well," said Number One, "you've certainly given us something to think about. I'm not so sure, though, to be perfectly honest, that we are ready to take on an offensive posture here at Golden Gate. So far we have managed to stay pretty secure by building a strong defense and not stirring up the pot. We believe in being strong and in keeping up a strong defense."

He looked at me quite directly as he said that.

"Good shields but no photon torpedoes," I said.

"What?"

"You know. Star Trek? Office culture?"

He stared at me incomprehensibly. Obviously, I did not belong to the Federation.

Number One stood up. My genuine resume was still in his hand.

"Your actual technical qualifications seem very good. Your experience is impressive. So is your false experience. You would be close to what we are looking for, but you present us with a basic philosophical change of direction I am not sure we want to make. Boris, would you show Mr. Bishop out, please?"

He looked down uneasily at my computer with the SDR waterfall still showing all his wireless signals. I removed the HackWave from the USB port and closed the screen. I thought about telling them all to live long and prosper, but I decided against it.

Boris took me all the way to the street.

"We have an Uber driver that we keep almost on retainer. He is faster and cheaper than the cabs. I will call him for you to take you to the airport. There's a little coffee shop just down the block where you can wait. He won't be long. I'll give him your name."

Whatever tell-tale expressions I had seen in his face before had disappeared. Now I stared into stone.

"See you again at Blackhat," he said. He did not extend his hand.

"If you don't hear from me before," I said.

He knew exactly what I meant.

My walk to the coffee shop was all too brief. The weather was delightful even if the air was moist. I hardly had time to order a black french roast when a Corolla pulled up to the curb and an eager looking man in a zombie apocalypse tee shirt stepped out.

"Augustus?"

Only after the plane had taken off and turned east did I realize that Boris had given the Uber driver just my first name. That was part of the informality of Californians. Everyone went by his first name, but Boris had given him my full first name, my formal name. He did not know to call me 'Gus'.

It was back in the office before seven o'clock San Francisco time. I wondered if Boris was still in his office. Morgan was gone, but he had left a hand-written note tucked under my keyboard.

"How did it go?"

I answered his note with a text.

"Delivered the message in person. Think it had the desired effect. Pacific Daylight Time will tell. Don't think I'll get the job."

I spent a couple of hours looking at server and firewall logs. I checked the server where we had first found the malware for any more Redhat patches. There were none. Nothing looked amiss. I looked for TheSands.com. I could not find it by domain name or by IP address. Emails I sent to Frank.Sinatra@TheSands.com came back undeliverable. Boris had worked fast and erased all his tracks. I checked my own email for any unusual messages. Everything seemed in order. I spent my last couple of hours perusing the Dark Web and watching the SIEM. Finally, about eleven-thirty Austin time, I went home with a qualified sense of security. I decided to walk home home to erase the effects of seven hours of airline seating.

No one stopped or called out to me on my way.

27 - Burial Grounds

When I returned from San Francisco, I changed my diet for awhile. I abandoned hot food and tried more mellow fare. Yet, after a brief season of macaroni and cheese, mashed potatoes and gravy, meat loaf, chicken fried steak, and fried chicken; I went back to the Thai. I lingered awhile in the comfort, but I returned to the spice.

"Joe! Where have you been?" Joe said when I walked in the door of MyThai. "I thought maybe you were dead. Or on a diet. But you're not dead, and you're sure not on a diet!"

I looked down. You could see my navel under my tee shirt.

"I've been under a little stress," I said. "Maybe I better take it easy on the noodles."

"Maybe you better take it easy on the beer."

I shuddered, but I nodded. Joe had a point.

I sat down at the table by the counter and waited. Things had not developed so very badly after all.

Boris had apparently disappeared from our network. Either my warning had worked, or he had gone so deep underground that he had exceeded my abilities to detect him. As Morgan said, they called it Computer Science, but that was mostly marketing.

Golden Gate Software offered me no employment. I really hadn't expected to get a job, and I had no plans to accept one if they had offered it. Yet, I was still disappointed. I could not help but wonder: was it my aggressive approach to computer security they did not relish, or were they put off when I used Star Trek against them?

"It is so obvious," I told Morgan, "that they are not boldly going anywhere."

"Their whole foundation is shaky," he said, "but somehow they remain standing. Of course, you remain standing on a shaky foundation yourself. I was afraid we were going to fire you because of your little email debacle."

But I had kept my job. FairWare's IPO had been delayed, but rumor in the office said that it was still in the works. We were all waiting for the company to issue stock and make us all rich. George had not moved his Ferrari out of the garage, but it appeared he had waxed it in anticipation of the day when he could hire a mechanic and the car would run once more.

"The trouble is," said Morgan, "you don't get enough credit. Everyone knows you were the target of the emails. No one knows you thwarted a much more serious intrusion."

It was true. More than once, I had almost told Paul about the greater episode surrounding the emails, but each time, Morgan had sensed where I was about to go and had warned me off that course with a simple shake of his head. The truth was, FairWare would have been no more pleased with my methods than Golden Gate had been.

"You know what you did," Morgan said. "So do I. What is the old saying? Virtue is it's own reward? That will have to be enough because no one else, except Boris himself, is ever going to know."

The trouble was, it was not enough. Self-knowledge and self-awareness did not equal self-sufficiency and self-satisfaction. Morgan's support notwithstanding, I was alone, and I was not confident that I had actually done enough to stop the intrusion. In fact, maybe I had not done the right thing at all. For one thing, Boris was still at large. Nothing stopped him from attacking FairWare again in a more subversive and destructive manner. Nothing stopped him from attacking me again, at FairWare or another company where I might later work. He could steal my identity and ruin my credit score. He could implicate me in a computer hacking scandal and demolish my reputation. Nothing stood in his way to prevent him from doing any of these things, only my little threat and my personal vigilance. Neither seemed adequate for the task. Maybe I should never have gone to San Francisco to confront him. Perhaps, I should not have counter-attacked at all but merely hardened my defenses and not antagonized my opponent. Maybe I should have asked him why he chose me to attack. What had I done to deserve such attention?

Robert had tried once when I was twelve to teach me Judo, the Gentle Way. I had been beleaguered by bullies. So had he, he said, when he was in junior high, and he gave me a basic lesson.

"It does no good to resist someone who is stronger than you. You cannot overcome him. If you give way, however, you throw him off-balance. That puts him, temporarily, in a position of weakness, and at that moment of weakness, you may have sufficient strength to overcome him."

"Makes sense," I said, but I could never make it work. I myself was perpetually off-balance so that I was never in a position to exploit the imbalance of my opponent. More than that, the whole idea never really made sense to me even if I had said that it did. How could gentleness, another name for weakness, ever overcome anything? So, I asked for Kung Fu lessons instead of Judo, and Robert, my long suffering benefactor, my unrecognized father, complied. It seemed to me much more effective to kick a bully in the face than to give way before him, but even in this martial art wherein lay the secret power of Bruce Lee and Jackie Chan, there was an element of giving way, of gentle deflection waving each blow aside rather than stopping it with a solid block. I was never able to master it either, and even though I did beat George Ramirez in a tournament, I was soundly defeated in the finals. I never made black belt. I was unable to embrace gentleness, and my strength could only take me so far. So, how could I hope to overcome Boris with the mere promise of force?

Besides, what had gentleness ever won for Robert but defeat. I decided martial arts did not deliver as advertised. I studied chess instead. I became a master at sacrificing pawns.

"Joe, did you ever learn Karate, Tae Kwan Do, or Kung Fu?"

"No, Joe learned Tae Kwan Spoon."

He held up two big kitchen spoons and crossed them in an X above his head.

"Joe also studied the ancient art of Colt 45 and concealed carry. He studied the martial art of Harrison Ford, not Bruce Lee."

He swung one of the spoons around like a flourished sword. Then, he lifted his finger like a gun and fired. The spoon fell.

"So you don't believe in the Gentle Way?"

"It depends. No one convinces son to give up Goth clothes and stop loving death without being gentle. Sometimes soldier gives up life on the battlefield and wins more for his country than killing dozen enemy. Sometimes gentle is only way. Jesus was gentle."

I just shook my head. Jesus had never been my favorite religious figure. He reminded me too much of Robert.

As I left Joe's MyThai, I wondered if I should get a gun. Then I looked down at my Buddha belly. There was no room to stuff another thing into my waistband. I could not bend over to pull anything out from the cuff of my pants. All the gun ranges were out in the suburbs where no civilized man should go if he could avoid it. Besides, bullets could not kill computer viruses, and those were the substance of the perfect zombie apocalypse.

I crossed Brazos and walked along the sidewalk between the Catholic Church and the Presbyterian Church. What was I afraid of? Why was I still bothered by my contest with Boris? I had won. Why did it seem like I had lost?

I saw a woman coming towards me walking her dog. I thought she lived in my building even though I had never seen her in the lobby or the elevator. She reminded me of Susan except Susan would have smiled and spoken to me right there on the street even if I were a perfect stranger. A perfect stranger. She would have said something provocative or slightly inappropriate in passing. I remembered how she talked to me on the phone that first time I had called her about the Saturday security incident. That had been the occasion, to my mind, when we had really met. She made me out to be the hero. I had protected her from being penetrated by forces coming out of the mists of the Dark Web. I had continued that role at Blackhat. I had kept her digital virtue intact throughout the convention only to fail when we returned home. Instead of being her knight in virtual armor, I had become the attack vector against her, and what happened? She had been fired, and I had survived. What kind of hero was that?

I stopped in the street and watched the Susan-like woman disappear around the corner. She had not noticed me. She never would have noticed me. In India they had the untouchables. In Austin there were the unnoticeables, my caste. Maybe I was wrong. Perhaps, this time the woman had noticed me. She had noticed me all too well with my tight tee shirt stretched over my abundant belly and the mark of digital compromise written all over my face, and she had hurried away before I could smile at her or attempt to hack into her phone.

I started walking again headed south, my Thai dinner jiggling in my stomach. I crossed Sixth Street and kept on going. Halfway between Fifth and Fourth, however, I stopped, caught in a crisis of geographical identity.

I had always tried to be normal by Austin standards. I prided myself that I resonated with that keep-Austin-weird vibe, and I had searched relentlessly for just the right dissonant chord to fit with the city's dominant minor key. I discovered, however, you needed a keen aesthetic sense to create an off-beat image that stood out from all the other off-beat images competing for special attention in this city. That was hard enough, but what made it doubly difficult was that you had to do it without violating the city creed. More and more, however, it seemed to me that the only way to stand out and be different was to go against the creed. Yet, breaking with the creed would not gain you positive recognition in Austin. The City Fathers entrusted with the keeping of the Sacred Weirdness would not celebrate you if you ventured outside the creed. Rather, they would send you into exile. I personally had known a few people who had been banished to Round Rock, a city built upon the very brink of that abyss known as the Republican Party. Could there be anything worse?

As a computer professional, as a resident, yea even an owner, of a downtown condo, I told myself that I belonged, that I lived and thrived on the cutting edge of progressive Austin culture, but the further south I walked from Sixth Street, the harder it became to remain convinced of that. The more out of place I felt. Now, I was approaching the convention center with the new hotels and the upscale restaurants, the center of haute cuisine east of West Lake. You could still hear the sounds of a band playing from the rooftop of a Sixth Street bar, but from Fourth Street that Sixth Street minor chord began to sound more like a minor seventh, and the sacred weirdness became merely quaint. It was like a slow motion Doppler shift. Subtly, everything dropped in pitch. Whenever I drove my Fiat Abarth with its custom exhaust down East Seventh Street, it roared like a Ferrari. On Third Street my Italian car sounded like a mere imitation. If I turned west, however, things would only get worse. The city still held its edginess, but the edge became sharper. Even if you took a Car2Go, or better yet, a red rented bicycle and headed towards Lake Austin, you would be bleeding before you ever made it past Lamar. I shuddered as I looked towards the setting sun, and then I turned east to cross under the interstate.

The interstate was the great dividing line in Austin, but the highway had not created the divide. It had only traced the boundary that was already there. The boundary was prehistoric. It separated two distinct geologies. On the west side was the rock whence came the granite that built the capitol and the limestone that built houses along Lakes Travis and Austin. The east side, however, had what every gardener in West Austin wanted: dirt. That is, soil. In west Austin, the man in the limestone house had to pay to truck in the soil to support his roses and his heirloom tomatoes. You couldn't even construct an LCRA approved septic system in West Lake without bringing in east Austin dirt. On the east side that golden soil was just lying around. There it just came naturally, and it supported trees, gardens and even farms without much special effort. It did not, however, provide a good substrate for building houses. The east Austin earth settled in the dry weather and contracted. While west Austinites built new houses cantilevered off the sides of hills supported by columns of rock, east Austinites watered the shrinking soil around their houses to keep their foundations from cracking—when the city could spare them the water. The west side was full of Californians who had cashed out of their native market to build new houses on hills that were immune to mudslides because west Austin, having no soil, had neither any mud. The only mud in west Austin was over the septic field planted in the front yard of the limestone house cantilevered in back off the side of the hill. And that soil trucked in from east Austin to build the west Austin septic, had been delivered and spread out by Hispanic workers. They lived on the other side of I35 because the geological fissure between dirt and rock was also an ethnic boundary.

For years, going back to the time the capital of Texas moved to

Austin, the city had consigned the Hispanics and later the freed Blacks to the east side while the whites lived west of what later would become I35. By the time I had moved in, the ethnic separation had broken down, but, nevertheless, the character of the city changed when you crossed the freeway. Even I could feel it, I who was immune to most of what was intangible, I who insisted upon remaining firmly grounded on the scientific age. In East Austin I felt relief. A weight lifted from my psyche. It was as if the air contained more oxygen and less humidity, as if some UT lab had found a way to vaporize lithium and disperse it into the atmosphere to alleviate the melancholia the city celebrated every year on Eeyore's birthday. Maybe it was just the trees. Of course, West Austin had trees, but as I crossed the feeder road on the far side of I35 and moved deeper into the east side, the shade collecting under those eastern trees seemed more inviting, even in twilight. The street in front of my condo building was well lit at night, and if I walked just a few blocks to Eleventh and Trinity, I could stand under the light of a moon tower. East Austin had street lights too, but the trees dampened the illumination. No one seemed to mind, though. East Austin seemed less afraid of the dark. I inhaled the night air and tried to absorb some of the confidence of the natives.

East of I35 was also the home turf of many downtown panhandlers, especially the ones who worked the intersections by the interstate. Those who did not sleep on the streets beneath the downtown condos or pay the seven dollar a night rental fee charged by The Austin Homeless Shelter came back here after dark. Maybe they needed to feel the soil under their feet instead of concrete. I didn't recognize any of the men that I passed. None of them begged me for any money. Once back in East Austin, perhaps they, too, rested.

I worked my way past several trendy restaurants: barbecue, tortillas, sushi, and Thai. These were places that I had intended to visit one day, places where the west of Austin had begun encroaching on the east side, but I tonight I was not hungry, and even though I had walked well over a mile, I was not thirsty. However, the evening was drawing to an end. At Navasota Street I decided it was time to work my way back. I turned north on Onion to head back up towards Tenth Street. By that time I was feeling a little lost, so I decided to consult my iWatch. Somehow it did not seem quite right to rely so much on technology here. Austin was a high tech town, but on the east side the cutting edge did not cut quite so deeply. Here a person might be able to walk by an innate sense of direction without a smart phone. He might even be able to see and navigate by the stars. But I was still a child of the west. I raised my wrist to my mouth and spoke into my watch.

"Siri," I said, "where am I?"

She told me the street names on the sign I could read for myself. I decided to be a little free with the virtual female on my arm. There was no one else on the street to talk to.

"Siri, if I ask you for directions, does it mean I am asking for directions from a woman?"

"I'm not sure I understand the question."

"All right. All right. Where am I headed?"

Before I heard her voice, I knew the answer. There directly ahead was The Texas State Cemetery, and it was almost night.

I avoided driving on I35 whenever I could, but when I did and when I headed north, I saw the edge of a cemetery from the road. That was a different cemetery, one filled with the ordinary, not the extraordinary, dead. To me it did not matter much. The dead were dead. Above ground some of them had taller monuments, but below ground they were all at the same level. Here though, the ground was filled with famous Texans, ones celebrated by their reputation, not just by the height of their granite markers.

"Siri, why are all the cemeteries on the east side of I35?"

I don't know what I expected her to say? "It's easier to dig where there is dirt? In death all races are equal?" Of course, she said neither of these things.

"I'm not sure I understand the question."

"You don't understand the question? Don't you know that Steve Jobs is dead, too? Are you dodging the issue?" Then, I heard the answer to my question, as clearly as if Siri had spoken it through the iWatch.

"It's because West Austin does not like to be reminded of it's mortality."

I looked around expecting to see a ghost, perhaps William Travis risen from the grave, stepping out of the earth to see how his memorial state office building was doing or Bob Bullock going to take in an exhibit in his museum. Instead, a saw a woman, a Mexican woman, a nun standing beside me on the sidewalk holding a string of beads. Something told she was Mexican. I told myself that was wrong, that she was Hispanic, but I could not quite believe my own objection.

"I think if you ask your question in a different way, you will find that there are cemeteries in West Austin. I know one or two in Cedar Park, and there's one off 2222 in far northwest Austin. But that one is small, and it may be full—if you're looking for a place to be buried. I would prefer a cemetery on this side of town myself. It is more peaceful over here."

"I'm not looking for cemeteries," I said. "I have no interest in being buried. And I don't know about peaceful, but it certainly is dark."

"Are you afraid of the dark?"

"Of course not."

I thought for sure she was going to hit me with a follow-up question: "Are you afraid of death?" But she didn't, not verbally anyway.

"What are you doing here?" I said. I wanted to add that nuns didn't walk around in Austin in twilight, but this was East Austin.

"Don't worry. I'm not a vampire."

"I know that. There's no such thing as a vampire."

"No, not in East Austin, but how about in West Austin?"

"Well," I said, "I have to admit I've known one or two who self-identified as vampires, but you know how that goes."

The nun smiled.

"I do. I think I've met some myself. I'm not dead," she said. "I live here. Not in the cemetery, but across the street from it. I live in Our Lady of Guadalupe Convent."

When she said "Guadalupe" she said it like she was speaking Spanish, not English with mangled Spanish words. She did not pronounce it "Gwah dah loop" as people called the street on the west end of the UT campus.

"There's an actual convent here?"

"Yes. Just up that street."

"Why are you out here when it's almost dark?"

"I'm not afraid. I've come on purpose. I am praying for the dead."

"Praying for the dead? I thought you were supposed to pray for the living. It's too late for the dead."

"No. The dead need our prayers. The dead want our prayers. It's the living who think it's too late for themselves. Sometimes they even hope it's too late. Why would they think like that?"

"Because they don't believe in God?" I almost said, "Because they know there is no God," but I wanted to be polite to this silly young woman. That was another thing I noticed about her. She was young, and she was actually pretty. Nuns were all supposed to be old and ugly.

"No, because they don't want to change."

"And the dead? They want to change?"

"Some of them—yes."

"And the others?"

"Those are the ones in Hell."

"And they don't want to change?"

"No. They just want to get out, but they don't want to go where they would have to go in order to get out."

The temperature seemed to be rising, not cooling, as the light dimmed. Maybe it was the humidity. Beads of sweat were beginning to form on my brow. I decided to change the subject, but with the cemetery stretching before me, there seemed to be no other subject available.

"Have you ever been in the cemetery?" I asked. It was like asking if she had ever been to Chicago.

"Oh, yes. Have you?"

"No."

"You should go to this one, when it's open. Texas history comes alive. So to speak."

I smiled at her joke, weakly. The sweat on my brow began to roll down my face. I wonder how the nun kept from perspiring in that getup she wore, but I was not going to ask.

"Come," said the nun, "walk with me. You can accompany me back to my convent, and I will show you your way."

"How do you know where I want to go?"

"You are trying to go home. Right?"

I nodded meekly.

"Come," she said. She held out her hand. I took it. I could not remember when I had held a woman's hand. I had shaken a few women's hands at Blackhat, but that was not the same thing. For all our time on the bed, Susan and I had hardly touched.

We turned to the west and walked along the iron fence on the sidewalk.

"To visit the cemetery, you will have to come back in daylight. Of course, some people do come in at night., but I don't recommend it."

Was she going to warn me against satanic rituals, something involving virgins and chickens?

"You would have to climb the fence. Climbing the fence is not all that dangerous, but I wouldn't do it. People like to come to cemeteries at night to be scared."

"Yes," I said. "People like being scared."

"It's a way to deal with the fear of death. What is it that frightens you?"

I was afraid to say. I muttered something vague. I wanted to say, "Nuns," but not only would that have been offensive, it was ridiculous. I was still holding her hand, more like a child than a lover. We turned right on Navasota. My eyes darted from the sidewalk back to her and then rapidly past her through the iron bars to the graves beyond. She didn't take her eyes off me. She followed the sidewalk by dead reckoning or by divine guidance and not by looking. As we walked I thought of caves, of losing my job, of being alone, of lying cold in the ground forgotten by the living. All these fears seemed to rise up silently from within me like dead Texas heroes rising up from the ground and looking around to see if there was now any relief to be had from the fears that had driven them underground when they had lived. I did not know the answer.

"Here is my convent," she said. We had just gone a couple of blocks. "As you can see, it is only a short walk to the cemetery—a short walk and a constant reminder. Too close to your way of thinking?"

"Yeah. Way too close."

"Perhaps you are still closer than you would like to be. No?"

I didn't answer. I didn't have to.

"Now, getting home—you just keep going up Navasota two more blocks and you will hit Eleventh Street. Eleventh Street will take you all the way across the freeway and into downtown. You will pass Franklin's as you go. It's not open this time of night but the smell is heavenly. We think of it as local incense. Once you get across you will still have several blocks before you get to Brazos. You will be tired by then, but a left turn and three blocks, and you are home."

I smiled, but with the cemetery there at my right hand, it was a weak display. Yet, across the street was the convent, and though I did not want to let go of the nun's hand, I was unwilling to follow her any closer to her door.

"Good evening," she said. "You have a long way to go yet, I know, but I will be praying for you."

She squeezed and released my hand. I watched her cross the street towards the convent, but I did not wait to see her enter. I turned my face north and looked straight ahead as I walked. The graves passed by in my peripheral vision in a perpetual stream. Those ahead of me pulled me forward and inclined me towards the fence. Those behind me clutched at the back of my neck. Over my left shoulder the convent burned like an unseen sun. On my right I felt a chill. Fire and ice. I kept to the center of the sidewalk. It was only a block and a half until I reached Eleventh Street and turned left. The cemetery tugged at my collar all the way across Navasota and then made what seemed to me to be a reluctant release. However, both the burn and the chill remained with me all the way to I35. There were several little restaurants that tugged at me as I walked, but I was driven to get home. I smelled the wood smoke of Franklin's from across the street as I crossed the intersection of San Marcos and Eleventh. The smoke rose like incense to heaven but reached across the street to give me a little foretaste. I decided I would have to take off work one day and get up early enough to stand in line for lunch there. Man did not live by Thai alone.

What was it man did not live by alone? Robert used to tell me.

"Bread."

What was it that he did live by?

"Every word."

I watched the cars pass under the bridge as I walked over. The traffic was heavy, but it was moving. Still, I felt independent being on foot. Even so, I had checked my iWatch to see if there were any Car2Go vehicles waiting between me and Brazos. There was not been a single one.

At Red River, Eleventh Street rose dauntingly. My pulse rose to over a hundred as I climbed. If I had paused to eat on the way, I probably would not have been able to make it to the top. I barely noticed the little Orthodox Church across the street as I leaned into the incline. I thought I saw cab drivers at the La Quinta Inn laughing as I huffed past on my final stretch. But then, just across San Jacinto, there was St. Mary's. The flowers planted along the sidewalk seemed to drain some of the heat from the pavement. I felt cool air on my brow. At the corner I hung a left instead of crossing at the intersection and hugged the border of the cathedral staying on the opposite side of the street till I had crossed Tenth and Ninth and was directly across from my building. I crossed Brazos in the middle of the block. There was no traffic, but I had forgotten to look. I skirted the bumper of a Car2Go as I stepped up on the curb, and as I entered the lobby, the elevator was waiting.

I went to bed, and I slept what Robert must have meant by the sleep of the righteous, yet another of his old sayings that I had never understood.

"I've never known it," he said, "but I have hope that you will."

I had made it my goal to defeat him in his hopes for me, but now I was beginning to think that I had failed.

I slept all night without any bad dreams. It was not until I had climbed into that same Car2Go still parked in front of my building from the night before, that I asked myself the question.

How had that nun known where I lived?

28 - The IPO

"Did you see?" Morgan said when I walked into the office. "No, of course you didn't. You don't park those Cars2Go in the garage. You don't go in the garage."

"No," I said, "and therein lies the beauty. See what?"

"If you had driven in and used your complimentary parking space like any other mortal, you would have noticed something was missing."

"Missing? Something was missing in the garage? What? The parking stripes? The exit signs? Your car? Your car that you left here last night because you had too many margaritas downstairs after work to drive it home?"

Morgan shook his head at each preposterous suggestion.

"Not my car."

We both snapped our fingers.

"The Ferrari!"

"Very good. If this were twenty questions, you would still be in the running."

"George's Ferrari is gone."

"Right. And that can mean only one thing."

"The IPO!"

Morgan clapped his hands and nodded his head.

"Wait," I said. "Do you know this for a fact?"

"I know for a fact that the car is not there."

"No, I mean that the IPO has gone through. Has there been an announcement?"

I checked my text messages and emails from my iWatch. There was nothing.

"Not yet."

"Did you ask Paul?"

"No. Paul keeps everything close to the vest these days."

"Did you ask Butch?"

I knew the answer to that before Morgan could say it. Paul Cassidy no longer answered to the name 'Butch'.

So, we waited for the news. I devoted my morning to studying new attack signatures and checking our software versions to see if we were patched yet to resist them. FairWare would need all the more protection when she became a corporation. Yet, the paid software vendors we used were scarcely more caught up than the open source providers. I wondered if Boris was up on all these new attacks. He no longer used the name Frank Sinatra. Maybe he had changed his name to Tony Bennett and stayed in San Francisco. Maybe he had quit singing completely. I was slowly beginning to believe that my little visit to him had done some good.

About one in the afternoon, the phones began to ring, first on this desk and then on another. The person at the desk would answer, rise and head in the direction of the enclosed offices, disappear for a few minutes, and then return to work. No one spoke, but no one was crying. Some barely suppressed a smile. Morgan's turn came around three PM. When he came back and sat down, he gave me a knowing look. Around 3:30 PM, people began to leave. There had always been those who came into the office unthinkably early and left before the rest of us, but their numbers were never so large as this. By 3:45 PM, the entire office was practically deserted. Just before four PM, Morgan got up. His face was the only one I had seen that had borne any concern.

"I'll see you in the morning," he said and left quietly. At 4:29 PM all the lights went out although the office was still filled with natural light. Slowly, as the evening wore on, that began to fade.

I waited until the cleaning staff had finished, and then I went home. My long walk through East Austin had caught up with me. I was tired and did not go out. I went to bed by ten.

The next morning Morgan greeted me much more casually than

he had the day before. Yet, I could tell that he was sitting on something, waiting for the right time to spring it.

The right time, apparently, was about 10:30 AM.

"Did you talk to George?"

"No. Why should I talk to George? I don't have anything to tell him."

"I thought maybe he had called you into his office."

"No. Thankfully not."

"Well, then, did you talk to Paul?"

"No. Not since a few days ago. Why?"

"I just wondered."

"Did you talk to George?" I asked.

"Yes."

"When? Today?"

"No. Yesterday."

"Did you just go to speak your mind?"

"No, he called me in."

"Really?"

Then, I recalled Morgan disappearing for a few minutes the day before."

"Oh. That's where you went yesterday."

"That's where I went."

"Well, what did he say? Anything?"

"Oh, this and that. Actually, we talked mostly about the IPO—and related items."

Then I remembered how everyone else had disappeared yesterday as well, one at a time.

"So, he told you about the IPO? You just suspected before. He told you it was going to happen?"

"Yes, he was very excited about it."

"Why didn't you say something?"

"I didn't want to spoil the surprise."

"Well, you have now, apparently. Or, maybe not. What related things?"

"Oh, about the party."

"Party? What party?"

"The one last night. After work."

I remembered how everyone had left early.

"I didn't hear about the party. No one mentioned any party."

"We weren't supposed to talk about it. It was supposed to come from George."

"Well, apparently, someone was overlooked."

"That's strange."

"That's true," I said. "It's not like he doesn't know who I am."

"That's right," said Morgan. Then, he was quiet. We both were.

There was silence in the office for about a half an hour.

I was the one who broke the silence.

"How was the party?"

"It was good. You know. It was an office party. I'll bet some people are hung over."

"What were you celebrating?"

"The IPO."

"Yes," I said, "but why were you celebrating?"

"Me? Why not? It was a party."

I didn't say it, but Morgan was not a party animal. Even in Las Vegas you could see that he kept himself somewhat aloof from all the constant festivities.

"I was happy for all of you," he said.

"Happy for us? Why should you be happy for us?"

"For the company."

"Morgan, you're a contractor. As long as the company can pay your contract rates, why should you care about what happens to it?"

He didn't say anything.

"For that matter, why should any of us care? We are employees, not owners—unless we are getting shares."

"Well, as a matter of fact, there was something else. There was the stock."

"The stock?"

"Yes. Employees are getting shares of stock once the IPO takes place. And after that there will be an employee stock ownership plan you can join."

"How much are the employees getting?"

"It depends. I'm not getting any. I'm a contractor, as you pointed out."

"So, George called you in to tell you everyone else was getting shares but not you?"

"Not exactly. He told me that the employees were getting shares of stock in varying amounts, but I wasn't eligible, so he was giving me a bonus."

"A bonus?"

"Yeah. Pretty sweet, right?

I let another half hour pass before I asked my follow up question. It was an even more uncomfortable silence than the last one, but discomfort worked to my advantage.

"Why did he give you a bonus, Morgan? I mean, why in particular? Was he afraid you would feel left out?"

"No. He thanked me for my work in getting us past the email scandal and in re-securing the computer system."

The next silence was not as uncomfortable as the prior two had been. For reasons I could not grasp, I was simply glad to know the truth.

Morgan and I did not speak for most of the rest of the morning. Shortly before noon, he disappeared for awhile. When he returned, he said, "Why don't we take a little walk before it gets any hotter?"

Outside under the direct sun, I asked Morgan a direct question.

"Where did you go?"

"I went to talk to George. I asked him about you. I told him that you had played a major role in securing us after the email and that you deserved a reward."

"You said that?" Morgan rose another several points in my estimation. I almost told him so. "What did he say?"

"Did Golden Gate offer you a job?"

"No."

"If they do, you should take it. George said, 'He still has a job, doesn't he?'"

"Did you tell him about Boris?"

"No."

"Or the malware?"

"No. George couldn't spell malware. And I didn't tell him about your little trip to San Francisco. Should I have?"

"No. I suppose not. No, definitely not."

The sun was already becoming fierce. I wished I had brought my Las Vegas hat. I hoped Susan had kept hers. She needed it worse. I still had a job.

"You know," said Morgan as we headed back to the office, "the world needs heroes. But sometimes being a hero can suck."

I did not reply.

"That's why I think sometimes there does need to be a heaven. For people who never get their rewards in this life. For the saints. Saint Gus."

"You were part of all this, too."

"But I got my reward already. Or, I will when they deposit the money. But you're still waiting. In fact, you're not only waiting, you're suffering for doing the right thing. I not only think there ought to be a heaven, I think there ought to be a hell. But, then if there were a hell, I ought to be warning people to stay out of it. What I really want to do most of the time, though, is just smile and wave. Wave bye bye. I suppose that's the wrong attitude."

As we walked those few blocks, the temperature seemed to rise several degrees. I could feel it on my scalp. I wondered if my hair was thinning. When we reached the door to our building, Morgan's phone dinged. He held back and pulled his Android off his belt.

"What do you know? They've already deposited it."

"That was fast," I said.

"Yes, it was. Look, I'm not going back in just yet. I've got something I want to do. I'll catch up with you later."

With that he smiled, raised his hand to his forehead and made a kind of salute. From where I stood, however, it looked more like a wave.

Morgan was gone for the most of the afternoon. After he returned, he left at his normal time. Judging from the number of billable hours he was willing to forgo, I was able to estimate the size of the bonus. I stayed late as usual, past the time the cleaning staff was active with their trash carts and vacuums. This was my favorite time at work, after all, when everyone else had gone home and only that far off droning reminded me that humanity still existed somewhere in the distance, somewhere I could not quite reach. Was it humanity that kept its distance, or had I chosen to dwell in No Man's Land?

I stayed until all sound had subsided, even the cooling crinkle of window glass and the hum of air conditioning. I made sure that the network infrastructure was free from assault, that there were no undetected programs or scripts scuttling like scorpions across bare tile floors, betraying their presence with only the faintest of rustlings when they encountered a bit of paper or foil. The security guard greeted me with "Good night" as I emerged from the elevator on the ground floor. He seemed to recognize a kindred spirit. We were in the same business. He roamed the halls and kept vigil over the door. I roamed the network, the servers, and kept watch over the firewall and the computer ports. Neither of us was recognized by those who lived and worked in safety because of our efforts. Both of us did our best work alone.

I wondered, though, as I walked out the door: did the guard get a bonus?

29 – The Dark Side of the Road

The summer of the IPO moved into autumn, and the weather cooled below the hundreds. The office had cooled even more, so much so that I took to wearing long sleeves. That meant I could not walk home from work in the evening without breaking a sweat. Why did it have to be this way? Why was perspiration in Austin inevitable? The trouble was that I seemed to be the only one doing it. No one else broke a sweat in the normal course of life. They reserved their exertions for the gym where perspiration became an end in itself. To avoid the afternoon sweat going home, I tried driving in for a few days. After all, everyone else drove in. They commuted from garage to garage to avoid the sun. Why couldn't I do the same? When I roared into the garage in my Abarth, however, I saw the population of BMW's had doubled. Paul was driving an Acura. George's Ferrari was back in prominent display. It had been waxed, and now it could start and move without being pushed. People said you could hear it from the elevator when he ascended the ramp in first gear.

I gave up driving on the third or fourth day. I preferred walking despite the temperature, and if I drove, I relished parking outside on the street. There was no designated parking for a Car2Go, yet there was always a place to park. I floated above the parking issues of mere Austin mortals when I drove one of those ad hoc vehicles. I might have to circle the block to find the next available instance of the car, but I would usually find one whether I used the locator app or searched by sixth sense dead reckoning.

Sometimes as I circled I had to wait at the garage exit while my co-workers poured out like bats from a cave, but that only happened when there was a late meeting. There were more of those than there had been in the private equity days, and I found that I was not always the last one to leave the building. My co-workers were finding it harder working for the shareholders. I fancied that I was the last man in the company who still worked for the private enterprise. For me nothing had changed in that respect.

One Wednesday I decided to leave earlier than normal just to prove to myself and to those still at their desks that I could. I even considered making it a habit. Nothing I could do between six and eight o'clock would cause the stock to open higher on the NASDAQ the next morning. Furthermore, no one cared what I did. As far as the stock market was concerned, I was my own man.

During that fresh exercise of freedom, Lloyd London motioned to me on the sidewalk as I left the building. He was about half a block south of the front door, out of range of the security camera. He hailed me as I was about to head north.

"Hey," he said. "I've got a car around the corner with a few minutes left on the parking meter. Do you like The Oasis?"

He took me aback as he always managed to do. I realized he was inviting me for dinner.

"I've never been. It's pretty far. Besides, it's best, I hear, at sunset. We wouldn't make it in time."

"Maybe not. There's always Central Market."

I shrugged unenthusiastically. I could tell I was making him work for this meeting, but I was past caring about any inconvenience my outlook put upon anyone else. At the same time, I was hungry for grilled meats and some kind of conversation. In the end I knew I was going to go with him.

"I know. How about the food trailers on Riverside?"

I shrugged again with a different shoulder and a neck motion nuance which said, "Why not?".

I didn't say a word during the drive. Lloyd whistled a little and made a few comments about the drivers or about the women standing on the sidewalk. He smiled and shook his head in admiration as each one receded in one or the other side view mirrors. Easy come, easy go. To me each was like a little poignant missile aimed nowhere in particular but which always found its way into my heart. There was a sharp, sudden pain to each missile as it entered and another pain as I pulled it out. There were more arrows at the food court with all the unattached women standing about. Arrows fell in sheets like rain while we stood in line at the truck serving lobster po' boys. With every step I took towards the counter, I think I left a little pool of my own blood.

We took our food to a corner of a picnic table under an oak. I wondered if Lloyd had manipulated Google Maps to clear a spot for us under that huge tree. It took me a couple of swallows before I finally found my tongue.

"This is not your usual modus operandi, is it Lloyd?"

"How so?"

"You usually manage to show up wherever I'm going. I arrive, and there you are."

"I met you at the corner after work. What more do you want? Besides, you never go anywhere."

"What do you mean I never go anywhere? I go where's. I mean, I go places."

"No you don't. I see your bills. You haven't bought a beer on Sixth Street in two months. You buy bourbon and beer at the liquor store on the way home, and home is where you consume it. You eat Thai almost every night, but you don't eat it by the take out counter like you used to. You take it home and eat it sitting out on your balcony watching the hipsters go by. Some nights you don't eat anything at all. I'll spare you the actual percentage of skipped meals. Oh, and you don't sleep. You spend more time than you used to in the bed, but you aren't sleeping. And you're not doing anything else in it either."

"I don't skip any meals," I said. "Those nights you think I've skipped, I ate what was in the fridge."

I knew better than to argue with his data collection, but I could cast doubt on his analysis and interpretation.

"There isn't anything in the fridge. You never go to the grocery store."

"I pay with cash. It doesn't show up on my credit card, and the store therefore doesn't record who's made the purchase."

"No you don't. The twenty dollar bill you paid for this meal has been in your pocket since you went to an ATM and drew out the cash for your last premium. You never go to movies. You never see anyone except at work. You watch TV but only whatever is on at the moment. You don't do Pay for View. You don't do Netflix. You don't even use the DVR. And, when FairWare launched its initial public offering, you didn't participate. I know. You didn't put any extra funds in the bank. You didn't add any shares to your brokerage account. You didn't get any shares. You didn't get any raise, and you didn't get any bonus. You went to San Francisco for about four hours three months ago. That was basically your last trip. I don't know what all that was about, but I know the signs of depression when I see them. Although…."

"Although what?"

"Everything is billed as depression these days. It's a 'medical condition.' Being in the business, I see things differently."

"The business?"

"Everyone assumes today that the feelings and behaviors we call depression are an abnormality. You should feel good despite the fact that you didn't get a promotion, that your wife is cheating on you with a guy in her office, and that the city has raised taxes to pay for more bike lanes to make the roads more narrow."

I winced as he said that. I didn't even have a wife, and bicycles always made me feel guilty. Secretly, I wanted to run them down.

"You aren't 'depressed,' said Lloyd as he made quotations with his fingers around the word. "You, my friend, have a severe case of disappointment."

He put down his po' boy and pointed at me from across the picnic table. I wished he would lower his voice about bike lanes and depression. We were in south central Austin.

"No one considers philosophy any more. No one remembers Nietzsche."

"Nietzsche?"

"Nihilism, my friend. 'God is dead!' God is dead, and everything is permitted. Okay, that part's not Nietzsche. That's Dostoevsky, more or less."

He paused, and I considered. I had heard that name somewhere.

You remember those Russian names even if you can't pronounce them or understand what they wrote.

"Everything is permitted, but nothing is worth doing. That is Lloyd London."

He bowed from his bench as if he had said something profound from a podium and leaned into his po'boy for another bite. I sat immobile, my lobster growing as cold as the seas from which it came.

"I must admit, though, it's good for business."

"I thought you said no one knew philosophy. So how could anyone know about nihilism to make it good for business?"

"They don't know it. They live it, but they don't know what they do. That's Jesus Christ. So, they mope around on Zoloft or Wellbutrin thinking there's something wrong with them."

"Well, maybe—"

"Then one day they get an epiphany. This is just the way life is, and there's no point in expecting they ought to be happy. They ought not to be happy given the circumstances, and they ought not to expect or pretend any differently."

"They ought not to expect," I repeated trying to understand the words. "So, do they stop expecting and pretending?"

"At that point, yes."

"Sounds dismal."

"Sounds like a Bergman movie, that's what it sounds like."

"Then what happens?" I said. I had never seen a Bergman movie.

"Then they feel better because now they know the secret."

"How could that make someone feel better?"

"How? By lifting the burden."

"The burden? What burden?"

"The burden of thinking the world could be or should be any different than it is. The burden of thinking that the burden is worth carrying."

"I don't get that."

"The burden of thinking that there is anything worth caring about. Once you get past that, life becomes a lot easier. Like that book said, life is hard, but once you understand it is hard, it isn't so hard."

"What book was that?" I said. That line sounded familiar.

"I don't know. Some book back in the seventies."

I remembered a book on Robert's shelf: The Road Less Traveled. Was that the book? I picked it up often and read the first line. I didn't know if Robert ever finished it. Maybe he just lived it.

"What if someone uncovers the secret?" I said. "What if he decides that life...just isn't worth it?"

"Well, if he is our client, he doesn't ever have to come to that realization. I know. I am being inconsistent. I mean, here I am complaining that no one knows what they do anymore or why they do it. That frustrates me. I think there should be understanding. But there isn't. Even the task of coming to understanding about your own life has become a burden that people can't bear, or don't want to. So, we fill the demand in the marketplace. That's the beauty of it. See? We lift the burden of you having to understand for yourself that the burden is not worth carrying, but if you do realize it, then the service we provide becomes all the sweeter to you. For me, that is the best reward. I reach my highest level of satisfaction when that happens."

"But what if you don't know? I mean, Big Data can't tell you everything You said yourself that you don't know why I went to California. You can read my credit card statements and my bank account, but you can't read my mind. What if the client does realize that life is not worth it, but you don't see it? What happens to him then? Isn't he left in the place of despair with no hope?"

"Well," said Lloyd, "in that case he could contact his agent, and he could file a claim himself."

"He files a claim? What happens after he files the claim?"

"Well, then we send out an adjuster just like we would if we determined the client's state of readiness ourselves."

"A claims adjuster?"

"Yes."

This time I was the one who took a bite. Cold lobster was not as bad as I had imagined.

"Except I don't do it quite that way. I make my own evaluation first—either way. I always balance the one side with the other. I compare what the data tells me with what I observe myself in the client. More often than not, it is very clear, and there is no discrepancy. Even when the client files his own claim, the corroborating evidence in the data usually follows within days, if not hours. People may still make their decisions and come to their realizations in the privacy of their own hearts and minds, but soon after, they put it on Facebook or in their blog. There isn't that much lag time. You would be surprised. But when that happens, when the person makes his own decision before Big Data can catch it, I always make a personal evaluation."

"Why? It's clear. The data tells you, and the person has said it with his own—Twitter account."

I could have sworn that London reached across the picnic table and put his hand on mine, but he didn't.

"Two reasons. First, I owe it to him. He's my client."

He poked his chest with his forefinger.

"My client! My client. And I owe him a personal, human evaluation. I owe it to him to make sure, to confirm for him what he knows already in his own mind. Also, we humans still need to verify that the computers are not wrong."

I nodded in agreement.

"I have to say," I said, "and don't you dare tell anyone, I am impressed with your personal integrity and professional dedication."

"Didn't you hear a word I said? Life is meaningless. There's no personal integrity. Professional dedication in the end is arbitrary. I don't know why I do it. Maybe I'm just a rebel."

A piece of lobster slipped out from the end of his sandwich. He turned the bread around and drew it into his mouth with his tongue.

"And there is also the second reason."

He didn't wait for me to ask what the second reason was, and he didn't pause to finish the last of the chunk of lobster.

"Paying off the claim is not the only proper response when the client realizes that life is not worth living. Some people find in that knowledge an opportunity, an opportunity to live in freedom. After all, everything is permitted. Some benefit from just living in the freedom in the moment. After all, in the final analysis, if life is not worth living and everything is meaningless, it may make no sense to live, but neither is there any value, any meaning, in an untimely death. There are two necessary responses to the nihilism, but both are equally invalid: life or death. Life is meaningless, as we said, but some think that by choosing death they are either demonstrating their superior grasp of the truth or they are protesting the meaninglessness by destroying something of value, namely their own life. But their life has no value, and there is no one to protest against. After all, God would be the only person worth protesting against, and he's already dead. It all ends up the same. Death wins in the end, and there is no value in trying to embrace it. So, some people decide to embrace the freedom for awhile, and they live as if everything is permitted. I like to give those people that opportunity. I know what's coming in the end. We are still going to be paying the death benefit of the policy, but I enjoy that special freedom for awhile. It gives them a kind of philosophical kinship and historical continuity with some of the great free men and women of the past."

"And who were those?"

"Oh, Jack the Ripper, the Marquis de Sade, Vladimir Lenin, Margaret Sanger. It makes no true difference to me. For the company it's a few extra premiums, but if we let money get in the way, we risk failure to meet our obligation to our clients. That's what I tell my fellow agents, and they know that the relationship to the client is sacred to me. Besides, some of the clients who file a claim but then decide to delay receiving the benefit make the best claims adjusters. I am the most successful recruiter of claims adjusters in the company, and I choose my adjusters carefully. Rest assured that when your claim is paid, you will have one of the best adjusters in the business. In fact, I promise, you will have the very best available at the time. I will see to it. I take good care of my clients."

I sat back, as much as you can on a bench, and tried to take in what I was hearing. Darkness came over that sylvan glade of a food court. It filtered down through the leaves of the trees. It filled in the spaces between the glass bulbs strung between trunks and enveloped the clear Christmas lights woven in among the branches over our heads. It surrounded us, and every bite of po'boy passed through it on the way to our mouths. Was everyone else just oblivious? I still saw people moving about. They were laughing. They were eating and drinking in groups and pairs. They were young, but those who were not so young still acted young. I doubted there was a single one among them who had yet taken the precaution of purchasing life insurance. Of course they hadn't. They had no dependents to protect.

Neither had they taken out entire life, for they did not yet appreciate the limits of their own entire lives. Then, I noticed how, despite all their enthusiasm and dance-like movement, they stayed near the light more like moths than bats. As the darkness descended, they huddled beneath those bulbs, hemmed in by the night. Maybe they ignored it deliberately. Maybe they didn't see it. How can you see something that by nature is without light? But to a person, they all reacted to the dark, and each one shrank away. Lloyd London saw it too. He looked out on the crowd as if it were a field ripe for the harvest. I could just see him sharpening his actuarial scythe.

"I don't understand," I said.

"What don't you understand? Tell me."

"Who are you?"

"I am Lloyd London, and I proudly represent a company which offers the most unique product in the world. Who else on the face of the earth can ensure the quality of your life and give protection against the greatest enemy a man faces in his life?"

"What is that?"

"You know what it is. It is the fear of death. The fear of the very thing that can bring you relief. Just the relief from the fear can add years to your life. It also adds to the quality of your life. Our actuaries have tried to correlate the two. How much quality can we add? Can quality even be measured and put on a spreadsheet? How much living time comes with an increase of quality of life? Some say the good life is a bearable life, and a bearable life yields a longer existence. I personally don't think quality of life can be measured. I am not sure it adds time to life. Perhaps it consumes life faster, but without the fear of loss, there need not be any dread in that consumption."

"But—"

"You know what? I'm not sure you're hungry after all. In fact, you look very tired. I think I had better get you home. You could use a good, long night's sleep. Chamomile tea, or warm milk—that will help."

Then, we were back in the car, and we were just as silent as before. I wanted to ask questions. Where was I in my life? Had my situation become intolerable, but I just didn't know it? Or did I know it? Robert used to tell me that we knew things we did not admit to ourselves. I, of course, never believed him, but now I had to wonder. Did I know something before I realized that I knew it? Whether I knew it or not had my own life lost all its value, and was I on the way to having my claim adjusted? Why did I not find that thought very comforting?

Surely not. Surely Lloyd through his street-side proxies would be collecting many more premiums from me for many years to come. I wondered how much it cost to adjust a claim. Probably, I had not paid in enough premiums yet for the company to break even. Lloyd may have been dedicated to his clients, but he had to make a profit. Besides, the company would not jump in and pay a claim on such paltry evidence: the lack of a bank deposit and lower credit card bills. What if I stopped paying the premiums? That would put an end to Lloyd and his Big Data analysis. That would keep the company from paying my claim. But hadn't he foreseen that possibility when he sold me the policy? Hadn't he already figured out that angle?

Then, the obvious possibility struck me. Maybe this company never paid a claim. Maybe all they did was collect premiums until the customer realized that life was pretty good after all, that he didn't want to die just now, and that this whole thing was only a scam. That would be pretty good for Lloyd. He would collect a few thousand dollars and then move on to the next person who was depressed. I had not been depressed, however, when Lloyd first approached me. I had been on a search. Why would Lloyd go after a person who was neither depressed nor disappointed? It was the depressed person who was apt to buy a policy, but it was also the depressed person who was apt to file a claim. What kind of a business model was that?

Then another possibility struck me, only this one was not just a possibility. This one was a fact. I had bought the policy without being depressed. Why? It must have been because I was already wondering about life. I was already wondering how it was going to turn out, and I had already sensed that there was something missing. Had I bought the policy because I knew something was missing and that there was the distinct possibility, even the actuarial probability, that the missing element would never be found? Or, was I still looking for the missing piece?

I remembered the joke about life insurance. You are betting you will die. The agent is betting you won't. You hope he wins. This entire life insurance inverted the formulation. I was betting I would want to die. Lloyd was betting that I would want to live and pay more premiums. Yet, every premium I paid seemed to make a contradictory statement: that I wanted to die, albeit without dread, and yet that I wanted to stay alive.

Lloyd took us down Fifth Street to get back to my condo. Fifth Street—it was another Sixth Street in reverse. Slowly, we moved from the hip near Lamar to the bohemian near Congress, but I noticed another progression, or, rather, a regression. The people on West Sixth were engaged in an accelerated pursuit of pleasure and social recognition. Moving east people slowed down but became more desperate. As we turned on Brazos a woman started to cross the street in front of us against the right of way. Immediately, she saw us and lurched back. She appeared to be on something that reduced her capacity to receive the live feed of reality. Instead, everything for her was buffered like video on a computer with insufficient memory. She wore a light, loose kind of blouse with no bra. Under the blouse her body moved in time delay to her erratic movements on the street. It was evening but she looked like she had been on the street all night, all day, and was about to be out all night again. She was young. She was pretty albeit a bit haggard. She was vulnerable. No doubt she would be available given the right inducements. She could use a good bed. I could give her a warm bath, a decent meal, and then I could give her that good bed. Afterwards, I could give her thirty dollars so she could buy herself more buffering, and I would spend less on the whole evening than if I had met her on Sixth Street in a bar. The trouble was she would come to me again wanting more money for more buffering, and then I would become vulnerable. So, I would have to make sure there was only a first time. I could take her for a ride, take her someplace she had not been before, someplace from which she could not easily return, someplace, in fact, from which she would never return. Or I could just give her more money: seventy-five, a hundred dollars. Then, maybe she would take care of my problem herself and buy so much of what she used as her buffer that she would never need to buy anymore ever again. That way, her pain and my vulnerability would both be permanently relieved. It would be a form of cheap insurance. It all seemed so perfect.

This must have been what Lloyd London meant about living in freedom.

But when I looked in the mirror again, the girl was gone, She was not hovering at the curb still trying to cross the street, nor was she lying in the middle of the intersection, a victim of the next car. She had successfully crossed the intersection and disappeared down Fifth Street. I decided not to ask Lloyd to let me out two blocks early to try to find her.

"One more thing," he said when we reached the curb in front of my building, "I'm not necessarily supposed to tell you this. It's another thing that falls within my personal discretion. Remember when I told you about the person we would pair you with so that you could cover one another?"

"No."

"You know. You take out a term life policy that covers someone else's entire life policy, and he does the same for you?"

"Oh," I said. I had forgotten all about that aspect of my coverage.

"Well, we just paid the term life benefit on your partner. Since you are his beneficiary, the money goes to you. We used it to prepay your entire death benefit."

"I don't understand. What happened to the other guy? I don't even remember his name. I never met him. Did he die?"

"Of course."

"Did you pay his claim?"

"Actually, not the entire life death benefit. You see, he was what we call self-adjusting. It pains me to say it, but we did not catch him in time. Sometimes that happens. Some agents like to think that in those cases the client self-adjusts, but it was still due to our coverage. We, through our coverage, helped give the client the confidence and freedom to perform that self-adjustment. I still can't help but consider it a failure. I don't think we should ever let a client get to that point. These things can happen suddenly. I understand that, but usually there are warning signs. But what can I say? The man was not my client. Don't worry. It won't happen on my watch. But, as I said, his term life benefits accrued to you. So, you don't have to worry."

"I still don't understand?"

"Well, let's say you lost your job. You started getting behind on your mortgage. You might think that you couldn't keep up your premiums and might be tempted to the let the policy lapse. That would be a real shame because that is precisely the kind of situation in which you need your coverage. Well, thanks to the term life benefit that accrued to you from your policy partner, you don't have to worry about that. Your entire life premiums are prepaid."

"Really? For how long?"

"Long enough for us to adjust your claim, which is what you really want."

"But what if it weren't what I really wanted? What if I were to change my mind?"

"I don't see that happening."

"But suppose I did."

"Normally, if the client who stops paying premiums has not accumulated enough cash value in his policy to cover the costs of adjustment, he lapses. I've had to let clients walk away because they didn't understand the benefits they gained by having the policy, the daily relief from the fear and the empowerment to embrace freedom. I had to let them go. It is the hardest part of this job. But that is academic in your case. You cannot lapse. Your account is paid in full. You can lose your whole life by not making payments, but you can't lose your entire life. When the time comes for you to collect, we will be there to pay you your benefit."

"But what if I don't want the benefit?"

"That is impossible. You may not understand it. You may not appreciate it, but you cannot not want it. We are tapping into the deepest longings of the human heart here, but that is immaterial. Our actuaries have devised a means to assign calculable value to each human life. Eventually, all life loses value, and when it does, we cover that loss. We cover it whether the client realizes when he has suffered the loss or not. As I said, you are prepaid in full. Even if you decide you no longer want the whole life or term life, the entire life is yours. We will pay your claim, and you will collect."

I paused there on the sidewalk. There was silence again on Brazos Street, there on that little section of Austin.

"I'm not saying I've changed my mind. I'm just asking a

hypothetical."

Lloyd London nodded knowingly.

"But you said if I lost my job and couldn't pay the premiums, that would be a tragedy because I would lose coverage when I needed it. But I didn't lose my job. I'm not going to lose my job."

London nodded again.

Silence began to fill in the corners of the void. I thought for a moment that it might have something to say to me, but London broke it off.

"Take care of yourself," he said.

The car pulled away from the curb.

I walked through the lobby and entered the elevator. The door was open. I pressed four, and I felt the elevator lift upwards. I realized in that moment in the quiet of the elevator that even if it stopped on the second floor and any one of several gorgeous women got on and rode with me, it would not matter. Even if George were to pull up in his newly repaired Ferrari, run up the stairs and meet me as the elevator door opened with five hundred shares of FairWare Incorporated, it would make no material difference.

Even if the elevator was rising, I myself was still descending.

30 - Shots in the Dark

This time it was Paul who called me into his office, not George, but the summons was just as ominous. I tried to think of him as Butch as I made my way over, but the camaraderie of our old gang was gone. He stood nervously behind his desk once again looking more like Strother Martin leading a string of mules in Bolivia than Butch Cassidy. In fact, he appeared to me more of a Saul than a Paul. I wondered if there were a connection between the two names other than the fact they rhymed. My mind searched in vain for a movie I might have seen that tied them together.

"Gus, close the door please. It is just going to be us."

He smiled weakly. I sat down. He motioned towards the chair after I had sat in it. I strained my attention towards him with all the effort I could muster. I knew he was going to be hard to hear with the words of Lloyd London echoing in my ears: "Well, let's say you lost your job."

"This is difficult for me," Paul said.

It didn't look that difficult.

"The time for our association—the time. Gus, the company is changing direction. We are no longer a private company. We are now a corporation, a public corporation. We are on the NASDAQ. It is an exciting time. When we went public and made our initial public offering of shares, George gave a bonus to all the employees who have been with us up to now. Each got shares in the new corporation. You were the sole exception. I cannot tell you how much that grieved me, but under the circumstances, in light of the recent security events, we did not see, George and I, how we could justify giving out shares of stock to the very man who had been the nexus of the attack. Not when that man was the very man charged by the company with preventing the attack."

"San Francisco."

"What did you say?"

"It doesn't matter."

"Whatever. I had hoped that you would join in anyway. I had thought that you might buy some shares on your own and partner with the rest of us, but you did not see fit to do that. So, as I said, the direction of the company is changing. The culture is changing. I think we are becoming a little less Austin and a bit more...San Francisco."

I looked at him incredulously.

"Or, Palo Alto. In any event, we are no longer the same as before, and all of us must become different men and women to stay in step with the company. Rather than ask you to make a change that your heart is clearly not interested in making, I have come to the difficult decision to give you your freedom."

He picked up a piece of paper from his desk I had not noticed before and handed it to me. My stomach wrenched.

"I'm sorry, but you leave me with no other choice."

"You're firing me?"

"No, your position has been eliminated. We have decided to contract with a data security company to monitor our defenses. Morgan will say on to help make the transition, and the security company will give him the option of joining them. He is such a contractor at heart, however, I doubt if he will do it. As for you, we no longer need any full-time employees and company owners—"

He smiled at this.

"—that's what we like to call ourselves now—filling the security role. George believes it will dilute our energies, so it is best transitioned to professionals who devote themselves exclusively to it."

I wondered what else I had been doing to dilute my company energies.

"You are firing me!"

"We are not firing anybody. We are reorganizing and trimming down."

"You're firing me because I wouldn't buy any IPO stock?"

"I told you the company is shifting focus."

"Who else are you trimming away?"

"I'm afraid that information is confidential. I have secured you a generous severance package. We are giving you one month's salary and keeping you on our insurance plan for the same month. After that you have six months to buy a COBRA plan or just go with a government broker."

He reached out his hand across one corner of the desk, but there was still a couple of feet of mahogany between us. When I didn't take his hand, he dropped it, but his weak smile remained.

"Good luck."

When I returned to my desk, I found I had been logged off my computer. When I tried to get back in, my account had been disabled.

"Sorry, man," said Morgan.

"It's all right. Seems like the scummy contractor is the only friend I still have in this company."

"That's right."

"It also seems as if Boris Burns has won after all. I may have driven him out of the network, but he was able to deliver one final, fatal blow. Now that I am gone, he may come back since I won't be here to carry out my threat."

"I would execute it in your stead if it came to that, but, under the circumstances, I doubt that will ever happen."

"Why? You think he won't bother to attack the company again because I am not with it anymore?"

"No, I think he won't attack FairWare again because he is dead."

"What?"

"Yes, it seems that his own employer, Golden Gate found out what he had done, and they were not too happy about it. That guy who interviewed you, Number One, put two and two together after your visit, and they confronted Boris. I think they threatened to sue or to prosecute."

"And?"

"Boris did a very grand and traditional San Francisco thing. He left Golden Gate Software jumped off the Golden Gate Bridge."

I froze in my chair. The room spun a little around me.

"You all right?"

"Just a little vertigo. I can't believe it."

"I wanted to tell you earlier, but I wasn't sure how you would take it."

"How do you know all this?"

"I have friends all over: the brotherhood of scummy contractors. One of them went to work at Golden Gate after Boris left. He heard the whole story one night from the guys in the office over vodka and sushi."

"I didn't tell them when I was there. I told them theoretically what I would if the hacker bothered FairWare again. They didn't know I was actually talking to one of them."

"I know. I believe you. You told Boris B. in veiled terms what you would do if he misbehaved again. No one else in the room had a clue what you really meant. But apparently they found a clue after you left. I told you that you should go to work for them. They seem to be sharper than some of the other knives in the drawer. Than in this drawer."

"They didn't offer me the job."

"They may now."

"I doubt it."

There wasn't much to say after that. I didn't have much to pack. Morgan found me a paper box with a good lid next to the printer. I filled it up, and I walked out. It was early afternoon.

If I had been in a movie, I would have walked out of the building carrying my box and headed east on the sidewalk. Instead, I stopped in the Mexican restaurant on the ground floor and ordered a shot of Don Julio. From the elevation of the bar stool, I could see from a higher perspective. All I was facing was the liquor stock, but what I saw was the fact that I was unemployed. I couldn't afford Don Julio anymore. So, the next shot I ordered was Cuervo Gold. After that, I switched to the house tequila. By that time I was feeling conspicuous with my box at my feet, so I found a table in the corner and slid the box underneath. I was halfway through the shot when I realized someone was standing over me.

"Hi, Geek. Buy me a drink?"

I turned, and there was Susan. I looked up at her face, and she was smiling. Then, I looked down at her belly. That flat stomach I had seen by the pool was now convex.

"I know," she said. "It does draw your attention a little lower, right?"

She turned to give me a view in profile.

"What happened?"

My mind shot back to what had not happened between us a few months before in Las Vegas. This could not have been my work.

"Woody?" I asked, but then I realized I should never have asked such a question.

Susan, however, answered with enthusiasm.

"You betcha! Old Woody rose to the occasion."

I think I turned a little red. I felt a faint trace of heat in my face.

"I forgot. You decided to call him Glen."

"I did for awhile, but then he did this. I told him he was Glen for about five minutes, and then he went back to being Woody again. Only this time there was no irony. Hey, how about that drink? Can you make it a double? I am pretty dry."

I raised my hand and got the attention of the waiter. Since we were the only customers, it wasn't that hard.

"Two—"

"Two Topo Chicos," Susan said. "No tequila. I'm not going to set you back that much, and until I deliver, I have to lay off the sauce."

She sat down and looked at me earnestly.

"I think I'm allowed to drink while I'm nursing, but then I've heard I may have to lay off the jalapeño because it will upset the baby. We mothers are always being called upon to make sacrifices."

She shook her head in an if-it's-not-one-thing-it's-another sort of way.

"But it'll be worth it," she said.

I wasn't at all sure I could agree, but I found myself nodding nonetheless. She was obviously happy about all this, and I could almost see why.

"How is Woody taking it?"

"Woody is ecstatic. Woody is ready to start working on the second one before the first one even arrives."

"What about your job?"

That was another misstep, but Susan took my every misstep in stride.

"I'm not worried about that. I haven't been looking."

"You haven't even looked?"

"No. In case you haven't noticed, I'm a little late coming to this game. I may still be a ravishing beauty, but I'm on the late side of my child bearing years. I put it off for so long that now I think I need to give it a little attention. Besides, I'm having too much fun. I can't wait until people start putting their hands on my belly in the elevator."

She looked at me as if she realized she had failed to invite me to a party.

"It's a little early for that now. I'll come back to see you when I am farther along, and then you can play pat the Susan and the baby."

I felt the heat in my cheek again. On the plane and on the bed, our shoulders had scarcely brushed.

So, you're just living on Woody? I mean, on his salary?"

"When we realized I was pregnant, he went out and found a better job. For now, we don't even need to move although I guess eventually we will have to start thinking about schools."

"I don't know what to say."

"I didn't come here for you to say anything. Not about this. I came here because I got wind of what was going to happen to you today. I see the box under the table."

"You heard?"

"I saw George the other day at Book People. I've been reading a lot lately. I can't imagine that he does. He tried to act like we were old friends. We're not, but I don't want to bear any grudge. He's supposed to keep his mouth shut about personnel issues, but he couldn't quite help himself. I think he felt a little guilty about me being the one to bear the brunt of the whole little email incident, so he dropped a few hints to indicate that I would not be the only person to go out the door over it all and to lose out on all that IPO stock. I could tell those hints he was dropping were about you, so I thought I should come over here and try to catch you on your way out. I was hoping you would turn up here in our favorite bar. I think it was the Holy Spirit."

"The holy what?"

"I came to tell you not to worry, and not to blame yourself. I've landed on my feet. It worked out for the best. I don't regret a thing. Okay, there are some things I should have done differently, but this is so much better than what we had before. The same can be true for you, but you still have a ways to go before you see it."

I tried to smile, but my lips barely budged on the edges. Yet I found myself nodding again. I half believed her. I believed the part that concerned her being better off, but not the part about me.

We sat there in silence drinking: her drink, soft and effervescent, full of sparkle; mine, hard and dulling,

"How can I not?"

"How can you not what?"

I paused for another sip.

"How can I not blame myself? There's more to this than you know."

"I don't doubt that. I'm sure you and I were not the subject of all those emails because someone thought we made such a cute couple by the pool. Maybe you did have more to do with it than I did, but there was some other motive for that attack. You and I were just the opportunity."

"So, you admit that I have the blame for some of this."

I had to rescue some culpability.

"I have no doubt."

"But you tell me not to blame myself."

"Not about me being fired. Not about you being fired either. I don't believe for a moment that was justified. Don't forget I was a manager. I have some sense of these things."

"Then, what can I blame myself for? Do I let myself off the hook?"

I remembered our conversation in the lobby when she left Blackhat abruptly.

"No, you just don't accuse yourself for things that aren't your fault. That's one of the things the priest told me in Vegas. Blaming yourself for things that aren't your fault is a way of deflecting."

"Deflecting?"

"Yeah. It's a way of avoiding responsibility for the real stuff."

"Real stuff?"

"Yeah, the stuff that really is your fault."

It seemed the floor in the bar dropped a foot or two right out from under me, and I came down hard on top of it.

"So there is stuff I can take the blame for?"

"Oh, yes. You bet."

"And what do I do about that?"

"Confess!"

The floor shifted again. I looked to see if my tequila had spilled, but it rested securely within the rim of the glass.

"Hey, don't do anything I wouldn't do," she said. "Or, don't do anything I didn't do. One of those two. Maybe it's both."

That was the trouble, of course, about the idea of confessing. She had done it.

My mind went back to a bridge in California and fell into the dark waters below. Was this her way of reaching in and pulling me out?

Susan drained the last of her first bottle of Mexican mineral water.

"Unlike last time," she said, "I can take this other one with me."

She put the second bottle unopened in her purse. Then, she placed her hand on her belly again.

"You know, I consider you to be the cause of this—not the root cause, but a pre-cause. No, that doesn't sound right. Precursor? Catalyst? I'm not sure which. I just know that things came to a head in Las Vegas, and I made a sharp turn. Thanks to you. Now, I was hoping I could somehow help you do the same."

"I appreciate that," I said.

I did not appreciate that at all.

"But this is about as far as I can go right now. Take care, Gus. When the baby comes, I'll bring him by for a visit. Or her. I don't know which it is yet. I think I want a boy, and Woody wants a girl. But every few days, we both flip. We're never in sync."

I tried to make a comeback, but I could not think of anything clever, so I resorted to science.

"It's like Schroedinger's cat," I said. "It's both possibilities at once until you take a peek, and then it is just the one thing. Just the one."

"And we both have our preferences, but when her or she finally comes, we will both have the same love. I may tell Woody about that Schroedinger thing," she said, "but I'll have to change it up. Woody is allergic to cats."

She put one hand on my shoulder, kissed me on the cheek and walked out of the bar. At the moment all my uncertain probabilities collapsed into just one thing, and I knew that Susan was no longer my boss, my lover, or my fantasy. She was my friend, and that certainty for me seemed both a gain and a loss.

It was uncertain, however, what I was going to do with it.

31 – The Double Slit

After Susan left I wandered around till evening. Towards dusk I sat down on a low retaining wall where homeless men gathered to watch the clubbers work their ways up and down Red River. They did not speak to me, neither the clubbers or the homeless. They merely tolerated my presence. To the club goers, I was another one of them, only maybe a little too tired to keep up the pace. The homeless, perhaps, knew I was in transition just as they had once been. I sat there with them, watching the same flow of drinkers and music lovers, and I felt naked just as they had felt when they left behind any pretense of being useful in the world. I had left my usefulness behind with my computer and my security officer privileges in the office, and somewhere out on the Dark Web, someone was eyeing the new corporation I had just left. Before I even got out the door, it had begun. Back when George's long awaited IPO announcement was made, the TOR browser opportunists had begun shopping for new internet burglary tools, and soon after FairWare opened on the NASDAQ, they had gone to work knowing that a new company was an unstable company loaded with new secrets and enclosed within an uncertain perimeter. They were already checking every door and every lock, and I was powerless to prevent it. I could only sit by the curb and watch in my mind's eye.

Sometime after ten PM, one of the homeless men turned to me and asked a probing question.

"You got any spare change?"

I nodded and reached into my pocket. I had $1.55 in quarters and dimes.

"You got anything bigger than this? This will buy me a twenty ounce coke from the machine, but it won't get me no dinner or bed. It won't get me anything better to drink."

I found a ten and a five in my wallet. This, I thought, was a transaction that Lloyd London could not trace.

"Thanks," he said. "Say, isn't it time you went home to bed?"

I looked down at myself. I was still too well dressed to be homeless, and, for the time being anyway, I still had a home to go back to and a bed to sleep in, lonely as it was.

"Yeah," I said. "I guess I do." So, I got up and went home.

The condo seemed particularly empty. I missed the company of the street, so I tried sleeping with the curtains open. No one on the other side of Brazos could see into my window from the Presbyterian Church or even from the glass office building beside it, and I wanted still to be a part of the town and its goings on. Some time after midnight, however, I got up and closed my curtains to block out the light. Dark as it was, the light still hindered my sleep. There was nothing left for me now but to pursue sleep, sleep that was deep and undisturbed by any of the false hopes of life or what people called energy.

During the night Boris Burns tiptoed into my room. I could hear the water dripping on the hardwood floor from his hair. I sat up to tell him not to ruin my hickory floor with all that Pacific salt water, but he waved his palm at me as if he were pushing me away. Then, he opened my curtains into two slits. I laid back down and pulled the cover up to my eyes. Yet, even with my eyes closed, I could see light through my lids. I opened them to a squint. There on the wall above my head were bands of light and dark spread out on the wall. It was the light from the moon tower on Eleventh and Trinity. The Catholic Church had bent that moon beam around St. Mary's Cathedral by means of general relativity so that it streamed through the two openings in my curtains to paint its photo interference pattern on my bedroom wall. I looked at Boris incredulously.

"There's no need for uncertainty," he said, "I'm authorized in the State of California to to perform the Double Slit Experiment." He held up a diploma in physics from U.C. Berkeley.

"But how did you get in?"

"The window was transparent. Don't worry! I will let myself out."

With that he disappeared into a higher energy state and was replaced in the room by another figure more shadowy than he.

"Who are you?" I asked.

"I read on a website that there was dark matter here for the taking."

"Dark matter?" I said. "You read wrong."

"Well, I paid twenty dollars for the exploit key to come and look. So, if you don't mind, I will just take a peek around while I am here."

I did mind, but I didn't know how to say so.

"It's a wonder anyone could find any dark matter here. There is too much light."

He closed one slit in the curtain.

"There. That's better. Now I can see."

The room grew darker as if the moon tower had been eclipsed. The light on the wall coalesced into a single band on the wall just to the left of my head. He was right. With less light in the room, it was easier to see.

"But all of Boris's work," I said as the dark figure stumbled and rumbled around in my darkened room. "You have removed it."

I jumped out of bed to reopen the other slit. Yet even as I spoke, the light changed again. The moon tower bulb was pulsing one photon at a time. I saw each one emerge through the single slit in the curtain, traverse the room like a slow motion photon torpedo from Star Trek, and stick like luminescent glue to the wall. I opened the other slit again to let in more light. Gradually, Boris's band pattern returned as the photons took turns on which slit each one went through. Or, was it that the slits were taking turns admitting the photons? Or did the photons replicate so they could go through both slits at once?

The intruder was in the bathroom now. He dropped a bar of soap on the floor of the shower. He rummaged through the drawers of the vanity. I could hear my toothbrush and razor being knocked over. I think my comb fell into the sink. I jumped back into the relative safety of my bed, pulled up the covers, and tried to cower under one of the dark bands on the wall.

The intruder returned to the bedroom from the bath.

"Man! Is it cold in here!"

He looked at the light and dark bands on the wall.

"What an awful paint job," he said. "Your decorator has piss poor taste. If it were me, I'd want it painted black. There's no dark matter here. You can't trust anything you read on the Dark Web."

He paused for a moment at the foot of my bed. Yet, even as he paused he seemed to flutter around the room. Each word in his sentence came from a different direction.

"Well, I bought some credit card numbers that I think belong to some of your neighbors. I think I'll go check up on them. That way the night won't be a total loss. Have a nice evening."

I was alone again with the bands of light. The moon tower had stopped its pulsing. The bands of light grew brighter, but the dark bands grew darker. I sat up in bed to see what would happen. I tried to scrunch myself into one of the dark bands so as to hide from the next intruder, for I felt certain there was going to be a regular procession coming into my room. The band was too narrow to hide within, and so the adjacent band of light on either side played across my face. I moved my head back and forth so that the light fell on one eye, then the other. My movements were erratic as I moved from light to dark, but the same light pattern that was on the wall formed on the back side of my eyelids. I held one eye open, and the interior pattern became one wide illuminated swath displayed like white light on a movie screen from a projector. I closed that eye and held open the other eye, and the projection screen transferred to the eyelid which had been open but was now closed. I opened both eyes again, and the dark bands reappeared. I opened one eye and then the other back and forth in rapid and unpredictable succession. The bands of light and darkness persisted in my brain on the backs of both eyelids.

"You're going to have to decide?" said a voice. It came to me in an instant when both eyes were closed but one ear was open. I could not be sure.

"Which is it? Is it light or dark?"

I was no longer confined to the bed. I was flitting about the room. I was out in the street. I came back into the room through the narrow slits in the curtain, sometimes through one, sometimes through the other, sometimes both. I went into the bathroom, jumped to the kitchen, touched the shower wall, sat in the living room chair, ran along the ceiling and laid beneath the covers of the bed. The dark man was right. It was cold in the room.

"Take a look at your self."

I did, and I was no longer flitting about the room. I was standing in one place but I did not seem quite still. I moved at an indeterminate speed towards another part of the room.

I said to Siri, "How fast am I going?"

"Let me measure," said my iWatch. "You are traveling at two feet per second."

"Thank you," I said, but I no longer knew quite where I was. Perhaps it was the bathroom. Maybe I was in bed. Maybe I was stubbing my toe against the night stand which was obscured in a band of darkness.

"Look…..at………..yourself!"

"…….Where...am…….I……..going?"

Suddenly, I was not moving. I was still, and I was painted in bands of light and dark.

"You have to choose. We used to wake up in the dark, but now you have to decide either to stay in the dark or move into the day light."

It was Robert. I could not see his face, but I recognized the situation. It was early morning, and he was waking me in the dark. I didn't know exactly when.

"You like to hide in the dark. You pass through the light as quickly as you can so you can hide again. I used to hide, but I learned to live in the light.

"I happen to like the dark."

"Live in the light."

"That's easy for you to say. You're supposed to be dead."

"That's easy for you to say. You're supposed to be alive."

"Life is overrated."

"Death is overrated. You will see that soon enough."

We jumped and dodged about the room. I tried to stay in the dark bands, but I couldn't avoid popping up in the light. Whenever I did, there was Robert illuminated in moon tower light.

"You can keep your precious light. I'm going to stay in the dark." I found the window and closed both slits.

The room went totally dark, darker than I expected, darker than I really wanted. I tried to open the curtain again, but I could no longer find it. No longer was I flitting about the room, but neither did I know where I was. At least I had gotten rid of Robert. He would have to leave, ghost that he was, to stay in the light he craved. But I was wrong, because there he stood before me, illumined in his own light while I stood in his shadow. No, it was not quite his shadow for some of his light fell on me.

"The truth is, death can be very underrated, but it all depends on how you approach it. You have to live your way into it."

"Is that young man going to come and visit us?"

I heard that second voice in the room. I could not see the speaker, but I recognized him. It was Robert's father. The two of them were in my room: Robert's father, dead from old age and the lingering scars of World War II, and Robert, dead of cancer and a broken heart.

"You two are ones to talk. You both died, and you both did it in a long, unnecessarily painful way. I'm not going to follow in your footsteps."

"If he does, he'll be entirely welcome."

"No," I said, "I don't want to be welcome. I just want to die when I want to without any pain, and I don't want any damned family reunion on the other side spoiling my demise."

"It won't work," they said in perfect unison, the old man and the son.

"You can't escape from life by dying," said the father.

"You can't escape from death by dying," said the son.

"The hell I can't. I have insurance."

"Did he say he had assurance? That's good."

"No, Dad. Insurance."

"Insurance? I had insurance. I still got old and died."

"I know. I had it, too. It made all the difference for him."

"But what's he got to insure?"

"Nothing in the normal sense, Dad. I think that's the point."

"No, it isn't," I said. "I have a condo downtown. I have a high performance car. I'm a highly paid professional—"

They looked kindly at me, those two ghosts, casting their gentle lights upon my face. They looked kindly, but I was filled with rage. It burned up in me like the Bastrop fire, but it cast no light. It was dark energy, the product of the dark matter the burglar was searching for minutes ago. Then, it died away, the dark fire. It burned itself out, and I was left standing in the lights of my unacknowledged father and grandfather. They hovered close to one another, so close that they became like a double slit in themselves, and the light passing through them cast dark and light bands directly upon me. I was exposed like film in a camera.

"Okay," I said, "I was a highly paid professional. I have a car I don't drive. And I have a condo, but I'm only three years into a thirty year mortgage. My net worth may be negative for all I know. But that is why I have insurance: so I can turn my insecurities into a total loss."

Now they looked at me quizzically, as if what I had said made no sense.

"Is he talking about life insurance or car insurance? I had a car wreck once. It never was a good car, and when it wrecked, I just wanted the insurance company to total the thing and be done with it. But they wouldn't do it. They said it could be fixed. Son—I mean Grandson—I mean Young Man—"

"It's okay, Dad. I think he has figured out who we are and who he is."

"In that case, Grandson, it sounds like you bought car insurance to cover your life and you're trying to make it a total loss."

"That's a stupid analogy."

"He does have it figured it out, Dad. No one talks like that to someone who isn't family."

"You said yourself," I said, "the car was no good, and you just wanted to write it off, but the company was too cheap."

"But it turned out that they were right. After they fixed it, the car drove great. Better than ever."

"Oh, what do you guys know about it? You're already dead."

"What do you know about it? You're still alive. Worse yet, you're young and alive."

"Worse? I thought those were good things. According to you dead people, it's good to be alive. And it's good to be young. It used to be."

"It still is good, but not in this case. Not from a perspective point of view."

"You're right there, Son. I enjoyed being young and alive until I went into the war. I enjoyed it again after the war was done, but over the years, I got something else. I got perspective like you say. And having seen both—"

"Perspective is better."

"That's right. We called it wisdom. It's worth the waiting."

"It's worth the effort."

"That's right. Best car I ever had after they fixed it."

"Don't be in a hurry to cut your losses."

"Die wise."

"Don't be in a hurry to die."

"It will come soon enough."

"Wise up while you can."

"Best car."

"Then, you can join us."

"And you'll be entirely welcome."

And those two ghosts, who were so much more reserved and bound by the cares of life while they were living but who had become so much more frank, open and chatty in death, returned to silence and faded from view. And I? I returned to darkness and to the comfort of my bed, but my bed was not so comfortable as before. There was so much dark matter under the sheet I could not even stretch out my legs. Darkness is not nearly so comforting when there's dark matter crowding the bed. But then the light reentered my room. It streamed in again from the moon tower at Eleventh and Trinity, bent around St. Mary's and came in through the slits in my curtain, but now there must have been just the single slit because the light formed one band on the wall several feet away from my head. I lay awake with one eye open staring at it until the entire wall was lit and the sun, even through that single slit, had managed to fill the room.

Then I woke up and realized I had been asleep.

I spent the morning upgrading the software on the Windows PC I had once used for gaming. It had fallen dangerously behind on the patches for everything from Adobe reader to Windows OS. It was no longer internet worthy, but I needed it to start looking for jobs. So, I devoted morning and midday into bringing it back up to all the current releases. By early afternoon, however, when the sun was overhead and no longer pouring in through the condo window, I began to have trouble seeing. My eyes were strained. I could read the screen, but I could barely see anything written on paper. I had never realized before how bad the light on the desk was because I always had used the laptop and could take it to any part of the condo I needed to see. The gaming PC, however, was immobile. The overhead light was too dim, and the twenty-four inch screen, too bright. My condo which faced the morning sun went dark by noon, and I had never upgraded the light fixtures to compensate.

Dark matter aside, I needed more light.

32 - The Lamp

There were home furnishing stores on West Sixth Street, and no doubt one of them could have transformed my condo into a well lit showcase of downtown living, but I had no prize artwork or furniture to illuminate, and no one to show it to if I did. I just needed to see to work. Besides, I was unemployed, and the Abarth had a full tank of gas. It was the same gas that had been in the tank for weeks, and it needed to be burned. It was a little past two o'clock in the afternoon when I slipped down Eleventh Street. As I crossed over I35, I had an impulse to keep going into East Austin. I remembered someone telling me there was a home renovation thrift store over there, information I thought I would never need. However, instead of crossing under the iron arch and working my way east, I turned left and punched the gas up the access road north onto the freeway.

The commuters were still in their offices. The lunchtime traffic had passed. It was a rare opportunity to drive almost unencumbered in Austin. I drove through north Austin with all the trees hiding the neighborhoods on the east side of the highway. I passed the old Mueller Airport without having to stop even once. The old radar antennas lined the service road as if they were still looking for aircraft wanting to land, but there was no landing space to be had anymore, not even in the box store parking lots that had replaced the runways. I could have begun my shopping there, but I had my heart set on a more distant pilgrimage. Even the shops of Pflugerville and nearer Round Rock were too close, too accessible for my purpose. I drove practically to the border of Georgetown and entered into the land of

IKEA.

I had never been to IKEA, but Paul had told me about it.

"Don't park near the entrance. That does you no good when you come out with your stuff. Park as close to the exit as you can get."

"The exit and the entrance are not the same?"

"They are not the same. The way in is not the way out."

I took his advice and I hovered in the parking lot till I saw someone emerge from the store with a flat bed cart loaded with long narrow boxes. I pulled into the spot nearest those sliding glass doors. Fortunately, the lot was not full, and the Abarth was easy to park. Even so, it had taken me ten minutes to get the lay of the land. That was due to the fact that the IKEA parking lot was the most regulated I had ever seen. The old airport I had passed could not have been more orderly. There was just one way in to the shopping center from University Boulevard. From that entrance I approached the store from the back. I could see the parking lot but I could not enter. I had to drive all the way around the huge store to the front. There was one way into the lot itself. Once you were in, there were sections designated for different types of cars. I envied the section reserved for electric cars and hybrids until I realized that Paul's advice took me even closer. Still, I did not understand why the exit and the entrance had to be separate until I got inside.

When you walked into Academy or HEB or Target, the whole store presented itself to you. Numerous paths forked off from the entrance, and you scanned the aisles until you found the one most promising. IKEA had one sliding door into the store, and once you entered, there was just one path to follow. You might have come to look for a desk lamp or maybe a floor lamp, but the store designers knew better. They figured you could not be fully prepared to see their lamps until you had made your way past every other group of items that they sold. Apparently, they thought that it was not good for man to buy a lamp in isolation without having seen the bedroom furniture, the kitchen cabinets, and the shelving. It reminded me of a ride at Disney World in which you followed the course from beginning to end and were not allowed to veer off or skip anything along the way. The store, I thought, could have been built inside Airman's Cave, if the cave had been higher, wider, drier, and brighter. It was certainly long enough.

I followed the linear path through the store: linear because it was one thing after another but not because it was a straight line. The path curved as space curved drawing you in like gravity to one grouping and then another. I broke free from the orbit of the kitchen cabinets only to fall into an arc around mattresses and bedroom furniture. I began to feel lost. Lost? How could I be lost when there was one direction to follow? Would I ever find what I was looking for, or would I discover that I was actually looking for something else? I saw lamps, but they were not in a lamp section. They were presented in the context of the bedroom or the kitchen work surface or the chair. I feared that I would find just what I wanted but not be able to buy it because it was anchored in its proper setting and could not be removed. Was I supposed to take a picture on my phone and show it at the register. Where was a register? Did anyone work in the store? Were there guides, or was the herd of shoppers self-guided through the maze with a single path?

Then, I saw her. She was wearing a blue polo with the store name on it. She was talking to customers and moving up and down the path as if she were its master, now entering the orbit of this chair and end table, now breaking free without so much as firing a rocket and landing on a bed. There she deftly showed how the lamp cantilevered off the overhead storage could swing freely to illuminate a book which leaned against a small stack of books in the shelf beside the pillow on the bed.

I cried out in hope and desperation.

"Maize!"

Even in a polo and without the green shoes and T-shirt covered in mud, I recognized her. Long ago, before Las Vegas and Boris Burns, she had disappeared from my life. Now here she was, here to lead me to the lights, and, perhaps, beyond.

"Maize!" I cried out even louder.

She did not respond.

I pushed my way past two women who were looking at the storage crates and stumbled over the blue futon trying to catch up with her. The twenty-something with the shaved head looked at me as if I had emerged from some alternative reality that was out of phase and out of step with this world tripping as I was over store displays and calling women by names to which they did not respond.

"Maize!"

"It is not a maze!" said a woman with a pierced lip and blue hair. "It is a linear progression. You just need to stop, breathe in, and follow the path. Stop yelling as if you were lost. It is impossible to be lost. All paths are one."

I smiled and squeezed past her as quickly as I could.

"Maize!"

At that moment, Maize turned around, but it wasn't the sound of my voice that changed her direction. She reached back to adjust a pillow on a sofa and saw me as I avoided the ottoman.

"Oh, hi," she said. "I'm glad you came in. I've been wanting to talk to you."

Did she remember who I was? Did she mistake me for someone else. I didn't dare ask.

"I get off at six. Can you meet me in the cafeteria?"

"Yes, but I need a lamp."

"Silly boy. Your condo was too dark."

She showed me a desk lamp. I realized I had no proper desk, not compared to the wonder of design and efficiency that the lamp was resting on. So, she found a desk that tucked neatly into a corner with a keyboard tray that pulled out and stored underneath when not in service. I did not dare tell her I was unemployed and shouldn't be spending so much money.

"But where do you get these?" I said. There was not a shelf in the place that was not itself for sale.

She led me to the warehouse. There we dragged a four by three foot box off a lower shelf onto a flat bed cart. She herself reached up to get a three foot by 8 inch box down from a high shelf on the rack. As she stretched and reached I saw why she had not responded when I called. Her name tag said, "Mary."

She led me by a shortcut to the cashiers. I felt as if I had learned the secret path to enlightenment from my own personal guru.

"Six o'clock. In the dining area. She pointed to a cafeteria at the end of store."

"Six o'clock," I repeated, wondering how I would endure until then. It was only three-thirty.

I was out of the store and rolling towards the parking lot before I realized the obvious. My four by three foot box was not going to fit into my Fiat 500 Abarth, not easily. I had to fold down the back seats and fold the front passenger seat forwards to do it. And I still had two hours and fifteen minutes to kill. I drove around the parking lot for awhile. There was a Spec's liquor store in the complex, and I wandered around looking at the tequila and beer, but the choices were so many I couldn't make up my mind. The silver tequila reminded me that I had gas to burn, so I left the store and headed east on University until I reached the toll road. There I drove up and down varying my speed between seventy-five and ninety-five. I wanted to go all out as if I were on the Autobahn and push the Abarth to its limit, but I was afraid of getting a ticket I could not afford in my present financial state. Besides, I felt strangely confined within myself, and I seemed to hit my own limits well before the car did. I noticed as I drove how short the throw was on the shifter. As I moved up to third, my knuckles stopped just inches from the dashboard. The distance from third to fourth was practically the flex of my wrist. As I pressed down the accelerator, I noticed how small the car really was. Despite the fact that I was more accustomed to a Smart Car, the Fiat felt confining. The faster I drove the shorter it seemed to get. How close the windshield seemed to my face. How enclosed my heart was in my chest. At ninety-five I reached the end of my little race course more quickly than I would have liked. I turned and went back to Round Rock. It was the work of mere minutes. I ran the whole course again. If was as if I were a kid on a bicycle confined to a single stretch of sidewalk bounded by streets I could not cross. The whole exercise in freedom only highlighted my boundaries. Even the thrill of acceleration was reduced to the backwards drag of inertia.

I returned to IKEA and parked in the shade of the back of the building.

***

I didn't know how to begin with Maize. We sat across the table lifting our eyes to one another across two plates of meatballs.

"These things are really good."

"I know. I've gained seven pounds since I started working here."

I couldn't see where she put it. If anything, she looked better than before: more rounded.

"You eat here a lot?"

She nodded. The prices were great, and maybe she got a discount.

"But I thought you were a vegetarian."

"No. Why did you think that?"

I remembered seeing her at Whole Foods. She had been handling beef.

"Just an impression. I guess vampires can't afford to be vegans."

"No, that's true. But I'm not a vampire anymore. I buried that identity months ago."

"Put a stake through its heart."

"Yes."

"And you changed your name."

"No, I didn't. Oh, that's right. You met me when I was calling myself Maize. I did that for awhile. I liked the whole wind-in-the-fields-native-american-organic vibe. Maybe that is why you got the impression I was a vegan."

"Maybe so."

"My name is Mary. It always has been, but I've been in rebellion."

"Why?"

"It sounds so, so pure. You might get the impression I'm a virgin."

I wanted to say that didn't matter, but I stuffed my mouth with a meatball just in time.

"I'm not, you know."

I nodded as if I did know. My mouth was still full, so I could not speak. I think my face was turning red.

"I've slept with a lot of guys. I've slept with a few girls. I almost slept with you."

I almost choked. So close. I had come so close.

"I was going to crawl in bed with you that night after the cave, but you fell asleep. You were so tired, and I remembered that someone had to go get your car and bring it back. So I left to go get it. That was a bit of a trick."

"I wish you had stayed."

"I know. It's better this way."

"How is it better?"

"Because now we can be fresh with one another. Hopeful. Not once joined then ripped apart. I've been ripped apart too many times."

"I'm sure once is enough," I said.

"Once too many," she said.

Of course. It was a stupid thing to say. I had only stupid things to say. Then, I had an idea.

"What if I were to offer to marry you, Maize. I mean, Mary."

"Oh," she said. "Really?"

"Sure," I said.

"That may be the sweetest, the most gallant, the most wonderful thing anyone has ever said to me."

She grabbed my hand in both of hers. I wished it had been me grabbing her hand, but I hadn't thought of it. My offer had been too spontaneous.

"No one has ever, ever asked me to marry him before. I had a woman ask me once, but I turned her down."

She leaned forward and whispered.

"It's not the same. Besides, she really didn't mean it."

"I mean it."

"I know."

What was I doing? I was unemployed.

"It almost makes me want to go outside with you and get in your car and make love right there in the shady side of the parking lot."

"Why can't we?"

"Because I've seen your car. And I've seen what you have stuffed in it. I helped you find it in the warehouse. Remember?"

"I'll pull it out and set it down on the ground."

She shook her head and smiled.

"What about your car? It's got plenty of room."

"No, it doesn't. I don't have that car anymore. It finally died. Besides, it would have been a sauna in there."

"What kind of car do you have now?"

I was sure that whatever kind it was, I could make it work.

"I don't."

"You don't have a car? How do you get around? Do you need a ride?"

Of course. Her place. I could take her home to her place.

"No. I've got my scooter. Finally. It's so wonderful. I can get around again—except for on the freeway or the toll road. It's not big enough for those places. But for eighty miles per gallon, you can't complain."

"A scooter?"

She nodded.

"You are sweet," she said.

I nodded.

"But I can't be sleeping with you."

I started to nod but stopped.

"It's not you."

For some reason Robert came to mind. Why would Robert come to mind at a time like this?

"Of course," I said. "We should get married first. That's how people used to do it. We can restart an old tradition. I will wait till then. I can wait for you."

I might as well wait. In fact, at that moment I almost thought I could marry her and still wait, keep right on waiting. Lloyd, did you get that on the IKEA cafeteria camera? I'm planning for the future. I hope to live. I'm finding meaning in life.

"Oh," she said squeezing my hand. She smiled. A tear rolled down her cheek. She let go of my hand.

"We can't."

"Why not? I'll get another job."

"Another job? Why would you need another job?"

"It's a long story."

"Where would we live?"

"In my condo."

"I'd have to give up my job here. I can't ride my scooter to Round Rock on the freeway. Remember?"

"You could drive my car."

"Thanks, but no."

"Or, I could get another place. Up here."

"That would be awfully far for you, especially with the traffic."

It was far.

"I could do it."

"I wouldn't want you to do that. Besides, I can't marry you. I'm thinking of becoming a nun."

"You're what?"

"I'm thinking of becoming a nun."

"But you just said you wanted, you almost wanted to— "

" —to sleep with you?"

She sighed.

"I know. I did. I've got a long way to go."

"But you never told me you were Catholic."

Actually, she had never told me a lot of things, had she?

"I'm not."

"You're not? Then, how are you going to be a nun?"

"Well, first I'll have to become a Catholic."

"Why would you want to do that? Wait! I know. It's so you can become a nun."

Lloyd, never mind.

No, wait. I didn't mean that. But Lloyd couldn't read my mind. He said so, essentially, after Las Vegas. But he could read the signs.

"No, that's just the progression. You know, Catholic to nun? I think the reason I want to become Catholic is because of the blood."

"The blood?"

"Yes, you remember I was a vampire? We talked about that."

"Yes. You had room in your suburban to put a coffin."

"After I ditched that notion, I wondered what I had ever seen in it. I had thought I was attracted to death, but that wasn't it at all."

"What was it then?"

"I wanted life."

"But blood is about death. You bleed, and you die."

"True, but that is only because blood is about life. We think about death when we spill blood, but that is because we see the life ebbing away. The life is in the blood. The blood is about life."

"What's that got to do with you becoming being a Catholic?"

"Catholics drink the blood of Jesus Christ."

"You mean out of a glass?"

"I think it's a metal cup."

"Does it taste like blood?"

"I don't know. I haven't tried it yet."

"But," I said, but I didn't finish the sentence. I reached across the table and grabbed her hand as if we were lovers and not just two people who crawled through a muddy cave together and washed off in the same shower.

"But what?"

I could almost hear the word "darling" at the end of that sentence as if she meant to say it but hadn't.

"But what does this have to do with being a nun? All Catholics are not nuns. I know some who aren't nuns."

Technically, Raj could not be a nun, but I didn't mention that. Practically speaking Susan could not be one either.

"I heard somewhere that Catholics don't believe in birth control. Well, logically that means they do believe in sex. At least, they believe in married sex. But that's okay. I—I'm willing for that. You still could. We still could."

Her eyes were filling with anticipation like tears of joy without the wetness. I realized I was making an argument but not quite a proposal. Robert told me once about proposals.

"When you propose to a girl, you've got to be definite. You have to say it like you mean it."

"Mary," I said. Mary was her name. Did she even know my name? I would have to tell her later.

I realized I should be on my knee before I continued, but we were in an IKEA cafeteria. Everyone would be watching. I supposed this was the dilemma faced by many men over time, and they had paid the price. I slid my chair aside. It scraped on the floor. I got down on one knee. I did not let go of her hand.

"Mary, would you marry me? Me? Gus Bishop?"

Her smile grew larger. An actual tear dripped down one cheek.

"Gus, I can't."

"Mary, it's all right. I don't mind. I liked you when you were a vampire. I would love you even if you were a Catholic. I might even…."

What might I?

"I might even put up with the birth control thing."

"You might not have to."

"Why?"

"I sold my eggs."

I thought of a carton of green Styrofoam in the refrigerator, but that wasn't what she was talking about. She took a couple of deep breaths. I held her hands and waited.

"I sold my eggs to a fertility clinic. I was desperate. I needed the money. Now I may not be fertile any more."

My mind raced. I thought back to what little I knew of female reproductive biology. A period once a month. Ovulation. Puberty. Menopause. Most of these memories of mine came from crude jokes, but I pieced it all together and stirred in a little math.

"But you couldn't have sold them all yet."

She looked up at me. I thought I saw either hope or confusion in her eyes.

"Every month you produce an egg, right? Or release an egg. Anyway, you do that from age thirteen to age—I don't know—forty-seven. That is thirty-five years. Times twelve that's four hundred and twenty. If you sold an egg a week it would take you eight years to sell them all. You didn't sell that many, did you?"

She shook her head.

"But—"

"I know. You sold some. You may be fertile for fewer years, but you haven't lost it entirely. Don't worry. You can still have babies."

She still didn't appear to be that comforted, so I tried a different tack.

"You can still be a nun even if you are more fertile than you thought."

Another tear fell. Mary smiled through the tears, the pair of them.

"Careful," I said, "you'll dehydrate."

She smiled again. I fetched her a cup of water.

We parted in the parking lot. I walked her to her scooter. We waited there in the shade of the building until all her tears had dried and she could see clearly once again. Then, she smiled and put on her helmet. We shook hands, and she started the engine. I followed her with my eyes as she wound around the building back to the exit of the parking lot, but I did not attempt to follow her in my car. I did not have her number, and I did not know where she lived. She said I could come by to see her at the store again at six Tuesdays through

Fridays. I said I would but that it would be difficult to do when I was working. I knew she still didn't know what I meant by that. Yet, I felt responsible to her. Once I had another job, I would not be able to drive to IKEA by six. Until I had another job, I had nothing to offer her. I didn't remember Robert saying this, but somehow I imagined that he would have. You could be married to a woman in poverty and want, but you couldn't ask her to marry you until you could support her. Then, there was the other paradox. I wanted to marry Mary, a paradox in itself, but I also wanted her to be happy, and it did not seem as if her happiness lay in lying with me. But if I let her go, I would be letting go of the last hope I had.

I drove home and went to bed. The next day I arose around noon and began assembling my new desk and mounting my new lamp. Somehow that task took me most of the afternoon. I couldn't decide how to rearrange the room to make space for my new furniture. I could not set my mind to the discipline of following the directions which blurred from time to time from my tears. Every twist of the Allen wrench tightening a bolt increased the pressure on my heart. Finally, about six o'clock I finished the desk. Twenty-two miles away Mary was getting off work. Did she eat in the cafeteria, or did she ride home to make a salad? There was no way for me to catch up with her in time no matter what she did, so I went downstairs and round the corner to order Thai.

I did not speak to the woman at the register. I had never seen her before. I stood there in silence until Joe told her from the kitchen what my usual order was. Then, I sat in my spot at the table. When she brought the food, I nodded once and ate in silence. I sat there at my empty plate for a long time and left a twenty dollar bill as I stood up. I had no income. What did I need with money? I went back around the corner and up the elevator to my condo. I put my old gaming PC on the new desk and booted it up. I did not look for jobs or check the forums to see who was hiring. I did not play any games.

My new lamp hovered over the keyboard at just the right angle to illuminate the board and the desk, but I did not turn on the light.

33 - The Claim

I awoke with one sure purpose in mind: to contact Lloyd London. It was still dark. I was slumped in the easy chair I had parked in front of my computer screen. The screen still glowed like a portal into the Dark Web, like the entry point into secret knowledge. Outside the street was quiet. I could not see any clocks, not without budging from my chair, not without breaking from my stasis. If only I had opened a Facebook account, I could have posted my condition. But now I could not bear going through the process of opening an account and, worse yet, of asking for friends. Perhaps Lloyd would see such an effort as an act of desperation in itself. On the other hand, the thing he had warned me about so clearly was going offline. Perhaps internet silence was the best beacon I could deploy. The problem was I could not stand the quiet, not for the amount of time it would take for Lloyd to know I was good and internet dead. Besides, I was afraid that out of the silence would come voices, and the voices, I was certain, would say things I could not bear to hear.

That's the trouble with nihilistic despair. Nothing you can choose to do because of it can ever be worth doing.

I should have been a blogger. I should have opened a Twitter account when I had the chance and developed a following. I should have had virtual friends and followers so that I could express my anguish to my insurance agent who collected the data on my life unseen and made his quiet actuarial determinations. This wasn't supposed to happen. I wasn't supposed to reach this place of loss and desperation. Instead, I was supposed to pass painlessly into sweet oblivion at the first sign of unrelievable distress. Not like Robert, not like he had died and, for that matter, not like he had lived. For Robert, my progenitor, my father, had lived with trouble and crushed hope. My mother had never treated him with anything but disdain, and he had suffered for the loss of her. I had never realized that before, but now I could see what in the past I had either not understood or had simply ignored. Robert had suffered the loss of the woman he had continued to love. She hated him, but he never hated her back. And he had suffered another loss besides. He had lost me. I had absorbed her indifference and disdain. Now, I could see what I had been an unwitting party to all along. Robert kept me in clothes, bicycles, and education funds, but he had never been allowed to admit, not to me and not to the world at large, that he had been my father. No, that wasn't it, not entirely.

He had never been allowed to confess to me that I was his son, and I had never admitted that fact to him or to myself. Yet, despite the silence, he had been my father until he died. Did it even stop then? Did his fatherhood stop upon death? No one else ever said, "I had a father, but I don't have one any longer." They just said, "My father is dead." Robert had become more of a father to me after he was dead than when he had been alive. That was just like Robert to be better dead than alive. He should have realized that and done something about it before he got cancer and went through all that suffering. Too bad Lloyd London wasn't in business back then, but then Robert could never have afforded the kind of insurance I had. He would have had to pull the trigger himself.

But he did have insurance. He had the old fashioned kind of life insurance: term life. I was his benefactor. But what if he had committed suicide? What would have happened to me? Would the company have paid? That was a question for Lloyd or for Google. On the other hand, if he had been so predisposed to suicide, would he ever have bothered to buy insurance at all? Would he have cared for me the same, or would he have been preoccupied with his own despair? Robert lived on the edge of despair all the time. Or, rather, he always had reason to despair, but somehow he never did. I would have done it. I had done it, and my life was nowhere near as hard as his, not even now. He should have spared himself all that suffering, but if he had spared himself, would I have reaped such benefits, either during his life or after?

Then, a truly sobering thought came to me at my brand new IKEA computer desk. What if Robert's suffering had been part of the whole transaction? What if, in some bizarre, parallel alternative universe way, his suffering had been the mechanism that enabled him to give me the gifts that he had? What if Robert had been my father all along, in sickness and in health, but it had taken his death to make me his son? Wasn't the whole thing with life insurance that you had to die before it would pay? That life insurance policy, however, had not even been the half of it. Everything Robert had ever given me cost him his life. With every pair of jeans, every pair of running shoes, every school activity fee, he had died a little more. Every time he met mom in the HEB parking lot to pick me up or drop me back off, he left a little of his blood on the asphalt. So, here I was alive, and there he was dead, but what good had it done? He had successfully given me the means to live, but what reason had he left me to continue to do it?

I sat there in a state of tension, caught between the odd, sudden sense of joy that comes when you finally figure something out and the pervasive sorrow that the quick stab of joy has pierced. I was wounded by that joy, a deep and painful wound, and I was offended to have my old familiar sorrow so abruptly disturbed. But the old injury remained and the pain only moved deeper below the surface beyond the reach of any ointment.

The next thing I knew I had awakened from a deep sleep. The darkness was gone. The room was full of light—not lamp light or dawn light but daylight beating down and heating up from directly overhead. I felt like a vampire who had overslept and now found himself exposed to the sun. The fear of death came upon me as if I were that vampire caught in the light. Wherever I looked, I saw no dark place to escape, but I could not stay where I was.

My computer screen had gone dark. There was no browser internet session behind that opaque screen, but my iWatch came to life with the flick of my wrist. I checked my vital statistics. My pulse was 185. I might as well have been running a 10K race, but I hadn't moved in hours. My pulse rate was due to panic. Then, I understood. I did not need to be posting my anxiety on social media for my insurance company to detect it. My watch was giving me away. Lloyd certainly knew now that my time had come, and his failure to detect my need sooner would bring him all the more quickly. I had to welcome him. I had to escape.

I jumped up from the chair. The room seemed to rotate about me in frames. My entire body vibrated. My limbs trembled. I began to pace about the room in quick random paths like an electron in a high energy state. I seemed to be everywhere and nowhere. Yet, everywhere I went, there was death waiting. So, I ran. I bounced off the wall like a bird at a window and fluttered along its length until I found the bedroom door. I ricocheted about the living room in indecisive jolts: the kitchen, bedroom, balcony, bath, and through the front door. The elevator was open in the lobby and waiting, but the sight of that confining little space appalled me. I ran to the stairwell and flew down, down, down, down to the lobby and out onto the street.

Traffic on Brazos flows north. I turned south. At Eighth Street I dodged right in front of the Omni Hotel and ran east to Congress. There a nice, leisurely progression of pedestrian traffic flowed north on the sidewalk. No one hurried, not even to cross the intersections. I slowed down to match the pace, but my arms and legs were surging with adrenaline, and I could not remain in that laid back late morning groove. I passed everyone on the sidewalk ignoring the walk signs at the intersection, and so I found myself at Eleventh Street with the Capitol looming before me. I didn't want to wait for the light, so I ran across Congress and down the sidewalk by the Governor's Mansion. I turned left on Colorado, and there I slowed down to consider my options.

What if I threw my hands up in the air, screamed, and charged the mansion. Would the DPS take me out? Could I commit suicide by cop? Or, would they merely tackle and cuff me. Then, I might just lie there still on the street until a car came to take me to jail. How long would I be trapped in that car? How long would I be down on the ground? How long would I have to wait before I could escape? How would I ever explain? What if they just let me go? Better to keep my hands in my pocket, look straight ahead, and keep moving, keep burning adrenaline.

Then I remembered: I could text, and to Lloyd's big data analysis, a text was as good as a Facebook post. I pulled my phone out of my pocket, and I found Raj's message thread. Our last exchange had been before I entered the cave when I had become sick in the bathroom.

"Cant go on. Dont want 2 go on. Must not go on."

Raj was right there with his reply.

"What's wrong? R u afraid?"

"Panic. Fear Im going to die. Fear wont die fast enuf."

"What is it?"

What if he thought this was all just a joke? Was he taking me seriously? It didn't matter as long as Lloyd did, and Lloyd had my ongoing pulse rate and Geo-location to corroborate his assessment.

"My life over. Nowhere to go. All closing in. Cant run fast enuf."

"Did u lose your job?"

"Yes."

"Did u meet a woman you cant have?"

"Probably."

How did he know these things? Was he psychic? He was a Catholic Indian, not a Hindu guru type of Indian. His real name was Thomas. I only called him Raj to make him seem more Indian to me. But what the psychic Indian didn't know was that I had lost more than a job and a love. I had lost whatever was beneath even those things. Everything I had taken for granted and even solid things I had denied now tilted and sank into soft, shifting sands that were giving way beneath my feet. I tried to flee, but I found no footing. And in my agony the sand could not swallow me fast enough.

"Wait till I get there."

"Dont know where I will be. Cant stay still."

"Will find u. Text u when I get to town."

"OK," I wrote, but I did not intend to wait. I might not even answer when he texted back. I was not waiting for Raj. I was waiting for Lloyd London. Lloyd London—I didn't have his email address or his phone number. Yet he could see these texts. The signs were unmistakable. He would come. Maybe he would not come in person, but he would come. Lloyd, with whom I had sat down and eaten several meals, would send me relief. Raj and I—we had never spoken a word to one another. We had seen each other at the front door of our building, in the hall, in the parking garage for weeks without acknowledging one another existed. Then, one day I had texted him.

"Look down the hall to ur right."

He turned to me. I nodded, phone in hand.

He nodded back.

"How did u get my nbr?"

"Have ways."

"U a hacker?"

"Sort of."

"White hat?"

"More gray."

That had been the beginning of our textual relationship. Though we lived on the same hallway, neither of us ever knocked on the other one's door or even said, "Good morning." That had been our rule of interaction. Now, he was leaving work in midday to rescue me from my dread. What could I say to him now?

At Sixth Street I turned left. There was no live music in the middle of the day. Maybe in the piano bar at the Driskill Hotel. I turned left on Brazos to see if I could hear any music coming from the hotel. Perhaps I could have gone in just to check, but that would have meant waiting. I had to keep moving in the open until Lloyd could find me. I checked my pulse again. It was over two hundred now, but if I were continually moving, would Lloyd just think I was exercising? I had to depend on the texts to do the trick. Surely, they revealed my despair. Surely Lloyd would realize he had to hurry before Raj arrived to keep me from fleeing from the fear of death into the arms death itself.

Once I was past the Driskill, I slowed down. My body could no longer keep up the pace, but my mind never stopped racing. When I was still, I wanted to be moving. When I moved, I wanted to be waiting. Every direction I could choose held just as much promise and just as much futility. So, at Seventh, I paused and tried to catch my breath. It came back to me in a few minutes, but the tingling and rushing of my blood never abated. I pressed on slowly, almost staggering as if I were drunk. I crossed another street, and there I was right back in front of my own building.

Then, I heard the first voice to address me in more than twelve hours.

"Man, you better hurry. He be after you."

I looked around, no longer able to tell the direction from which sounds came. There on the sidewalk in the shade of a small tree stood my homeless man, the one whom I encountered going to work. I reached for my wallet instinctively knowing full well I couldn't spare twenty dollars now when I had no job. But why couldn't I? It was not like I was saving it for the future.

He just held up his hand and shook his head.

"I ain't never seen you in this big a hurry, but you better just keep on runnin'."

"Running? I'm not running? I wasn't running. It's too hot to run."

Surely, he could see the sweat stains on my shirt.

"No, man. I know the run. I seen it before. I know what you done. You bought the policy, and now it's time to collect."

"Policy? What are you talking about?"

"The life policy. You been payin' the premiums. I seen you do it. I used to be a collector myself, but I just couldn't do it anymore. Most of them policy holders would last maybe nine months, even a couple of years. Then, it would just go dark, and they'd be gone."

"Dark?"

He laid his palm upon his heart.

"Dark. In here. And when it goes dark, it's time to come to terms. What I couldn't understand was why they kept on payin' the premiums. When they was feelin' good and seein' hope, why didn't they just change their minds? But don't stand here listenin' to me. Get going. He's on your tail."

"Who?"

I had been running, true, but I hadn't really thought that I was running from anyone, not from anyone on two feet or in four wheels.

"Who am I running from?"

"Can't you see? Look at you. You're runnin' around in circles just as the day is getting hot. You're in a panic. You don't know where to go, but you don't want to stay where you are. You're sendin' out clear signs, and so they have sent him to get you."

"Who have they sent? Who is they?"

"The company, man! The company. They know it's time, and they have sent him to pay up. In full. I've seen it before."

"I don't know what you are talking about. This company—"

"Don't shine me on, Man. I've seen you payin' the premium. I know how it works. You pay by the week just like you was a black man on the east side with a burial policy. It is a kind of burial policy. You pay the guy on the street until you just can't stand it anymore. Then, they pay up, and you collect."

"Can't stand what anymore?"

"Livin'! You got your condo and your loud little car and you can't stand it anymore, so they come for you. That's what you paid 'em for, right? So, now, you reached the end. You got nowhere else to go, but you're afraid. Man, are you afraid. You so afraid you can taste it. Right here."

He touched his lips and tongue with his finger. He was right. It was that same metallic taste I had known in the cave.

"He's comin'. I've seen this guy before. This is his territory. They always send him to this part of town. You're not the first. There's been others, and I've seen him come for them."

"Who? Who have you seen?"

"The agent of death."

Now the taste on my tongue became sickening. Numbness spread from my mouth and weighted my arms and legs. I felt immobile, and yet I had to flee.

"Where can I go? What do I do?"

"Right now you better run. Run somewhere you don't normally go. Then, calm down and decide."

"Decide what?"

"Decide you want to live."

I nodded and started to go. I was halfway down the block when he called out to me.

"Hey. Hold on. Hold on. You won't get far with that."

He pointed to his wrist. I looked at my watch keeping track of my pulse, my every step, and my Geo-location. I undid the band and handed to him. I started to go again.

"And the phone! He's trackin' you."

"You're right. I know it."

I handed him my phone.

"Wait," I said. "Won't he just come after you instead?"

"No. He knows I ain't you, and I didn't buy no policy."

I turned again. As I resumed my stride I called back over my right shoulder.

"Three-nine-two-six-one-four. That's the number to get into the phone. I've got unlimited calls, but there's only half a charge on the battery. You're welcome to what's left."

"Thanks, Man. I can get it charged. I got my ways."

I felt lighter. My feet moved faster than before, but I was going the same direction. Too predictable. I turned and went back to Congress, but this time when I reached Eleventh I crossed the street and kept going onto the state capitol grounds.

The air there, at least, was cooler. There was intermittent shade and grass all around. Even though I wasn't dressed for jogging, I didn't look quite so ridiculous running here as I did on the city sidewalks. The walkways here moved in gentle arcs and forked off in different directions. I took the fork to the left and ran easily down hill.

Then, I saw him, the agent of death. He had on a white hat, off white pants and shirt. It had to be he. He was coming towards me on the path I had just been on, so now he would have to walk past my position and turn right to follow me on my new path. My heart began pounding. I tried to quicken my pace, but my legs wouldn't move any faster. I looked over my shoulder. He was about thirty yards back. He seemed to be in no hurry. Did he think I would just stop and let him catch up? I imagined him coming up beside me from behind, putting an arm around me and greeting me as if we were, if not friends, at least compatriots, fellow travelers. And then?

But he didn't overtake me. He just kept following.

I took the next right and headed towards the capitol itself.

I reached the path that went around the building, and I began walking that loop. There were more people here, even a few troopers. I thought about going into the building itself, but what if he came up to me while I was waiting at the metal detector? I kept going on the outside around the building.

When I got to the far side of the capitol, I left the loop and took a path that headed for the perimeter gate. I wanted to put that iron fence between us, even if only for a moment. I looked over my shoulder. The agent hadn't veered off to follow me. Had I been mistaken? Was the man in all white not the agent? He was still on the loop, and I was still headed for the gate. I slowed down a little and almost strolled to the iron fence. I even touched the nearest gold star as I left the inner capitol grounds and turned left back towards Eleventh Street. I felt a little more secure with that metal boundary between me and the supposed agent. My relief lasted but a few moments. Without someone concrete to fear, fear itself came on me as an all pervasive dread. Only now, I had no energy left to run and nowhere to go to escape my ubiquitous doom.

I passed another gate and turned back into the capitol grounds. Immediately on my right there was a series of steps leading down to a grassy depression. I read once that the capitol had contained a small pond. The pond had long since been drained, but now I was walking on what had been the bottom of it, headed once again towards the main entrance along another curving path. There were lots of trees with people lying on the grass in various spots in this depression, some with lunches and some with books. They were calm, enjoying what was essentially a park. They had hope. Whether any single one of them had a future or not, I couldn't tell, but they acted as if that did not matter. How could it not matter? Who could be relaxed and implicitly hopeful without a future? Without a future, you were at the end.

And then I saw I had been wrong, for now the man in white was on another sidewalk that would intersect with mine. He had not turned away. He had found a path from which to cut me off, and whether I kept going south or turned back north, he would meet me at either crossroads, and then would come my reckoning, the payment of my claim.

I stopped. He stopped on his parallel path. I waited as if I were enjoying the scene. I left the path a little to look at a tree. There was no way to climb it, but I looked up as if I were admiring its branches. I think there was a little plaque to describe the variety of the tree, but I didn't bother to read it. I reached up to touch the bark. I leaned into the trunk. The agent of death also left the path and began walking straight towards me. I waited till he had nearly reached the tree. Then, I bolted for the sidewalk and began walking briskly towards the main gate. I looked back once over my shoulder. The agent was on the path and following me. It felt good to have my fear objectified in a person who had a definite location. Halfway to the main gate, I darted off the path and ran across the grass towards one of the side gates. If the agent were going to follow, he would have to leave the path as well. If he continued towards the main gate in hopes of cutting me off again, I would have him fooled. I was going to turn the other direction. If he had that move figured, I would turn to the main gate and leave him behind. How would he ever know which way I would go? By the time I was through the gate, however, I had realized the desperateness of my gambit. Whichever way I turned, Big Data would have predicted it. So, I turned neither way. Instead, I crossed the four lanes of Eleventh Street against the light. The agent would not be so foolhardy to follow me until the traffic cleared. That would give me time to duck into an alley and pop out on the other block. If I could just make it around a brick building corner, I could lose him. Maybe I could get back to my condo and my car. I could grab a Car2Go, but he could track those. I had to be more careful. I had to be more unpredictable.

I was just ten feet from the curb when a car whizzed past behind me. I could feel the suction as it passed. The tire just caught the heel of my shoe and pushed it down to the pavement. I thought I would run out of my crippled shoe, but it stayed on my foot like a flip flop sandal. I stumbled onto the sidewalk. People were pointing in amazement. They weren't sure if they should marvel at my narrow escape or condemn me for my stupidity.

One of them said, "Did you see that? That car had no driver."

I looked back. The agent must still have been on the capitol grounds behind the fence. I hoped he could not see me. I ran down the road on the east side of the governor's mansion until I reached Tenth. I limped across it in my damaged shoe. At Brazos I was about to turn south towards home, but I decided against it. It was simply too predictable. So, I crossed Brazos and found myself in front of St.

Mary's Cathedral. A steep flight of concrete steps led up to a pair of imposing wooden doors. The doors were shut, but then one opened with a creak, and a man trotted down the steps and turned right on the sidewalk. I looked back over my shoulder. The agent was nowhere to be seen, and I was nowhere he could see me. I climbed the steps, opened the door, and entered with one shoe firmly fastened and the other just held to my foot by force of habit.

The inside of the church was cool and dark. I sat down on a bench and tried to recover my other shoe.

34 – The Bruised Heel

My shoe was beyond hope. The leather upper was so compressed onto the sole that the two were practically fused together. The back of my sock was quite torn away, but that was not the worst. The entire outer layer of skin had been sheared from my heel. The blood was beginning to ooze onto the floor.

Lloyd and his agent had missed but by inches. I could hear him in my head as if we were eating at another Austin venue and speaking of life and of terms.

"Don't worry. Next time we won't miss. Remember! We will take good care of you. That is what you paid us for, and you are paid in full."

The door creaked open, and a man rushed in wearing a state ID badge and sun glasses. He walked past me and went through another set of doors. I suddenly felt very vulnerable sitting out in the foyer, so I followed him inside. There I found myself in another era. All around me there was stained glass peopled by figures in ancient or Middle Age costume, the light shining through each one. I didn't recognize anybody in the windows. Down the center isle in the front there was a gold cylinder with a dome on the top, and behind that, high on the wall, was a cross with a man hanging on it: Jesus, I supposed. He was suffering. He obviously had never had insurance of any kind, and yet even though I had, I felt something like him. Or, rather, he seemed to feel like me—except he was merely suffering, and I was suffering and afraid. Seeing him there, my fear quieted a little, but not completely.

I was standing in the middle aisle, and there was no one else visible. Where had the guy I had followed in gone? I looked to the right and the left. Along the wall on either side there were two lines of people waiting to go back into the foyer. My guy was on the right. I went over to the line on the left. There I leaned into paneled wall. The room was quiet, quieter than anyplace in downtown could be, quieter than my condo at midnight.

The woman at the head of my line went through the door, and everyone moved forward a space. I realized that my hiding place in this queue had an end point. My turn would come, and I would have to exit. Perhaps I could change my mind and go sit on one of the benches towards the front. Maybe no one would notice me there, and I could hide for a little longer. Perhaps the quiet would seep in, and when I finally had to leave, I could carry it with me. It almost seemed as if the quiet had ears and had heard what I had not even said. My fear left me and took a step back. Now, it stood behind me, separate but still waiting for an opportunity to return. I decided I didn't like being in this line. I had picked out a place to go sit when someone else came through the door and walked over to stand behind me. Now I was trapped.

The line moved again. Just one more step before I would be the one standing at the door, waiting my turn to exit. The guy behind me smiled. Why was he smiling at me? There must have been some unspoken, secret camaraderie of those in the line. I wasn't sure I really wanted to be included, and yet with this guy standing behind me fear had taken yet another step back. Fear now was at the end of the line, and with fear, even a short distance made a huge difference.

The person in front of me stepped through the door, and I stepped to the threshold. However, he didn't go out of the church. He went through another door along the very back wall of the foyer that had just swung open and closed it behind him. So there was yet one more place of respite before the final exit. I turned to the smiling man behind me, and I smiled back albeit nervously.

Outside the main doors I expected the agent of death was waiting, and inside, behind my smiling compatriot in line, fear was waiting to drive me into the agent's arms. For now, however, we were at a truce. Jesus on the cross did not move, and neither did I.

"Are you going in?"

I turned. The man behind me was speaking to me.

"What?"

"Are you ready to go in?"

"I don't know."

"It's your turn."

I looked. The door just beyond the threshold had swung open. At the same time I could hear the outer door of the church swinging closed. Fear seemed ready to pounce. Then, I had an idea.

"You can go first," I said.

"No. That's okay. You go. I'll wait, or I may go over to the other side. There's only one guy over there. You go. Take your time. I'll be fine."

He smiled again. I could hardly have been more disarmed than if Maize/Mary herself had smiled at me. I also could not have been more trapped.

I turned and entered into a tiny closet of a room through the open door in the foyer. I closed it behind me leaving Jesus and my line friend behind. There was a little wire screen in the wall to my right. There was nowhere to sit, but there was a little padded ledge under the screen close to the floor. I realized it was a place to kneel. A voice on the other side of the screen said something I did not understand. I placed my knees on the pad, and I waited.

"My son," said the voice, "do you have something to confess?"

Confess? Did I have something to confess?

"I'm afraid," I said. "Or I was."

"Yes."

Silence ensued. Outside the door I could hear this tiny fan generating white noise. I could almost have fallen asleep.

"Is that what you have to confess? That you are afraid?"

"I suppose."

"There is not necessarily anything sinful in being afraid. It is an emotion. But do you let it rule you?"

"Oh."

"Well, do you?"

My hand felt back to my bare heel.

"I'm not sure. Maybe."

"The Lord wants to rule in your life with his peace in place of your fear. Why are you afraid?"

"The Lord? Who's that?"

"My son? Are you a Catholic?"

"No. I don't think so."

How could I be?

"Have you come to confess?"

"I don't know."

"Why are you here?"

"I lost my job."

"I see. And that is why you are afraid?"

"Partly.".

"Did you do something wrong that caused you to get fired?"

"I wanted to sleep with my boss."

"Did you?"

"No."

"Did you make an advance?"

"Almost. She almost made one towards me."

"What happened?"

"She threw me out of her room, and the next morning she went to church to confess. You see, it was in Las Vegas."

"So, she changed her mind."

"I suppose she did."

"Since you are not a Catholic, I cannot absolve you for your sin, but I can tell you that your boss gave you a great gift."

"I wanted to sleep with another woman, but I did ask her to marry me."

"Why did you want to marry her?"

"Because she seems so fragile. She needs someone to take care of her. She used to be a vampire, but now she's just underemployed and barely getting by. I don't mean she was a real vampire—"

"I know what you mean. Is there anything else you would like to confess?"

"I think I killed a man."

"You think you killed a man? How did this happen?"

"I told him I would expose him if he broke into our computer systems again. I didn't, but when his boss found out what he had done, the man jumped off a bridge."

"Was it your intention to kill this man?"

"No."

"Perhaps you didn't choose the best means to deal with this man, but you are not guilty of his death. You can be sorry about what happened to him, but do not blame yourself any longer."

"Thank you," I said, and as I spoke, I felt stress released from my body as if I had had a massage. Then, something else began to bubble up inside.

"Is there anything else you need to confess?"

"I took out an insurance policy to end my life when it has lost its value."

The man behind the screen paused.

"I'm not sure I understand. You bought a policy for when your live is not worth living? Like an assisted suicide?"

"Actually, it was supposed to save me from suicide. The company has all sorts of data analysis capabilities, and so can tell when—"

I halted in mid-sentence.

"—when the best time has come for me to stop further pain and futility."

"This company is going to determine when you should die and then kill you themselves?"

I had never heard it put so bluntly.

"Yes."

"So you could avoid pain. When you took out this policy, were you in pain?"

"No. I just anticipated."

"Did your life seem no longer worth living?"

"It was worthwhile enough. I guess."

"So, you took out this policy because of fear."

"I suppose so."

"And yet, here you are. Fear has driven you here in spite of the policy."

It had indeed.

"My son, this is a grievous sin you have committed. You hired someone to murder you so you would not have to face death yourself. I don't know what you paid for this policy, but whatever it was, you sold yourself cheaply. And, it didn't help. You are still afraid."

"Yes. What can I do? The policy is paid in full. I can't just change my mind."

"Yes, you can. It wasn't just fear that brought you here. It was also love. You have known love in your life. You didn't recognize it as such, but you have. I think you have also discovered that love sometimes involves pain because love is perfected in self-sacrifice. Do you want to love?"

"I don't know. Yes."

"Then, go and pursue love. But ask yourself this. What if you could live as if you have already died? What power would the fear of death have over you then?"

But how could I do that? Could I crawl into my father's grave and come out again?

When I left the little room, the line was empty. There were people still entering the church, but they were coming in and sitting down. I heard the door next to me open and my confessor leave, but I did not see who he was. I opened the ponderous wooden door and stepped out of St. Mary's into my own Austin high noon.

I saw him just as soon as my eyes could adjust to the light. The agent of death stood directly across the street next to a parked car. I tremblied, but I descended the steps. The agent was wearing reflective sun glasses like the man with no eyes in Cool Hand Luke. His face was expressionless, yet I imagined that somehow he was grinning. I turned away from him and headed west towards Brazos. The walk light was already counting down as I started across the street towards the Fox TV station. I heard the car when I stepped off the curb. I turned and saw a white Suburban coming up Brazos from the south. The light for north bound traffic was red, and I was crossing with the green light, but the Suburban was not slowing down. The grill was wide and high. There was no license plate on the front, but that was the least of it. There was no driver either, only an empty cab with a steering wheel. I froze in the crosswalk waiting to collect my death benefit.

Then, I heard another sound like a silent rushing wind. Another car coming west on Tenth entered the Brazos intersection, turned left against the one way sign, passed inches from my bleeding heel, and stopped between me and the oncoming Suburban. The big SUV lurched forward as the hidden driver slammed on the brakes. It stopped just short of the driver's side of the car, a blue Prius. The passenger door to the blue car opened, and a human voice spoke.

"Get in!"

It was Raj.

I jumped into the car. Raj started forward even before I could close the door. The Suburban began to follow him in slow motion. Then, he threw the car in reverse and hit the accelerator. We spun around and sped south on Brazos going the wrong way backwards and dodging the oncoming cars. Those same cars came upon the empty Suburban as it attempted to make a U-turn in the middle of the road. They stopped, honked, and blocked the Suburban from making its turn. It turned back north again and made a left on Tenth. Raj backed all the way through the Seventh Street intersection, stopped, shifted into forward, and turned right. We hugged the left lane and passed the homeless shelter and the police station at legal speed, but once we were over I35, he accelerated again. We took a hard right turn onto Waller, and from there we wound our way down pleasant wooded streets until we reached the Habitat for Humanity Re-Store. Raj pulled into the lane on the south side of the store where you get in line to drop off donations and stopped.

We both turned towards one another.

"Man, I was looking all over for you. I went down Congress and up Lavaca. Then, I said, "This is nuts. Where would I go if death was on my heels? So, I circled down to Tenth, there you were coming out of the cathedral. Somehow I knew I had to catch up with you before you crossed Brazos, or it would all be over. I saw that Suburban without a driver, and I knew that was the assassin. What's going on? Why is Amazon trying to kill you? Did you send back one too many Prime orders?"

I didn't answer. I looked at the brown face of my neighbor down the hall, the man to whom I had never spoken before, and his face was to me like the face of God.

35 - The Lonely People

When we came back up Brazos and made the left into the condo parking garage, the Suburban was gone. Only when Raj had pulled into his parking spot and set the parking brake could I relax. All the way home from the Re-Store, I was sure his car would be hacked and we would end up running full speed into a stone wall or a cinder block bar on Sixth Street. But, we didn't.

Since I no longer had my phone, my life was reduced to essentials. I considered sending Raj an email to see if he wanted to get dinner, but I found I did not know his email address. I never had that. I had sent all my texts to his phone, and I had lost his phone number with my phone. I only knew his physical address. So, I had to go down to the end of the hall on my bruised heel and knock. We ordered Thai on his phone and ate it together at his kitchen table. After that we made a pact to eat in. Raj was a passable cook. My repertoire consisted of microwaved pastas and boiled water. We took turns using each other's kitchens. I praised his cooking with carefully measured phrases; he never said anything contrary about mine.

Two weeks to the day after my escape from the agent of death, I ventured outside for the first time. There on the north corner of Seventh Street I heard a voice calling after me as I crossed the intersection going down Congress.

"Gus! Hey, Gus! Yo!"

Never before had I heard someone on the street know and use my name. I turned and saw it was my homeless friend. How did he know my name? Then, I saw he was holding something aloft in his hand. It was my phone.

"I've been looking for you. I heard the agent missed and that you been layin' low. I ain't seen him around since, so maybe it's safe to give this back."

"I don't know what to say."

"You been gettin' text notices. It's about time to pay the bill."

"Okay. I'll look into that."

"You also ought to change your password. I know it, and I can't say some other brother didn't look over my shoulder while I was opening it. You know how the street is."

He turned to go.

"Wait a minute," I said. "What is your name?"

"Tommy. Tommy Washington. But folks call me Eagle cause I'm always watchin'."

"You sure are."

He turned back north towards the capitol.

"Uh'm, one more thing," I said. "The watch?"

"Oh, yeah. The watch. I don't have it."

"I see."

"I kept the phone because I could use it, and I figured, if you survived, you'd be needin' it again. But the watch? I pawned it."

He reached into his pocket.

"Here's the ticket. I'm pretty sure you're behind on the payments, but if you get down there and catch up, you might still get it back. It's like your soul; it's gotta be redeemed."

"Yeah," I said. "I may have to do that."

"Oh, and I texted some of your friends."

"You did?"

"Yeah, I figured you wanted them to know you was still alive."

Did my friends have any doubts about that? Maybe they did.

"Eagle. Say, if you see—"

"The agent? If I do, I'll be lettin' you know."

"Thank you."

"Maybe I'll be sendin' you a text. Soon as I get me another phone."

I smiled. At this point, I had little doubt that this resourceful man would manage to get another phone.

That evening Raj had to work late. He texted me to say I would have to fend for myself for dinner.

"How did u know I got my phone back?" I asked.

"U sent me a text this afternoon."

I started to text back that it hadn't been me. It had been the homeless man who held my phone while I faced down my own appointment with mortality, but I decided the whole thing would be too difficult to explain. Especially in texts. Sometimes you just have to let your friends speak for you, even the ones you didn't know you had.

So, that night I texted Joe's to order Thai on the strong suspicion that he was just another such friend.

To my surprise, Joe himself answered back.

"You been gone too long. Tonight we accept an order from you only in person. No takeout. No delivery."

I was taken aback.

"Too long? It's only been a week."

"A week?" said Joe. "A week on the edge of eternity you mean."

After an answer like that, what else was I going to do? I went down in person. I stood at the counter, and I deliberated as if I didn't know what I wanted. Joe stood there behind the counter with his cashier and waited patiently while my eyes went up and down the menu.

"I think I will have the vermicelli noodles."

"Nope," said Joe.

"No?" I said incredulously. That was what I always ordered. That was what the girl at the counter always rang up without even asking me.

Joe shook his head. We were playing a little game. I smiled and tried again.

"Okay. Not noodles. Khao Pad, then."

"Nope."

"All right. Pad Krapow Moo Saap."

"Not that either."

I began to be a little concerned. Robert had once told me of a restaurant in New Orleans that had one single dish on the menu, different each day of the week. Had Joe changed his strategy?

"Gaeng Keow Wan Kai?"

"Not that one!"

"What's the matter? You out of pad and wan?"

"You just keep trying till you get it right."

"Kai Md Ma Muang?"

"Uh-uh."

"Gaeng Daeng?"

"Wrong."

"I give up. I don't know."

"You don't know? You give up easy."

Joe looked at his girl at the counter. I saw her name was Jen. I had seen her name tag a hundred times before, but I had never paid attention to it.

"Tell Mr. Joe what he wants to eat tonight."

"Tom Yum Goong!" said Jen triumphantly. Joe mouthed the words with her and nodded his head.

"But that's not on the menu. You don't sell that."

Joe just stood there smiling.

"Okay. I'll play along. I will have the Tom Yum Goong."

"And you eat it here."

"Well, actually, I was thinking I would take it out if you've got a container—"

"No, you eat here. It's on special. You eat it here."

"If you insist."

I reached for my wallet.

"No charge. On special. On the house."

I went to sit down at the same table I had used so often before.

"Not there. In here. In the kitchen. Now. It's ready. Come on back."

He stepped from behind the counter and beckoned for me to follow. We passed through a plastic bead curtain. Joe took me to a little corner of a table that was even smaller than the place outside where I usually sat, but he smiled with pride as if I were an honored guest while Jen brought me the Tom Yum Goong.

So I did sit and eat.

"This is amazing," I said after the first bite. Joe's normal fare had always been good, better than you would expect, but this was on another level entirely.

"When I start selling this, I want to name it after you: 'Joe Yum Goong'."

"But with that name, you could be naming it after yourself."

"That's true, but my name is not really Joe. Your name could be."

"My name is Gus, not Joe."

"No, your name is Augustus. But your middle name is Joseph."

I started to speak, but Joe, not real Joe, cut me off.

"Don't try to deny it. Your name is Augustus Joseph Bishop. Don't you know I have your credit card memorized? I see it often enough. You, Joe, are more Joe than me. You know?"

I think I coughed a little. I know I was pressed back in the chair by the sheer force of the revelation. Why was I always surprised by people who knew who I was?

"Why would you want to name a dish after me?"

"Because you inspire me. You love my food, and you sit out there at that little table. I see you there, and I think. 'All the lonely people'. So, I think I want a sit down restaurant so lonely people like Gus/Joe can come and be together. I also want to serve all those Joe's better food so they can enjoy even more. And also I can charge them more money."

"I'm overwhelmed," I said. It seemed I had no secrets, but it also seemed that being known was not as bad as I had imagined.

"So, are you going to expand this place?"

"Not expand. Move."

"Move? Where are you moving?"

"I'm gonna open a new place on Fourth Street called Four Star Thai. Four star on Fourth. Pretty good, right?"

"Pretty good. But where am I going to eat?"

"You can't drive to Fourth? You drive your Fiat to Fourth, and I give you valet parking. No charge. If you walk, we drive you home."

"I don't know. This place is so handy. You make downtown living possible being right here around the corner from me. I am going to miss this place."

"You don't need to miss. You need to buy."

"Buy?"

"Yes. Buy Joe's MyThai. Well, maybe not buy, not outright. Buy a share. This Joe needs some capital, so I'm gonna have my own little IPO. I'm gonna sell shares. Minimum share size is one fifth. I give you special option. I sell it to you cheap. Well, maybe not cheap, but a good price."

I smiled at that.

"I wish I could, Joe, but I don't have the money."

"Oh. Well, that's too bad. Okay. I still name Joe Yum Goong after you."

"I don't know how to run a restaurant. I don't know how to cook. I'm in computer security—at least I was."

"I see. You're in transition. Tough break. Too bad. Of course, you don't need to cook. I want you to hire my cousin."

"I'm not going to hire your cousin, or one fifth of him. What's his name? It isn't Joe, is it?"

"Ed! And Jen here wants to stay. Only she want to work in the kitchen and be apprentice to my cousin. We need a new counter man. That would be on you—if you had money. Then, you serve all the lonely people on the corner by the condos. You talk up Four Star to all your customers, and then they bring their loneliness upscale. You give me good recommendations. You tell them Joe taught you everything you know."

"Joe, it's sounds great, but I'm not sure I can even afford to stay here myself. I may have to sell my condo."

My condo?

"Never mind Joe. You eat. Joe Yum Goong is not so good cold."

I put the condo up for sale. It was gone within the week. With my three years of equity growth, I made a hefty profit. Without the condo, I had no place to park, so I sold the Fiat. Now, I had cash and nowhere to go. For a few moments I was homeless, but then Raj offered me his spare bedroom. Unlike me, he bought a two bedroom condo and used the second room for visiting relatives. He was not expecting another relative for at least nine months.

"So, you can take your time."

I told him about the offer from Joe to buy one fifth of his takeout place. I expected Raj to laugh, shake his head or say something dismissive like, "Well, that was a nice offer." He didn't. He offered to put up enough money to make it two fifths. I knew I could say no to the whole thing, but at that moment no other direction made sense. I seemed to know for the first time in my life where I was and where I was going. The only question was how fast.

Raj and I bought two fifths of Joe's MyThai between us. Of course we kept the name. Thanks to Ed the traffic in and out barely took a dip. After a month or so, Ed introduced a new menu with fourteen different entrees. I had eaten the same thing almost every time, but we soon had a clientele who rotated through the entire menu every two weeks. I began to feed Eagle Tom Washington from the scrapings of the pans. He stood just up the street at the corner and began to tell people where they could find parking and what the special of the day was. I didn't know we had a special of the day, but thanks to Eagle, we added one. We called him our concierge. Instead of handouts, people offered him tips. I began to wonder if he could work behind the counter, but he seemed to enjoy his post by the corner.

He was still watching.

I stayed with Raj in his condo for about six months. Curry seemed to repel claims adjusters as well as garlic did vampires. Gradually, my fears subsided and my cash flow increased. I found a room for rent in East Austin. It was just a couple of blocks from the Texas State Cemetery. I avoided the cemetery for the first few days, but I got over that at least during daylight. I began walking around it in the morning. Even a cemetery is less morbid in the morning. I didn't pay much attention to the graves. In fact, I only glanced at a few near the fence. I put most of my attention on the outside of the perimeter. I was looking for the nun I had met there before, but I never saw her again. Perhaps she could only come out in the evening when I busy. Maybe she had already managed to bring all her dead to life.

Once a week on Saturday evening I took a Car2Go up to IKEA to have dinner with Mary. Every time I did I wondered if Lloyd was going to hack into the car and send me out of control into oncoming traffic. It gave me some comfort to know that the steering, at least, was not on a wire, and even at full throttle, I would have plenty of time to steer the car away from danger.

I told Mary about the restaurant business. Sitting there in the IKEA cafeteria as we were, I lowered my voice.

"It's better food than here."

She seemed doubtful. Nothing I could say would sweep this girl off her feet. So, I started bringing her MyThai. We had to eat it outside despite the evening heat; it was better that way. Our conversations became more intimate. I began to learn how to have an intimate conversation. It was harder than I expected, and easier. Sometimes we ate in my little rented car. I lifted the hatch, and we sat in the storage compartment with our legs dangling over the bumper like UT tailgaters. Sometimes we sat on her scooter. That is, I sat on her scooter, and she sat on the scooter beside it. I wanted to suggest that we go to her apartment to eat, but I never did. I wanted her to invite me back to her place to spend the night. It never happened. Instead, I found within myself a growing resolve to woo this girl or be wooed by whatever direction our relationship took.

"This food is good," she said, "much better than the meatballs. I was beginning to get tired of them. Your restaurant should do well."

"You could come and help me. You could work in the kitchen or make deliveries on your scooter. I might even buy a Smart Car and turn it into a delivery vehicle. Or, maybe even open a food truck. Either way, I need people to help me expand."

She stared off into the parking lot towards a row of electric cars. There were three of them in an impromptu green row. They had all decided they would rather have the shade than the prestige of the designated parking IKEA provided for them in the front of the store under the full afternoon sun. Then, she turned and smiled.

"I can't. The rent is too high, and I can't commute on my scooter, not on I35. Besides, I'm in RCIA."

"You're in what?"

"RCIA. Rite of Catholic something."

"Why are you doing that?"

"Don't act so surprised. It was your idea."

"My idea?"

"Yes. I told you I was thinking of becoming a nun, and you said I would have to become a Christian first. So I am."

"A Catholic first."

"Yeah. Whatever."

"Well, how long does that take?"

"Probably nine months."

"Nine months?"

"Yeah, until Easter, at least."

"Nine months?"

"Yeah. I feel like I'm pregnant."

"And after nine months you give birth to a nun?"

"No, after nine months I'm a Christian. Then, we talk about nunhood."

I couldn't convince her to come back to town and work with me, but I did get her to accept a gift. It was a pay-as-you-go phone. I figured she would not consent to being added to my plan. That was too intimate, too presumptuous. But, she took the phone, and once she had it, I could give her additional gifts in the form of air time cards. In that way, I made her accessible. However, we never had a single conversation on the phone. All we did was text. Those texts became a record to me of our relationship and a journal describing the process she was going through.

"God is 1 but he is also 3," she wrote.

"How is that?" I answered. I might be an atheist, but I was a monotheistic atheist.

"God is luv. U can't be luv and be alone."

I shook my head at the iPhone screen. She was really taking all this in. Honestly, however, it wasn't the idea of three-in-one that I found so incredible at that moment. It was the idea that anyone, whether he be only one or three-in-one, could be undivided.

36 – The Loss

Even though the restaurant was practically an all consuming enterprise, I wondered if I would ever resurrect my computer security career. Then, I reminded myself. I had been the apparent cause of an email attack that had nearly derailed my company on the very brink of its IPO. Word of things like that got around in a high tech venture capital town. There was also the additional complication that I could not tell anyone how I had dealt with the attack. Even if I had started to break my silence an interview, the thought of Boris Burns sinking into the dark, cold waters of the San Francisco Bay would have closed my lips. I could see his face disappearing into the depths, and he was speaking to me.

"The insurance we had was not enough."

"I know."

You just can't go to an interview with a conversation like that playing in your head.

Yet, I was glad of the reminder. Looking down into those waters in my mind, I could feel the chill, but I was still in the sun.

Then, one Friday at noon a man came in and ordered coffee. He handed me his card. I swiped it once. I swiped it again. I tried a third time with a careful stiffness in my wrist.

"I'm sorry," I said. "Your card has been denied."

He didn't act perturbed, indignant or even surprised. Instead, he pulled a twenty dollar bill out of his wallet and handed it to me. I noticed there was a complete set of twenties in the fold.

Why had he even tried to pay with a card? Why didn't he have another card? I noticed, too, he was wearing a ball cap with the bill pulled down more than normal. The cap was plain blue with no log on it. I wondered where he even found such a featureless cap and why he kept his head down towards the counter. He didn't look at me when I gave him his change, and he left without saying a word. The situation did not add up, so, I did the only logical thing. I logged onto our computer with my administrative account and began downloading diagnostic software. Late in the afternoon I found what I had half suspected. There was a script on the credit card that had invaded my computer through the card reader. It was a rather crude point of sale attack, a script which collected the credit card numbers that I swiped on the card reader and stored them in a file. It wasn't a very sophisticated script. I was able to find it for sale on the Dark Web for about twenty dollars in bitcoin. Later in the day, another man would show up and would pay for coffee with a credit card. His card would also be denied, and he would pay with cash. However, his bad card was going to pull all the card numbers off my reader from the collection file assembled by the first card. It was a technique that originated years before, but it was cheap, and as long as the merchant was unprotected and unawares, it worked.

I deleted the card numbers from the collection file, and instead I filled it with a little program of my own. Right before closing time, a man came and ordered coffee. He also wore a plain ball cap only his was red. I know our security camera took his picture from its perch on the wall behind me, but, just like the other man, this one kept his head low and his cap bill declined over his face.

"Your card has been denied. Do you want me to call the company and see what the problem is?"

"No. That's okay."

Then, he also paid with cash. Instead of twenties, however, this man's wallet was fat with ones and fives. I wondered how many coffees his partner had bought during the day. If you walked into a store to buy clothes or groceries or even gum, you could leave the items behind when your card was denied and not have to spend any money in order to leave your card collection script. In our shop, you could not very well leave your coffee at the counter. We would get suspicious.

It made me wonder if I should stop selling coffee.

When the second coffee drinker left MyThai, he left with a cup of Joe's special blend, a formula Joe had bequeathed to me with the restaurant as a special gift. He also left with some thirty-five cents in change, but he did not leave with a set of credit card numbers from my loyal customers. Nor did he take any numbers from my brother merchants. My program deleted them all. At least I hoped it did. I couldn't test the script without trying to collect card numbers myself, but I did do some verification. I got a screen scraping program to mine the popular Dark Web sites for the credit card numbers the thief had tried to steal. When none of them showed up on any sites after three months, I deleted my copy. I was amazed at how unburdened I felt to get rid of that data which, by all rights, I was not supposed to have. Even when you think you have put on the white hat, when you look in the mirror, you find you are wearing black.

I dreamed I sold the card numbers myself. I met the buyer underground in Airman's Cave. We huddled in the Aggie Art Gallery around a little clay figurine that looked like a pagan fertility goddess made in some ancient Assyrian art class. My buyer gave me five dollar bills one at a time, and I fed him card numbers one by one. The process seemed interminable because I had so many numbers, and he was such a loathsome character.

But then I wasn't selling him numbers. I was selling my script, my Point of Sale Protection Software to a Mexican restaurant owner in the Frost Bank tower. His customers could never use the same card twice because every card was stolen once he had rung up their enchiladas and swiped their cards in his reader.

When I awoke I wondered if I could sell my script. I texted Morgan to see what he thought of the idea. I had not spoken to him since the day I was fired. Morgan did not text back. He called me on the phone.

"I'm glad you are back in the game," he said, "but this idea is not going to work."

"You don't think so?"

"Would you let some guy down the street come into your shop and put some piece of code he said he had written himself on your credit card machine?"

"But I'm not just some guy from down the street. I have security certification."

"Are you going to pull the certificate out of your back pocket and waive it in his face? No one is going to buy your script. People will buy malware off the Dark Web, but they won't buy bonware from a cold call, door-to-door security salesman."

"I guess you are right. Thanks for the perspective."

"Is that it? Is that the only reason you called?"

"What else? You told me what I wanted to know."

"You wanted me to tell you that you are a loser? That's why you called?"

"No," I said. "That would not quite be the truth, would it?"

"The truth? When did you get into the truth."

"It's the new thing on my bucket list. Before I die, I want to know the truth. It's not as easy as it sounds."

"I should say not. But wait. Don't hang up. I may have something for you."

"You do?"

"Yeah. I may need some help. Some piecework, you know?"

"Really?"

"Yeah. I've got a contract, and I've got more than I can do. I'm working on a set price for a month at a time. I can hire someone if I want."

"Is someone going to let you hire me for their security work?"

"They will if I vouch for you. They will if I tell them I will take the hit."

"You'd do that?"

Morgan paused.

"Yes. I suppose I would. Hard to believe, I know, but after all, one scummy contractor has to take care of another."

Morgan's sub-contract kept me busier than ever, but I still made it up to IKEA to see Mary once a week. For some reason none of these various occupations conflicted. One thing seemed to sharpen the other. I became more attuned to details at the takeout, and I began to approach my security work from a place of calm rather than from an implicit desperation. I'm not sure why I was able to do all this. I think it helped to approach life without a backdoor exit in mind. I told

Mary as much without mentioning Lloyd London or the ensurance policy. She, on the other hand, was much more forthright.

"I was in love with death," she said. "That's why I have to make such a drastic change."

At first I cautiously contradicted her. I thought I could steer her hopes back towards me. As time went on, however, I found I cared less what she thought about me and more about what she actually wanted. I followed her trajectory, and when she wavered, I steered her back. Eventually, I realized that my own efforts were sabotaging my own desires.

Fortunately, I came to this realization at the Thai takeout counter. In my ideal world Mary would have been there to witness it. Instead, it was Jen who saw the epiphany written on my face.

"Boss? What's wrong? Are we going broke?"

"No."

"Good. You don't know what a relief that is. I've been learning to cook, and I found out I had screwed up the Pad Krapow Moo Saap."

She pinched her thumb and forefinger together and held them aloft over a virtual pot.

"Not enough holy basil."

I shook my head.

"So, if we are not failing, what is it? Are you dying?"

"Not yet."

"Are you in love?"

I stared hard at the counter.

"No. Not now."

She looked at me with the penetrating gaze of the woman.

"I think you still are."

"Well, if I still am, I can't just turn it off."

"Why would you want to turn it off? You don't want to stop loving, but loving is not always keeping."

I grasped the edge of the counter in a death grip with my left hand, and I brought my right palm down hard. The card reader shook.

And then I let her go. I let Mary go. I kept meeting with her on Saturdays. I continued to read her texts. I encouraged her in every way that I could. I was there the night they poured the water over her head and dressed her in the white robe. I was there at the corner to help her load her suitcases onto the bus. She had found a monastery that was willing to take her as a novice. Of course, it was out of state.

"I guess I will never see you again," I said.

"That's ridiculous," she said.

I hung my head.

"I know."

How did I know?

"I'll miss your texts," I said.

"I will write to you."

"Write? Letters? I'm not sure I can read handwriting."

"You will learn."

"I'm not sure I know how to write myself."

She looked at me dubiously.

"Okay. I'm being melodramatic."

Then, my eyes began to moisten. Mary grabbed my hand in both of hers.

"Don't worry. We'll always have Airman's Cave."

When the bus pulled away at the curb, Raj was there waiting in his car. We drove to the IKEA parking lot once again. He handed me the key fob to his car. I handed him the key to Mary's scooter. She had given it to me, title and all, but I didn't know how to ride. Raj was an old hand at small motor two wheeled transportation. We took the back roads from upper Round Rock back to East Austin. He parked the scooter behind my apartment, and then we traded keys. I was uncertain at first, but after a few days of running around the neighborhood, I was riding it to the restaurant. I say the scooter was a gift. Mary said she was going to take a vow of poverty and could no longer afford the payments. I needed transportation, so, I took over her payments. Mary's poverty was financial. Mine was of a different kind.

37 - The Austin Geode

I had to lose Mary to find her. Eventually I realized my own life worked the same way. To gain my life, I would have to lose it. No policy Lloyd London offered could do that. There was just one way I could think to do it, but I resisted. In the end it was Susan who gave me the final push. She called me up one day. I hadn't seen her since the day I had bought her two Topo Chicos in the bar.

"You're probably wondering why I'm calling."

"I didn't know you had my number."

"Of course, I have your number. You called me before. Remember?"

"Yeah. Computer security. You can't be wanting to go to Las Vegas again."

"No. That didn't turn out so bad though. I still use that SDR radio. You won't believe this, but my neighbor locked himself out of the house. I hacked his garage door opener. At first he was so happy to get back into the house, but after that, he started looking at me funny. You do a good deed, and people get suspicious."

"Tell me about it."

"Don't have to, do I? But I didn't call about that."

"You went back to work and want to offer me a job?"

"No. I wanted to tell you Woody is being baptized just before the baby is born, and I thought you might like to come."

On one hand I was outraged at the suggestion. On the other hand I was flattered. Once again, however, I was too polite to say no, not to Susan. Not now.

"It's Saturday night, the night before Easter. It goes from about eight thirty till nearly midnight. Don't worry. There will be tons of people there, and you won't have to sit with us. That would be a little embarrassing."

"What does Woody—I mean, Glen, think about this?"

"He thinks it is a good idea. He might even shake your hand after it. He'll be in a pretty forgiving mood."

"I'll have to see how things go. I'm pretty busy these days."

"What? Just a minute. Gus, can you hold on just a moment? Woody is trying to tell me something."

I think she put her hand over the phone, but I could still hear her side of the conversation.

"Tell him what?"

"Woody is listening?"

"He says you can put it on your bucket list."

I got Raj to go with me. After all, he was going anyway. I watched from a safe distance. I could barely see Glen get wet, but I could see Susan well. She was so big by that time she would have floated if the priest had tried to push her under.

After that, there was only one thing left to do.

I went back to St. Mary's and met the priest face to face.

"Bless me, Father," I said. "I'm afraid I may want to become a Catholic."

"Why?"

"Because I want to live."

Raj became my sponsor. He went to every class with me. He even went to class when I stayed home pacing the floor trying to talk myself out of it. When it was time for me to go through my first rite, my initial entry, he coached me on what to say.

"What do you ask of the Church?"

"I don't know."

"Faith," he said.

"All right. Faith."

"And what does faith offer you?"

"Eternal life."

That was in April. By December, I was beginning to gain a sense of what eternal meant. The nights became longer and colder. One cold

December Wednesday night, Lloyd London met Raj and I near the base of the steps from St. Mary's.

"Good evening. Nice brisk night we're having," he said. "Good a time as any to die."

I tried to step back up the steps and stumbled, but Raj caught my arm. Then, I regained my balance.

"I'm not dying. Not as far as I know."

"Not as far as you know."

"Did you come to take me out to dinner again? If you did, I'm afraid I'm not hungry. Besides, I have a friend with me, and he would have to come, too. Since I'm not paying premiums anymore, I'm sure you don't want to pay for the extra meal, and he doesn't want a policy. So, under the circumstances, good night to you."

"You're not going anywhere," Lloyd said. "You have already gone too far. This is the end."

"What do you mean? You tried to pay the death benefit once, but I wasn't ready to collect. I escaped. I've changed my mind. I don't want to collect."

He started to speak, but I interrupted him.

"No, I don't want a refund. You can keep all the premiums I paid. But you don't need to watch me anymore. I no longer require your services."

"I think I am the better judge of when you require my services and when you don't," said Lloyd. "Remember? I told you before. You are paid in full, and we still owe you your death benefit. I held off awhile to see what you would do with a little more time. That was my decision. You didn't elude me. You can't elude me. I keep my promises."

"I don't believe you. I escaped. You no longer have a reason to pay the benefit because my life has changed. It's better. It has begun to have meaning."

"Meaning? What's that? But you're partly right. You did change. I'll grant you that. I congratulate you. You have done well. Till now."

"Till now? Oh, this is not the end. I'm just getting started."

"No, you aren't just getting started. You are near finality. That's why I have come to see you in person this one last time. There's nothing I like better than rescuing a client from a long, painful, wasting, unfortunate end especially after a nice, pleasant interlude. That's all we can expect from this life: an interlude between non-existence and oblivion. You've got your interlude now, but not for long. I warn you, if you go through with this thing—"

"With what thing?"

He gestured towards the church looming behind me like a big brother.

"This affront to good sense and sound reason, this antithesis to human freedom."

"I don't understand. When I crawled into a cave just so I could say I did it, you didn't object. When I tried to bed my boss in Vegas, you didn't warn me that maybe this wasn't the road to happiness and fulfillment. When I tried to beat the Chinese at poker, you didn't tell me to consider the odds. I could have become a serial killer, and you would have approved because you think that is the height of freedom."

Lloyd didn't answer, but he smiled. I could see, even in the dimming light, that he agreed.

"So why does this bother you? I even fell in love with a girl who wanted to be a vampire, and you didn't warn me. Why does this get under your skin?"

"Maybe because there are no vampires. I reserve my warnings for things that are real."

"What do you mean by that?" I said, but Lloyd London did not reply. He seemed to realize that he had said too much. He stepped backwards off the curb and crossed the street without ever turning around. He kept his eyes fixed on mine as he receded beyond the light of the moon tower into the night.

"What did that guy want?" Raj asked.

"He wants to pay off the claim on my insurance policy."

"Does that mean he is going to give you some money?"

"No, it means he thinks it is time for me to die."

"Well, then, that's just what you'll have to do."

***

I arrived early Saturday night for the Easter Vigil with my brown robe. We sat in darkness holding candles while ancient history passed before us. Then, it was time to cross through the water. I had always heard that a drowning man went down three times before he succumbed. That's what Robert told me when he pulled me out of the water.

"Don't worry", he had said. "You only went under once."

This time I went under three times. I came up with water in my ears and eyes. Yet, I could hear applause as my ears popped. I could see a blurry Raj smiling. Behind him in a corner I thought saw Robert and his father standing for a moment. They also smiled and nodded to me before my vision cleared and they faded away.

When it was all over, after I had dried off and put on a white robe, after the priest had smeared me with oil, and after we sang a song to the holy dead asking them to pray for us, the not yet holy living, I found that I was wide awake. It was just past midnight when the reception ended. Raj and I left the bishop's hall, turned south on Brazos, and walked down to Sixth Street to see if we could burn off enough energy to be able to go to bed.

I could see a few women here and there wearing pastels. Other than that, no one seemed to know it was Easter. I watched people pass from one dimly lit doorway in the darkness to the next. It struck me that the doorway was the brightest part of a bar, just a little illuminated passage between darkness outside leading to darkness inside.

Someone came out of the inner darkness of one of the bars into the light of the door. His eyelids fluttered a little as his eyes adjusted. Then, he saw at me, and he smiled.

"Fancy seeing you here," he said.

It was Cro Magdon, the South Austin Cave Man.

"I've been right here all along."

"Maybe you have, but I just got back from Brazil. I've spent the last year doing tours of Abismo Guy Collett. Deepest quartzite cave in the world. More than 670 meters. Great gig—until that unfortunate event. Well, they threw me out of the country. So, now I'm back in Austin, and what do I find? Airman's closed. I'm been reduced to leading the wild tour at Innerspace Caverns and working at Whole Foods part time."

He leaned over to us and lowered his voice.

"I'm also looking for an alternative entrance to the Lakeline Cave, but don't tell the Cedar Park police."

"That sounds like a good way to get thrown out of Cedar Park and Austin both."

"Maybe so. I'm negotiating with the Austin Parks Department about Airman's, but until that ice thaws, the fact remains that you, my friend, are the last person to see the Austin Geode."

"I am? Are you sure you've got the right person? Gus Bishop?"

"Yes. Your tour was the last tour into that cave, and you were the last one on the tour to make the final push to the very end of Airman's to see the geode. Don't you remember?"

"Yes, as a matter of fact. I do, but I didn't know I was the last one."

"You were. Several folks in that group didn't even go. They stayed in the clay. They were too tired. They told me they weren't interested. One actually told me the geode at the end of the cave was a myth, and that he had been satisfied with the Aggie Art Gallery. Can you believe that? To have gone so far and then to stop short of the prize? But you, you went the distance. That's why I've been hoping to run into you. I lost your email address. Go to my web site and send me an email with your physical address so I can mail you your certificate."

"Certificate?"

"Yes. I pretty well have it memorized. Do you want to know what it says?"

He cleared his throat.

"Inasmuch as Augustus Joseph Bishop has journeyed into the furthest reach of Airman's Cave beneath the City of Austin to behold the underground jewel, he is therefore elected into the Order of Subterranean Luminescents. By the authority invested in me as Cave Master under The Texas Spelunker Society and in association with the Austin Parks Department, I now recognize him to be a Seeker of Light in Dark Places. Congratulations. I never thought you'd make it."

He smiled a wry little smile.

"Send me that address," he said.

With that he disappeared down Sixth Street. I shook my head in disbelief.

"Luminescents?"

"Aren't you going to send him your address?"

"I don't know. A spelunking certificate? Seems kind of silly now. Where would I put it?"

"No! You've got the wrong attitude about this. You need to get that certificate, frame it, and mount it on your wall. Let it be a reminder to you. You are Augustus Joseph Bishop, a seeker of light in dark places. Now isn't that the truth?"

I looked at him in amazement. He was right. I was.

CPSIA information can be obtained
at www.ICGtesting.com
Printed in the USA
FSOW01n2313250817
37845FS